Another Time,
Another Life

www.transworldbooks.co.uk

Also by Leif G.W. Persson

Between Summer's Longing and Winter's End

Another Time, Another Life

THE STORY OF A CRIME

Leif G.W. Persson

Translated from the Swedish by Paul Norlen

Doubleday

LONDON · TORONTO · SYDNEY · AUCKLAND · JOHANNESBURG

TRANSWORLD PUBLISHERS
61–63 Uxbridge Road, London W5 5SA
A Random House Group Company
www.transworldbooks.co.uk

Originally published in Sweden as *En annan tid, ett annat liv: En roman om ett brott*
in 2003 by Piratförlaget, Stockholm

First published in Great Britain in 2012
by Doubleday, an imprint of Transworld Publishers

A CIP catalogue record for this book is available from the British Library.

ISBN 9780385614191 (cased)
9780385614207 (tpb)

Addresses for Random House Group Ltd companies outside the UK
can be found at: www.randomhouse.co.uk
The Random House Group Ltd Reg. No. 954009

The Random House Group Limited supports the Forest Stewardship Council (FSC®), the
leading international forest-certification organization. Our books carrying the FSC label are
printed on FSC®-certified paper. FSC is the only forest-certification scheme endorsed by
the leading environmental organizations, including Greenpeace. Our paper procurement
policy can be found at www.randomhouse.co.uk/environment.

Typeset in Dante MT
Printed and bound in Great Britain by
CPI Group (UK) Ltd, Croydon, CR0 4YY

2 4 6 8 10 9 7 5 3 1

For Mikael and the Bear,

What's the use of warning someone who can't defend himself?

—*The Professor*

Part I

Another Time

I

On Thursday the twenty-fourth of April 1975, death came during office hours, and oddly enough in both female and male form. Which is not to say the men weren't still in the majority. Death was attractively and neatly dressed, and to start with behaved both courteously and urbanely. Nor was it by chance that the ambassador was at his place of employment, which was otherwise far from always the case. On the contrary, this was the result of careful planning, and key to the whole affair.

The embassy of the Federal Republic of Germany in Sweden is located on Djurgården in central Stockholm, and has been since the early 1960s. In the northeast corner of the area that goes by the name Diplomat City, with the Swedish Radio and TV building and the Norwegian embassy as its closest neighbors, it hardly gets finer than that as Stockholm addresses go. There is nothing remarkable, however, about the embassy building itself. An ordinary, dreary concrete box in the sixties' functional style, three stories and just over twenty thousand square feet of office space with entry on the ground floor at the north end, it is far from the most prestigious foreign posting in the German Ministry of Foreign Affairs.

The weather was nothing to write home about that day when death came to call. It was a typical Swedish spring with biting winds, restless clouds under a pewter-colored sky, and only a vague promise of better, warmer times. For death these were ideal conditions. Best of all security at the embassy was almost nonexistent; it was a building that was easy to occupy and defend but difficult to storm. Best of all, a solitary, rather worn-out attendant manned the reception area where, if worse came to worst, the glass doors of the security passage could be forced manually. Granted, the weather conditions would not help the perpetrators when it was time to leave.

At some point between quarter past eleven and eleven-thirty in the morning things started to happen, and the fact that a more precise point in time could not be established was also owing to the poor security. Whatever. Within the course of a few minutes, six visitors arrived in three groups of two people each, young people between twenty and thirty, all German citizens of course, and they all wanted help with various matters.

In their homeland they were notorious. Their likenesses and descriptions were on thousands of wanted posters all across West Germany. Their faces were also to be found in airports, train and bus stations, banks, post offices, and basically any public area where there was vacant wall space available. Their images were even on file at the embassy in Stockholm, in a folder in a desk drawer in the reception area, however useful that might be. But when they actually showed up no one recognized them, and the names by which a few of them introduced themselves were different from their own.

First two young men arrived who wanted advice on an inheritance issue that concerned both Swedish and German jurisdictions, and it was clear, if for no other reason than the bulging briefcase one of them was lugging, that this was no simple matter. The guard in the reception area told the two men where they could find the official they needed and let them into the embassy.

Immediately after this came a young couple who wanted to renew their passports. A routine errand, one of the most common at the embassy. The young woman gave a friendly smile to the guard as he opened the door for her and her companion.

But then things became more complicated. Two young men showed up looking to acquire work permits. The guard explained that this was not an embassy matter but rather a question for the Swedish authorities. Instead of listening to him the two persisted. One of them even got a bit stubborn when the guard didn't want to let them in. While they stood there arguing, one of the embassy employees, who was going out for lunch, appeared. As he exited, they both took the opportunity to slip in and immediately disappeared up the stairway to the upper floors, without taking any notice of the guard shouting at them to come back.

Then everything happened very fast. The six congregated in the stairwell outside the consular department on the second floor, pulled on balaclavas, and took out pistols, submachine guns, and hand grenades. After that they cleared the offices of superfluous visitors and personnel; a few introductory rounds in the ceiling making the plaster spray was sufficient for the majority of the staff to flee head over heels out onto the street, and the twelve who remained behind were gathered together and herded into the library on the top floor, with military precision and without wasting time on any pleasantries whatsoever.

At eleven forty-seven the first alarm about "gunfire at the West German embassy" came to the Stockholm police command center, and this unleashed an all-out response. Uniformed police, detectives from the central detective squad, the homicide squad, and the secret police, in effect all personnel that could be called out were ordered there; blue lights, sirens, and screeching tires all headed for the West German embassy on Djurgården, and the alarm they are responding to is already clear enough. The West German embassy has been occupied by terrorists. They are armed and dangerous. All police are urged to observe the greatest possible caution.

First on the scene was a radio car from Östermalm precinct, and that it arrived at eleven forty-six according to the submitted report was not because the patrol commander was psychic; his watch was two minutes slow when he noted the time, and considering what happened later this was a minor error.

By twelve-thirty, after a little more than forty minutes, the police had already surrounded the embassy, secured the basement and lower floors inside the building, set up barricades in the area outside the embassy to hold back the quickly growing crowds of journalists and curiosity seekers, set up a temporary command center, and begun to organize their radio and telephone connections to police headquarters, the embassy, and the government offices. The head of the homicide squad who would be leading the effort was on the scene, and as far as he and his colleagues were concerned they were ready to get going.

The six people inside the embassy hadn't been twiddling their thumbs either. They had led the twelve employees being held hostage, including the ambassador himself, from the library to the ambassador's office in the southwest corner of the top floor of the building, and as far away from the entry as they could get. A few of the female employees had to help by filling wastebaskets with water and stopping up the sinks and toilets with paper towels to prevent an expected gas attack via the water pipes. Two of the terrorists primed blasting caps at strategic places on the top floor while the others guarded the hostages and the door toward the stairwell. And after all that they were ready at approximately the same time as their opponent.

The terrorists made the first move, opening with a simple, unambiguous demand. If the police did not immediately leave the embassy building, one of the hostages would be shot. The head of the homicide squad was not a man to get worked up unnecessarily, and his self-confidence was great, if not unlimited. Besides, he had been present at the drama on Norrmalmstorg a year and a half before, and there he had learned that if the culprits only had time to get to know their hostages, then the strangest feelings of camaraderie could arise between them, and the risk of violence would be greatly reduced. This interesting human mechanism had even been given a special name, "Stockholm syndrome," and in the general psychological delirium no one gave any thought to the limited extent of its empirical basis.

Therefore the head of homicide thought he was on a solid behavioristic footing when he sent word that he had made note of the terrorists' wishes and was willing to talk things over. But his adversaries had different, more violent ideas. After only a few minutes a volley of shots echoed from the top floor of the embassy. Then the door to the upper corridor opened and the German military attaché's bloody, lifeless body was thrown out down the stairs, coming to rest on the halfway landing. That done, the terrorists again made contact.

The demand remained. If the police wished to retrieve the corpse, that was fine, provided that at most two police officers did so, dressed only in underwear. And if they did not wish to retrieve more dead bodies, they should leave the building immediately. What extraordinarily depressing people, the head of homicide thought as he made his first operational decision in a crisis situation. Of course the police would leave the building. Of course they would see to removing the body. Of course. It was already under way.

Then by radio he contacted the chief inspector of the central detective squad who was leading the forces inside the building and asked him for three things. First, to send a suitable, clearly visible number of men out of the building; second, to see to it that those who remained behind regrouped discreetly on the basement level; third and finally, to appoint two volunteers who were willing to play the part of EMTs in underpants only.

Assistant detective Bo Jarnebring with the central detective squad was one of the first who, with service revolver drawn, and with a warm heart and a cool head, had rushed into the embassy building, and he was also the first to volunteer. His boss had only shaken his head. Even an almost naked Jarnebring would be far too terrifying a spectacle in this sensitive initial phase. The assignment had gone instead to two of his older colleagues who had a more jovial, roly-poly appearance. Jarnebring and two other like-minded colleagues would try to provide cover for the stretcher bearers and if necessary fire their weapons toward the upper corridor.

This duty suited Jarnebring much better, and he quickly crawled up the stairs and took position. His two colleagues succeeded with some difficulty in rolling the lifeless, bloody body up onto the stretcher that they pushed ahead of them. It was not exactly simple to do lying curled up on a stairway, but it worked. After that they very carefully started to ease back down the stairs with the stretcher dragging after them while Jarnebring held the sight of his service revolver aimed steady at the door to the upper corridor. It was at approximately that moment that he acquired his lifelong memory of the German terrorists' occupation of the West German embassy in Stockholm. There was a smell of burnt telephone.

Suddenly he glimpsed the barrel of an automatic weapon in the door opening, and just as he tried to change position to get a clear shot at the person who was holding the gun he saw the flames in the muzzle of the barrel, heard the reports boom in the narrow stairwell and the ricochets buzzing like angry hornets around his ears. But it was his nose that remembered best the smell of burnt telephone. It was not until the next day when he and a few of the others returned to the site to help clean up that he became clear about the reason for his memory. The staircase banister was covered with black Bakelite, and about eighteen inches above the place where his head had been the bullet from an automatic weapon had carved a yard-long groove in the banister.

The Swedish police lacked both the equipment and the training for this type of effort. The combined practical experience of the police force amounted, counting generously, to no more than three similar events: the murder of the Yugoslavian ambassador in Stockholm in April 1971, an airplane hijacking at Bulltofta outside Malmö in September 1972, and the so-called Norrmalmstorg drama in Stockholm in August 1973. That was when an ordinary Swedish thief had taken the personnel of a bank hostage in an effort to force the release from prison of the bank robber most lionized by the national mass media. Both the airplane hijacking and the Norrmalmstorg drama had ended happily in the sense that no one had died, but in this new case other rules clearly applied; only an hour after the situation had begun the head of the homicide squad had a corpse around his neck and this he greatly disliked.

He therefore decided to change tactics and lie low, very low, as low as possible, if for no other reason than to give the Stockholm syndrome a second chance to have its full effect. Deep down, because he himself was a good person, he had a hard time letting go of that thought. As afternoon changed to evening he had therefore allowed his forces to conduct the police variation of the Swedish hedgehog, and he had mostly talked on the phone. With his own police command, with people from the National Police Board, representatives of the government and the Ministry of Justice, basically with anyone and everyone who managed to get in touch with him.

Late in the afternoon two colleagues from the German secret police showed up at his temporary command center. After a brief description of the situation they left him to form their own impressions. Only a

quarter of an hour later an out of breath chief inspector from the uniformed police came to report that the "German bastards" were going
around doling out high-caliber American army revolvers as a gift to their
Swedish colleagues. So that they would have "more substantial hard-
ware to hold on to than a lousy Walther pistol when things got serious."
The head of homicide sighed and told the chief inspector to break off
these "philanthropic activities" as quickly as possible and take care to see
that any gifts already doled out were rounded up.

"Otherwise the boys from tech will go crazy on us," he added both
judiciously and pedagogically. For regardless of how things went with
those inside, there would be a forensic investigation at the crime scene at
some point, and much of that would involve attributing discharged bul-
lets to the right weapon. This he knew better than almost anyone else,
because he had devoted more than twenty years of his career to investigating serious crimes of violence.

The opponents inside the embassy had not in any event expressed
any active dissatisfaction with the police command's new tactical
arrangements. They had their hands full with monitoring the situation
at the same time as negotiations went on with their own government
and the Swedish government about the demands that had been made:
immediate release of twenty-six comrades from German prisons,
among them the leaders of the Baader-Meinhof group. Transport by air
to a friendly host country plus twenty thousand dollars on top of that for
each and every one of those released. If their demands were not met,
they would start shooting hostages, one each hour starting at ten o'clock
that evening. It was as simple as that.

There followed hours of waiting without anything in particular happening while the clock ticked on toward ten. It was decided, for lack of
anything better to do, to hasten the preparations for the tear gas attack
that had been under consideration for the past few hours.

The time had reached quarter past ten before the final word from
the German government in Bonn—via the Swedish government in
Stockholm—reached the terrorists at the embassy. Only a few minutes
later someone inside must have got tired, went and fetched the
embassy's trade attaché, led him up to a window, and shot him from
behind.

One of the police detectives, well situated in a so-called nest at a neighboring embassy, saw the trade attaché being murdered, and when he reported his observations—"I think they shot him in the back or the neck"—the head of the homicide squad suddenly lost heart. The promised effects of the Stockholm syndrome, this good, consoling cigar, seemed more remote than ever. It had been less than ten hours and already two of the hostages had been murdered.

A while later he started to hope again. Eleven o'clock passed without anyone else being shot, and only a few minutes later the terrorists inside the embassy suddenly released three female secretaries from among their hostages. A ray of hope in the gathering April darkness, and . . . maybe still, thought the head of homicide, for a tear gas attack was not something he was looking forward to. That could only end with further misery. At the same time the authorities had a good idea of how many hostages there were. A rapidly shrinking group, which would not last longer than early morning if the terrorists made good on their promise to execute one per hour.

The release came at a quarter to midnight. The head of the homicide squad had left the construction shed where he had set up his temporary command room to finally stretch his legs, take a breath of fresh air, and smoke yet another cigarette. First he saw the flash of light from the embassy building, then he felt the shaking in the ground below him, and only after that did he hear the series of explosions. The clouds of glass splinters, building material, smoke, and last of all the screams from the people inside the building. People climbing out of windows, throwing themselves out, jumping, clinging to the façade, tumbling, falling, getting up again, or remaining lying. That was how he remembered it when he thought back, in just that order: the flashes of light, the shaking, the detonations, the smoke, the screams, the people.

In contrast to the TV reporter who led the live broadcast from the scene, the head of the homicide squad had not jumped off the ground, and whether his feet did rise or spread was none of his doing in any event. On the other hand he had thought a bit. I'll be damned, he thought, despite the fact that normally he never swore. Then he put out his cigarette and returned to his chair in the temporary command center. Clearly high time, for inside it was already a complete circus.

Half an hour later it was almost all over, and wonder of wonders, with one exception all of them—the terrorists and their hostages and his colleagues down in the basement of the embassy and in the vicinity of the building—seemed to have survived the explosion. A number were wounded, a few were even seriously wounded, but they were all alive.

The terrorists were seized, and if he and his colleagues weren't completely mistaken, it was a clean sweep. In any event everyone his detectives and investigators had been able to observe and count up earlier in the day and evening. One was still inside the embassy; he had just been found, or at least half of him, and he had been identified several hours previously. Four of the culprits were seized in the parking lot behind the embassy building, where they had most likely gathered in a vain attempt to flee in the rented car in which they had driven there twelve hours earlier—which was stupid of them because the police had already secured that car in the afternoon.

The fifth and last of the terrorists was seized as he was staggering around in the garden of the Norwegian embassy. Sooty and with clothes smoldering, hair singed off, burned all over, blinded, completely confused, he was at first mistaken for one of the hostages. But that part had been sorted out. Three of them were taken to the hospital, one in poor and one in miserable condition, but two had been in good enough condition to be sent directly to the jail in police headquarters after bandaging. All of them were in handcuffs, and two of them with ankle shackles to be on the safe side.

Jarnebring had left just after two in the morning, one of the last from the squad. Remaining were his colleagues with the uniformed police who would attend to guarding the barricades, and the technicians who stood trying to stay warm while waiting for the fire department to finish up. At home a worried wife was waiting, on the verge of climbing the walls, along with three small sleeping children of which the oldest had passed out from excitement in front of the TV several hours ago but without having been the least bit worried.

He himself felt strangely absent, and when his wife told him that his best friend and closest colleague Lars Martin Johansson must have called ten times during the afternoon and evening, he only nodded and pulled the telephone cord out of the jack to be on the safe side. Then he fell asleep, slept without dreaming, and woke up six hours later. He was completely clear in the head despite the strange persistent feeling that what had happened had not concerned him. The odor of burnt Bakelite was still there too. It will pass, he thought. It will pass.

During the Second World War the English leader Winston Churchill would often maintain that "He who is forewarned is also forearmed." During the most difficult years he had repeated this almost like an incantation, in Parliament, in his cabinet, and in public speeches to his severely tormented population: "He who is forewarned is forearmed." And in hindsight, considering how it all actually ended despite the initial miserable odds, this must have been true for him in any event, and for a sufficient number of his countrymen. But this time, in Sweden, it did not apply, for when something did happen it seemed to have come as a total surprise, despite the fact that the warnings had been arriving thick and fast for several years.

II

The first government official who found out what was going on was not the minister of justice—which it should have been—but the prime minister. It turned out that way owing to the simple workings of human nature.

As soon as the dispatcher on duty at the police command center was sure this was serious and not just another false alarm, he pulled out the list of procedures that applies in such situations from the folder on his desk. The rest was routine. First he called the head of the homicide squad, who was his immediate superior at the police department in Stockholm. The homicide chief answered on the first ring, hemmed and hawed a few times, and asked the dispatcher to get back to him as soon as he knew anything more. Then the dispatcher called the contact person at the secret police who, in accordance with instructions, phoned the assistant undersecretary at the Ministry of Justice who was responsible for the practical aspects of the ministry's and the government's contacts with the secret police.

There was a busy signal at the assistant undersecretary's office, and while waiting for the call to go through—because the seconds were ticking by painfully slowly, and so that he could at least have something better to do if the bastard on the other end of the line was to continue gabbing for all eternity—he moved the beeping receiver to his left hand and with his free right hand used his other telephone to dial the direct number to the prime minister's undersecretary. The undersecretary

13

answered at once and was informed in less than a minute. And just as the secret police officer put down the receiver he heard the previously occupied assistant undersecretary shouting "hello" in his left ear, and what happened after that was completely in accordance with instructions.

As stated, this departure from procedure was never discovered, much less pointed out. It lacked any significance whatsoever for either Swedish or German contemporary history, and the officer from the secret police had not thought much about the matter himself. On some occasion he mentioned it, as a small detail in a good story in the company of trust-worthy colleagues, after a nice dinner along with the second cognac and the coffee. But it had never been more than that.

The prime minister and his undersecretary were involved from the beginning; the minister of justice would take the conviction that he had been "the first to find out" with him to the grave. While the afternoon of the embassy takeover gradually passed into evening and then night, a growing troop of members of the government, high-ranking police officers, and officials in the government offices gathered at the prime minister's office, none of them particularly happy. Life felt heavy and unjust, for this event did not directly concern them and the Sweden that they, in established democratic order, had been given to lead.

First there was the murder of the Yugoslavian ambassador, involving Croatian extremists and separatists, and a dead Serbian ambassador, and in any event, Sweden had no responsibility for all that. Then other Croatian terrorists hijacked an SAS plane to free the murderers of the ambassador, and in the process risked the lives of almost a hundred ordinary Swedes. The plane finally landed in Spain, where the hijackers immediately gave up and turned themselves over to the police. And now: a half-dozen crazy students calling themselves the Socialist Patients' Collective, who wanted to overthrow German society by force and who chose to do so in Stockholm, of all places. This was not just, and it was un-Swedish with a vengeance. The fact that in between all that a domestic piece of talent from the traditional criminal lumpen proletariat took hostages in a bank on Norrmalmstorg was something they would have to put up with.

First there had been discussions in the prime minister's office about how the hostages could be rescued without further unnecessary bloodshed. There was more than enough as it was. Ideas were in short supply, but at last the prime minister, who had been a reserve officer in the cavalry, suggested that the police should storm the building. But the idea was immediately dismissed by a unanimous top police command. Swedish police lacked both equipment and training for such missions, despite the fact that, as the national commissioner so alertly took the opportunity to point out, funds for such operations had been requested by the department on several occasions and for several years running, but no money had been granted. Now they had neither equipment nor training, despite apparent willingness.

"It would be a pure suicide mission," the national commissioner clarified in his rasping dialect, and an even greater gloom settled over those assembled.

When the West German government then gave their reply categorically rejecting the terrorists' demands, the mood quickly reached a low ebb, and at last, for lack of anything better and because something had to be done, it was agreed that a little tear gas should be fired into the building. While this effort was being planned, however, things resolved themselves of their own accord when the top floor of the embassy building was literally blown into the air. It was unclear why, but that was a question for later that others could answer. Because for the most part those inside the building seemed to have pulled through, there were more important questions on the night's agenda.

At that point they moved over to the government's conference room, and the discussions quickly took a new direction. Namely, how they could be rid of the five surviving terrorists as quickly as possible. The very thought of having them in Swedish prisons, with the prospect of constant attempts to free them through new airplane hijackings, kidnappings, and all the other outrages their comrades might conceivably think up, was just about the worst thing that could be imagined.

"They've got to go. There's nothing to discuss," as one of the older cabinet ministers summarized the matter even before the deliberations had begun.

The only one who raised objections was the advisory cabinet minister in the Ministry of Justice, the government's own judicial expert, and as it happened the same man who had written the terrorist legislation that would be the basis for the immediate deportation. According to him the problem was not complicated at all. If the government's intention was to use the terrorist law, then there was no legal basis for deporting the five terrorists, but because this was no time for judicial subtleties a united government, including the legal consultant, decided to immediately deport the five using that very same Swedish terrorist law that actually applied only to foreign citizens and therefore was not even an issue for the Ministry of Justice.

"You can't have the statute book under your arm in these kinds of situations," as the cabinet member responsible for "foreigner issues" so elegantly summarized the decision. She was a woman besides, the youngest in the government, the youngest cabinet member ever, and as decisive as male colleagues twice her age.

For her, Friday the twenty-fifth of April was a day filled with practical tasks from early dawn until long past midnight. First she had to try to get a little order in the jurisprudence, to the extent possible, and then clear up a thousand and one practical details in connection with the deportation itself. The Germans, for example, had promised to send over an airplane to bring home their countrymen, but the fact that it never showed up was of minor importance. From the start the Swedish authorities had decided that a Swedish plane would be on standby at Arlanda, fueled and ready, with an eager, rested crew and accompanying nursing personnel.

The medical condition of the deportees was a problem. None of them was in wonderful shape, but for three of them at least the doctors had given the go-ahead, and it was even simpler with the fourth one. He was so severely burned that if the bed he was lying on had been moved a few feet he might as well have been killed on the spot. It would be necessary to wait a week until his condition was stable enough for him to survive the trip home to West Germany. Letting him die en route was not an option. That was the sort of thing that made people want to take revenge. But after a week he was allowed to go home, and once home he had the good taste to spend another week in a German hospital before he died.

It was the fifth one, the female participant in the occupation of the embassy, who represented the major problem, for on her case the opinions among the medical experts were sharply divided. The first doctor asked saw no problem at all in proceeding with her deportation, but when the cabinet minister responsible, a large number of police officers, and the necessary nursing personnel went to the hospital to pick her up, the senior physician responsible started to dig in his heels. Finally he played his trump card and simply refused to discharge her. If she were to be taken away, someone else would have to take the medical responsibility, and he wanted an affidavit from the cabinet minister attesting that he was opposed to the transport.

If it was his patient's well-being he had in mind, this was not very smart of the doctor—it suggested a significant underestimation of his opponent, for in a situation like this you do not win any victories if you go around with a statute book under your arm. Without changing her expression, the cabinet minister took out a pen and wrote out the order for deportation. Then she wrote a brief affidavit for the doctor, and she and her entourage took his patient to Arlanda. Immediately after three a.m. on Saturday the government transport plane finally lifted off toward its secret destination in West Germany with its cargo of four German terrorists.

What had happened was definitely not a cheerful story, but in the general misery the government could be happy that public opinion was united behind them. In addition, for once the goodwill was shared by the populace and the media. The man on the street was, to put it simply, furious. The whole thing was very un-Swedish, and at the same time it was typical for the Germans to foist their problems on their peaceful neighbors—something the Germans unfortunately had been in the habit of doing for far too long. In brief, you got the terrorism you deserved, and besides, everyone who had been abroad in winter knew that the Germans always push ahead in the lift lines at the most popular ski resorts, despite the fact that these were in Austria and Switzerland.

In the media various editorial writers and so-called experts were feasting on the shortcomings of the German government. Not only had the German government avoided taking any responsibility; it even had the gall to shift the responsibility onto the Swedish government, the Swedish police, and the Swedish people. In addition, to be on the safe side they were so completely and utterly incompetent that the only reasonable conclusion was that the German embassy in some mysterious way must have self-ignited, and that the terrorists' contribution to the matter was to be seen more as an effect than a cause.

Considering what had happened, the media reception was almost phenomenal, with only one exception, found of course in the major conservative morning newspaper. On its editorial page, "the nest for generally retarded and inverted opportunists," as the prime minister used to summarize things when he was in one of his extravagant moods, a brief contribution appeared in which the writer had the gall to compare the German terrorists' occupation of the embassy with the blowing up of the English strikebreaker vessel *Amalthea* in Malmö Harbor by Anton Nilson and his comrades sixty-seven years earlier.

This piece of writing upset the government's minister of finance to such a degree that a week later he grabbed a firm hold of his suspenders during a fine bourgeois dinner at home with the business elite and took the opportunity to "read the riot act to the newspaper's editor in chief." According to witnesses who were present, it was superb entertainment and, considering the limited social establishment in the small country of Sweden, completely logical when seen against the background of what had happened. But it never really went further than that. The whole matter was far too un-Swedish.

III

It was not a bad police investigation, it was a truly lousy investigation, and considering that it concerned one of the most serious crimes in postwar Sweden, this was not really easy to understand. One of the explanations discussed within the top police command, including in confidential conversations between the national commissioner of police and his closest younger colleagues, was that the government, in some mysterious way, seemed actively disinclined to touch the subject, and that this in turn had rubbed off on the police. Here was a crime with clear political overtones, at the same time a government that was very clearly pushing the whole matter away, and what could the police do with that?

The head of the Stockholm police department's homicide squad was not a man who devoted himself to political theorizing. That sort of thing could be left to other people, and the government's attitude on one issue or another left him cold. He didn't usually even vote for them. On the other hand he was indignant because the government had meddled in his investigation and repatriated his perpetrators. How could a crime investigation be conducted if there was no opportunity to question the suspects?

The homicide chief had personally looked forward to being able to talk with them—in peace and quiet, in proper sequence, and as many times as needed to put all the pieces in the right place. He had managed this countless times before, and he was convinced he would have done so this time too, and without even needing the help of an interpreter. For in contrast to his colleagues he actually had a diploma, from Whitfeldska secondary school in Gothenburg no less, and his old school German was still impeccable. What the government had been guilty of in terms of technical investigation was pure sabotage. And the damage was not mitigated by the fact that they were certainly completely unaware of that fact.

So he and his colleagues basically had to be content with conducting a technical investigation under conditions that were far from ideal. Immediately after the explosion it appeared as if all hell had broken loose. According to what the terrorists had mentioned on the phone during one of their extortion calls with the government, they were supposed to have brought at least thirty pounds of TNT into the building and there was nothing at the scene that belied that assertion.

The efforts of the fire department, however unavoidable they were, had not made matters better—pouring tons of water on top of all the other debris was not good. But what had disturbed him and his colleagues most were all the more or less extraneous individuals running around at the crime scene. Their German colleagues, for example, hadn't added much to the affair, even if he made allowances for their involvement. If you were to be formal, the crime scene was actually German territory, so he had no right to simply tell them to leave.

It was the same way with the "felt slippers" from Sec and their irritating (to say the least) bad habit of always standing and glaring over his colleagues' shoulders when they were only trying to do their job. When in addition they had the gall to offer him their own technicians, he really put his foot down, because if you worked that way it would all turn out to be a muddle, and personally he did not intend to spend his time pissing in the woods. Others could do that, and if they didn't want to rely on him and his men, they could take over the whole damn case themselves.

But it had not been good, and when the police chief, after more than a week, on the same day they took away the outer barricades, informed the homicide chief that the continued investigation would be run by the secret police, he had actually experienced it as a relief.

He and his colleagues, on the other hand, had managed to establish a fairly good idea of the reason for the explosion. There was nothing to point to the terrorists' having deliberately blown up the building. Instead most everything suggested an accident, carelessness, and ignorance combined, and the one who probably caused the discharge was the terrorists' own "explosives expert" who, like all children, put his fingers in the wrong place. He never would have passed an ordinary Swedish rock-blasting examination, as was shown with enviable clarity by the wiring and connections that survived the explosion, even if the tabloids had praised his expertise in this area.

But there was never more to it than that, and as far as the homicide chief was concerned it was really all the same. As mentioned, what the secret police actually accomplished in the investigation they took over was unclear. In any event nothing was done that led to judicial proceedings or legal actions; instead as usual they "worked in silence," and if anyone were to ask the homicide chief about it he was convinced that, as so often before, they had not accomplished much of anything. You didn't need to be a police officer to figure out that there must have been more individuals involved than the six terrorists who occupied the embassy building itself.

Who otherwise could have left the message that at one o'clock in the afternoon on Thursday the twenty-fourth of April landed in the mailboxes of three different international news agencies housed in the Swedish News Agency TT's office in the first Hötorget skyscraper, less than two miles and no more than five minutes by car from the West German embassy out on Djurgården? The six people inside the building— "commando holger meins" as they called themselves with lowercase letters throughout—could not have done it in any event.

The head of the homicide squad had thought a good deal about what must have happened before the six had entered the embassy. They must have had somewhere to stay; they must have done reconnaissance on the scene, likely tracked those who worked there and mapped out their routines, investigated suitable ways to get there and to flee if something went awry. They must have had a roof over their heads, beds to sleep in, tables, chairs, and eating utensils, vehicles to ride in, food and drink and all the practical nastiness in the form of weapons, explosives, and false documents. All combined, the preparations for the operation must have taken at least a month or two.

In a word, the terrorists must have had help. Probably from several individuals. Probably from individuals with a connection to Sweden and Stockholm. Individuals who spoke Swedish, who were familiar with the area, with the surroundings, with local customs, usage, and everyday necessities such as buying a ticket for the subway or shopping for large quantities of food in a grocery store without attracting attention. Ordinary, anonymous people their own age without a criminal record who looked and thought the way they did.

The head of the homicide squad was not one to complicate matters unnecessarily. In his profession he had learned that the simplest explanation is most often the right one. A group of young students, he thought. Radical, motivated, with self-discipline and minds in good working order. Perhaps they even lived together in one of those strange collectives he had read about in the newspaper. And a not terribly bold guess was that they were Swedes.

When he turned over the case to his colleague at Sec who would be assuming responsibility for the investigation, he brought up his musings. Simply a few words in passing, which of course he should have spared himself. His colleague was not a real police officer but rather a legally educated police superintendent of the usual self-confident type and his reaction was familiar.

He had nodded with the expression of a man who always knows best, sighed wearily, and drawn a well-manicured index finger along his long nose. "I'm sure that thought has occurred to us too," said the police superintendent deliberately, but that was it. Before long the head of the homicide squad thought less and less about the whole matter, and after a few years it was not even included in the assortment of heroic police stories he used to tell when he encountered real policemen. Nowadays there were newer, better ones.

Otherwise the secret police should have had a few things to work with. The warnings that German terrorists were planning some form of action on Swedish soil had arrived with increasing frequency during the year preceding the embassy occupation. It was a jumble of high and low, just as it ought to have been: anonymous leads, information from various informants, and even a report prepared by one of Sec's own undercover agents, but they all had one thing in common. There was nothing concrete or tangible to get hold of, and during the spring it had seemed most likely that the whole thing had settled down. All was quiet on the informant front; not even their best informants had the least little thing to bring in.

A few leads and observations had also arrived via colleagues within the open operation. Mostly they concerned "mysterious vehicles" and "shady individuals" who had been observed at and around the West German embassy before the terrorists' action, but despite investing a lot of time in following them up, they had not led to anything. It was exactly as usual, in other words, for leads of this type almost never led to anything. This is in contrast to activities you initiated and guided yourself in the form of surveillance, infiltration, and the organized gathering of information through telephone monitoring, other types of eavesdropping and radio surveillance.

The recurring assertions in the media that the secret police had ignored a clear threat were discussed at several of the secret police's command meetings, and also in the secret police's parliamentary committee. As so often in the past it was possible to show that this was pure nonsense, baseless idle speculation intended to damage the operation. Measures had been taken that there was reason to take, and for a few weeks, when the host of rumors was at its strongest, the West German embassy had been entered on the list of highly prioritized surveillance objects.

The result of that measure had been unambiguous. No indications whatsoever had emerged that something was in progress, and the allocated extra surveillance had been withdrawn, which was a gift from above because the Russian squad suddenly had an unexpected need for extra personnel. The parliamentarians in the committee were completely satisfied with the report they received. The occupation of the West German embassy was an isolated incident, planned and executed by a faction within the West German terrorist underground that could best be described as a collection of fanatical loose cannons from the University of Heidelberg. According to information Stockholm authorities had received from their colleagues in the German secret police, many of the faction's more established comrades—in the regrettably extensive circle of radical elements—had taken strong exception to what had occurred. The embassy occupation had not benefited the common struggle.

Leading that struggle to a successful finish demanded better planning and more organization. The Swedish secret police, strangely enough, drew the same conclusion in the report that was submitted to their committee less than a year after the embassy drama. "For this reason, among others, the risk of another, similar event on Swedish territory, directed against German or Swedish interests and executed by German terrorists, is judged to be very small." There were "other risks that [were] significantly more serious," and regardless of whether this was true or false, it would have been bureaucratic suicide to maintain the opposite. And the secret police's investigation of the embassy drama was thereby concluded.

IV

What remained were the memories. Police memories.

Jarnebring remembered the smell of burnt telephone, but because that was an extremely unusual smell even at his place of work, less common even than the odor of madeleines, that was not what would bring up the images in his head. Other things did, or nothing at all. Sometimes, most often in his dreams, the memories of those minutes in the stairwell of the embassy would come crowding in on him without his having the least idea how or why. It was no big deal, for fairly soon he stopped talking about what had happened, and not long after that he also stopped wondering about it. We human beings are fortunately constituted in that respect, he thought.

His best friend and closest colleague, Lars Martin Johansson, a newly appointed detective inspector as of a month before the embassy occupation, also had his memories despite the fact that he had not even been in the vicinity of the West German embassy. On Thursday the twenty-fourth of April 1975 he had taken comp time to take care of his two small children who were too runny-nosed to go to day care. He had followed the embassy drama from the couch in front of the TV in his living room on Wollmar Yxkullsgatan on Söder. And he had definitely not phoned Jarnebring ten times, despite what Jarnebring's wife at the time maintained. He had phoned three times, neither more nor less, and not to satisfy his curiosity either but to ease his worry about what might happen to his best friend.

In a way he too had become a victim of what had happened. In his line of work there was no merit in sitting at home taking care of sick children while all of his comrades who were able to stand upright were in position with service revolvers covering the embassy. The gibes had come pouring in and had continued for quite some time. They reached their peak about a month after the embassy drama, when someone furnished the name plate outside his office with a printed label with his name at the top, and below that his new title: DIRECTOR OF THE GRASS SNAKE DAY CARE CENTER.

For a time what had happened was also played out in some quiet bickering with his best friend and closest colleague. When the phone rang in their joint office—often because someone wanted to speak with a different Lars Johansson than the one who happened to sit with Jarnebring in the police headquarters on Kungsholmen—it would be resolved by waiting as long as possible to answer. Usually it was the caller who gave up first.

But not always, and when the ringing at times got too persistent, Lars Martin Johansson would glance up from whatever papers he was occupied with at the moment, sniff like a foxhound, and look questioningly at his best friend and colleague.

"Am I the only one who thinks it smells like burnt telephone?"

And after that Jarnebring would always pick up the receiver.

Someone else who had strong memories of the embassy drama, besides having been involved from start to finish, was then police constable Stridh. Stridh was driving a patrol car on Östermalm, and Djurgården was part of his area. Stridh was also in charge of the patrol car that arrived first at the West German embassy, according to his own notes up to the moment before central command sent out the alarm he was responding to, and only due to the fact that his watch was a few minutes slow.

Stridh's quick action had greatly surprised both his bosses and his colleagues, among whom Stridh was best known—to put it gently and collegially—for his thoughtfulness. His colleagues had nicknamed him "Peace at Any Price," and he was not someone who had become the human face of the Stockholm police department's rapid action out in the field. There were others who had done that.

The reason that he had been the "first man on the scene" at the West German embassy was not due to the fact that he normally patrolled in that area and thus, purely statistically, ought to have had at least a decent chance of doing so. He was actually a master at avoiding such things, and especially in spring when there were many of his motorized and considerably more ready colleagues who would take the opportunity for a drive out on Djurgården. There was a different reason.

The week before the embassy drama he had responded to a simple, rather harmless request over the radio. There was a guard at the Norwegian embassy who had observed a suspicious personal car prowling around the area and wondered, "Was there anyone in the vicinity who would check the vehicle in question?" Because this sounded innocent enough and the car it concerned was only fifty yards ahead of them on Djurgårdsbrunnsvägen in line with the Maritime History Museum, Stridh and his colleague had taken the assignment. They stopped the vehicle and conducted an ordinary, routine traffic check.

It was a fairly new, far from inexpensive Mercedes. It was being driven by a young man, about twenty-five, and beside him sat an even younger woman. All papers were completely in order, and the young people in the car were pleasant, a bit giggly and a little nervous, as decent people easily get when stopped by the police. Without his having asked the question, the young woman explained that this was her parents' car and that they were just out for a drive with no particular destination. Stridh had no further questions. He nodded amiably as he gave back the young man's driver's license, and when he and his colleague had driven away he thought about spring and youth and love. Then they drove to the station to take a coffee break, and if it hadn't been for what happened a few days later, he would certainly have forgotten the entire incident.

His colleague on the radio had called again. The same guard had observed the same vehicle he had seen a few days before, and he asked if there was possibly a car in the vicinity that could keep an eye out for the vehicle in question and preferably also take a swing past the embassy and talk with the person who had called. Stridh had taken the assignment, and to keep things simple he had driven straight to the embassy without looking for any Mercedeses en route. There were plenty of cars of that make in that particular area.

At the embassy Stridh had spoken with the guard who had called the police. He was about thirty-five, Norwegian, a nice guy who without asking served coffee and cookies while they were talking. Norway, Norwegians, and the Norwegian embassy did not have a score to settle with anyone, yet the embassy guard had observed the vehicle in question on at least four occasions in as many days. Considering that the Germans were right across the street, after his second sighting he had decided to call the police.

"Have you talked with your colleague at the German embassy?" asked Stridh.

He had not. If he could avoid it, he did not talk with Germans for personal reasons. He preferred to talk with the Swedish police.

"They put my father in Grini," he explained, and that was good enough for Stridh, whose major interest in life was not police work but modern European history. In contrast to some of his colleagues he had never had any problems with his historical sympathies.

"I know what you mean," said Stridh with a Norwegian intonation and smiled. Nice guy, he thought.

When he drove away half an hour later he first intended to write a few lines about the matter, but on closer consideration he decided to let it be. A simple mental note would have to suffice, for regardless of whether the guard seemed to be a good, reliable fellow, his information was far from certain. Thus he could not say without a doubt that it had been the same car all four times. Two times it was, for then he had managed to get the license plate number. And unfortunately he had a rather uncertain memory of the driver. The first time it was a young man who drove, and he had someone beside him in the passenger seat; this the guard was "rather certain" of, but he had not managed to see if it was a "boy or a girl." The second time that he had taken the license plate number he was "almost sure" that the car was being driven by "a boy" and that he was alone in the vehicle, but if he was also the same young man as the one who had a passenger with him on the earlier occasion he could not say.

After having pondered the matter further, Stridh decided that there must be some banal, natural explanation and to refrain from the mental note as well. Right before lunch on Thursday the twenty-fourth of April 1975, he changed his mind. The next morning, despite the fact that he was dead tired after working far into the night, he drove to the station, borrowed a typewriter, and wrote a lengthy, completely perspicacious summary of his observations and his conversation with the guard at the Norwegian embassy. This he gave to his boss, who nodded and promised to pass it on to "the spies up at Kungsholmen."

After that nothing happened. No one called, and as time passed he forgot the whole thing. You just had to assume that one of the secret police colleagues had checked the whole thing out and reasonably come to the same conclusion that he himself had at first—namely, that there was some banal, very innocent explanation.

Therefore he had been extremely surprised when almost fifteen years later, in the middle of December 1989, a Commissioner Persson from the secret police rang the doorbell to his pleasant little two-room apartment on Rörstrandsgatan and wondered whether he had time to talk about the observations he had made in connection with the events at the West German embassy in April 1975.

Part 2

Another Life

1

Thursday evening, November 30, 1989

It turned out to be an alarm with a number of obstacles, and considering that it also turned out to be a murder it was unfortunate that it took so long before the police arrived at the scene. In the normal course of things, it might have been possible to save the life of the victim, or at least arrest the culprit and thus avoid a lot of inconvenience. But things were not normal, and so it turned out the way it did. At Stockholm Police Department's command center it was agreed, however, that it was not Charles XII's fault.

A few days earlier the legal department of that same police agency had granted permits for two different demonstrations, and both decisions had been preceded by considerable legal and mental exertion and extensive strategic and tactical consideration.

In the first application to arrive, various "patriotically minded organizations and individual Swedish citizens"—which was how they described themselves—wanted to "pay homage to the Swedish hero-king on the anniversary of his death." This was to occur in the form of a torchlight procession from Humlegården to the statue of Charles XII in Kungsträdgården, with massed standards, the laying of a wreath and speeches at the statue itself, and the whole thing was planned to start at 1900 hours and be finished at 2100 hours at the latest.

The very next day another application arrived. A number of political youth organizations, representing with one exception all of the parties in parliament, wanted to conduct "a broad, popular manifestation against xenophobia and racism." So far so good. But for reasons that were not completely clear, in any case not evident from their request, the intention was to conduct this demonstration on that very same Thursday, the thirtieth of November, between 1900 and 2200 hours. There would be a gathering in Humlegården, a march down Birger Jarls-gatan and up Hamngatan, concluding "with speeches and a joint procla-mation" at Sergels Torg, all of 400 yards from the statue of Charles XII in Kungsträdgården.

As far as political opinions were concerned, the participants in the two demonstrations were, to put it mildly, dissimilar, to the point where they could easily be sorted into two different piles based solely on their appearance. And this nonexistent common interest would evidently be expressed at the same time and the same place. The sharp minds in the legal department were struck by this. In brief, trickery was suspected, and in order to prevent difficulties, the good old police rule of thumb was followed to separate even presumptive troublemakers.

This plan primarily affected the group of the "patriotically minded." There was no question of playing political favorites—of course, no offi-cial authority could support such things. The decision was made solely on the basis of police department estimates of the relative size of the two groups. Democratic decisions were after all in many respects made based on a question of size, and the friends of the fatherland were con-siderably fewer in number. As the chief inspector on the detective squad in charge of estimates summarized the matter, it concerned at the most a few hundred, "a few old queers from the Finnish Winter War plus their younger, skinhead comrades," which was not "very much to hang on the Christmas tree if it's democracy we're talking about here."

So true, so true. And in a time of severely strained police resources the patriotically minded demonstrators were thus granted permission to gather at the pier below the Grand Hotel at 1800 hours, walk in forma-tion about a hundred yards to the statue of Charles XII, where of course it was fine both to lay wreaths and to give speeches, provided that the event was over at 1900 hours at the latest and that the crowd then "dis-persed in good order." They could even sing the national anthem if they wanted to, despite the fact that, probably due to a simple omission, this activity had not been included in the application.

On the other hand, they could forget about the torches. "You don't really think we're dim-witted," as the same chief inspector remarked in explaining the rejection when one of the organizers phoned him to discuss that particular detail. And as far as flag-waving was concerned, it was assumed that this would be kept within reasonable bounds.

On the other hand, because the participants in "the broad popular manifestation," exactly as promised and according to a similar police department calculation, could be assumed to amount to several thousand, based on the same democratic principles the authorities had been considerably more generous. On the condition that the gathering really commenced at 1900 hours, and in no event earlier, it was fine for the demonstration to set off from Humlegården. And the demonstration could end at Sergels Torg if the crowd took Kungsgatan and Sveavägen instead of Birger Jarlsgatan and Hamngatan.

All available police personnel were then called up, and to be on the safe side they were reinforced with a few hundred men from around the country. An "iron ring" was formed around Kungsträdgården, and the route of the counterdemonstrators was secured yard by yard and well supplied with mobile reserves behind the front lines. Literally everything was being done, it was being done by the book and in the best way, and already by eight p.m. complete chaos prevailed in Stockholm City: rock throwing, window breaking, battered cars . . . swollen lips, bloody noses, black eyes, broken arms, scraped knees, even a knife cut. There were howling sirens, flashing blue lights, yet at the command center they managed to keep a straight face when in the midst of it all an elderly woman phones and maintains that someone is murdering her neighbor.

Between 2005 and 2020 hours, she calls the emergency number 90 000 a total of three times. She is quickly transferred to the police command center. Already during the first call she sounds very upset but nonetheless she starts by saying in good order what her name is and where she lives: "Rådmansgatan . . . up by Engelbrekt Church, you know." After that she says, verbatim, according to the police department's time-logged recording of the conversation, "You've got to come at once. Someone is murdering my neighbor. I think he's dying."

The female radio dispatcher tries to calm her as best she can and asks her to stay on the phone while she dispatches the alarm on the radio, but while she tries to find someone to send out, the call is cut off. Probably because the woman who called hung up.

The next call comes at 2014 hours, and the old woman's voice sounds close to tears. "You've got to come. You've got to come," and in the midst of the general muddle that prevails this call too is cut off and no available patrol car has yet been reached.

The third and final call comes at 2020. Now the woman is screaming loudly into the telephone that "the murderers are knocking on my door," and this is the situation when detective inspector Bo Jarnebring has mercy on his colleague, the radio dispatcher, who has started to sound more and more stressed, takes the microphone out of its holder on the instrument panel, breaks his radio silence, and responds to the call from central command.

Inspector Bo Jarnebring was a few miles from the center of events. At eight p.m. on Thursday the thirtieth of November, he had been sitting for a couple of hours along with a female colleague in one of the detective squad's most discreet cars, keeping an eye on a restaurant fifty yards farther down the street. The first hour they had been accompanied by an additional surveillance vehicle, but then the growing chaos down in City had forced the officers to respond to more pressing assignments instead.

Jarnebring and his partner were sitting there because of a tip that had come in the day before. This was, incidentally, the most common reason for anyone's spending time in this way, and if any one of the growing number of bureaucrats in police headquarters ever got the notion to produce statistics on this activity as well, then he (for it was almost always a he) or (in exceptional cases) she would have discovered that as a rule the sitting was in vain. It was exactly like hunting or fishing, uncertainty and waiting were basically the whole idea, and whether or not you got anything it was, at least to start with, exciting enough.

The catch that their informant had promised this time wasn't bad either. According to the informant, who in the name of discretion lacked all identifying features but in reality was almost always a man with a criminal record, an internationally wanted Iranian drug dealer at the wholesale level would show up around six p.m. to have dinner and discuss a little business with a like-minded countryman.

Jarnebring, who had neither been born yesterday nor recently fallen off a cart, had of course asked the informant why in such a case the Iranians would choose to hold this get-together at a restaurant that with good reason was known for its Swedish home cooking, but the informant had an answer: "Saddam is an ace at not giving himself away, likes sort of exotic settings you know, and besides he's crazy about Swedish meatballs."

Sounds almost too good to be true, Jarnebring had thought. Because he was also an incorrigible optimist and interested in both hunting and fishing, he had been sitting there for the past two hours. The last half hour, however, had felt a little long, and to get a break from the tedium he had turned on the police radio to listen to the action playing out down in City.

Despite the cacophony on the radio he had also heard the call about an ongoing violent crime in an apartment on Rådmansgatan, but because he was familiar with the address and those who lived there—a nice block with conscientious middle-aged, middle-class residents—he understood at once that the person who had called was certainly an older woman who would not get worked up unnecessarily.

He still thought that when the second call came in, but he also noted that the voice of his female colleague on the radio was starting to sound a trifle dejected. So when a short time later she dispatched the call for the third time, now actually sounding a little beleaguered, he sighed, took the radio microphone from its holder, and replied.

"Jarnebring here," he said into the microphone. "Can I help you, little lady?" What meatballs, he thought sourly.

So the Iranian lived on, and presumably he and the informant were sitting in a completely different part of the city chowing down couscous and roast goat, or whatever that sort usually ate, while they laughed their heads off at all the dumb cops cultivating their hemorrhoids in the worn-down front seat of an increasingly chilly unmarked car.

"Let's forget about the gook," said Jarnebring to his colleague. "Drive to Rådmansgatan."

She merely nodded without answering. She looked surly, thought Jarnebring. Probably because of that "little lady" remark. She was rather good-looking, if you liked dark-haired ladies. Personally he preferred blondes. And the occasional redhead, provided she was a genuine redhead. Although of course they weren't that common, he thought.

But she could drive a car, he had to admit that, for in just over two minutes and after two U-turns she had taken them from the west end of Tegnérgatan to the address in question on Rådmansgatan. And en route he had obtained an entry code to the outside door from the "little lady" at the command center. On the other hand she had not produced a key to the apartment door, but he could take care of that with the help of the bag of police accessories he kept in the storage compartment of the car.

"Let's do this," said Jarnebring as she stopped the car outside the entryway on Rådmansgatan. "I'll take the walkie-talkie and check the apartment, and you kill anyone who tries to sneak out onto the street."

Now she actually smiled. She really is good-looking, thought Jarnebring as he disappeared through the entryway with his bag and the walkie-talkie. While he was sprinting up the stairs he suddenly felt more exhilarated than he had in a long time.

His delight was short-lived. Jarnebring stopped at the third floor to get an overview: rectangular stairwell, four apartments, two doors at an angle to each other at each end. The name of the victim was Eriksson and his door was farthest away. To the left of it was an ornate brass plate with the surname of the person who had called central command and introduced herself as "Mrs. Westergren, Ingrid Westergren."

Jarnebring tiptoed up to the door to Eriksson's apartment. Silent as a grave, not a movement anywhere. He carefully tried the door handle. The door was locked, and when he bent down to peep in through the mail slot, at the same time as he loosened the holster strap that secured his service weapon, in the corner of his eye he saw a faint dent not half an inch long in the dark glazed wood on Mrs. Westergren's door. Because the dent was at a level with Eriksson's door handle and the door lacked a doorstop, he realized at once what had happened.

The perpetrator or perpetrators had not tried to break into Mrs. Westergren's, as she had told the radio dispatcher. On the other hand it was probable that someone had thrown open Eriksson's door in great haste, whereupon his door handle had struck Mrs. Westergren's door. Without thinking about it, he buttoned the strap on his pistol handle again, carefully opened the mail slot slightly, and peeked in.

He had done this a hundred times before during his life as a police officer, and on a few occasions it had struck him that this might just be his last action on the job, because he might find himself looking straight into the barrels of a shotgun. But he did not think that way very often; fortunately he did not have that disposition. And it hadn't happened now. What he saw was good enough.

There was a light on in the hall. Straight ahead was a living room behind a pair of open, glazed double doors.

In the living room there was a couch, and in front of the couch a coffee table, approximately twenty or twenty-five feet from the outside door. The coffee table had been overturned and there was a lot of blood on the light parquet floor. Squeezed between the couch and the coffee table was a motionless man on his stomach. It was not a comfortable position, and you didn't need to be a police officer like Jarnebring to figure out that the man had not chosen to lie down there voluntarily.

Oh shit, thought Jarnebring, straightening up. People never can behave decently to each other.

Then he tapped out the hinges on the door and went into the apartment.

First he made sure the victim really was dead. He was, even if he did not appear to have been dead for very long. He had bled heavily from both his nose and mouth. His shirt was soaked through with blood from a wound that seemed to be high up on the left side of his back.

Probably stabbed with a knife, thought Jarnebring. Lungs, heart, major organs were penetrated; trying to resuscitate him would be wasted effort, he thought.

Then he straightened up, drew his service weapon, and carefully searched through the apartment to make certain that the victim was not only dead but also alone at home. Three rooms, hall, kitchen, bathroom, separate toilet, a large clothes closet, a total of about a thousand square feet, strikingly clean and neat, and there was nothing to suggest anything other than that the victim had had sole use of the apartment.

Jarnebring was careful about where he set his feet, and he kept his fingers under control the whole time out of consideration for the crime technicians, but this didn't prevent him from peeking under the bed, behind the shower curtain in the bathroom, and in the darkest corners of the clothes closet. He had found more than one perpetrator that way over the years.

But not this time, this time it was empty.

The rest was pure routine. He made contact with the command center on the radio. They promised to send people—"on the double"—from the duty desk and the tech squad, as well as reinforcements from the uniformed police. A murder took precedence even over degenerate political demonstrations.

On the other hand, the canine patrol that Jarnebring tried to requisition could not be mobilized. The four-legged colleagues that were on duty had been busy with other things between their jaws for the past few hours. On the other hand, taxi drivers would be questioned as to whether they'd had any interesting fares to and from the victim's address.

While they waited, Jarnebring and his female colleague did what they could. The first crime scene barriers were put in place. They searched within the building and out toward the street where the victim lived, the courtyard and back building as well. They checked interesting entryways in the vicinity and noted license numbers on all cars parked in the area, in case the perpetrator was in such a hurry that he had not managed to take the car in which he might have arrived. The growing crowd of curious people who had gathered down on the street were gradually questioned, and very soon the plan was to start knocking on doors in a more organized manner.

Half an hour later Jarnebring and his colleague had done everything possible, and given the conditions no one could have done it better. But because neither the people from the duty desk nor tech had shown up yet, he already suspected whom he was waiting for, and that things would soon change.

2

Thursday evening, November 30–
The night of Friday, December 1, 1989

Bäckström was short, fat, and crude whereas Wiijnbladh was short, slender, and dapper. Together they complemented each other splendidly and they were also happy working together. Bäckström thought that Wiijnbladh was a cowardly half-fairy—you didn't even have to raise your voice, and he still did what he was told. Wiijnbladh in turn viewed Bäckström as mentally challenged and bad-tempered—a dream to work with for anyone who preferred having the situation under control himself. Because they were both solidly incompetent, no disputes arose on either factual or other professional grounds, and to sum up, they made a real radar unit.

Bäckström was a detective inspector and normally worked on the homicide squad, but because he was a bachelor, had no children, and his finances were always shaky, he took every opportunity to sign up for a little extra duty. He was no numbskull either, so the thirtieth of November was a day he normally would have avoided, but because it was getting toward Christmas he had no choice. These were hard times, and they would not get better for a long while.

It had turned out just as badly that night as he had feared. His colleagues in the uniformed police shoveled in piles of the worst kind of rowdies. Lots of snot-nosed youngsters who thought that rock throwing was a democratic right and began every attempt at conversation by threatening to report the interrogator for assault and making reference to Daddy, who was either a senior physician at the psych clinic, a technical adviser at the Ministry of Justice, or an editorial writer at *Dagens Nyheter.*

To begin with Bäckström had managed nicely—not so strange in itself, given his experience—but he had to work like a tightrope walker to keep out of the way, and he basically pulled out every trick he had in his considerable repertoire. First he locked himself in the john to leaf through both *Little Pravda* and *Excessen* in peace and quiet—the only place imaginable where a person could read such shit. Then he slipped down and took a nap for a while at registration, but when he came back to his office he was immediately forced to snatch up a dead telephone receiver and sit humming and nodding while a couple of half-apes from the riot squad stood in his doorway and more or less tried to stare him out. He waved dismissively at them several times but they didn't even react. How the hell did those guys get to be police officers?

The chief inspector on duty arrived like a rescuing angel, surly as usual and a fundamentalist. He was a bastard of course, but in a crisis situation you couldn't be too particular.

"Stop your monkeyshines now, Bäckström," said the boss. "I have a murder for you. Some wretch in an apartment on Rådmansgatan has checked out. We have a shortage of cars, so you'll have to ride with tech. Luck of the draw. Let's hope for our Lord's sake the victim doesn't have any relatives," he said piously as he was leaving.

Rådmansgatan. Sounds good, thought Bäckström. Not a high gook alert at that address, and if his luck held maybe it would prove to be something really juicy. Worthy of an old pro like himself.

On the way out he took the opportunity to sneak into the break room and liberate the last Danish pastries. A whole bag, in fact. Who wanted to risk landing in a murder investigation on an empty stomach? Besides, there was plenty of time for a pot of fresh-brewed coffee with Wiijnbladh up at the tech squad while he explained to the miserable half-fairy what this was about before they began the evening's exercises.

Wiijnbladh was looking forward to a calm, quiet evening filled with edifying reading. True, there were demonstrations out in the city, and apparently an awful commotion, but a major advantage of even violent uprisings was that they seldom gave rise to a lot of forensic misery, the need for such disappearing naturally in the general confusion that prevailed in such contexts. In relatively undisturbed peace he would thus be able to go through old issues of the *Annals of Forensic Science* in hopes of finding some good hints for how, in a completely risk-free manner, he might be able to eliminate his wife. Some kind of poison, thought Wiijnbladh. Definitely not the usual messiness with blunt objects and firearms. He had seen more than enough of that at work. Some effective, discreet poison that he could sneak into her completely unnoticed, and that would preferably cause severe pain when it was too late to do anything about it. She so deserved that. And who of all his half-moronic, visually handicapped colleagues would be able to detect something like that? None of them, thought Wiijnbladh with emphasis, turning the page in his thick book just as his phone rang.

The call was from the duty desk where a murder had come in. At first—in a moment of terror—he got the idea that it had happened during the demonstrations and he would have to spend the night outside in a merciless November wind, but when he understood that the crime scene was indoors, in an apartment on Rådmansgatan, he heaved a quiet sigh of relief. Until that horrid fat slob Bäckström showed up. Waving a lot of sticky pastries squished down in a sack, more or less forcing him to brew fresh coffee while they "talked over the strategy."

What did he have to say to such a person? But then again, what choice did he have? A man of peace like him, an educated man like him, now being sent out into the cold by a stern fate with this police department Neanderthal who had already managed to consume two pastries before the coffee was even ready.

Poor man, thought Wiijnbladh, and it was the murder victim and not himself he had in mind. Let's hope he doesn't have any family.

So it had started as it always did when he and Bäckström had to march out to the field.

"Maybe we'd better get moving," said Wiijnbladh, glancing nervously at his watch.

Bäckström didn't even answer. How could he with his mouth full of

Danish pastries? He simply shook his head and waved his fleshy, hot dog-like fingers dismissively.

"I heard it was Jarnebring who responded to the alarm," Wiijnbladh said carefully. "So maybe it's best—"

"That fucking idiot," said Bäckström, but evidently that remark made an impression, for as soon as he'd finished chewing he got up and started buttoning up his coat around his fat stomach. Then he just nodded and finally they were on their way.

Jarnebring was standing in the entryway to welcome them when they arrived at the murder scene. He looked like a wolf. A big, hungry wolf, with eyes narrow as loopholes, deep-seated eyes set wide apart among the sharp angles of his lean face. He had shoulder blades like guitar cases and arms that started at the wrists and only ended where his thick neck started. He was also dressed in a mid-length black leather jacket, worn blue jeans, and heavy boots. And as far as Wiijnbladh was concerned, he might just as well have worn a black hood and carried a scythe over his shoulder.

"Did you crawl here?" he asked courteously, looking at the watch that fit tightly around his bony wrist, and Wiijnbladh felt the cold fingers of death groping for his heart.

"Nice to see you, Jarnebring," said Wiijnbladh as he tried hard to smile amiably and hold his voice in check. "The traffic is awful, as you know." Whatever you do, do not look him in the eyes, he thought; he had learned that at a course on how forensic technicians could avoid being bitten by mad dogs.

"How's the door knocking going?" asked Bäckström. "If you take care of that, Jarnebring, then Wiijnbladh and I will see to putting some order into the investigation." And then he only nodded curtly and continued up the stairs.

Say what you will about Bäckström, thought Wiijnbladh with sudden warmth, falling in behind his fat back before the grim reaper could get hold of him.

Jarnebring did not say anything, didn't move, didn't even blink. He shrugged his shoulders and nodded at his female colleague. Poor bastard, he thought, and it was not Bäckström or Wiijnbladh that he was thinking about.

Jarnebring and his new, and temporary, female colleague—and that was how he viewed her without the question even being discussed—devoted the majority of the evening of the thirtieth of November to knocking on doors, which had always been their intention, in fact, regardless of what Bäckström thought about it. They spoke with almost all the victim's neighbors, a total of about twenty people in the building facing the street and ten or so in the back building. Almost everyone who lived there was at home. They were mostly older people, many of them living alone, and with a few exceptions they had been sitting in front of the TV at the time their neighbor was murdered.

When the police rang their doorbells they were without exception friendly and obliging, and in a number of cases truly exerted themselves to answer the police officers' questions. In a practical sense the door-to-door inquiries went easily and smoothly, but in a factual sense it was an unmitigated catastrophe. No one had seen anything, no one had heard anything, no one knew the victim, the majority did not even seem aware of his existence. The one who seemed to know him best, his closest neighbor Mrs. Westergren, who had called the police, had for the most part only said hello to him on those occasions when they met in the stairwell.

Jarnebring and his female colleague started with her, and Jarnebring suggested that perhaps his partner ought to lead the questioning. The witness was extremely agitated and he had an idea that a woman—despite the fact that she was half the age of the witness—might perhaps make the witness feel more comfortable. Which proved to be true. His younger colleague handled the questioning in an exemplary fashion and Jarnebring just sat there and listened. It felt unusual, but not at all unpleasant. The new generation is taking over, Jarnebring thought philosophically, and concentrated instead on appearing as secure and confidence inspiring as possible.

First they talked about the witness herself, Mrs. Westergren. Then about the victim, her closest neighbor Kjell Göran Eriksson, who had just turned forty-five at the time of his demise, according to the information that Jarnebring had received from the duty desk a while earlier. Only after that did his colleague bring up the events that had led Mrs. Westergren to call the emergency number. The entire conversation was conducted in a careful, systematic, professional manner and the results were as thin as gruel.

Mrs. Westergren herself was sixty-five years old and recently retired from a job as an official at a bank in Stockholm. She lived alone, had no children, and had moved into the building after her divorce some ten years earlier.

"My ex-husband and I had a house out in Bromma," she explained. "When we separated and sold the house, I bought this apartment. It's a condominium."

Then she told what little she knew about Eriksson. He had moved into the building a few years later, and that was when she had her only long conversation with him. She had knocked on his door to welcome him, and he had invited her in for a cup of coffee.

"I was on the association's board, after all, the condo association that is, and I thought that it was appropriate. Yes . . . and then he was my closest neighbor too."

But there had not been much more.

"He introduced himself of course, but I already knew what his name was. I'd seen it on the paperwork when he bought the apartment. Yes . . . then he said that he worked at the Central Bureau of Statistics. With labor market statistics, as I recall. But he didn't actually say much more than that. He seemed rather reserved. Yes, not disagreeable or anything, not really, but far from talkative."

He must have riled up someone in any event, thought Jarnebring, but of course he didn't say that.

What was he like as a person?

"As a neighbor he was almost ideal, I guess, if you appreciate peace and quiet. He never made any fuss. He never went to the association meetings or anything. I don't think he knew anyone here in the building."

Did he have any friends that Mrs. Westergren had noticed?

"No women in any event. I don't believe I ever saw him with a woman during all the years he lived here. Sometimes I saw that he had visitors, but it was always men his own age. There were some that I've seen on at least a few occasions. But it really didn't happen very often that I saw him having visitors. The last time must have been several months ago. Yes . . . and this evening then . . . a few hours ago." Mrs. Westergren had become noticeably paler.

What was it that made her call the police?

"I heard that he had a visitor. I had just come in the door. I'd been out shopping. It must have been some time around seven. I was standing in the hallway hanging up my coat when I heard someone ringing his doorbell. Yes . . . he opened the door and said something and then the door was closed."

Had the visitor said anything? Did she have any idea who the visitor was?

She did not. The murder victim's mysterious visitor had not only been unseen but unheard as well. The witness herself had not thought any more about it. Besides, why should she? Her neighbor had a visit from someone that he knew, and, true, it wasn't common, but it was no more than that. She had gone out into the kitchen, made a cup of tea and a warm sandwich, which she brought into the living room. She'd had her sandwich, finished her tea, and then read a magazine she had bought when she was out shopping. She preferred reading, you see, and she almost never watched TV.

"It must have been about then that it started . . . right before eight o'clock. I remember that I was looking at the clock, because at first I had the idea that it was his TV that I was hearing. But of course it wasn't that. . . . I realized that. I heard how he was screaming . . . how he bellowed right out . . . Then I heard thumps from the furniture as if someone was falling or as if . . . Yes, as if he was fighting with someone then . . . Yes, my neighbor, I mean. It was only him that I heard. Not the other one . . . although they must have been fighting. What is it the lawyers always say—it's in the nature of things—although that was what was so strange." Mrs. Westergren shook her head.

What was it that had been strange?

What was so strange was that he had not sounded afraid. Angry, furious, crazy with rage, but not afraid. Their witness had become noticeably paler as she spoke, but at the same time it was very clear that she was truly exerting herself to remember what she had heard.

"No," she said, shaking her head. "Not afraid, he sounded more like he was angry . . . or furious . . . He just bellowed in rage . . . although I didn't hear what he was screaming."

"And you're certain that it was your neighbor you heard? Not the one who was visiting him?"

"Yes. It was Eriksson who screamed. He sounded completely insane actually. The other one I didn't hear. He was quiet, I guess."

But it was only when the neighbor's bellowing had ceased that she had phoned the police. By then she had heard him moaning loudly, and it sounded as though he was crawling around on the floor in the apartment. It was then that she made her first call to the police.

"It never stopped. It felt like an eternity. It sounded as if he was dying in there . . . and he was too.

"You never came," she said, and for some reason it was Jarnebring and not his colleague she was looking at when she said that.

Had she noticed anything else? Anything about Eriksson that struck her? Some observation that she had made? Any speculations she'd had?

Anything at all, thought Jarnebring. Give us anything at all because we're not picky. Just give us a little piece of thread that we can start pulling on.

"No," said Mrs. Westergren, suddenly looking guarded. "Like what?"

She's hiding something, thought Jarnebring, feeling the familiar scent in his nostrils, but before he managed to ask the question, his colleague got there first.

"Let me put it like this, Mrs. Westergren," she said with a friendly smile. "In my job the people we encounter are rarely completely black or completely white . . . in a moral sense that is. It's more complicated than that. I'm thinking about what you've told me and my colleague. Everything you've said indicates that it was someone who knew Eriksson who attacked him. Why? Eriksson doesn't appear to have associated with any crazy people. What was it about Eriksson that might provoke someone he knew to the degree that he—"

"Murdered him." Mrs. Westergren looked pale as she finished the sentence.

"What I mean is . . . what was it about him that could have caused someone to do that?"

Well done, thought Jarnebring. She has not said "murder" the whole time. She was really good-looking too. Although maybe a little thin?

"I don't really know," said Mrs. Westergren. "I have no idea what it could have been."

His female colleague just nodded without saying anything, simply looking at the older woman who sat across from her. Friendly, cautious, encouraging. Now then . . .

"I had the feeling," said Mrs. Westergren hesitantly, "that he had started to drink a great deal recently. That something was worrying him. It's not like I saw him drunk or anything . . . but there was something. The last few times I saw him . . . he seemed really nervous." Mrs. Westergren nodded in confirmation, and looked almost relieved herself.

Well, well, well, thought Jarnebring. Then we'll have to find out what sort of thing it was, and then the prosecutor can take over.

When the door knocking was finally finished it was almost midnight and they had gathered in the victim's apartment for a first go-through. The corpse had already been carted away, leaving only the impressions of his upper body and head on the blood-covered parquet floor where he had been lying. It was clear that effort had been devoted to searching for fingerprints—that flagship of police work—because moldings, handles, and cupboard doors were smeared with black traces of carbon dust. For some reason they had also tidied up—the overturned coffee table, for example, was now standing in its usual position, and it was only to be hoped that Wijnbladh had managed to take photos before they'd rearranged the furniture. Bäckström sat and smoked as he wallowed in the largest armchair in the room, talking on the victim's phone while trying to make a show of not noticing either Jarnebring or his colleague. Wiijnbladh too was his usual self. Little, gray, and fussy as a sparrow that had just stopped pecking for a moment.

"Step right in, just step right in," said Wiijnbladh, waving a hand, his head at an angle. "Make yourselves at home. I realize that you want to take a look."

Fucking idiots, thought Jarnebring. How the hell can anyone like them become policemen?

Jarnebring and his new, temporary colleague made the rounds of the apartment, and considering that Eriksson was supposed to have been a bachelor it was a remarkable place. Not the least like Jarnebring's own two-room apartment over in Vasastan. If you disregarded the disarray created by the crime and the traces of Wiijnbladh's and the others' work, the place was quite tidy, neat, almost overfurnished, and in a taste that Jarnebring neither shared nor would have had the means for.

"Strange fucking place," Jarnebring said to his new colleague.

"What do you mean?" she asked.

"To live in," said Jarnebring. "Hell, I don't live like this."

"Imagine that," she said. "Believe it or not, I didn't expect you to."

Wiijnbladh displayed his finds, lined up like trophies on the coffee table. Although he looked like a sparrow he was still proud as a rooster for he had "secured both the murder weapon and a great number of other interesting clues."

"Yes, we found the murder weapon in the kitchen. The perpetrator had thrown it in the trash." Wiijnbladh pointed at a large carving knife with a black wooden handle, its shiny blade black with dried blood.

Congrats, thought Jarnebring sourly. This is almost too much to expect from someone as blind as you.

"Is this the victim's knife?" asked Jarnebring's colleague.

"It appears to be so, yes, it appears so," said Wiijnbladh, nodding insightfully. "The blade is almost a foot long, after all, so it's hardly something you would carry around."

"Sabatier," said Jarnebring's colleague. "French brand, kitchen knives, very expensive. I saw that the other knives in the holder out in the kitchen were also from Sabatier."

"Exactly, exactly," said Wiijnbladh, trying to look as though he were appearing on "Nobel Minds."

What the hell are they up to? thought Jarnebring, looking at his watch. It was past twelve and high time to hit the sack before a new day with fresh mayhem and misery, and here they are yakking about the victim's choice of kitchen utensils. Even a child could figure out where the knife had come from.

"I'm hearing that you were in the home ec program out at the police academy," said Bäckström to Jarnebring's colleague. "It didn't exist in my day, but maybe we can stop talking domestic science and try to get something done.

"I've talked with your boss, Jarnebring," Bäckström continued, "and he has promised that both you and your girlfriend will help out. So if we could meet at homicide tomorrow morning at nine, I'll thank you ladies and gentlemen for a pleasant evening."

Watch out, you little shit, thought Jarnebring, but he didn't say it.

There really were no major faults with his new, temporary colleague, even if she was a woman, thought Jarnebring as they drove away. First she had offered to put their car back in the garage at the police head-quarters on Kungsholmen—she lived nearby so that was no big deal—and on the way there she had driven him home.

"How does it feel to start working as a detective?" asked Jarnebring, who didn't want to be outdone.

"Good," she said, nodding. "I think I'm going to like it."

"You worked with the uniformed police," said Jarnebring, and this was more a statement than a question. Strange I didn't notice her, he thought.

"No," she said, shaking her head. "That was a long time ago."

It couldn't have been that long, thought Jarnebring. How old could she be? A little over thirty, tops.

"I worked at Sec," she said. "As a bodyguard."

The hell you did, thought Jarnebring, but naturally he didn't say it.

"And now you've wound up in a murder investigation," Jarnebring stated. With two real fools, he thought.

"It's my first one," she said, "so it will be interesting."

"With two real fools," said Jarnebring.

"You mean Bäckström and Wiijnbladh," she said and smiled. "I'd actually heard about them. Although it's only now that I'm starting to believe it's true . . . what I heard, that is."

"Bäckström is a known douche bag," said Jarnebring. "Let me know if he messes with you and I'll slap him around."

"No need to worry," she said, smiling wanly. "I can do that myself."

Strange gal, thought Jarnebring. Where the hell is the police department headed?

"So you can then," said Jarnebring, "in a pinch?"

"Yes," she said, nodding with her gaze directed straight ahead and her hands steady on the wheel. "I can. In a pinch."

When she dropped him off outside his door and before he had even managed to think up a suitable farewell line, she simply drove away.

"See you first thing tomorrow morning," she said and smiled. "Sleep tight now."

Jarnebring watched the car as it disappeared down the street. Anna Holt, he thought, Inspector Anna Holt. Strange he hadn't run into her before. After all, he'd been a policeman his entire adult life.

Bäckström had surprised Wiijnbladh. He had offered to stay behind and make sure the crime scene was locked and sealed before they drove away.

"Aren't you going to ride with me?" asked Wiijnbladh.

"No," said Bäckström, smiling mysteriously. "I've got a little something going if you know what I mean. And you have to drop off what we've confiscated up at tech. So I'll see you tomorrow."

"That's nice of you," said Wiijnbladh. What if I was to sleep at the office? he thought, but obviously he didn't say that to Bäckström.

. . .

Finally alone, thought Bäckström, and as soon as the little half-fairy Wiijnbladh disappeared out through the door with his bag and baggage Bäckström locked himself in and searched through the corpse's clothes closet. The bastard had cases of expensive alcohol. Bäckström thought about calling a taxi, but at the same time a real pro took no unnecessary risks. Who knew, there might still be some reporter outside on the street. Whatever. There would be other occasions to return for more bottles—rather that than the goods ending up in the general inheritance fund for any relatives the victim appeared not to have had. The bastard.

Good thing he had brought his winter coat. The be-all and end-all of crime scene investigation gear, thought Bäckström with delight, an ample coat with deep pockets. He put some well-chosen bottles in the pockets and then locked up from the outside with the victim's keys, pasted sealing tape on the door, and took off.

When he got home he sat down on the couch in front of the TV and inspected the goods he'd brought with him. Then he pondered how to set up the investigation so that he could mess with Jarnebring and that skinny police dummy he'd had with him.

"Cheers," said Bäckström, raising his glass of malt whiskey toward the blurred mirror image of himself in the dark TV screen. True, he didn't have any expensive furniture like the corpse, and it was high time that he brought home a whore who liked to clean and could get laid for clearing away the worst of it, but all in all he had it good enough. We're drinking the same alcohol, the corpse and I, thought Bäckström and sneered. Although I'm alive while he's dead. So he poured another ample shot before taking a pee, and just as he swallowed the last swig he saw the light. Suddenly he understood exactly the way things were, clear as water, the motive, the whole nine yards. Lit up like a plain under a flaming sky he saw the truth spread out before his eyes. Hell, thought Bäckström with delight. This is going to be fun.

3

Friday morning, December 1, 1989

Jarnebring's day had not started out well, but it got much better as it went on. At the end of the day things got a little shaky again, and if he hadn't pulled himself together as evening approached and showed some determination the day might have ended really badly. But there was finally a good end to it and a very promising weekend lay ahead. The reasons for this were complicated but were in all essentials connected with his love life, and personally he preferred not to think about it, much less talk about it.

For almost four years Jarnebring had been engaged. His fiancée worked as a uniformed police officer at Norrmalm. She was beautiful to look at, fun to be with, had considerable household talents, and led an orderly life. Besides, she was very much in love with Jarnebring, and so far all was well and good. The problem was the engagement, and time's more and more rapid flight, drawing him into some kind of strange union that he couldn't seem to get a handle on.

To start with, everything had been peace and harmony. Jarnebring moved in with his sweetheart. He had been extraordinarily well taken care of and seen their engagement as an omen of an imminently approaching marriage, eternal future harmony, and peaceful domestic happiness. Then he put on ten pounds, the ring on his left hand suddenly felt irritatingly tight, and their relationship started to flounder.

Unfortunately he had also discovered new sides to his "girlfriend," such as the fact that it annoyed her when he called her his "girlfriend" instead of his "fiancée." If that was how things stood for him, she had said, if he saw their engagement as just a ploy to gain time, he might just as well "come out with it immediately" so she'd have the opportunity to arrange something else instead. So he'd moved back home again, they had reconciled, he'd moved back in, moved home, and so on as time literally rushed onward. At the moment he was living at home, but their plans were no more definite, and personally he would have preferred not to think about the future. But on this particular morning he had no choice, as soon as he opened the refrigerator door at a quarter past six in the morning.

Jarnebring never slept more than five or six hours even when he'd partied. When he got out of bed he was always alert and rested, but above all hungry and in need of an ample breakfast. Even as he was standing in the shower he had unpleasant premonitions, and when he looked in his refrigerator those premonitions were confirmed.

It did not look good. Yesterday's roll lay collapsed in a bag—who could be so dense as to put bread in the fridge?—in the company of a wedge of cheese, a trickle of apple juice, and a very tired, soggy tomato that had clearly given its all. The only consolation in this wretched state of affairs was an almost full carton of eggs. When he saw the miserable prospects for a dizzyingly brief moment he considered calling his girlfriend despite everything—she lived on the way to work after all—but then he steeled himself, pushed that thought aside, and made the best of the situation.

As a policeman I have to approve of the situation, thought Jarnebring, without really feeling convinced of that. They're not like we are, and the ones he had in mind were the great human collective among which his fiancée could also be counted. They're like children, damn it, he thought with irritation as he put the pan on the stove and poured in enough water for both coffee and the eggs.

Half an hour later he was on the subway en route to work after a breakfast of instant coffee without milk, half a glass of juice, almost an entire tomato, yesterday's roll with a few shavings of cheese and five soft-boiled eggs. He was prey to conflicting emotions, only partly connected to his first meal of the day.

When he arrived Holt was already in place behind her desk, and evidently she had been sitting there a good while because she had managed to do searches on the victim, his neighbors, and the cars that had been parked on the street.

"Haven't come up with anything, unfortunately," said Holt, shaking her head.

"Hell," said Jarnebring. "Have you been sitting here all night?" He nodded toward the thick bundles of computer printouts on her desk.

"I got here an hour ago," said Holt, smiling wanly as she shook her head. "Nicke is with his dad this week, so I had nothing better to do."

I could have fixed that if you'd come by, thought Jarnebring, although mostly from habit and without feeling that old conviction he used to feel before he got engaged. Damn that too, he thought with irritation.

"Nicke," said Jarnebring questioningly.

"My boy. Haven't I told you about him? He's six and he'll start school next fall."

"Great age," said Jarnebring vaguely. "Does he have any siblings?" What was I thinking about just now? he thought.

"Just Nicke," said Holt. "None on the way and none planned."

I'll just bet, thought Jarnebring, who had carried on that discussion on a number of occasions in recent years.

"Well well then," said Jarnebring, smiling. What the hell should he say? "Has anything else happened?"

"Yes," said Holt, digging out a yellow message pad. "Our colleague Danielsson at homicide called and wondered if you could go see him before the meeting."

"I see," said Jarnebring, taking the slip of paper. Must be that idiot Bäckström, he thought.

"Danielsson," said Holt. "Is he the guy they call Jack Daniels?"

"Yes," said Jarnebring, nodding. "Although I don't understand why. He doesn't drink more than most of the others and he can hold considerably more, even though he'll soon be retirement age."

"See you at the meeting," said Holt, as she resumed leafing through yet another bundle of papers in the pile on her desk.

"Sit down, Jarnebring," said Danielsson, nodding toward his visitor's chair.

"You look energetic, old man," said Jarnebring with warmth in his voice. There's a real policeman, he thought.

"What the hell choice do I have," said Danielsson, "as expensive as schnapps has gotten." He was just as big and burly as Jarnebring. Twenty years older, sixty pounds heavier, blue-red in the face, and with a tie like a snare around his bull's neck.

He must be built like a woodstove, thought Jarnebring, looking appreciatively at the medical miracle before him.

"What did you have in mind?" he asked.

Nothing in particular as it turned out, just the same old same old. A little talk about this and that between fellow police. An opportunity to thank Jarnebring for wanting to help out. Danielsson was nonetheless the assistant head of the squad.

"Nothing's the same here since they killed Palme. You may be wondering why our colleague Bäckström is the lead detective. If he starts any foolishness just say the word and I'll kick some sense into the little bastard."

"It'll work out," said Jarnebring. "I can arrange that myself in any event."

"I would think so," said Danielsson, grunting appreciatively. There's a real policeman, he thought.

Then the old man brought up his favorite subject. Things had been much better before and best of all in "Dahlgren's day," referring to the legendary old squad chief who had closed up shop more than ten years ago. The one who had ended his life by his own hand and with the help of his service revolver to save society unnecessary nursing expenses and himself an undignified life. Although that particular detail was not usually talked about, not even at the time when it was fresh in people's memory. Back then you could still talk to the crooks, who had surnames that weren't all consonants, even if Danielsson chose to formulate that linguistic problem in a different way.

"Do you remember those days, Jarnie," said Danielsson, "when you could spell the crook's name? And understand what he said?"

"Sure, sure," said Jarnebring, smiling a little. Although Blackie, Genghis, the Pistol Gnome, and Charlie Cannon weren't always so fun to deal with either. Sometimes you could keep a straight face.

"Lars Peter Forsman . . . and Bosse Dynamite," said Danielsson dreamily. "Even the Clarkster, that fuckup from Norrmalmstorg, although maybe that wasn't exactly his fault. Do you remember when they wrote on the front page of *Little Pravda* that they'd given Bosse Dynamite an intelligence test and he had an IQ like a professor? Do you remember how furious Dynamite got? That was one talented guy. Completely normal. He didn't want to be compared to any crazy academics. He should have sued those bastards."

He's the same as ever, thought Jarnebring, sneaking a look at his watch.

"Fine lads," said Danielsson and sighed nostalgically. "And what the hell do we have now? A lot of Yugos and Polacks and Turks and Arabs and guys like that fuckup Bäckström who's going to take charge of all the misery. And on the shelf there"—Danielsson nodded toward the bookshelf behind his desk—"I have two rows of binders with unsolved murders. Damn, Dahlgren would have killed me if he'd lived. Although he never even swore at you."

"Dahlgren was good," Jarnebring agreed, despite the fact that he was always going on about his diploma, he thought.

"Sure," said Danielsson. "And here I am talking shit."

Then they went their separate ways. Jarnebring went to his meeting and Danielsson leaned back, looked at the clock, and wondered whether he could slip down to the liquor store before lunch so he could avoid standing in line for hours. In recent years he'd had an awful ache in his knees, and it was the weekend anyway and soon it would be Christmas. . . .

The first meeting of the invesitgation team with lead detective Bäckström had astounded all those who knew him. He was alert and freshly showered, despite what was for him an early hour, and radiated both effectiveness and a strong odor of menthol-flavored throat lozenges.

"Okay then," said Bäckström energetically, opening up his folder of notes. "Allow me to welcome everyone. We have a murder and we have to like the situation."

And not make things unnecessarily complicated and mistrust the chance coincidence, thought Jarnebring, something touching his heart at the same time as he thought about his best friend, police superintendent Lars Martin Johansson, and his three golden rules for a murder investigator. I'll have to call Lars Martin. It's been awhile. What the hell has happened to Bäckström anyway? He must have put vitamins in his nightcap, thought Jarnebring.

"Let's see now, said blind Sarah," Bäckström said, leafing among his papers with his fat right thumb. "First we have our corpse . . . Eriksson, Kjell Göran, born in 1944, single, no children, no known relatives whatsoever . . . that we could produce in any event." Bäckström gave Holt an inquisitive look.

"No," Holt confirmed, without needing to consult her own folder. "No wives, no children, no relatives."

This is almost too good to be true, thought Bäckström, feeling how the keys to the victim's apartment were keeping warm in his right pants pocket.

"Worked as some kind of bigwig down at the Central Bureau of Statistics over on Karlavägen. Isn't that the monstrosity at the intersection down by the Radio and TV building?"

New nod from Holt, although more hesitant this time.

"Not exactly a bigwig," she said. "He was bureau director, hardly a bigwig."

Typical, thought Bäckström. Fucking attack dyke. As soon as you're a little nice to them and extend a hand, they try to tear off your whole arm.

"Yes," said Bäckström. "Bureau director. Wasn't that what I said?"

"I don't recall," said Holt, "but a bureau director is hardly a bigwig," she clarified. "That must be the lowest management position they have. Like a detective inspector with us." Watch out, you fat little schmuck, she thought.

"He's dead anyway," said Bäckström. They always have to talk back, he thought. Thank the Lord he had resisted the pressure and was still a free man.

"Where, when, and how," said Jarnebring, looking encouragingly at Bäckström. So we can get out of here sometime, he thought.

"Exactly, exactly," said Bäckström with newfound energy. "The scene of the crime is the victim's residence. More precisely, the living room in his apartment on Rådmansgatan. Of that point we can be completely certain."

Wiijnbladh nodded in agreement, without Bäckström condescending to give him a glance.

"So then there is the time," Bäckström continued. "If we're to believe our witness and the call she makes to the colleagues down in the pit, the whole thing seems to have gotten going about eight o'clock, quarter after eight, yesterday evening." Bäckström let his gaze sweep across those assembled, but no one seemed to be of a different opinion.

"Cause of death . . . one or more knife wounds in the chest area . . . from the back. Wiijnbladh?" Bäckström looked inquisitively at Wiijnbladh, who nodded obligingly.

"Yes, well, I'll be meeting the forensic doctor later today, but that's my definite opinion as well," said Wiijnbladh. "And I believe we've found the knife."

"Okay then," said Bäckström, leaning back in his chair and clasping his hands over his fat belly. "Then only two questions remain out of six. Who did it and what's the motive. As far as the latter is concerned I already have my ideas, but there are a few things I've asked Wiijnbladh to check before I get back to that. We still have to flush out the perpetrator, and I don't think that will take very long." Bäckström looked shrewdly at those gathered.

Nice to hear, thought Jarnebring, for personally he had been part of more impressive detective teams than this one.

The smaller of the two conference rooms at the homicide squad held a total of nine individuals that morning, considerably fewer than would usually be at the first meeting of a new murder investigation: lead detective Bäckström and his little squire Wiijnbladh, who would take care of

the technical aspects; Jarnebring and Holt; one of Bäckström's coworkers in the squad, whose name was Alm but who was generally known as
Blockhead and was not considered a shining light; a female civilian office
worker, Gunsan, who would take care of filing the preliminary investigation material; plus three younger talents who were on loan from the
uniformed police. The idea was that they would do all the other things
that weren't very important but still had to be done, and because all of
them were almost jumping with eagerness despite the fact that they
were still sitting down, evidently none of them had figured out what had
been planned.

"Okay then," said Bäckström, closing his folder. "Any questions?"

"Should we work this weekend?" asked Jarnebring.

"I'm sorry," said Bäckström, making a brave effort to look gloomy.
"We're still short on cash since they shot that socialist down on Sveavägen, so there's no question of overtime." In any case not so it extends to
you, you incompetent bastards, thought Bäckström, having already
filled out the overtime forms for the weekend on his own account. "So
we'll have to meet on Monday morning. Unless something comes up.
Then I'll be in touch." You can forget about that, he thought.

"Yes?" Bäckström looked questioningly at Wiijnbladh, who had actually raised his hand. A careful little wave of his little handsy-pandsy, typical for that half-fairy, thought Bäckström.

"Are you coming to look when we undress the body, Bäckström?"
Wiijnbladh asked. The question was not as strange as it sounded
because it had been a tradition since old Dahlberg's days that at least one
of the squad's heavy-duty murder investigators was there for the
autopsy.

"Thanks for asking but I have to pass," said Bäckström, who had
other, more important matters in mind. "You and I can talk later."

4

Friday morning, December 1, 1989

The survey of the victim's personal characteristics is the very hub of the steadily rolling wheel of a murder investigation, and considering this particular victim's appearance, Jarnebring and Holt had decided to start with his coworkers, without even needing to discuss the matter in more detail.

First they talked to the head of the department at the Central Bureau of Statistics where Eriksson had worked. Naturally he was shocked. The whole thing was inexplicable, for according to him, Eriksson had been not only an ideal colleague but also an extraordinary and generally well liked individual. Besides which he had been active in the union at work, with a strong, genuine commitment.

Who at the bureau had known him best? Was there anyone he socialized with outside of work?

Eriksson's boss had given them two names. A woman and a man who sat next to Eriksson and were part of the same statistics-producing unit. But he couldn't think of anyone else. And as far as things outside the workplace were concerned, perhaps it was best to ask his coworkers directly. Personally he had not seen Eriksson outside work. Had never even run into him in town, now that he thought about it.

Holt questioned the male colleague and Jarnebring the female one, and considering what they said about Eriksson it would have been enough to speak with either one of them.

Neither of them had anything bad to say about Eriksson. He had done his job, even if his union obligations naturally occupied a good deal of his time. Neither of them had socialized with him privately. Neither of them had seen him at all outside of work, and they could not name anyone else who had either. Eriksson had always been correct, maintained a certain distance from his surroundings, was courteous of course but at the same time a man of high integrity.

You don't say, thought Jarnebring.

You don't say, thought Holt.

On the way out through the reception area, when it was time to return to police headquarters, they finally got a lead. A doorman in his fifties who was standing bent over a copy machine behind the counter in the lobby had given them that lingering gaze that every true detective learns to recognize early on.

Jarnebring slowed his pace, smiled and nodded amiably, giving the doorman the extra moment that such people always need. Medium height, slender build, with thin medium blond hair and forward-leaning body posture, Jarnebring noted without even thinking about it.

"I heard that Eriksson was killed," the doorman said without looking at them, as he filled a carton with paper.

"You knew him," said Jarnebring, and this was more a statement than a question.

"Hmm," said the doorman, nodding.

"Should we meet down in the cafeteria in five minutes," said Jarnebring, and this was more a suggestion than a question.

"There's a café in the Radio and TV building," said their prospective informant. "It's quieter there. Give me ten minutes."

Fifteen minutes later they were sitting by themselves in the most remote corner of the café, each with a cup of coffee. Holt started their conversation with a police-style scissors kick.

"With or without filters?" said Holt, smiling at their prospective interview victim even before he started digging in his pockets with his skinny, nicotine-stained fingers.

"Preferably with," the doorman said, and Holt immediately conjured forth a pack of Marlboro Reds and a lighter. Then everything went like clockwork.

Holt doesn't smoke, thought Jarnebring with surprise, and on that point he was almost certain.

What had Eriksson been like as a person?

"This stays completely between us, right?" the doorman asked, drawing his fingers through his thin hair.

Jarnebring nodded, Holt nodded, and the doorman took a deep, contemplative drag before he nodded too.

"What Eriksson was like as a person," said their source. "Well . . . I don't really know how I should put it."

"Try," said Jarnebring, smiling his famous wolf grin.

"You meet a lot of people over the years. I've worked at this place for almost thirty years now . . . and . . ." The doorman smiled wryly, shook his head, and tapped the ash off his cigarette, while both Jarnebring and Holt waited in silence. Oh well, thought Jarnebring while in his mind he watched the line running out from the reel.

"Kjell Eriksson," said the doorman. "What was he like as a person? If I put it like this . . . Kjell Eriksson was probably the absolute smallest person I've met here—and the absolute biggest asshole." He nodded with emphasis and looked at them, evidently delighted now. "That man was one exceptionally large asshole."

"I'm interpreting this as meaning it wasn't you who killed him," said Jarnebring, grinning cheerfully.

"Oh no," said the doorman, shaking his head. "Why would I do that? A child could see that someone was going to do it sooner or later, and the only thing that's a little mysterious is why it took so long. He must have worked with us for ten years at least. Talk about living on borrowed time. Well, damn . . ." Eriksson's former coworker looked at them with eyes shining with delight.

"What was it with him?" Holt asked.

Lazy-ass, wheeler-dealer, chicken, ass licker, stuck-up, bully, gossip, backbiter, thief, and just a bastard in general; he even had bad breath.

But he did not seem to have had any other faults. Not that the doorman could think of now in any case.

"Sounds like a nice guy," said Jarnebring.

"Eriksson was a bad person," said his former coworker seriously. "But he was no ordinary idiot. He was a shrewd bastard."

Bäckström had held a press conference up at homicide. Not especially well attended, half a dozen journalists from the newspapers as well as some from radio, but none of the TV channels had done him the honor. That was a shame, because those few times he had appeared on screen it had immediately resulted in a number of odd jobs when he was at the bar showing the flag. Lazy and incompetent, thought Bäckström. They get to report the weather on the screen for a week, and then they think they *are* the weather.

He had not had much to say himself. Of course the investigators were covering a lot of ground without preconceived notions at the same time as a number of promising leads were being followed up, and conclusive evidence had of course been secured. If he were to say something off the record, it would only be that he was personally convinced that this would be cleared up soon.

"Can you tell us how he was murdered?" asked an older female reporter who was sitting in front.

"Not at the present time," Bäckström said heavily. "This is the sort of thing I want to be able to confront the perpetrator with."

"Do you know anything about the motive?" asked a middle-aged male journalist who was sitting farthest down by the door.

"I have my own definite ideas about that," said Bäckström. "But even at this point it is too early to say anything."

"Have I understood you correctly if I say that it's exactly as usual at this point. That you're fumbling around in total darkness?" A younger talent with an irritating smile who had not sat down but instead stood leaning against the wall moping.

Bäckström looked at him sourly.

"No comment," said Bäckström. "We'll leave it at that." Fucking asshole, he thought. Those bastards ought to be boiled for glue.

"I don't know about you, ladies and gentlemen," he continued, "but personally I have a great deal of work to get down to, so if you have no more questions, then . . ." Bäckström had already stood up, nodded heavily at them all. None of them had any objections.

While Bäckström was holding his press conference, his colleague Alm was organizing the incoming tips.

As soon as the media had informed that Great Detective—the General Public—that citizen Eriksson had been murdered, ordinary people would start calling the police like crazy, because they always did, despite the fact that they almost never had anything sensible to say.

"Keep that in mind as you're sitting there by the phone," said Alm, nodding at his younger colleague with the uniformed police who had been given this responsible task. "Whatever you do, don't start arguing with them, because you'll never be finished. It's only a lot of bag ladies and drunks and other riffraff."

"Doesn't anyone ever call with something important to say?" the borrowed police constable asked, looking at Alm with youthful seriousness.

"Not that I can recall," said Alm. "It has never happened to me in my twenty years at homicide, so just keep it short so they don't get a lot of ideas in their little heads. And as far as the two of you are concerned, you should complete the door-knocking from yesterday." Alm nodded, looking like a general, at the two remaining younger colleagues from the uniformed police. Just as well to explain this so they won't sit here moping, he thought.

"Yes, I'm wondering—" said one of them.

"Talk with Gunsan and you'll get a list of names," Alm interrupted.

" . . . if there's anything in particular we should be bearing in mind?" the second one continued.

Who are they recruiting nowadays? Alm thought sourly, staring at them.

"Bearing in mind," said Alm. "You can find the way to Rådmansgatan, can't you?"

"I didn't mean that," the one who had asked the question persisted. "Is there anything special we should remember to ask them? When we knock on doors, that is."

"Ask them if they've seen or heard anything," said Alm. "Is that so hard to understand?"

Apparently not when it came down to it, for all three had immediately left his office.

Well now, thought Alm, leaning back in his chair and looking at the clock. Suppose one were to take the opportunity to get the trip to the liquor store over with before lunch, to avoid getting varicose veins by standing around half the afternoon along with all the welfare recipients who don't have anything better to do.

5

Friday afternoon, December 1, 1989

As soon as Bäckström got rid of the journalistic mob he snuck out to a discreet lunch place in City where he met his own reporter from the major evening tabloid. He was a relatively normal character, considering his chosen profession, and he always entertained on the newspaper's dime. After a few beers and a generous portion of roast pork with potatoes and lingonberries, Bäckström recovered his good mood and, as a thank-you for the meal, lifted the veil of police secrecy a bit.

"Just between the two of us, I'd say he was stabbed to death," Bäckström said, nodding confidentially at his host.

"It wasn't a pretty sight," the reporter said expectantly.

An overturned coffee table, a little blood, and a stiff—that wasn't such a big deal. He had seen considerably worse himself, though he couldn't say that of course. You have to give the audience what it demands, thought Bäckström.

"Let me put it this way," said Bäckström. "It didn't look like your house or mine." Which was completely true, he thought.

"A knife, you said," the reporter said greedily. "So it was a real slaughterhouse then? Was it a big knife?"

"Between us . . ." Bäckström lowered his voice and leaned even closer. "It was a real machete . . . like a samurai sword almost." Bäckström indicated this by stretching out his fat arm.

"You don't think this might have any connection with the porno murders," the reporter said with eyes shining.

"What do you mean?" asked Bäckström evasively. This may be going a little too fast, he thought.

"There's a lunatic going around hacking up people with a big knife. There are at least three now. First that Negro on Söder, and then those other two who were jerking off in porno shops. One down in Vasastan and one outside the apartment where he lived. Hell, Bäckström . . . don't you see we have a serial killer on the loose?"

"Well, yes," said Bäckström. "I hear what you're saying, and that thought has occurred to me too." What the hell do I do now? thought Bäckström, and for some reason he also happened to think of his immediate supervisor, chief inspector Danielsson. It was not a pleasant thought.

"Was Eriksson involved with pornography?" Now his host was looking Bäckström right in the eye. "Was Eriksson involved with pornography?" he repeated.

Involved with pornography? I guess everyone is, thought Bäckström confusedly, but then he pulled himself together and nodded energetically at his host.

"Personally I've been thinking that there's a sexual motive," said Bäckström. For he actually had. He'd realized this as soon as he saw how the bastard lived. So far that was completely true, thought Bäckström. And pretty much everyone looks at pornography except old ladies of course. I'll have to see if I find any magazines or videotapes at his place. With those butt princes in their sailor suits, he thought, suddenly feeling livelier again.

"Great, Bäckström," said the reporter. "I get it, I get it. We'll do the usual . . . sources in police headquarters allege. It's cool. What do you say to a cognac with coffee, by the way?"

"It'll have to be a small one," said Bäckström.

Criminal Inspector Wiijnbladh spent the better part of the day at the medical examiner's office in Solna where he attended the autopsy of their murder victim, Kjell Göran Eriksson, and also secured the clothing the corpse was still wearing when the forensic examination started.

Normally these were rather pleasant affairs, during which you had the opportunity to exchange professional experiences and shoot the breeze with officers from homicide and the doctors who worked at the office. But not this time, Wiijnbladh thought gloomily. For it wasn't enough that he was there as the sole representative of the police, since that completely unrestrained binge eater Bäckström was overseeing the investigation. As soon as he stepped inside the door out in Solna he had been struck by yet another blow. The autopsy would evidently be performed by a new forensic physician in the department. A young woman, thirty-five at the most, it seemed, whom Wiijnbladh had neither met nor heard mentioned before. A short little person with unpleasantly searching eyes, who judging by the nametag she wore on her white coat was named "Birgit H.," just like some character in that incomprehensible novel he'd received as a birthday present from his dreadful sister-in-law, but who apparently preferred to be called "simply Birgit."

"My name is Birgit," she said, extending her steady little hand, "simply Birgit, and I'm guessing that you're Wiijnbladh."

"Okay then," said Wiijnbladh when the formalities were out of the way and they had taken their places at the autopsy table. "The professor himself is away at a conference I'm guessing?"

"The professor?" Birgit said questioningly. "Do you mean Dr. Engel? Or 'Esprit de Corpse,' as I've heard you all call him."

"Well, yes," said Wiijnbladh evasively. He didn't like people to be called by their nicknames. Especially when they themselves were not present. But certainly, at police headquarters and among police officers Dr. Engel was best known as Doctor "Corpse" or "Engel with two e's." An interesting man of somewhat vague German-Yugoslavian background, but with considerable practical experience according to what the police officers could tell, and known as a great joker besides, provided the joke wasn't about him.

Birgit shook her head.

"He hasn't gone away," said Birgit. "He fell off a loading dock."

"Good Lord," said a shocked Wiijnbladh. "How did it happen?"

"Eh!" Birgit shrugged her shoulders with irritation. "Work accident.

Going out to look at the scene. I guess it was one of his moonlighting jobs for one of those insurance companies that he fiddles around with instead of focusing on his job. And because he's almost blind he walked right off the end of the loading dock. Wrist fracture and concussion but none of his nobler parts."

"Blind," said Wiijnbladh. What did she mean? he thought.

"Precisely," said Birgit, fixing him with her black peppercorn eyes. "Our colleague Dr. Engel is acutely near-sighted and because he's as vain as he is he refuses to wear glasses. Among other things that's why he always says hello to the palm tree down in the lobby when he comes to work in the morning. Moving the palm is a popular prank among his younger coworkers, by the way. However not with me, and if you don't believe me or understand why, I suggest you go to a blind dentist next time you have a toothache."

"I really had no idea," Wiijnbladh defensively. What is that person standing here saying? he wondered. Blind? Could his old friend Milan be blind?

"Besides, he's not a professor," said Birgit. "He calls himself professor but that's not the same thing, and if you don't have any objection I was thinking about starting now."

"Of course, of course," said Wiijnbladh. What an unpleasant, pushy woman, he thought.

"Nice to hear," said Birgit as she let her gaze sweep over the gleaming implements on the instrument table, "and in contrast to Engel I am actually a professor, a real professor, so you can be completely at ease, Inspector."

What an extraordinarily unsympathetic woman, thought Wiijnbladh.

One thing was certain, however, thought Wiijnbladh reluctantly as she pulled off her rubber gloves two hours later: This wasn't the first time she'd done an autopsy. Personally he'd never seen anything like it, despite the fact that he had attended hundreds of them.

"Well then," said Birgit as she plucked the cassette tape out of the tape recorder into which she had dictated her observations during the course of her work. "Let's go into my office and talk. Don't forget to bring his clothes along. I don't want them left here making a mess."

She nodded at the bags with Eriksson's trousers, shirt, undershirt, underwear, socks, and shoes.

"Coffee or tea?" asked Birgit, nodding at the coffeemaker set up on a small table next to her desk. She had already supplied herself with black coffee and was sitting in her large desk chair with her legs resting on the desk.

"I'm okay," said Wiijnbladh. This is not a human being, he thought. This is a little ballbuster in human form.

"Good," Birgit said curtly. "You'll get the report next week when the tests are ready. But I'm guessing you'll want a preliminary statement."

"Yes, gladly, if it's all right, I mean," said Wiijnbladh, and for some reason he happened to think of Jarnebring, even though this specimen was only half as large as the dangerous lunatic on the homicide squad.

"Then that's what you'll get," said Birgit. "I'll do it in ordinary Swedish so there aren't any misunderstandings."

"Thanks," said Wiijnbladh, smiling wanly. "Thanks."

Eriksson had died of a knife wound or rather a knife thrust that had been administered at an angle from above.

It had struck him from behind, high up on his back, between the left shoulder blade and spine and passed between two ribs into the chest cavity, wounding the heart, left lung, and the aorta. The stabbing resulted in rapid, extensive loss of blood, dramatic drop in blood pressure; the victim lost consciousness and stopped breathing, which led to death within a few minutes at most. The knife blade had been held at an inclined horizontal angle when the knife struck the body, which thus argued for a thrust rather than a cut; a cut would have produced an incision that was vertical or inclined to vertical as a rule.

The weapon was a large, very sharp, single-edged knife with a straight blade at least ten inches in length and two inches wide where the end of the blade met the handle. These observations in connection with the autopsy matched the knife in the photo that Wiijnbladh had faxed over to her before he came. And as for that, by the way, there was something she wanted to say.

"I understand that the intention was good," said Birgit, fastening her eyes on Wiijnbladh, "but in future I want you to wait with this type of information until I ask for it. First, I want to form my own opinion. I'm a forensic physician, not a fortune-teller."

"Of course, of course," said Wiijnbladh.

"Was there anything else?" asked Birgit, inspecting him up and down.

"The time," said Wiijnbladh. "Can you say anything about the time?"

"When you got the alarm. Around eight o'clock. Nothing I've seen contradicts that time. I thought it was you who wrote the fax I received? At least your name was on it." Birgit shrugged her shoulders.

"I've been thinking about something," Wiijnbladh said carefully. "Eriksson was five foot ten inches tall, and in my mind I see a perpetrator who must be considerably taller than Eriksson, and have considerable body strength besides. Considering the angle of incision and the depth of the cut, that is," Wiijnbladh clarified. Surely she must be able to take all that in. She has an academic degree, after all, he thought.

Now she looked pleased in a manner that Wiijnbladh experienced as deeply disturbing.

"So that's what you see in your mind," said Birgit.

"Yes," said Wiijnbladh. "A big, powerful perpetrator, very tall, about six foot three, considerable body strength, violent stab . . . or else a thrust then . . . so to speak."

"I see," said Birgit tranquilly, inspecting her neat, short trimmed nails. "Personally I might imagine that Eriksson was sitting on that couch I saw in one of your pictures. As far as the stab wound is concerned, no particular strength would be required for that. A sharp knife slipped in between two ribs. The perpetrator sneaks up behind and just makes a thrust. If it had been me who'd done it I would have been very surprised at the result."

"Could it have been a professional of some type?" said Wiijnbladh. "Considering where the stab went in, I mean. In my opinion this suggests considerable anatomical knowledge."

"Where do you get all this from?" asked Birgit, sighing. "Is this the sort of nonsense that you and your colleagues sit and blabber about with

Milan? It was pure luck, or bad luck depending on how you look at it. Call it what you want. How could the perpetrator see where the victim's ribs were? The poor man had his shirt on. Unless you think that the perpetrator came up and squeezed his chest cavity before he stabbed him?"

"No, that's clear," said Wiijnbladh. What a horrid person, Wiijnbladh thought, and to top it off he had started to sweat too.

"Was there anything else?" said Birgit, nodding courteously at the clock on the wall of her office. "Otherwise I actually have a lot to do."

Good Lord, thought Wiijnbladh. Bäckström's question.

First he felt almost desperate, but then he breathed deeply, pulled himself together, and asked it, because it had to be done anyway, even if he gladly would have switched places with that fat runt from the homicide squad.

"Just one more thing," said Wiijnbladh. "I was wondering . . . during your autopsy here . . . did you make any observations that suggest that Eriksson . . . the victim, that is, . . . that he was . . . well, homosexual? So to speak."

"You mean whether he had a tail," said Birgit, looking at Wiijnbladh with an amused smile.

"No," said Wiijnbladh, smiling nervously. "Perhaps you understand what I mean?"

"No, actually not," said Birgit. "I can only guess. You're wondering if I found anything that indicated that he, for example, was regularly penetrated in the rectum in connection with anal intercourse."

"Just so," said Wiijnbladh. "For example, anally, so to speak."

"Or if I found semen in his rectum or made any other terrifying observations regarding his penis?"

"Yes," said Wiijnbladh, and now he felt the sweat running down between his skinny shoulders. "Did you?"

"No," said Birgit. "So you and the other boys up there on Kungsholmen can be completely at ease."

"Well, okay then, then I'll just say thanks," said Wiijnbladh.

"It was nothing," said Birgit.

After their visit to the Central Bureau of Statistics, Jarnebring and Holt went to the SACO union headquarters in Östermalm. When they inquired about Eriksson's doings, Eriksson's boss answered that the day before, the same day he was murdered, Eriksson was supposed to attend a conference on current issues in labor law hosted by SACO. This also proved to be true.

"He was invited as a representative of the academics employed at Statistics who are organized within TCO," the woman who took care of the practical details in connection with the conference confirmed.

Then she retrieved the conference program and the list of participants. It was a one-day conference that began at nine o'clock in the morning and concluded at five with a break for lunch between twelve and one. It had been held in the SACO offices and had featured current issues in labor law as stated, which was always interesting to the union and its members. There had been fifty-some participants besides Eriksson.

"And you're quite sure that Eriksson was at the conference?" Jarnebring asked.

He had registered in the morning and received his conference materials. Of that she was quite certain because she had taken care of that detail herself and she recognized Eriksson from previous, similar meetings. On the other hand she was uncertain if he had been there the whole day.

"It's not unusual for people to come and go," she explained, and personally she'd had other things to think about than Eriksson's presence, even if naturally she didn't put it that way.

With the help of her two coworkers the details were soon cleared up.

Eriksson had been at the conference until lunch. He should have stayed the whole day, but at the short smoking break before the last lecture before lunch he had excused himself and reported that something had come up at work and he was going to have to depart at twelve, which meant he wouldn't have time for lunch.

"Did you get the impression that something had happened? Did he seem upset or anything?" Holt asked the conference hostess with whom Eriksson had spoken.

Nothing strange at all, as far as she could recall. He had been happy and pleasant, almost exuberant, and because people basically came and went the whole time, it wasn't strange that Eriksson too had departed, was it? She'd made a note to inform the kitchen that there would be one person less for lunch. That was it.

Jarnebring and Holt thanked her and went to a nearby restaurant to get some food in their stomachs themselves. While they were waiting, Holt leafed through the papers they had received from the conference organizer.

"Well," Jarnebring said, grinning, "find anything interesting?"

"The chairman gives a welcome, the head of legal affairs at the labor ministry reports on some developing trends in Swedish labor law during the eighties, the secretary of the labor law committee reports on the requested oversight of the Codetermination Act—"

"Thanks, thanks," Jarnebring interrupted. "I understand exactly why he left before lunch."

"Lunch, yes," said Holt. "For lunch there were veal roulades with boiled potatoes and lingonberries. And a vegetarian alternative for those who wanted it."

"Veal roulades can be damn good," said Jarnebring, who five minutes earlier had ordered beef patties with fried onions and felt how his stomach was growling precariously. "Are there any interesting names on the list of presenters and attendees?"

"Besides the already mentioned head of legal affairs and the secretary of the labor law committee, both men of course, we actually have a female lawyer who lectured on a recently concluded case in the Labor Court as well as a whole pile of ombudsmen from every nook and cranny . . . and Kjell Eriksson as an invited guest from TCO."

"Good, we'll deal with that later. Let's not talk with our mouths full," Jarnebring decided, catching sight of a waiter who had a steaming plate in each hand and his eyes trained on their table.

Over coffee they talked about other things. The list of who had been at the conference did not seem particularly exciting, and regardless of that any further research could wait until the excellent Gunsan had looked up the names on the police department's computer. Instead Jarnebring brought up Holt's somewhat bewildering smoking habits.

"I've never smoked," said Holt, shaking her head when Jarnebring asked the question. "Why should I do that? It's pure craziness to smoke."

"So the ciggies you offer are just a tactical instrument in police work," Jarnebring marveled. "Something you learned at a course when you were working with the felt slippers in Building B?"

"You might put it that way," said Holt. "Although it was not in a course. It must have been something I saw on a detective show or something like that. Isn't there anything you use when you're going to talk with people you meet on the job?"

"No," said Jarnebring, trying out his wolf grin. "I don't meet any people on the job. I only meet crooks. Plus a loaded Joe Six-Pack or two, and they're often the worst to deal with."

"What do you do when you want to develop a rapport with them?" Holt asked curiously.

"Scare the shit out of them," said Jarnebring. "And then when I'm nice to them they look like they've gotten a whole carton of cigarettes." Jarnebring nodded and did not appear at all dissatisfied with his approach. "Cheap and good, and it saves time too."

"That's the difference between you and me," said Holt. "Not even if I wanted to, which I don't, would I be able to do it like that."

"Feminine wiles," said Jarnebring.

"No," said Holt. "I'm just that way. It's nothing I've chosen."

Like I believe that, thought Jarnebring.

"I'm a bad person myself, so what do you think about trying to make glue out of the culprit we're looking for," said Jarnebring, looking at his watch.

"Track down and arrest the perpetrator," said Holt. "Sounds like an excellent idea."

When Wiijnbladh finally left the medical examiner's office in Solna he was worried, agitated, and confused. The first thing he did when he sat down at his desk was to call his old friend Dr. Engel to find out how he was doing.

Under the circumstances, well, according to the patient himself. Wiijnbladh told him about the unfortunate meeting with his colleague Birgit—"simply Birgit"—and the serious concerns for the progress of the investigation he had subsequently felt. Unfortunately the more he thought about his concerns the more serious they looked, and it was

even more gratifying to find that Milan completely shared both his perception and his apprehensions.

"You are completely right," Engel agreed. "She is not sane. She is
crazy. She lives with other women. She is a fucking dyke. She is totally
lacking in judgment. She is—"

"If you want I can bring the documents over and see you," Wiijnbladh interrupted cautiously.

Which he did. Half an hour later he was sitting with Dr. Engel in his
pleasant bachelor's pad on Sveavägen, analyzing the particular circumstances of Bureau Director Eriksson's woeful demise only twenty hours
earlier. Just as Wiijnbladh had suspected all along, Engel shared his
view of how it had happened down to the slightest detail. Translated
into comprehensible Swedish, in any event, according to the doctor's
opinion—based on science, common sense, and proven experience—the
victim was "a typical closet gay who picked up a big, strong and above all
very tall, violence-prone bum boy who stabbed him from behind with
one of his own kitchen knives."

In addition Engel had made a completely unique, independent contribution to the investigation that not even Wiijnbladh himself had
thought of.

"You said him Eriksson lived Rodmansgatan op by ze church?" Engel
asked, squinting sharply at Wiijnbladh.

"Exactly," said Wiijnbladh. "At the corner at Karlavägen."

"Hommelgarden," Engel said emphatically.

"Hommelgarden?" What does he mean? thought Wiijnbladh.

"Hommelgarden where all ze bum boys go pick up closet gays. Rodmansgatan is right in the vicinity."

"You mean Humlegården," said Wiijnbladh, suddenly feeling the
same familiar excitement he had felt so many times before when a
breakthrough in an investigation was near at hand. Why didn't we think
of that? he thought.

"An interesting thought you have there, Milan," said Wiijnbladh carefully, because he was reluctant to relinquish anything unnecessarily.

"It vas nothink," said Dr. Engel modestly. "Dat's my treat."

· · ·

After his nourishing lunch in town, Bäckström spent the remainder of the afternoon in peace and quiet, going through the victim's apartment on Rådmansgatan. It was an interesting experience in a number of ways, and productive in at least two. Bäckström was no expert on interior decorating, but he did understand that the furniture in Eriksson's apartment did not get there by chance and that it must have cost a lot of money. Everything from the paintings on the walls and the draperies on the windows to the gleaming copper pans in his kitchen and the thick terry-cloth towels in his bathroom. It was hardly surprising considering how types like Eriksson usually were, thought Bäckström.

Besides looking through shelves of books and neatly organized binders of papers in what was evidently his office, items that Blockhead or another one of his simpler colleagues could start digging through after the weekend, Bäckström contented himself with a quick sweep in his hunt for more interesting artistic works. Strangely enough he did not find the least trace of what he was looking for: no videocassettes in anonymous packaging with innocuous handwritten labels, no videocassettes whatsoever. No scrupulously concealed bundles of magazines with oiled-down butt princes in leather, chains, and shiny four-color printing. Nothing at all in that line, actually.

Wonder where he hid them? thought Bäckström, for they must be somewhere. But because he found so many other things of interest he decided to let this matter rest until after the weekend.

In the victim's bathroom he made his first discovery. A rather refreshing detail that had evidently escaped that blind bat Wiijnbladh the evening before. The fact that Bäckström's sensitive police nose had put him on the trail didn't hurt either.

At the bottom of the laundry basket was a dark blue terry-cloth hand towel with a yellow border, soiled with vomit. It was of the same color and pattern as the ones hanging on the hooks in the bathroom. What was strange was that it was farthest down in the large, woven laundry basket, despite the fact that the vomit appeared fresh. It was under a lot of other dirty laundry, including a number of similar hand towels, all brick red with wine red borders, probably put into the laundry basket when someone replaced them with a new, clean set in dark blue with yellow borders.

So that's how it is, thought Bäckström with delight. Someone's been sick and tried to conceal that he's been sick; as a weekend present for a blind technician this couldn't be better.

Bäckström fished the hand towel from the basket and set it to one side for the time being, in order to devote himself to more essential things, namely the corpse's quite unbelievable stocks of alcoholic beverages. I'll be damned if he doesn't have liquor everywhere, Bäckström thought excitedly.

In the clothes closet there were cases of alcohol. Some were unopened cases, others had only a single bottle missing, and still others had been nipped at longer and harder and most recently by Bäckström himself. Rows of bottles lined up on the floor: cognac, whiskey, gin, vodka, aquavit, as well as a lot of mysterious liqueurs and other shit that ladies and types like Eriksson pour down their throats.

Likewise in the kitchen: a whole pantry and two overhead cupboards full of wine and dessert wine. A number of full wine racks on the kitchen counter and alongside the stove. In the living room was an antique peasant sideboard which, judging by the contents, evidently functioned as a liquor cabinet. On the desk in the office there was a large tray of hammered silver with several carafes filled with amber-colored drinks.

Bäckström made a careful, very discreet culling of this unrestrained excess, but despite the fact that he was exceedingly moderate in what he took, he was forced to borrow an empty suitcase from the victim, as well as a pile of his clean hand towels, so that the contents wouldn't rattle too terribly much when he drove home.

On his way out he remembered the soiled hand towel and went into the kitchen and rooted among the bags under the sink to find something to put it in. What the hell do you do with soiled hand towels? thought Bäckström. Should they be stored in paper or plastic? Whatever, he thought. Eriksson appeared to have paper bags, and why should he have to do Wiijnbladh's job? He crumpled the hand towel into a paper bag and called for a taxi on the victim's phone. What else would you expect? This was a murder investigation, and he had signed for a whole book of taxi vouchers just in case.

On the way home he stopped at the tech squad and asked the taxi to wait on the street while he left the hand towel on Wijnbladh's desk along with a collegial, friendly note and wishes for a nice weekend. Then he could finally call it a day and go home.

It was nice to be able to avoid thinking about the liquor store on a Friday, thought Bäckström.

Paperwork was not Jarnebring's strong suit, and if he had the choice he would rather use his hands for something besides thumbing through binders. At the same time he was not one to desert a colleague either, so it was actually on Holt's own suggestion that he decided to swing by the homicide squad and check out the situation, see if anything interesting had come in. Nothing had.

Besides, homicide was basically deserted. The only one there was a young colleague from the uniformed police who was sitting by the tip phone, reading a tabloid and looking rather down in the mouth.

"Has anything happened?" Jarnebring asked.

Not much, according to the tip taker. A few bag ladies and drunks had called, but he had kept it short and was able to get rid of them pretty quickly, jotting down the names of anyone who wanted to provide them. Two individuals had also called and reported that they had known the victim. He had given their names to Gunsan for further processing. He'd be going home soon. His supervisor, Detective Inspector Alm, had promised him he could, when Alm had disappeared on urgent duties in town a few hours earlier.

"He said the duty desk would take over the tip line starting at six o'clock," he explained to Jarnebring.

"Go home and sleep, kid," said Jarnebring, nodding. "So that you're wide awake on Monday."

Then Jarnebring talked with Gunsan, who would soon be done with the entries on the neighbors that had come in after the additional door-to-door inquiries. It had gone unexpectedly well, considering that it was Friday. That was because almost everyone who lived in the victim's building was conscientious middle-aged or elderly.

The most interesting thing that had happened was that two individuals had called to say they knew the victim.

"Fine folks on the go," said Gunsan, smiling. "One of them is even a B-list celebrity you may have seen on TV."

Jarnebring did not have the faintest idea who either of them were, but he took all of Gunsan's papers with him anyway to read through in peace down in his own office.

"Isn't it time for you to go home too?" said Jarnebring, smiling at his female civilian colleague. She was the only real police officer in this place since Danielsson lowered the flag, thought Jarnebring. Why hadn't she ever applied to the police academy?

"Pretty soon," said Gunsan, smiling. "How about you, old man? Isn't it high time you went back to your little fiancée and looked after her?"

"It'll work out," said Jarnebring, and then he went down to his own office and his new colleague. Gunsan is actually an extremely attractive woman, he thought as he went through the door to the detective squad. It's a shame she's not twenty years younger, he thought. If nothing else this showed how prejudiced he was, as Gunsan was only a little older than he was.

"Okay," Jarnebring said energetically as he poured yet another mug of black coffee. "If we were to summarize the day, what do we know about our victim? So far?"

He didn't have a large social circle, or so it seemed. At the same time it was large enough to include—in all likelihood—at least one person who had murdered him.

He was unpopular with his coworkers, to say the least. You could read that between the lines of what his boss and closest coworkers had said. It came through pretty clearly in the doorman's story. At the same time there was nothing concrete to go on.

"He wasn't exactly the kind of guy you'd want to share an office with," Jarnebring summarized.

"It would be nice to have something more concrete," said Holt. "An example, I mean. The man can't just have been born bad."

"Don't be so sure," said Jarnebring.

. . .

Holt had been struck by one thing as she was plowing through all the papers. Considering his rather modest salary, for it was no more remarkable than her own or Jarnebring's after the customary police overtime, he seemed to have astonishingly good finances. According to income statements for the last five years, which was what she had produced up to now, he had capital income that widely exceeded his income from his job. He also owned a condominium worth at least a million Swedish kronor, and according to the tax form he had a fortune of the same magnitude in stocks, bonds, and regular bank balances.

"You saw his apartment," said Holt. "Strange as it may sound, I do actually know a bit about art and antiques, and I'd guess there's another million in the contents of his apartment. Which would mean he must have been worth three or four million."

"Maybe an inheritance," Jarnebring suggested. "Didn't he have an old mother who kicked the bucket in the mid-eighties? Art and antiques, isn't that the sort of thing you inherit if you've chosen the right parents?"

Holt just shook her head. The mother had died in 1984, and according to the estate inventory that the excellent Gunsan had already produced, the old woman had left behind four thousand kronor.

"His old man," Jarnebring suggested.

"Father unknown," Holt shot back. "Eriksson seems to have grown up with a single mother and a completely absent father. Poor thing. Think how that must have been." For some reason she sounded almost ready to burst into laughter.

Shit, thought Jarnebring. He hated cases like these. The victim at home with a knife in the back and someone he or she voluntarily let in usually involved drunkenness, agitated emotions in general, or jealousy and ordinary insanity in particular, and regardless of whether the latter was temporary or permanent, he and his colleagues would seldom need more than a week to put the pieces together and land the perpetrator in lockdown. But when money was involved it was almost never that easy, and if there was anything he wished for it was that Eriksson's inexplicable good finances had nothing to do with his death.

"It'll work out," said Jarnebring, smiling and nodding with more conviction than he really felt, as he rocked back in his chair.

"On Monday," said Holt, and she smiled too.

"On Monday we'll turn his apartment inside out," said Jarnebring, "and then I'm willing to bet a month's pay we find our perpetrator too. When we've got the telephone lists and all the entries and have gone through all his notebooks and scraps of paper and photo albums and old letters and God knows what."

"So isn't it time to step on the gas now?" Holt was still smiling, but the question was serious enough. "You've heard about the twenty-four-hour rule and all that, haven't you?"

"You watch too many of those American detective shows," said Jarnebring. "Let me say this," he continued. "Our colleague Bäckström is definitely no bright and shining light, but he does have a certain instinct for self-preservation. Besides, his boss has been around awhile and doesn't usually pull his punches when things get too far off course."

"Jack Daniels," said Holt, smiling.

"Yes, sure," said Jarnebring. "I understand what you mean. But assume we'd found Eriksson outside his apartment. Knifed in the entryway or out on the street. Then we would have had an all-out effort, and I can assure you it wouldn't have been colleague Bäckström behind the wheel."

"The murder of Eriksson isn't so difficult that it can't wait until after the weekend?" Holt looked at him inquisitively.

"I really don't think so," said Jarnebring. "At least it doesn't feel that way. Unplanned, not premeditated. A perpetrator who must have made lots of mistakes, and who knew the victim besides. We almost always nail that. And if we have really good luck then the culprit comes to us on his own when his conscience gets to him." Although it's a bitch that Lars Martin isn't here, he thought with irritation. Then we could have probably taken the weekend off because the perpetrator would already be sitting in jail crying his eyes out. Someone other than Jarnebring usually took care of that part.

"Sounds good," said Holt. "Then I can see my guy."

"What does he do?" said Jarnebring, smiling despite the fact that he had a rather hard to place and not altogether pleasant feeling about what she had said.

"The handsomest guy in town," said Holt. "Niklas Holt, six years old. Generally known as Nicke."

"Please send him my greetings," said Jarnebring, and then they called it a day. And it was just in time if he was to have any hope of making peace with his fiancée before darkness settled far too deeply over the city.

6

Friday evening, December 1, 1989

When Wiijnbladh and his good friend the doctor finished their discussion, he borrowed the telephone and called home to find out if he should get anything for dinner on his way back. But his wife had evidently already gone out or else she wasn't bothering to answer. Instead he drove past the office one more time, and on his desk he found a vomit-soiled, foul-smelling hand towel, bunched together and shoved into a paper bag from Lisa Elmquist in the Östermalm market, as well as a shameless letter from Bäckström. He remained at the office until far into the night.

First he had to complete a new form for the seizure of the hand towel. Then, after an initial preliminary inspection, he decided to conduct various chemical investigations of the same hand towel, and this too had required a tribute of forms. Last and finally he made sure the hand towel was packed correctly before it was sent on to the National Laboratory of Forensic Science in Linköping.

Then he made coffee and had the sandwich he had intended to have for lunch but that had remained sitting back at the office because he had simply forgotten about it. True, he was not particularly hungry now, but still he had paid for it. And when he finally mustered enough strength to get on the subway and go home, the usual thoughts started grinding in his already tired head.

I have to do something, thought Wiijnbladh. I can't live like this. It can't go on. He was thinking about his wife who had openly cheated on him and thereby robbed him of any possibility of a respectable life.

. . .

When Jarnebring arrived home he called his fiancée to mediate peace, but the conversation did not start particularly well. Icy voice on the other end.

"Hi honey," said Jarnebring. "Your old man is home again after a long day's struggle against crime. Soon to be a full day's invigorating murder investigation."

"So now my old man is hungry and wants me to cook dinner," she answered, and the way she said it was enough for frost to form on the receiver he was holding against his ear.

"Are you nuts, honey?" said Jarnebring, who had planned the whole thing with care. "Just start powdering your little nose, I'll be there in half an hour. I have a table reserved at your favorite dive, three courses, candles, and live music. I've arranged a tango orchestra, and I'm sure they're already on their way."

"You're hopeless," she said, "but all right."

And there was something in her voice that definitely gave him hope for brighter, better times. Easy as pie. Now it's only a matter of finding that tie she gave me the day after we met, thought Jarnebring, and hung up.

To be sure, the part about the tango orchestra wasn't true, but otherwise it all added up. And what do you need an orchestra for when your whole heart is singing? thought Jarnebring as he twined his fingers through hers, which were only half as big.

"Listen, Bo," she said, but because he already knew what was coming he just slowly shook his head, tested the old wolf grin, and took her other hand in his as well.

"In a few weeks it's . . . well, you know . . . an even number if I may say so." I can't sit here and say that soon it's four years, he thought. Never wake a sleeping badger.

"Yes?" She nodded seriously and looked at him.

"My suggestion is that we go away. Avoid having a lot of relatives and colleagues drinking up your money. I'll invite Lars Martin, you can invite Karin. Isn't she your best friend?"

"Is this a proposal?" she asked. Yet another, she thought.

"Yes, well," said Jarnebring and nodded, and there must have been something in the food for it felt as if something was stuck in his throat. "I know it sounds a little corny, but that's what it's supposed to be. A proposal, that is."

"In that case the answer is yes," she said, nodding.

They didn't bother with champagne. Instead they went home to his fiancée and future wife's place and played the film backward to the first days of their relationship. When Jarnebring finally fell asleep he felt like the sun was already about to go up on the other side of the curtains, but he must have been wrong because the red digital display on the alarm clock on the nightstand only showed three, and she was resting with her back and behind pressed against his chest and stomach, like a coffee spoon against a soup ladle, Jarnebring thought contentedly. In his world this was exactly as it should be, her head resting on his right arm and his left arm over her side and his hand carefully against her stomach. And when a dream finally took him and led him away he sensed the aroma of fresh-brewed coffee, fresh-squeezed juice, scrambled eggs and bacon.

It's going to work out, thought Jarnebring between sleep and trance, and then he slept just as securely as when he was a little boy and summer vacation had just begun.

7

Saturday-Sunday, December 2–3, 1989

Criminal inspector Anna Holt, age thirty-one, had spent the weekend with her son, Niklas "Nicke" Holt, age six. They had gone skating in Kungsträdgården, had junk food at McDonald's on Norrmalmsgatan, bought a new jacket for Nicke, played games, and been couch potatoes.

"This is the way it will always be for you and me, Mama," Nicke summarized the weekend when it was time for a bedtime story on Sunday evening.

Criminal inspector Evert Bäckström, age forty-seven, didn't wake up until Saturday afternoon with what was, even by his standards, a formidable hangover, which he attributed to all the alcohol he had unfortunately happened to pour into himself the evening before. First came malt whiskey, vodka, and cognac, and so far all was well and good. Unfortunately toward the wee hours he had also sampled—mostly out of curiosity—some bottles with contents unknown, which for philanthropic reasons he had rescued from the General Inheritance Fund.

When he went down to the convenience store to shop for a little late breakfast he was met by the major evening tabloid, which reported that an "insane serial murderer" had been running loose in the city for almost a year now and that he had just "butchered his fourth victim."

Where the hell'd they get that from? Bäckström thought, and contrary to habit bought a copy.

As he read it he saw Jack Daniels before him. It was not a pleasant sight, and he realized it was high time to drag himself off to work and execute a number of preventive measures over the weekend.

Jarnebring didn't even open a newspaper over the weekend. He and his future wife didn't leave their bed any more than was absolutely necessary, and when she parted from him outside work on Monday morning he couldn't remember when he had last felt so good. For breakfast he got fresh-brewed coffee with milk, fresh-squeezed orange juice, two fresh-baked rolls with a crisp crust, lettuce and ham, and a large plate of yogurt with fresh fruit.

I have to call Lars Martin and tell him, he thought as he went through the door to the detective squad.

8

Monday, December 4, 1989

"Have you seen the newspaper?" Bäckström asked, waving his copy of Saturday's tabloid as he stepped into Danielsson's office on Monday morning. Better to forestall than be forestalled. Go ahead, shit your pants, Jack Daniels, he thought with delight when he saw Danielsson's expression.

There were a number of indications that Danielsson too had seen the newspaper. Among others, there was a copy of the same newspaper in front of him on his desk. But after Bäckström's opening, the boss did not have much to say. Mostly he sat silently in his chair and glared at Bäckström, his swollen face purple and a vein as large as an earthworm wriggling back and forth on his left temple.

Soon his fuse will blow, thought Bäckström with delight, but of course he didn't say that. Instead he arranged his face in a worried frown and kept talking according to his carefully prepared strategy.

"My first thought was that the leak came from someone inside," said Bäckström, shaking his head. "As you know we have a number of new, unknown entities working with us. But then"—Bäckström shook his round head again—"then I actually read this crap, so now I don't think so anymore." Bäckström nodded for the third time and looked at his boss credulously.

"So why don't you think so?" Danielsson grunted, looking askance at his colleague.

"It's just too stupid," said Bäckström. "That some religious maniac would run around butchering homos with a . . . what the hell was it? . . .

samurai sword because he was sexually abused by a male father figure when he was a child. Or so says the psychologist the tabloid talked with."

"Samurai sword?"

"Yeah, you know, one of those things the saffron monkeys have," said Bäckström. "You and I and everyone else who knows anything know that Eriksson was stabbed with an ordinary kitchen knife. It's sitting down in tech for examination."

And there wasn't much more to it than that.

"Unfortunately I've got to run," said Bäckström. "I have a meeting with the investigation group."

Danielsson didn't say a word. Only stared at him.

"Okay," said Bäckström, leaning forward in his chair and looking energetically at the detective team assembled in full force in the room. "Let's start with Eriksson himself. What was he doing before he closed up shop? Jarnebring?"

Something must have happened to Bäckström, thought Jarnebring. Wonder if he's going to AA.

"We've found out a few things," said Jarnebring, pulling out a paper with handwritten notes summarizing what he and Holt had come up with.

On Thursday, November 30, Eriksson had first been at a SACO conference in City. Then, for reasons that were unclear, he had chosen to leave right before lunch, which was usually served at about ten minutes past twelve. At about three p.m. he had then shown up at the office in time for afternoon coffee. What he'd been up to in between was a blank. At work he had coffee for about half an hour with a number of coworkers, after which he went into his office, closed the door, and did some work. Shuffled papers and talked on the phone according to those sitting closest, if they were to hazard something that at the same time they couldn't swear to. At five thirty-five, on the other hand, it was certain he left his office. This was shown by the stamp on his time card and was supported by his coworkers in the office next door who saw him on his way out.

Right before closing time—they closed at six—he went into the Östermalm market, where he shopped for a number of food items but none that indicated he was having guests for dinner. Normal weekend purchases for one of the market's regular, single customers. Then there were a number of things that indicated he had walked directly home carrying his briefcase and a bag from the market: Humlegårdsgatan down to the corner of Sturegatan, then diagonally up through Humlegården to Engelbrektsgatan–Karlavägen, Karlavägen to Rådmansgatan and into the building where he lived. The customary police calculations indicated that he must have arrived home at about six-thirty and that he then began his solitary evening by having a portion of already prepared chicken with rice and curry, which he had purchased an hour earlier. With the chicken he had two bottles of German beer, and after the meal was finished he placed the dishes in the dishwasher and threw the empty bottles into the wastebasket.

At about seven, according to his closest neighbor, he had a visitor. Someone rings his doorbell, he opens the door and lets the visitor in. The witness's story and the little that had been produced about Eriksson so far strongly indicated that the person who came to visit was someone he knew. Probably also that the visit was prearranged.

"We'll have to see if we find any notes at his apartment or if his phone records might give us something. We can forget his office because all the calls go through the same switchboard. They're working on dumping the records," said Jarnebring.

"His office," said Bäckström, who was suddenly struck by a thought that he had forgotten to investigate. "His office, was there anything there?" Efficient and managerial. Something must have happened to him.

Maybe he's met someone, poor guy, thought Jarnebring.

"No," said Jarnebring, shaking his head. "No private notes in any case. Some that dealt with his job, mostly meetings that were noted on his desk calendar. But nothing exciting that we can see." Jarnebring exchanged a glance with Holt, who nodded in confirmation.

"So what's next?" said Bäckström, leaning back comfortably in his chair.

A prearranged visit from someone he knew, but that was all they had. No witnesses or technical observations that pointed to any specific individual. Eriksson's private socializing seemed exceedingly meager. Up to now two individuals had made contact and said that they were personal acquaintances. Both had known Eriksson for more than twenty years, both had met him at the university, and all three had spent time together. The one who made contact first by calling the homicide squad on Friday morning was named Sten Welander. He worked as a project coordinator at the TV editorial offices in the big building on Oxenstiernsgatan at Gärdet.

"I'm sure you all know who that is," said Gunsan, looking delightedly at the others in the room.

The reactions to her comment were mixed and hesitant.

"It's that red-bearded guy who produced that program about the police last spring," Gunsan continued. "That terrible person . . ."

"Is it that creep who looks like Gustav Vasa?" Alm asked.

"But skinny," Gunsan giggled. "Do you remember the ruckus after that program?"

"Leave it for now," Bäckström interrupted. "If he's the one who did it, I promise I'll treat you to cake and coffee. Who's the other one who called?"

Something definitely must have happened with Bäckström, thought Jarnebring. If he goes on like this there's a major risk we'll soon have someone sitting in the slammer.

The other one who had called was the director and principal owner of a stock brokerage firm with an office on Birger Jarlsgatan down at Nybroplan. Theodor Tischler, born and raised in Sweden but with a German name. Generally known as "Theo" among family and friends, and in financial circles, according to the all-knowing Gunsan, he was known as "TT."

"He seems to be rich as hell," said Gunsan.

"Good for him," said Bäckström curtly. "Jarnebring, do you have anything else? What's the story with our corpse after he chows his last meal?"

Eriksson's visitor had arrived around seven. At around eight a quarrel broke out, according to the witness, Mrs. Westergren. What had the victim and the perpetrator been doing between seven and eight? They'd had coffee, according to the technicians, and one of them had also had cognac.

Then the coffee cups, cognac glass, and coffeepot had been carried out to the kitchen, placed in the sink, and rinsed off. After which one of the two had a gin and tonic with lemon. The traces were found partly in the kitchen—a lemon that had been cut into strips, the empty ice cube tray that was normally in the refrigerator, an empty tonic bottle—and partly on the floor in the living room, where a half-empty bottle of Gordon's Gin was found with the cap screwed on, along with an unsealed bottle of tonic and a crystal highball glass. And the wet patch on the floor from gin, tonic, and perhaps melted ice.

"The drink was probably sitting on the table in front of the couch where they were drinking, and then ended up on the floor when the fight broke out and the table was overturned," Wiijnbladh stated, while looking portentous.

"Bravo, Wiijnbladh," Bäckström drawled. "Do we have any idea who was drinking these noble beverages?" *Besides me, of course, but you can forget about that*, thought Bäckström, giggling with self-satisfaction.

Judging by the fingerprints it was the host himself. On the other hand, whether his guest drank anything, and in that case what, was not clear from the evidence.

"Probably he took the glass, wiped off the fingerprints, and put it back in the cupboard. Eriksson had a very large collection of different glasses, by the way," said Wiijnbladh.

"It doesn't seem very likely," said Bäckström. "How the hell could he see which glass was his if they'd ended up on the floor in the general confusion? There was only one lemon slice if I remember correctly. Did he wipe off and dispose of his own lemon slice too? Either he drank something else or it was out of a different glass or he didn't drink anything at all. Compare that with the coffee cups. By the way, have you found any prints on them?"

Wiijnbladh looked offended.

"They were in the sink. They were rinsed off," he said indignantly.

"There, you see," said Bäckström contentedly.

The little fat boy has turned into a regular Sherlock Holmes, thought Jarnebring with surprise.

An hour together which, judging by the technical evidence, passed in at least relative harmony. You have coffee, one of you, probably Eriksson, has cognac as well, you clean up and proceed to further consumption. The host at least has a gin and tonic with ice and lemon. But then something must have happened.

"Thanks, Jarnebring," said Bäckström without taking the least notice of Wiijnbladh. For a half-monkey you did really well, he thought. "Well, Wiijnbladh," Bäckström continued, looking at his victim with delight, "may we hear what science has to say? What happened when things boiled over?"

"Quite a bit," said Wiijnbladh indignantly. "We have already produced quite a bit and quite a bit is in progress, as I said. I have received a preliminary report from our forensic physician," he continued, peeking in his folder. "The protocol is in process."

"Did Esprit de Corpse do it?" asked Bäckström.

"Unfortunately no," said Wiijnbladh. "It was some new, younger talent, some woman I've never seen before. But I contacted Engel. He and I have met and gone through the whole thing, and he has promised to keep a watchful eye on our case."

"Sounds good." Bäckström chuckled. "Esprit is supposed to have an eagle eye. What does he say?"

"That the victim Eriksson was killed with a violent knife thrust that was delivered from behind at an angle and struck him high in the back, penetrated into the chest cavity, cutting apart the heart, left lung, and aorta," Wiijnbladh summarized.

"Nothing else?" Bäckström looked almost a little disappointed. "No signs of a struggle? No other observations about our corpse and his little body?"

"No signs of a struggle," said Wiijnbladh, shaking his head. "No wounds at all except for the one that killed him."

"This woman that peeked at him . . . does she have the same keen eyesight as Esprit?" Bäckström asked, grinning.

"I reserve judgment on that," said Wiijnbladh stiffly. "Do you mean do either of them have any thoughts about the victim as a person?"

"Exactly," said Bäckström expectantly. "Did either of them have any?"

"Yes, Engel was of the opinion that the victim was homosexual," said Wiijnbladh.

"Imagine that," said Bäckström. "The same thought struck me when I saw the crime scene and the way he lived."

"Although his younger colleague, the woman who did the autopsy, thought that it was hard to find any physical signs of it," said Wiijnbladh. Best to say what's right, he thought.

"So I've heard," said Bäckström. "As for how things really stand, our local policeman will surely figure it out."

"I'm listening," said Jarnebring, who had toyed with the same thought himself.

"My gut feeling tells me we have an ordinary homo murder here," said Bäckström.

It's nice that you're starting to sound like yourself again, thought Jarnebring.

"I'm still listening," said Jarnebring.

"Single man, forty-five years old, no children, not a woman as far as the eye can see. Lives like a queer, eats like a queer, drinks like a queer, dresses like a queer. By the way, did you see those berets on the hat rack out in the hall? A whole bunch of fairy caps. He sits on the little couch with his boyfriend and has a few drinks and then they have a falling out and the little fiancé fetches his knife and sneaks up from behind and sticks it in. Then the perpetrator waltzes off to the kitchen, throws the knife in the sink, and hops into the bathroom where he throws up."

"Did he throw up in the bathroom?" said Jarnebring, looking questioningly at Wiijnbladh.

"We have secured a vomit-soiled hand towel," said Wiijnbladh evasively. "It has gone to the lab for analysis."

"Depends on what you mean by 'we,' " said Bäckström.

"I see," said Jarnebring. There was actually a lot in what the fat little toad was saying, he thought. Eriksson did not exactly seem to have been a normal man, not like Jarnebring and the other guys on the squad. "You're the boss," said Jarnebring. "How do you want us to proceed?"

"Let's do this," said Bäckström, leaning on his elbows, balancing forward on his seat. For a moment he almost looked like a bulldog, thought Jarnebring.

"I think we'll hold off on his social circle," said Bäckström. "We have to try to get more meat on the bones first. It's meaningless to go after types like this if you don't have anything substantial to beat them up with."

Couldn't have said it better myself, thought Jarnebring.

"You guys from tech done with the crime scene?" asked Bäckström, looking inquisitively at Wiijnbladh.

"Yes," said Wiijnbladh. "We've been done since Saturday." What is he looking for now? he thought.

"You seem to be a whiz at finding things, Jarnebring," said Bäckström. "Take Holt with you and turn his pad inside out. Who was Eriksson, who did he get together with, and which of them stabbed him to death? It's high time we find that out, and since we haven't gotten anything for free, it's probably best to start at his home."

"Sure," said Jarnebring. Just what I would have done myself, he thought.

"And in the meantime, we should see if the rest of us can't produce something more about his so-called orientation." Bäckström grinned and wiggled his fat little finger meaningfully. "You can bet your sweet ass that if we still had our old fag files we would have cleared this up already."

"Talk with the parliamentary ombudsman," said Jarnebring. "He's the one who told us to toss them."

"I should damn well think so," said Bäckström. "Typical gay lawyers. If it had been me I'd have carried them down to the basement without letting on. Fifty years of police work gets sent to the dump because the fairies don't want us to keep tabs on them."

"You're preaching to the choir," said Jarnebring abruptly, making a move to get up. "If that's everything . . . who has the keys to Eriksson's pad?"

"You must have them, Wiijnbladh," said Bäckström innocently. Which is why I gave them to you before the meeting, he thought with delight. So that you could give them to Jarnebring. He was already done with what he had to do, at Eriksson's home at least.

"Okay then," said Jarnebring, taking the extended keys from Wiijnbladh, nodding curtly, and leaving the room along with his new colleague Holt.

"Have you ever done a proper house search?" Jarnebring asked when he and Holt were on the scene in the hall of Eriksson's apartment.

Holt shook her head.

"I've been around and helped out a few times but . . ." She shook her head again. "Nothing like this, no."

"The whole thing is simple as hell," said Jarnebring, "and there's only one important part. It's going to take time, because if we don't do this properly we might just as well forget about it. When you and I leave here, there shouldn't be a dead louse we haven't found and checked."

"I see what you mean," said Holt, smiling.

"I'll show you what I mean," said Jarnebring. "Come here." He went ahead of her to the door to the living room and pointed at the draperies over the two windows facing the street.

"You see those curtains?" said Jarnebring.

"Yes," said Holt, nodding.

"Any idiot can peek behind the curtains and feel with his hand that there isn't something stuffed into a fold. We'll do that too, so don't misunderstand me . . . but in contrast to all the lazy asses, of which there are thirteen to the dozen, you and I are also going to unscrew the knobs on the curtain rods and look to see if anything was stuffed inside. They're hollow. See what I mean?"

"I see what you mean," said Holt, nodding.

"Everything we need is in my bag," said Jarnebring, tilting his head toward the large gym bag he had set down on the floor. "Drawings of the apartment with all the measurements indicated, flashlight, mirrors, folding rule so we can measure that the space we're checking matches the drawing, carpet hammer for tapping out hollow places, jigsaw, regular saw, and everything else we need to peek behind something. Feel free to tear off wallpaper if you think we need to, but make sure you have plastic gloves on, and if you find anything interesting, yell at me first before we even poke at it. Everything of interest we gather up on the table in the living room, write down where it comes from, take it along to the office, and later on we'll go through it in peace and quiet. Always allow for a margin of error. Better to be safe than sorry and have left anything behind. Report forms and bags and sacks are in the bag. Any questions?" Jarnebring looked at his new colleague and nodded.

"Strategy," said Holt. "Where do I start?"

"I'll start here at the outside door," said Jarnebring. "I'll take the coat closet, guest toilet, the hall, and the living room, in that order. You start in the bedroom, then take the bathroom, and when you're done there it'll be time for coffee. Then we take the kitchen and finally the office. I'm thinking that's our best bet because he seems to have his papers in there."

"And everything that can tell us something about Eriksson, who he was, how he lived, and who he associated with is of interest. Notes, notebooks, loose slips of paper, diaries, old calendars, photo albums, videos, books in his bookcase, the color of his socks," Holt summarized.

"That's not enough, Holt," said Jarnebring, trying out his wolf grin. "When we leave here we'll know how he thought. So help me God, we will have peeked into his head."

"I see what you mean," said Holt, and then they went to work.

Jarnebring and Holt had a late lunch at a nearby snack bar. Jarnebring was done with the coat closet, the hall, the guest toilet, and the living room minus the large bookcase, and he hadn't even found a dead louse. Why would he have? The order was pedantic, everything was in its right place, and in the victim's clothing in the coat closet he had found only an invitation to a gallery opening and a three-week-old, neatly folded receipt from the book department at NK.

Cheerless type, thought Jarnebring and sighed.

Holt was through with the victim's bedroom and bathroom, and had gone through an antique dresser and his closets. Neat, clean, tidy and well organized, expensive and tasteful trousers, shirts, jackets, and suits. Underwear, undershirts, socks, sweaters, ties, suspenders, belts, cuff links, three different watches, and a gold money clip which, in light of everything else, was almost indecent. All of the best quality and arranged in a way that would have made an old submarine officer feel hope and enthusiasm.

Holt had made the find of the day. At the very back of the drawer in Eriksson's nightstand was a neatly folded handwritten paper containing five hundred-krona bills, attached with a paper clip, and with a few notes made in a slightly crabbed but legible handwriting revealing that the person who kept things clean at Eriksson's was probably named Jolanta, that she apparently cleaned for him under the table one day a week, that she was due twenty hours' pay for the month of November, and that her compensation of twenty-five kronor an hour would hardly make her rich. She had a telephone and could probably be identified: "Give directions regarding Christmas cleaning," Eriksson's handwriting plus a phone number.

Jolanta, thought Holt. The neighbor Mrs. Westergren had not said a peep about her. Because she was a cleaning lady and didn't, in Mrs. Westergren's world, count as one of those Holt and Jarnebring had asked about? Because Mrs. Westergren wasn't aware of her existence? But why hadn't Jolanta herself made contact? Judging by the notes, Friday was her regular cleaning day. Had the police scared her away when she came to work? Or was there some other, much more tangible reason that she hadn't come forward?

"Check this out," said Holt, handing the paper to Jarnebring, who was trying to screw loose the mirror in the guest toilet.

"Good, Holt," said Jarnebring. "Call Gunsan and ask her to start with the searches, then we'll break for lunch. I'm about to starve to death."

Five hours times two and they had already found a Polish woman who cleaned under the table. We'll take care of this, thought Holt.

· · ·

"Tell me about these 'fag files,' " said Holt, pushing aside her coffee cup and looking expectantly at Jarnebring.

"That was before my time," said Jarnebring evasively as he shook his head. "It's an old story."

"Tell me anyway," said Holt.

Okay, thought Jarnebring, and then he did.

A very long time ago, in the forties or fifties—the history was vague—someone in the big police headquarters on Kungsholmen had set up a registry of male prostitutes and their customers. The reason was that the former sometimes robbed and assaulted the latter, and every year there would usually be at least one murder with such a pedigree.

"Seems to have been a popular sport among the hooligans at that time—knocking off gays," Jarnebring said, taking a gulp of coffee and continuing.

The registry had consisted of a growing number of boxes with file cards. At first it had been kept in the crime department in the old police headquarters on Kungsholmen, then it had grown legs and wandered over to the homicide squad before finally ending up in the early seventies at the office of the central detective squad, at which stage it contained at least a few thousand names.

"A few thousand names," said Holt. "Of individuals who amused themselves by knocking off gays?"

Unfortunately it wasn't as simple as that. Over the years maintenance of the registry had become a bit iffy, and toward the end, before the parliamentary ombudsman suddenly popped up like a bad omen, it mostly contained names of victims as well as any homosexual men who for some reason had attracted interest from at least one member of the force.

"Maybe they just wanted to do some preventive work," said Holt with salt in her voice.

"It's said that in the early fifties some playful colleague put Gustav V in the fag files . . . the old king, you know. It was in connection with those business deals the newspapers were rooting around in at the time. There was a real ruckus so of course they took him out again. But it's clear . . . I understand that Bäckström is grieving."

"Why?" asked Holt.

"He worked in the burglary squad before he wound up in homicide, and he was one of the most diligent suppliers of names to the old fag files. He must feel his work was in vain . . . Speaking of work by the way," said Jarnebring, looking at his watch.

"What do we do about Eriksson's cleaning woman?" said Holt as she got up, finished her coffee, and put on her jacket in a single coordinated motion.

"First we call Gunsan and see if she has produced anything. Then we take the rest of his apartment tomorrow. If there was any justice in this world, little Jolanta would already have been questioned."

Gunsan had produced the address of the apartment that the telephone number belonged to. It was in Bredäng in the southern suburbs, and the tenant was a Polish woman who had come to Sweden about ten years earlier at the age of thirty and become a Swedish citizen just a few years ago. Her first name was Jolanta and as for her surname, it would not have made Danielsson happy in any event.

"Okay," said Jarnebring. "Now we'll go and question her."

"I have to make a call first," said Holt, looking at the clock. It's almost five. What do I do now? she thought.

"In that case, I have a different proposal," said Jarnebring. "You go and fetch Nicke at day care and I'll go and question Eriksson's cleaning woman. Then I'll see you tomorrow morning."

"Are you sure?" said Holt, looking at him.

"Quite sure," said Jarnebring.

"Watch out you don't upset my worldview too much, Bo," said Holt. "But thanks in any case."

"It's nothing," said Jarnebring. I've had three kids myself and had to pick them up at day care all the time, he thought, which proved that his memory treated him with a large measure of indulgence. Bo, he thought. She actually used my first name.

First he had checked that she was at home. This he had done in the usual way, without needing to look into the barrel of a shotgun either.

Good-looking, smart, vigilant, he thought as she opened the door after the second ring.

"My name is Bo Jarnebring," said Jarnebring, holding up his police ID. "I'm a police officer and would like to talk with you about an individual for whom you work."

Jolanta smiled weakly, shrugged her shoulders, and held open the door.

"Police," she said. "I never would have thought. Would you like some coffee?"

The rest had been like a dance.

When and how had she come into contact with Eriksson?

Two years ago through an acquaintance of Eriksson's she was already cleaning for. He worked at TV. What his name was didn't matter, did it?

"I know what his name is," said Jarnebring, smiling his wolf smile. Welander, he thought.

"Let's do this," Jolanta suggested. "If you don't tell him that you've talked with me, I won't call him and tell him that I've talked with you."

"Just what I was going to suggest," said Jarnebring. "Tell me about Eriksson instead. What was he like?"

Apart from the fact that he had been her stingiest and most finicky client there wasn't much she could say, for the simple reason that she almost never saw him. Their contacts had been managed primarily through the little messages that he posted in the drawer of his nightstand. On a few occasions he had been at home when she came to clean. A few times he had phoned her at home because he wanted to change the time when she would come. Any other practical matters he usually addressed to her answering machine, for she was seldom home.

"Why didn't you quit if he was so stingy?" Jarnebring asked.

Because she had Friday morning free anyway, and an old, considerably better client later in the day who lived right in Eriksson's vicinity. She cleaned his office, and he didn't know Eriksson, and what his name was didn't really matter.

"He never tried to make a pass at you?" Jarnebring asked with an innocent expression.

Not Eriksson. Never Eriksson, but of course it had happened and it
happened all the time with men other than Eriksson.

"Why didn't he?" Jarnebring asked. "I would have."

"He wasn't interested," said Jolanta, giving Jarnebring an appraising
look. "He wasn't interested in women. He wasn't like you or other
men."

You don't say, thought Jarnebring, but before he had time to ask the
next question she anticipated him.

"And I'm pretty sure it wasn't because he was interested in men
instead of women."

"What was he interested in then?" asked Jarnebring.

"Himself," said Jolanta. "Power, money, bragging about how well he
lived. Not sex. He simply wasn't interested in sex. Some men are like
that, you know."

Actually I didn't, thought Jarnebring. Not at Eriksson's age in any
case.

"I believe you," said Jarnebring. Now it gets sensitive, he thought.

"How did you find out that Eriksson was murdered?" asked
Jarnebring.

"You want to know what I was doing on Thursday evening," said
Jolanta.

"Yes," said Jarnebring. "What were you doing on Thursday evening?"
Here we go, he thought.

"That's a little sensitive," said Jolanta. "I have an alibi," she continued, "but it's a somewhat sensitive alibi."

Sigh, thought Jarnebring.

"What is his name and what does he do?" said Jarnebring.

"He's someone like you," said Jolanta. "Besides, he's married."

Jolanta's alibi was a police officer who worked with the uniformed
police, and where didn't matter. About Jarnebring's age, married to

another police officer, two teenage children. No intention of getting a divorce. They had met three years earlier when Jolanta reported her car stolen. On Thursday the thirtieth of November, when Eriksson was murdered, they had been in Jolanta's bed in the bedroom next to her living room, where she and Jarnebring were sitting drinking coffee. Before that they'd had dinner in her kitchen. When he left her it was already past midnight. At seven-thirty on Friday morning—she was about to go into town to clean at Eriksson's—he had called her and told her. That's why she hadn't gone there that day.

"Though I suspected you'd show up," said Jolanta, smiling. "Would you like more coffee?"

"Yes, please," said Jarnebring, holding out his cup. "How did he get out of the general call-up?" Jarnebring asked. "I thought there wasn't a single uniformed policeman who wasn't in service last Thursday."

"He didn't have to work," said Jolanta. "He had some kind of overtime cap. But his wife had to work."

She smiled weakly, shaking her head.

"What's his name?" asked Jarnebring.

"I would rather not say, as you understand," said Jolanta.

"I understand," said Jarnebring. "But unfortunately I need to know who he is. And if it's as you say, I'll do what I can so that this stays between you and me and him."

"Okay," said Jolanta. "I understand. Let me think."

"Another thing while you're thinking," said Jarnebring. "Do you have any idea who might have murdered Eriksson?"

Not a clue apart from the fact that she hadn't done it. She had never met anyone that Eriksson knew, apart from the man at the TV company she already cleaned for. She didn't even know if Eriksson knew anyone else, but she had a definite idea that he didn't know very many people. So she had no idea who might have done it. Not even who might conceivably have done it if it necessarily had to be someone who knew Eriksson. How could they be so sure, incidentally, that he hadn't been robbed and murdered by someone completely unknown? Such things happened all the time in her old homeland.

Did she have any idea why someone would have murdered him? Now she took her time before she answered.

"Yes," she said, nodding contemplatively. "I can imagine that someone wanted to get free of him. Someone he had power over. Someone he was pressuring. He was like that. He liked having power over people, and he liked letting them know it."

No, not that too, thought Jarnebring. This should be simple and obvious.

"Okay," said Jarnebring. "We have one small detail left, and then I might ask you for a small favor too, and after that I promise not to bother you anymore. Though if you think of something I suggest you call me."

"A small favor," said Jolanta, raising her well-plucked eyebrows.

"If you have time tomorrow to come over and look at his apartment. If there's anything that's missing, if someone has changed anything. I'm sure you understand why. Then the technicians want to take your fingerprints too in order to eliminate them from the investigation."

"Sure," said Jolanta, nodding. "That's fine."

"Then only the one small detail remains," said Jarnebring, looking seriously at her.

"Only the one? Okay then," she said, nodding.

She gave Jarnebring the name of her lover, and an hour later the married police officer confirmed her alibi.

"What the hell do I do now?" he said, looking unhappily at Jarnebring.

"If I were you I'd keep my mouth shut," said Jarnebring, who knew what he was talking about from personal experience. "Personally, I'm going to try to find a place for this information way in the back of all our binders."

"Thanks," said his colleague, looking somewhat less unhappy.

"Although actually you deserve a kick in the ass," said Jarnebring. "You never intended to call any one of us in the investigation."

"No," said the colleague, looking unhappy again. "I guess I screwed up."

"Then we have to hope it doesn't happen again," said Jarnebring, grinning. Because one or the other of us would probably start to wonder, he thought.

. . .

Always mistrust chance—that was the third of his best friend's golden rules for a murder investigation. I have to call Lars Martin and tell him about the wedding, thought Jarnebring, humming happily as he strode in through the door of his prospective wife's apartment. But for various reasons, roughly the same ones that had occupied him the entire weekend, there was no time left over to do that tonight. It would have to be tomorrow, he thought, as he fell asleep with his prospective wife's head resting against his right arm and his left arm carefully over her hip while he held his hand lightly pressed against her stomach.

9

Tuesday, December 5, 1989

Jolanta was already waiting in the entryway when Jarnebring and Holt arrived at Eriksson's building early Tuesday morning, and when they went through Eriksson's apartment together she was thorough and took her time. There were three, possibly four things she was struck by, and the first was completely trivial. The coffee table in the living room was not where it usually was. Normally it would be farther from the couch than it was now.

"We're the ones who probably moved it," said Jarnebring.

"I should have realized that," Jolanta replied, noticing the abundant traces of dried blood still on the floor.

Her second observation was more interesting. The drawers in the desk in the office were unlocked. Usually they were locked.

"You're sure about that," said Jarnebring.

Jolanta smiled faintly and glanced at Holt, but when she saw that she was occupied by something else her smile became broader and she nodded resolutely.

"I'm sure. They're always locked. Curious, you know," she said, winking at Jarnebring.

When Jarnebring and Jolanta went through Eriksson's clothes closet, things got really interesting.

"A suitcase is missing," said Jolanta, nodding toward two other suitcases that were on the topmost shelf in the clothes closet.

"You're sure of that," said Jarnebring.

"They were there the last time I cleaned," said Jolanta.

"Large, small?" Jarnebring asked.

"In between," Jolanta replied, measuring a rectangle of about two feet by twenty inches between her hands. "Neither large nor small, light brown leather, nice looking. Definitely expensive. I'd like one myself—but I'm not the one who took it if you're wondering."

"No, why would you have done that," said Jarnebring.

"Nice looking," said Jolanta, shrugging her shoulders as she smiled a little. "I suppose you know what Swedish guys say about Polish women?"

"Anything else?" Jarnebring asked, pretending not to hear her question. "About the suitcase, I mean."

"He had his initials on it," said Jolanta. "Face-to-face monogram, KGE . . . only one letter that didn't fit," she added, shrugging her shoulders.

The final discovery Jolanta made was in the linen cabinet in Eriksson's bathroom, but she wasn't nearly as certain as she was about the suitcase.

"I think some hand towels are missing," said Jolanta. "I'm almost certain."

"You think so," said Jarnebring. It can't be a great quantity in any event, he thought as he looked at the well-filled shelves.

"May I look?" asked Jolanta, nodding toward the laundry basket on the bathroom floor.

"Sure," said Jarnebring.

Jolanta took her time and even counted through the towels that were in the cabinet and in the laundry basket. When she was done she nodded and looked more sure.

"A few are missing," she said. "Not a lot but at least five or six. Of the medium-size variety," she said, pointing to the towel rack next to the washbasin.

"Half a dozen hand towels," said Jarnebring. "Eriksson couldn't have taken them to the laundry himself?" Fucking Wiijnbladh, he thought.

"No," said Jolanta. "He never did. He was too good for that. Maybe your colleagues took them with them," she suggested.

"We'll have to check," said Jarnebring. "It'll work out."

As soon as she left, Jarnebring and Holt checked Wiijnbladh's report from the crime scene investigation. There was a notation that all the drawers in the desk were unlocked, that some of them contained "various papers," and that the top middle drawer was empty.

"Maybe Eriksson locked them just before he went out," said Holt. "I would too if that woman was cleaning my house."

A total of seven different drawers, thought Jarnebring. She would be coming to clean the next morning anyway. That's quite a lot of locking and unlocking, he thought. He might lock one or two maybe, because he needed something, but all seven?

"This may solve itself when we see what they contain," said Jarnebring.

"There's nothing about any laundry, nothing about any hand towels . . . apart from the one that Wiijnbladh mentioned at the meeting," said Holt, shutting the binder with the technician's report.

"We'll have to talk with the little man," Jarnebring decided.

After that Jarnebring decided that the bookcases in the living room could wait. The built-in bookshelves covered the entire long wall from floor to ceiling. In total there was more than 150 feet of shelf space and up to several thousand books.

"Think about it," said Jarnebring. "It's going to take the whole day."

"I realize we don't have to read them too," said Holt, who seemed rather cheerful.

They finished off the kitchen instead. Expensive china, beautiful glassware, every imaginable cooking utensil. So far it was like the rest of the apartment. The fridge, freezer, and cupboards were impeccable. Even the vegetables still seemed fresh, despite the fact that it would soon be a week since Eriksson had died.

But in general they did not find anything of interest. Wiijnbladh had already rooted through the garbage bag under the sink on Thursday evening, and according to his report even that appeared to have made a neat and tidy impression. The most exciting thing they found was a glass jar of preserves with an old-fashioned lid and a rubber ring, in which Eriksson apparently stored currency in smaller denominations, coins, and various receipts for alcohol and groceries.

But it took time, and as they stood discussing whether they should have lunch before they tackled the bookshelves, Bäckström called the victim's phone to ask if they had found any safe-deposit box keys.

"That fucking blind bat Wiijnbladh didn't find any," Bäckström explained. "But now I happen to know that there should be a couple."

Jarnebring had taken a wild chance and looked in the top middle drawer in the desk in the office. The key was way at the back, wedged between the frame and the bottom of the drawer, which was otherwise empty.

Strange, Jarnebring thought. If I stored my things in a desk like that, I would have all the ordinary stuff in that drawer, so why was that one empty?

"I found it," said Jarnebring when he returned to the phone.

"That's great," said Bäckström. "Bring it over right away. Then you can tag along on a search at Handelsbanken."

Holt chose to stay at the apartment. She nodded at the bookshelves in the living room.

"You go ahead, I'll start going through the books," said Holt, and without Jarnebring really understanding why, he almost felt a little disappointed as he got into their service car alone and drove up to Kungsholmen.

Bäckström was in a splendid mood. He had received a tip on the phone that morning.

"I hate it when I don't know what they've been up to," Bäckström explained. "Maybe you recall that we have three empty hours when Eriksson is unaccounted for between twelve o'clock and three last Thursday. After he'd left his conference and before he showed up at work."

"Yes, I have a faint recollection of that," said Jarnebring. "It was Holt and I who found that out, as maybe you recall."

"Sure," said Bäckström, who hadn't noticed to begin with. "But now that's cleared up in any case. He evidently has a safe-deposit box at the Handelsbanken office on Karlavägen, halfway between his office and where he lives, and he showed up there at one-thirty last Thursday, sat down in the vault, and went through his box before he left the bank at quarter to three. An hour and fifteen minutes he sat there. It was a gal at the bank who called and gave us the tip. She'd seen in the papers that he was murdered. An hour and a quarter," Bäckström repeated. "This is getting fucking interesting."

One hour later Bäckström and Jarnebring were down in the Handelsbanken vault, monitored by a very proper bank manager, looking on while a female employee with the bank's and Eriksson's keys lifted out a safe-deposit box of the largest available size.

"If you'll excuse us," said Bäckström overbearingly, pulling on a pair of plastic gloves, "I would like to look myself first."

Fucking idiot, thought Jarnebring.

The box was empty. There was nothing in it at all. Not even a dust bunny.

"Damn it," Bäckström hummed as they sat in the car en route back to the police station on Kungsholmen. "He must have emptied the box."

Congratulations, thought Jarnebring. Now I'm starting to recognize you.

"Doesn't sound completely unlikely," said Jarnebring. "Considering the fact that it was empty, I mean," he continued innocently.

"It doesn't take an hour and a half to empty a safe-deposit box, does it?" said Bäckström. "And five hours later some bastard kills him," Bäckström continued, sounding as though he was thinking out loud.

Always mistrust chance, thought Jarnebring, but because this kind of thinking was certainly too advanced for the little tub of lard, he had chosen to express this in a different way.

"Considering that it had been more than a month since he was there the last time, this is undoubtedly a strange coincidence," said Jarnebring.

"How the hell do you know that?" Bäckström asked suspiciously.

"I asked the manager," said Jarnebring. While you were trying to hit on that little teller, he thought.

Then he dropped Bäckström off outside the homicide squad's offices on Kungsholmsgatan, took the car down to the garage, hurried past his office at the squad to see if anything had happened—which it hadn't—and because his stomach had started growling ferociously he chose the simple way out and went down to the police department's restaurant and had a late lunch.

There he ran into a couple of his old colleagues who were now working at the national homicide squad. One thing led to another, they ended up in the break room at the squad, and when he finally returned to Eriksson's apartment on Rådmansgatan it was already late afternoon.

"How's it going with the books?" Jarnebring asked as he stepped into the living room in Eriksson's apartment.

"Good that you came," said Holt. "I just finished."

I'll be damned, thought Jarnebring, but of course he didn't say that.

"That was quick work," he said. "Find anything interesting?"

"I don't know," said Holt, "but it's strange anyway. How did things go for you, by the way?"

"Eh," said Jarnebring with feeling. "We'll discuss that later. Tell me now."

"I'll take it from the start," said Holt. " 'Cause otherwise I'm afraid it'll seem a little strange."

Do that, thought Jarnebring. So that you're quite certain that old uncle Bo understands what you're saying.

"I'm listening," he said.

Holt had leafed through all the books on the shelves to see if they contained notes or interesting inserted papers. None of them had. In purely general terms it was an ordinary, standard Swedish collection that could be found in any sufficiently prosperous, educated, middle-class home: all the great Swedish authors in bound collected editions, a number of classics such as Dostoyevsky, Balzac, Proust, Musil, Mann, Hemingway, and so on; a majority of the most celebrated modern Swedish and foreign literary authors; quite a bit of history with the emphasis on biographies of famous people, and obviously a few major reference works. In this respect everything was completely in harmony with Eriksson's taste in decor and clothing, eating and drinking habits. Of course the books were arranged in alphabetical order by the author's last name.

"What is so strange then?" asked Jarnebring.

"Those," said Holt, pointing to a pile of about twenty books that she had set on the table in front of the couch.

Bäckström was not one to let himself be discouraged by the fact that he had drawn a blank in the bank vault, and as soon as he sat behind his desk he assured himself that the investigations he had initiated the day before were being pursued with undiminished force.

Because those fairies at the parliamentary ombudsman's office had done away with that excellent fag file, for lack of anything better he told Gunsan to see if Eriksson could be found in the general plaintiff registry. Colleague Blockhead had been given the task of talking to the folks who worked at burglary, the detective squad, and the liquor commission about whether Eriksson showed up in any interesting, sexually deviant context. The three younger idiots from the uniformed police had finally been sent out to show pictures of Eriksson at the usual dives and clubs where the bum boys, butt princes, and all the other disease spreaders flocked together as soon as the lights were turned off. The results had been meager.

If Eriksson had been the victim of any crime during recent years he had not reported it. According to Gunsan, he was nowhere to be found in the police department's register of plaintiffs. What the hell use are old ladies? thought Bäckström.

Colleague Blockhead had nothing to say whatsoever, so on that point it was exactly what Bäckström had expected from the get-go. Someone like that you should just kill, thought Bäckström.

One of the three little shits from the uniformed police did eventually come up with something. At a club on Sveavägen one of the customers seemed to recognize Eriksson by the photo he had been shown. He also gave a tip about a place Eriksson might be expected to have frequented.

"He thought he reminded him of a leather queen he met last summer," the younger colleague explained. "They say they hang out at an S&M club up on Wollmar Yxkullsgatan on Söder. It's for those types that like a little harder stuff," he explained.

Fucking idiots, thought Bäckström, and those he had in mind were not the ones who featured in his clues but rather those sitting on the other side of his desk.

"I'll do it myself," said Bäckström. "Give me the paper with the address."

All the books on Eriksson's coffee table were dedicated by the respective authors to various recipients. All the authors were Swedish, and all the recipients also appeared to be Swedes. Or at least their names suggested that. The majority of the books were literary, but there were also a few biographies of famous Swedes, one historical work, and a few nonfiction books.

"Maybe he bought them at a used bookstore," Jarnebring suggested. "Aren't there people who collect dedication copies?"

"I thought so too at first," said Holt as she shook her head. "But there's something that doesn't add up."

"What's that?" said Jarnebring, and he couldn't keep from smiling as he said it.

"For one thing, all the books were written between 1964 and 1975," said Holt. "Second, it seems like no one has read them or even turned the pages, with a few exceptions," she continued. "And third—though I have to admit that I'm not a book collector—they cover extremely different areas. Aren't collectors usually focused on certain particular subjects?"

"No idea," said Jarnebring.

"Me neither," said Holt, "so I thought I would take them to the office while I think about it."

Whatever this has to do with the case, thought Jarnebring, for it did seem pretty far-fetched.

"Do that," he said. "Put the shit in a sack, then we'll call it a day and pick up again tomorrow."

When Jarnebring returned home to his and his prospective wife's cozy little den he had to eat dinner alone. No big deal in itself, because his beloved worked nights, but before she left the house she had prepared food for him, put a dish of delicacies in the oven and set a loving list of instructions on the kitchen table.

When he had eaten he sat down in front of the TV to watch sports after the news, but he didn't get any real peace because Eriksson kept on showing up in his thoughts.

Strange character, thought Jarnebring. What had he really been up to? And having come that far in his thoughts he happened to think of his best friend, police superintendent Lars Martin Johansson. Have to call Johansson, thought Jarnebring. It had been over a month since they had seen each other and there was a lot to discuss.

But no one seemed to be home at Johansson's, and apparently his friend had still not acquired an answering machine. I'll have to call him at work tomorrow, Jarnebring decided. Wonder if he's still at the Ministry of Justice. The last time they had met Johansson had told him he had an urgent investigation assignment for the department.

Before Bäckström left the homicide squad to scout for gays on his own, he had first considered taking his service revolver with him, but that was a weakness he almost immediately pushed aside. Besides, it would have been stupid considering that he'd decided to slink down to the usual dive afterward and knock back a beer or two and eyeball the ladies a little. If there's trouble you can crumple the fairies with your left hand, thought Bäckström, flexing his fat shoulders before he pulled on his big coat and put a photo of Eriksson in his pocket.

He took a taxi. This was a murder investigation after all, and he had more than enough taxi coupons. For investigative reasons he told the taxi driver to stop a little way down the street so he could walk discreetly to the address in question. And what normal person would take a taxi to a gay club?

There was evidently an entrance directly from the street, but the windows were shuttered, and the place appeared to be closed with the lights off inside. Not being one to immediately fall for such simple tricks, he pushed the doorbell for a while, and just as expected a man finally came and opened the door. He was a big, burly type in a checked flannel shirt, worn blue jeans, and a crew cut. A little reminiscent of those boys on the Marlboro ads minus the hat and horse, so he was probably the building manager or something, thought Bäckström.

"We're closed," said the man, glaring at Bäckström.

"I'm a policeman, so leave it," said Bäckström, glaring back. "There's something I want to ask you."

Apparently that was enough, for the man suddenly became interested and seemed almost exaggeratedly courteous as he held open the door for the detective inspector.

"Come in then," said the type. "I'll see if I can help you, Constable."

Something doesn't add up, thought Bäckström.

Oh hell, what a place, thought Bäckström, looking around the dark room. A real torture chamber. What kind of a country are we living in? Hooks on the ceiling, chains and cables and dangling shackles, the walls chock-full of whips and a lot of other shit the use of which he preferred not to guess. This kind of thing should be prohibited, Bäckström thought indignantly.

The man sat down on a thronelike chair, nodded toward a stool at his feet, and looked at the detective with interest. Something here is damn strange, thought Bäckström.

"Sit down," said the man, nodding toward the stool.

"As I said, I'm a policeman," Bäckström repeated. "And there's something I'm wondering if you can help me with." Who the hell does he take me for? he thought.

"I've helped a lot of policemen," said the man, and suddenly he looked rather amused.

Maybe he's a normal informant, thought Bäckström. This place must be a gold mine. Although there seems to be something mysterious going on.

"Do you recognize this person?" Bäckström asked, giving him the photo of Eriksson.

The man took a proper look. Even turned and rotated the picture. Then he shook his head and handed it back.

"Not my type," said the man. "I have a hard time with anything that skinny. He looks like Jiminy Cricket, poor thing."

"So this is not someone you recognize," said Bäckström. Damn, he thought, glancing at the door behind his back, for there was definitely something here that didn't add up.

"No," said the man, devouring Bäckström with his eyes. "I like to have a little something to work with."

"Let's take it fucking easy here," Bäckström shouted, holding up his hand to stop a possible attack. "Fucking easy!"

"I'm calm," said the man, grinning. "It's the little cop who is upset."

What a fucking place, thought Bäckström, taking a deep breath as soon as he had escaped onto the street again. And just as he was standing there breathing out, that fucking Lars Martin Johansson came striding down the street with some dark broad on his arm. What the hell is he doing here? thought Bäckström confused. And if he was on his way here, this is no place you'd drag a broad to, is it?

Johansson stopped and looked at him, and for whatever reason Bäckström suddenly remembered that some of his colleagues in police headquarters called him the "Butcher from Ådalen." Safest to lie low, thought Bäckström.

"Good evening, Bäckström," said Johansson, and he was grinning too, the bastard. "Are you out cultivating your more sensitive side?" Johansson nodded meaningfully toward the closed door behind Bäckström's back.

Bäckström collected himself lightning fast.

"Murder investigation," Bäckström said curtly. "We're working on a gay murder right now." Bäckström nodded to give further emphasis to what he had just said.

"Yes, I thought I saw something in the newspapers," said Johansson with a sneer. "You'd better take care, Bäckström." And then the bastard simply nodded and kept going with the girl on his arm. And as if that wasn't enough, she started giggling violently a little farther down the street, but what Johansson had said to her Bäckström never heard.

Lapp bastard, thought Bäckström with feeling, and then he hailed a taxi and went down to the bar.

10

Wednesday, December 6, 1989

Eriksson's office held lots of papers, neatly arranged in binders, organized chronologically with small labels on the spine indicating what they contained. As far as his extensive stock holdings were concerned, there were twenty or more binders that took up two entire shelves on the bookcase in the office. Binder after binder with sales notes and account statements from his good friend Tischler's brokerage firm, showing that in recent years he had made hundreds of stock trades large and small, and that he almost always managed to do so at a profit. Large trades with very small margins, and as a rule done in the course of a day.

"The guy seems to have been a real financial genius," Jarnebring observed. "Buys and sells shares the same day for hundreds of thousands, even millions of kronor, and when he hits the sack in the evening he's always earned a few thousand-kronor bills. Talk about taking risks."

"We must have misjudged him," said Holt smiling. "He seems to have been a real stock exchange matador. Completely unrestrained."

"I have a friend who works in the fraud unit at the crime bureau," Jarnebring said meditatively.

"Call him then," said Holt, "and ask him to come here."

"Brilliant, Holt," said Jarnebring. "Then you won't have to carry sacks of binders to the office."

. . .

The colleague at the fraud unit had nothing better to do. He had been working on the same tax case for the past seven years, so the prosecutor he worked for should allow him a morning off here or there. Besides, he didn't intend to tell her about it. Within an hour he was sitting at the kitchen table in Eriksson's apartment, thumbing through his binders while Holt made coffee and Jarnebring snooped around in the victim's office.

"Coffee's ready," said Holt, and evidently the colleague from the fraud unit was too.

"Is it okay to smoke in here?" he asked, nodding toward a crystal ashtray on the kitchen counter.

"Talk," said Jarnebring, nodding and sipping his fresh-brewed coffee. "Go ahead and smoke," he said. "I doubt if the corpse will have any objections, and my colleague Holt here is loaded with cigarettes."

"I'm dying of curiosity," said Holt, smiling. "No thanks, I've quit," she said when the colleague from the fraud unit politely extended his own pack.

The whole thing was not particularly complicated according to the colleague from the fraud unit. For an ordinary person like Eriksson, over the long haul it was impossible in principle to earn any money on short-term stock deals.

"It's a zero-sum game," he explained, taking a thoughtful puff. "You can make a profit, or even several in a row, but sooner or later you take a loss, and over a longer period it evens out so that in the best scenario you avoid ending up in the poorhouse."

"But if he was sitting on a lot of important information," Holt objected, "then he should have been able to—"

"I thought you said he worked with labor market statistics at the Central Bureau of Statistics," the colleague interrupted. "Forget that. That's completely irrelevant for anyone involved with these kinds of deals."

"His best friend owns the brokerage firm that he used," said Jarnebring.

"Why didn't you say that up front?" said the colleague from the fraud unit, sighing. "Then we could have done this on the phone."

"I'm listening," said Jarnebring.

"This operation is basically a player piano if you're a broker," the colleague explained. "You buy a block of shares. If the price goes up you sell them and take the money and all's well and good. If the price goes down you dump them with one of your clients who put in a purchase order and let him make a bad deal. If you made a really lousy deal there's probably some old endowment or foundation you manage where you can bury the shit. At least you're holding the cards during the day, and sometimes the stock exchange can turn quite sharply."

"I still don't understand," said Holt. "Say that—"

"I'll give you an example," said the colleague from the fraud unit. "Let's assume that you're my client and I'm your broker." The colleague pointed his fingers at Holt and himself for emphasis.

"In the morning, before the stock exchange opened, you called me and said that you wanted to buy a block of a thousand shares at a price of a hundred kronor maximum per share—let's call the company Mutter & Son—a well-known Swedish engineering firm." The colleague smiled.

"Sure," said Holt. "It happens every day, though I usually use Nordbanken because they take care of my salary of ten thousand a month after taxes."

"Let me make this simple for myself," the colleague continued. "Naturally there are unlimited variations that are both smarter and more profitable, but if I were to make this easy on myself, I'd start by looking through a bunch of sales orders from other clients that are sitting on my desk. Assume that I find someone who wants to sell a block of a thousand shares in Mutter & Son for at least ninety kronor. If I make it easy for myself I've already earned five thousand.

"He'll have his shares sold for ninety, you can buy them for a hundred. I keep the difference minus sales tax and commission, which comes to five thousand in round numbers."

"I'd keep the dough myself," said Jarnebring, grinning. "No way would I share it with someone like Eriksson."

"And that is exactly what they're doing the whole time," said the colleague with feeling in his voice. "Except for those few occasions when they want to help a buddy. And maybe help themselves at the same time."

"What do you mean?" asked Holt. "Help myself at the same time?"

"Say you earn a million per year for yourself like this. That's about where Eriksson seems to have been during the eighties. After tax you have about seven hundred thousand left. You give me an under-the-table commission of half. Three hundred fifty thousand right into my own pocket."

"This can't be legal, can it?" Holt objected.

"No, but basically it's risk-free," their colleague stated. "As long as both keep their mouths shut the risk that both will wind up in the slammer is nonexistent. And if anyone were to start talking with someone like me, then he would have to count on keeping the other one company when it was time for jail—and, by the way, it almost never comes to that. There are no special penalties for this kind of thing."

"Is this how Eriksson made his deals?" Holt asked. "Tischler was nice to an old buddy and made some cash on the side for himself."

"Pretty much." The colleague nodded.

"Tischler made use of Eriksson and gave him some cash for the trouble," Holt clarified.

"Hardly likely," said the colleague, shaking his head and lighting another cigarette. "Tischler must be good for at least a billion if the business pages can be believed. What would he do with a few hundred thousand? It would only be taking an unnecessary risk."

"So he helped an old friend," said Jarnebring. Wonder how much Lars Martin is good for, he thought. With all that old inherited forest money—and he did look out for himself where that was concerned—but it was probably not a question of a billion, far from it, thought Jarnebring.

"So people like us have picked the wrong friends, 'cause we only associate with each other," said the colleague from the fraud unit, squinting down into his coffee cup. "Is there any more coffee, by the way?"

"Tell me about it," said Holt as she poured. "My salary runs out on the twentieth and the month ends on the thirtieth. Why hasn't the union done something about it?"

"The interesting question"—their colleague from the fraud unit nodded thoughtfully—"is of course why someone like Tischler helped someone like Eriksson. Everyone has a buddy, don't they?"

"Maybe he was in love with him," said Jarnebring, grinning.

"They must have played hide the sausage with each other," said Bäck-ström when the investigation team met after lunch and Holt reported the latest results of their efforts.

"Tischler seems to have at least eight children, and he's married for the fourth time," said Gunsan, shaking her head doubtfully. "Not that I've met him, but it still doesn't seem especially likely, does it?"

"He probably doesn't know which locker room to use," said Bäck-ström jovially. "Rich and horny and jumps on everything that moves regardless of what it is, and because little Eriksson couldn't squeeze any kiddies out through his ass he slipped him a little dough as consolation. A million here or there is all the same to a billionaire, isn't it?"

"Well," said Gunsan, pursing her lips, "as far as that's concerned Tischler's ex-wives don't seem to be lacking for anything either."

"A generous earwig," Bäckström decided. "What else do we have?"

A number of loose ends that had to be tied together, Jarnebring summarized. Plus a number of question marks that had to be straightened out. But nothing that seemed simple and obvious and good enough for them to pick up the phone and call the prosecutor.

"We estimate being done with his apartment soon," he concluded. "This week we hope."

"Then there are a few people we thought about talking to again," said Holt. "A few people at his office, among others."

"Do that," said Bäckström, "then I'll scare the shit out of both of his friends, that horny banker and the red-bearded one at socialist TV."

There were four apartments on the floor where Eriksson lived. A few of the loose ends were also hanging there. The closest neighbor, Mrs. Westergren, was one of them, so Holt and Jarnebring went to talk to her again. Upon more careful consideration—and in answer to a direct question—Mrs. Westergren recalled that Eriksson had had a cleaning woman. She had even talked with her on one occasion. "I think she said she was from Poland," she said, apologizing that she had completely forgotten about this. She had hardly seen her, and the natural explanation was that on Fridays Mrs. Westergren visited her ninety-year-old mother at the rest home. "Which was when you said that she was here and cleaned," Mrs. Westergren declared, and otherwise she had not thought of anything since they had spoken the first time.

"You mentioned that you thought Eriksson had started drinking a lot recently," said Holt. "Have you thought any more about that, Mrs. Westergren?"

It was an impression she had, that was all. One time a month ago she thought she smelled alcohol when he greeted her on the stairway. Another time a week or so later she saw him get out of a taxi and thought he'd walked a little strangely when he disappeared into the entryway. She was already outside so they hadn't even said hello to one another. It had made her think because these were new observations that didn't jibe with her previous image of her reserved, well-ordered, and clearly sober neighbor.

An elderly couple also lived on the same floor. Despite repeated attempts by younger colleagues from the uniformed police, they could not be reached. But by talking with their neighbors Holt and Jarnebring found out that they lived in Spain during the winter and left Sweden as early as the beginning of October.

"Not so hard to find out," Jarnebring muttered.

"We did it," said Holt happily. "Didn't take us more than half an hour."

The third and final neighbor took longer than that, despite the fact that their younger colleagues had already talked with him on the morning after the murder. Back then they had received the brief reply that he had neither seen nor heard anything because he hadn't been home during the evening in question, and if there wasn't anything else then he preferred to be left in peace. And he would have been if it hadn't been for the meticulous Gunsan, who found his name in an investigation file that the Stockholm police had set up before the expected disturbances in connection with the celebration of the anniversary of the death of Charles XII.

The neighbor was born in 1920, retired major with the infantry. As a twenty-year-old he had served with the Swedish volunteer corps in the Finnish Winter War, and he had never made any secret of the fact that his political sympathies were quite far to the right. "Obviously not a Nazi but nationalistic like every true Swede," as he himself put it at an interview in connection with his application for a position with the Ministry of Defense staff in Stockholm in the mid-1960s. He had of course not gotten this job, and in response he had requested, and immediately been granted, discharge from the military.

For the last twenty years he had been a retiree, and he had apparently used his free time to give expression to his "nationalist sympathies" by promoting various societies and organizations. Finances had never been a problem for him both because he had wealthy parents and because as a youth he had inherited a large sum of money from an unmarried aunt. As with every real officer and gentleman "the pay was for keeping a horse." He was a rumor-shrouded, decorated hero from the Winter War and the main character in many stories of a highly doubtful nature that were still part of the standard fare in officers' messes around the country.

On Thursday the thirtieth of November he had taken part in the laying of a wreath at the statue of Charles XII, and a number of photos that police detectives had taken supported this. As soon as the celebration itself was over, the responsible police commander ordered him and his sympathizers—"under protest"—to be packed into a couple of rented busses, whereupon they were driven to the subway station at Östermalmstorg at a fairly safe distance from the counterdemonstrators in Stockholm City. From there he had walked straight home to Rådmansgatan and had arrived there at a quarter to eight in the evening, according to the detective who had followed him just to be on the safe side, and whom the irreproachable Gunsan naturally had sniffed out, despite the fact that he had not intended to say anything himself. Whatever. The major had been at home and not out as he had said, and because of that there were very pressing reasons for further questioning.

At first everything went beyond expectations. He was at home and opened the door and let them in when they rang. How often does that happen? thought Jarnebring. A short, austere, and very fit man who looked considerably younger than his almost seventy years. Who nodded brusquely at them as he looked at his watch.

"Go ahead and ask. I don't have all day," said the major.

But then things came to a dead halt. He had neither seen nor heard anything, and he firmly rejected all insinuations that he had previously given misleading statements.

"I came home about eight o'clock, as I told the young constable, so I don't understand what you're after, Inspector," the major said, training his eyes on Jarnebring.

Hadn't he heard that something was happening in the building? Had he, for example, not perceived that the police were conducting a rather extensive and far from silent crime scene investigation right outside his own front door? Had he not heard his doorbell ringing on at least two occasions during the evening? Had he not even peeked out into the stairwell through the peephole in his door?

Answer: no. For one thing his hearing was a little bad, like so many others who had fired thousands of shots without ear protection during a long professional career. For another thing he had been watching TV and as usual he'd had the sound at a rather high volume.

"I was looking at the news to see how much of our royal capital the police had let the hooligans tear down this time," said the major.

Then he had gone to bed and fallen asleep immediately as was his habit. He did not know Eriksson. He had only spoken with the fellow on one occasion, and after that conversation he had no reason to do so again. His neighbor had seemed generally unreliable and ingratiating, and his sudden demise left him cold. His own experiences were different.

"Which experiences?" Holt asked.

The major had seen better men than Eriksson cut down, and he himself had been wounded in the battle of Salla when he was only twenty years old, and had fought side by side with his Finnish brethren against the Russian Bolsheviks.

"No big deal in itself," said the major modestly. "I was on my feet within a week, which wasn't true of most anyone. It's a strange experience getting shot," said the major, and for some reason it was Jarnebring he looked at as he said that.

"I can believe it," said Jarnebring.

"The bullet entered my left side," said the major. "The outside of the rib. But it bled copiously, and blood stands out against the snow, especially when it's your own."

Jarnebring did not say anything, but for reasons that he did not at first understand he suddenly spotted the old-fashioned black telephone with a round dial that was on the major's desk.

"It took a while before my comrades could carry me out of there," said the major. "I don't think I've ever felt so alone, . . . and after what happened I became a different person. Neither better nor worse, but different."

"I understand what you mean," said Jarnebring.

"Yes, I suspected as much," said the major. "People like me usually see these things."

Given this and other experiences of a similar nature the major was not one to spend time agonizing over someone like Eriksson, who had obviously socialized in the wrong circles and had met his death in an unfortunate way that was causing trouble for those around him. But what else would you expect from someone like him?

"What do you mean by that?" It was Holt who asked the question.

"A run-of-the-mill disguised proletarian trying to play the gentleman," said the major. "He didn't fool me."

How did he know that? Was he familiar with Eriksson's background? Holt again.

"You can sense that sort of thing. The fellow was a wretch," the major snorted.

"Nice old guy," Holt giggled when they were in the car en route back to the office. "What do you think? I wonder, by the way, how many times he's told that hero story for his audience in the officers' mess."

A time or two, even if that's not what it's really about, thought Jarnebring, but naturally he hadn't said that to Holt, because she still wouldn't have understood.

"I don't think he killed Eriksson, even though he certainly could have managed it," he said instead. "It's as though there isn't space for that, and Eriksson already had a visitor when the old man returned home after having said his *Heils* for the evening."

"I get the feeling he knows something," said Holt.

"Or else it's just that you don't like him," said Jarnebring, who had been around considerably longer than Holt.

"I think he's holding something back," Holt persisted.

"Or else he's just generally delighted that someone got rid of a guy like Eriksson," Jarnebring countered.

"I still think he's holding something back," Holt repeated.

"Possibly," said Jarnebring. "If that's so, I don't think he intends to help by telling us in any event."

"Gloomy type," said Holt.

What do you know about that? You were never drafted, were you? thought Jarnebring.

"Where did you do your military service, Holt?" asked Jarnebring, smiling his wolf grin.

Despite what he had promised, Bäckström never had the chance to scare the shit out of anyone this gray afternoon at the beginning of December. When with his colleague Alm in tow he stepped unannounced into Tischler's tastefully decorated office down at Nybroplan, the receptionist told him that the banker was not available. Because Bäckström wasn't the type to take no for an answer, he persisted and finally got to speak with Tischler's own secretary. A stylish woman in her fifties who went well with the decor. She apologized, but the banker himself was in New York at a meeting and was not expected home until Friday morning.

"I know he is very anxious to speak with you gentlemen," said the secretary. "So I suggest that you call me on Friday at midday, and I will try to arrange a time for you as soon as possible."

Fucking stuck-up bitch, thought Bäckström. Who the hell do you think you are?

He and Alm did not have much better luck when they visited the TV building on Oxenstiernsgatan where Welander was to be found. The guard in reception paid hardly any attention to their police IDs, and after some negotiating they were at last allowed to talk to yet another secretary, but this time only on the phone. Sten Welander was occupied. He was in an important meeting and could not be disturbed. If they wanted to meet Sten Welander, she suggested they call to arrange a time, and it would surely be fine. After that she simply hung up.

Fucking communist cunt, thought Bäckström. Who the hell do you think you are?

In the car en route back to police headquarters that blockhead Alm started whining and coming up with a lot of suggestions about what they should have done instead.

"I told you, Evert, we should have called ahead," Blockhead moaned.

Fucking idiot, thought Bäckström. Who the hell do you think you are?

When Alm was about to drive the car down into the garage Bäckström jumped out on the street, hailed a taxi, and went straight home. What a fucking society we live in and what fucking people there are, thought Bäckström, leaning his full weight back against the seat.

As soon as Jarnebring returned to his and his prospective wife's pleasant little apartment on Kungsholmen he called up his best friend, police superintendent Lars Martin Johansson.

Johansson answered on the first ring and sounded almost elated when he heard who it was.

"Good thing you called, Bo," said Johansson. "I've tried you a few times, but I suppose you've been working, as usual."

"Yes," said Jarnebring. "There's been a—"

"What do you think about having a bite to eat on Friday?" interrupted Johansson. "My usual place at seven o'clock. Can you?"

"Yes," said Jarnebring. "I'd actually been thinking that—"

"Excellent," said Johansson. "Then that's settled. I have a few things to tell you."

I see, thought Jarnebring. Wonder what that could be? He hasn't heard anything, has he?

11

Thursday, December 7, 1989

Holt was already at work before seven o'clock on Thursday morning. Nicke had spent the night with his dad, who would take him to day care. Holt woke up as usual, showered, had breakfast, and even managed to read the paper in peace and quiet, but when she was done with that she was still an hour ahead of her usual schedule. She went to work, and for lack of anything better to do while she was waiting for Jarnebring, she resumed her investigations of the mysteriously dedicated books she had found in Eriksson's bookcase.

After half an hour of searching she found the addresses for all four of the recipients of dedication copies that she had been able to identify, and the mystery deepened further.

One of them, a woman born in 1935, had died a few years ago, but her husband was still living in the residence they had shared on Strandvägen. In the year 1974 a far-from-unknown author and member of the Swedish Academy had dedicated his newly published novel to her. The author was still alive, he was considerably older than his now dead "muse," and the two of them had probably had a relationship at the time he had given her his book.

Oh my goodness, thought Holt, continuing to search in her files.

All the other three recipients lived in the same area. One, now an eighty-year-old bank executive on Narvavägen, had received a book about the Kreuger crash of 1932 written by another well-known financier. An executive on Djurgårdsvägen had received a book about Swedish chapbooks from a historian to whom he had evidently given a research grant. Finally, a very well-known publisher who also lived on Djurgården had received a book of poems from a poet unknown to Holt; the poet did not make a secret of the fact that he was thinking of changing publishers.

One woman and three men, all fine people at fine addresses in the same limited area of Stockholm: Strandvägen, Narvavägen, Djurgården.

This is a real detective mystery, Holt was thinking just as Jarnebring came into the office, his large body positively quivering with zest for work, as can easily happen when you've started the day by first, at full throttle and high volume, having sex with the woman you love, and then gobbling down a perfectly formidable breakfast.

"Good morning, Inspector," said Jarnebring. "Have we captured any suspects yet?"

"Not yet," Holt replied, quickly hiding her papers under a pile of regular searches.

Why did I do that? she thought.

During the morning they talked with Eriksson's coworkers again. The tongues of several of them had now loosened, and in all essentials they confirmed what the doorman had already told them, though their choice of words was different. Eriksson had not been a good person. He had been sufficiently bad that none of them had had any desire to associate with him, but at the same time not so terrible that there was any reason to kill him.

"Just an extremely unpleasant person," one of Eriksson's female coworkers summarized. "He really did nothing but snoop around."

None of them had socialized with him, none of them even seemed to have known him outside of work, and none of them had had motive and occasion to bump off Eriksson at home in his own apartment.

How is this possible? No man is an island, thought Holt as they drove back to police headquarters on Kungsholmen.

When they returned to their office after lunch the excellent Gunsan had solved Holt's mystery of the mysteriously dedicated books, despite the fact that she wasn't even aware of the problem. On Jarnebring's desk was a typewritten sheet of paper on which Gunsan had compiled what she, with the help of the police department's telephones and computers, had produced about Eriksson's background. Jarnebring took it and started reading while Holt—for the millionth time—started thumbing through her own piles of papers.

"Okay, it's clear," Jarnebring suddenly exclaimed. "Look at this," he said, handing over the paper with Gunsan's notes on Eriksson's history.

It appeared that Eriksson had worked as a mail carrier in Stockholm during the years from 1964 to 1975. First as a substitute mail carrier and then as a temporary, at the two post offices whose delivery areas included Djurgården and the tonier parts of Östermalm. At the age of thirty-one, when he completed his part-time studies at the University of Stockholm with a degree in sociology, criminology, and education, he also quit the post office and got a job instead as an assistant statistician at the Central Bureau of Statistics.

"But why did he steal books?" said Holt, looking inquisitively at Jarnebring.

"Maybe he stole other things too," Jarnebring sneered. "Who cares? This is already past the statute of limitations, and he's dead anyway."

"But books," Holt persisted.

"I guess he liked to read," said Jarnebring, smiling.

Holt shook her head.

"I think he was snooping," she said. "I'm pretty sure that Eriksson was an extremely snoopy type."

In the afternoon the detective team met as usual and again took stock of how the investigation was going. As of yet nothing had been produced that was even reminiscent of a breakthrough.

"I don't understand this guy," Jarnebring muttered. "He doesn't seem to have known a soul. Well, besides those two you wanted to question," he added, looking inquisitively at Bäckström. "How did that go, by the way?"

"It'll work out, it'll work out," said Bäckström evasively, and instead launched into a lengthy exposition of his pet homo theory, on which he and his colleagues had evidently put in some comprehensive work. Gunsan had searched out a large number of conceivable murderers of gay men, identified those who according to the computer already had something else going, for example, were sitting in prison or in one of the mental institutions for the criminally insane, and turned the rest back to Bäckström, Alm, and the others who had already questioned a number of them. Without any results, however.

"We'll find him," said Bäckström credulously. "There's some little fairy out there that Eriksson had contact with or just picked up when he had the chance, and sooner or later we'll run into him."

The hell we will, thought Jarnebring doubtfully, and if a murder investigation could be compared to a soup, then this was pretty thin.

The checks on Eriksson's telephone were done and had not produced anything in particular. The calls he made from his home phone usually went to the switchboard at the brokerage firm that managed his stock transactions. There were also occasional calls directly to Tischler, Welander, or his cleaning woman's home phone.

The autopsy was complete, but if you disregarded Esprit and Wiijnbladh's so-called interpretations of the victim's personality, it basically conveyed no more than what Jarnebring had understood with his own eyes when he found Eriksson dead on the floor in his living room.

Same thing with the technical investigations. Prints from a small number of persons of which the two most common samples had already been identified as Eriksson's and his cleaning woman's. But none that could be found in the police files, and other clues were sparse as well. The hand towel that had been found in the laundry basket in Eriksson's bathroom was still at the crime lab. As usual they were overworked and a report was unlikely to arrive before Christmas, despite the fact that Wiijnbladh had called to nudge them.

Instead the team members sat around arguing about a lot of irritating details that would certainly prove to be completely uninteresting once things got to the point. A safe-deposit box key that was missing, for example. An entire half hour of sometimes animated discussion had been devoted to this, and it was Jarnebring who brought it up, although this had not really been his intention.

Supposing it was the case that Eriksson had been killed by a male prostitute he had picked up. Why was there nothing to indicate he had been robbed? As far as Jarnebring and Holt and even Wiijnbladh and his colleagues had been able to ascertain, nothing particular was missing from Eriksson's apartment. Apart from a suitcase, probably a few hand towels, and possibly a number of papers. Despite the fact that there were various things that ought to have tempted an ordinary robber. Three expensive watches and a number of other personal items, such as a gold currency clip.

"We don't actually know that," Bäckström objected. "I'm a hundred percent sure that he emptied his safe-deposit box that day, so he could have had piles of dough at home." Although it doesn't need to be that bad, he thought, almost feeling a shudder as he did so. That would be simply too annoying, he thought.

"I don't believe it," said Jarnebring doubtfully. "If there's anything that has disappeared it's probably some of his papers that someone has taken. That thing with the hand towels is far from certain, and as for the suitcase it may just be that the perpetrator needed it to carry away the papers he may have taken."

You really are a true detective, Jarnebring, thought Bäckström, nonetheless deciding to mess a little with the big ape-man, since he still had the victim's suitcase in his possession, although he had always intended to put it back as soon as things had settled down.

"What papers?" asked Bäckström, suddenly seeming rather contentious. "What kind of papers would they be?"

Jarnebring just shrugged his shoulders. He had never brought up the empty drawer in Eriksson's desk, though he had thought about it, while stupidly he had mentioned the missing safe-deposit box key instead. Eriksson had signed out two safe-deposit box keys from Handelsbanken. One had been found but one was still missing, despite Jarnebring's and Holt's dogged searching. Where was it?

The proffered suggestions ranged across the whole field, from that it had ended up in the murderer's own pants pocket to that it had simply been lost. Which by the way was often how things turned out when you had two identical keys, despite the fact that you only needed one. Didn't everyone know that from their own experience?

When they were finally done and everyone had had their say, the day was basically over. In a few hours it would have been a week since Eriksson had been murdered, and they still did not have their hands on any culprit worthy of the name.

12

Friday, December 8, 1989

On Friday morning Inspector Alm provoked his colleague Bäckström's displeasure.

Without talking with Bäckström, he phoned TV reporter Sten Welander at the national television news to set a time for a conversation about Welander's old acquaintance Kjell Eriksson.

Welander was friendly and businesslike; he looked forward to meeting with the police and pointed out in passing that he had called them first, as early as Friday morning a week ago, as soon as he had heard about the tragic event. Not because he thought he could contribute much in particular, but he could scarcely be the judge of that. If he himself could propose a time, it would be either within an hour or two or else in fourteen days, because he would be traveling abroad in connection with a major news story he was working on. And if they wanted to meet with him immediately it had to be at his office in the TV building as he had a number of other meetings later in the day that were already scheduled and could not be changed.

Alm excused himself and asked to call back within five minutes, after which he went into Bäckström's office and gave him the available alternatives. Bäckström was naturally sour as vinegar, but as he did not have anything else to propose, he gave in after some grousing. A pleased Alm returned to the phone, called Welander, and said that he and a colleague by the name of Bäckström would be at Welander's office within half an hour.

Welander met them down in the reception area and led them to a small conference room he had reserved for their meeting. He was a lean, sinewy fellow in his forties with a well-groomed, full beard and dark, intelligent eyes, and his first action when they sat down was to pull out a small tape recorder from his pocket and place it in front of him on the table. After that he leaned back, clasped his hands over his flat stomach, and nodded to them that he was ready to start.

It was Bäckström who had planned their tactics. He would run the questioning while Alm kept in the background and stepped in as needed. Alm had no objections whatsoever. He remembered Welander's TV program about the police department and was really looking forward to seeing how Bäckström's "interrogation victim" would massacre his fat little colleague.

Bäckström took his sweet time before he started. Arranged his own tape recorder, notebook, and pen, tested the recorder, asked Welander to say something, rewound it, and played it to check that everything was working.

"I'm going to talk roughly like this," said Welander, leaning back comfortably and speaking in a normal, quiet conversational tone.

"Okay then," said Bäckström, nodding curtly. "Interview for informational purposes with Sten Welander with regard to the murder of Kjell Eriksson. Welander will be questioned about—"

"Excuse me," Welander interrupted, smiling courteously at Bäckström. "I forgot to ask whether you gentlemen would like anything to drink? Water, coffee? I don't know if we have tea, actually . . ."

"What the—" said Bäckström, but before he even had time to answer, Welander had done it for them.

"If not, then I'm ready to begin," said Welander, nodding suavely at Bäckström.

Welander versus Bäckström, 1–0. thought Alm delightedly as he noted that Bäckström's face had already turned a shade redder.

How did Welander know the murder victim Kjell Eriksson? How long had he known him?

Welander had become acquainted with Eriksson more than twenty years ago, when he was teaching sociology at the university. Eriksson had been one of his students. A diligent one, so Welander had arranged a few side jobs for him at the department, in the mail room, as a test proctor. A little of everything.

"He was actually a few years older than me," said Welander. "Worked part-time and studied on the side. Came from simple circumstances, so I tried to help him as best I could. He was really exerting himself; he really wanted to change his life."

The friendship had persisted and even developed. Welander had worked less and less at the university and more and more as a researcher and reporter at the TV news department. By and by Eriksson finished his degree and got a job at the Central Bureau of Statistics.

How often did they see each other?

Not that often, according to Welander, but certainly considerably more often if viewed through Eriksson's eyes.

"Kjell was a very solitary person," Welander explained. "He didn't really have too many friends. We saw each other from time to time. Went out and had a beer together, talked about old times at the university, had dinner now and then . . . and we've continued that over the years. How often we saw each other? Yes . . ." Welander looked as if he was thinking deeply. "Spread out over all the years then maybe it was once a month."

"Once a month," said Bäckström with palpable doubt in his voice.

"On one occasion I recall that he helped me by producing statistics for a series of programs on unemployment that we did. That must have been ten years ago, and then I think we saw each other considerably more often. Perhaps once or twice a week for a few months."

"But otherwise you saw each other once a month," Bäckström repeated. "Once a month? Always?"

"No, not really," Welander objected, smiling and shaking his head. "There could be six months when I didn't even talk to him. Once a month is an average. Say that I met him approximately two hundred times in twenty years. That's two hundred and forty months. Two hundred divided by two hundred forty is approximately once a month. Less than once a month."

"Thanks, I can count," said Bäckström sourly.

"That's nice to hear," said Welander amiably.

Welander versus Bäckström, 2–0, thought Alm, noting the change of color in his colleague's face.

Did Eriksson have any other close friends? Anyone he saw more often than he saw Welander?

Welander looked as though he was thinking deeply.

"I'm afraid I don't really understand the question," Welander said.

"Why's that?" said Bäckström. "That shouldn't be so hard, is it?"

"You say 'close,' then you say 'more often,' " said Welander, almost sounding as if he were savoring the words.

"Yes? What's the problem?"

"Closeness is a question of feelings while on the other hand 'how often' is a question of frequency, and in these kinds of contexts that's far from the same thing, wouldn't you say?"

Bäckström did not reply. He was content to glare at Welander who, however, seemed quite unaware of this.

"Take your colleague Alm, for example," said Welander pedagogically, smiling at Alm, who took the opportunity to smile back. "I am certain that you see each other several times a day . . . on average . . . but are you best friends too?"

No, God help me, thought Alm.

Fucking asshole, thought Bäckström. Fucking assholes both of them, he thought.

Welander versus Bäckström, 3–0. This is a real walk-over, I should have brought along the white gloves and ammonia bottle, thought Alm delightedly, old amateur boxer that he was.

If it was frequency of contacts that Bäckström meant, then Welander could imagine that his and Eriksson's mutual friend Theo Tischler met Eriksson more often than he did, because Theo Tischler helped Eriksson with various private financial questions. Obviously he was taking into account the fact that all three of them sometimes met, and it was he, by the way, who had introduced Eriksson to Theo Tischler. He and Theo had known each other since school days. They had been in the same class both in elementary school and in high school. Norra Real at Jarlaplan, if Bäckström was wondering.

On the other hand, as far as the emotional aspect was concerned he was less sure. His impression was that Eriksson did not have any really close friends whatsoever.

"I know that he was tremendously attached to his old mother," said Welander, sounding almost mournful as he said it.

This guy is phenomenal; look at the footwork, thought Alm.

"No women?" said Bäckström slyly.

"Excuse me," said Welander, as if he had not really understood the question.

"Eriksson," Bäckström clarified, and suddenly his voice almost sounded friendly. "Do you know if Eriksson had any women? Did he meet any women?" Bäckström repeated.

"Socially?" Welander looked at Bäckström as if he still did not understand the question.

"Exactly," Bäckström agreed smoothly. "Yes . . . sexual contacts . . . with women . . . if you understand what I mean."

"No," said Welander, shaking his head. "As far as I know, Kjell never met any women. Not in that way."

"He didn't," said Bäckström. "Why didn't he . . . do you think?"

"I guess he wasn't interested," said Welander.

"He wasn't," said Bäckström. "He wasn't, not interested in women you say."

"No," repeated Welander. "To be honest I think he was completely uninterested in women . . . in that way."

"Men then," said Bäckström. "Was he interested in men?"

"Not as far as I know," said Welander neutrally. "In any event he never expressed any such interest in either me or Theo."

"But you must have wondered about it, didn't you? Both you and Tischler must have talked about it," Bäckström persisted.

"*De mortuis nihil nisi bene,*" said Welander, smiling to himself.

"Huh?" said Bäckström.

"De mortuis nihil nisi bene," Welander repeated. "Say nothing but good about the dead," he translated.

You don't say, thought Bäckström contentedly, before he asked the routine last question.

Welander was obviously not a suspect in Eriksson's sudden demise, but for the sake of formality and saving time and so forth, Bäckström was nonetheless compelled to ask what Welander had been doing on Thursday evening the thirtieth of November.

It seemed there was no problem whatsoever. Welander had had dinner at the Lidingöbro inn together with eight of his coworkers from the TV station, among them his immediate supervisor and the station manager. Dinner had begun with a welcome drink at seven o'clock and gone on until just after eleven, when they had moved on to the home of one of the participants for "a little follow-up gathering." This had gone on until two, and then Welander had taken a taxi home to his wife and their two children in their townhouse out in Täby. If Bäckström spoke with the secretary at the TV office she would see to it that he received a list of all the dinner guests as well as their telephone numbers. Welander had already forewarned her to expect such a request.

The guy is a world-class champion, thought Alm.

Wonder what that idiot is grinning about, thought Bäckström as he and Alm were driving back to the police station.

Absolute massacre, thought Alm. This I have to tell Jack Daniels.

Jarnebring and Holt had devoted the day to routine business, which unfortunately took considerably longer than they had counted on.

"We'll have to deal with the rest of the apartment on Monday," Jarnebring decided as the clock started dragging toward five. It was Friday and he had to have time to shower and change before he met his best friend, police superintendent Lars Martin Johansson.

13

Friday evening, December 8, 1989

If Welander had stuck to the truth when Bäckström questioned him about his acquaintance with Kjell Eriksson, there would have been at least certain similarities between the relationship he had with Eriksson and the one Jarnebring had with his best friend, Lars Martin Johansson.

Johansson and Jarnebring had also known each other for more than twenty years; in the last ten years they had socialized on average once or twice a month, and when they did so they usually met at a restaurant. During the early years it had not been that way. They had met at work at the central detective squad at the Stockholm Police Department, each one being half of a team of two, and for several years they had spent more time with each other than with their own families. But then their paths had separated. Johansson had made a career and disappeared straight up to the top of the police pyramid while Jarnebring stayed put in the detective squad and was still working with the same sort of crimes and the same sort of crooks as he had been twenty years ago.

In contrast to Welander and Eriksson, they had a relationship that was grounded in a very strong, close friendship, and if anyone had asked either of them who his best friend was, they would have had no problem at all with the answer. And as is so often the case with close friends, they were like each other in everything that really counted and unlike each other in other respects that were mostly superficial, personal characteristics that didn't really matter much when it came time to settle accounts.

Their most important common quality was that they were both—in an environment almost exclusively made up of police officers—unanimously described as "real policemen." They were heroes in a large number of so-called police station stories of at best varying degrees of veracity, and in contrast to their colleagues in the world of fiction—who associate with female intellectuals, listen to opera and modern jazz, and prefer nouvelle French cuisine—Johansson and Jarnebring liked regular ladies, preferably female colleagues, dance band music, and Swedish home cooking.

But of course there were also differences. If anyone had asked Jarnebring, for example, if he could imagine stopping the bullet meant for his best friend with his bare chest, he would have flashed his wolf grin and said that if it was his friend they were after the question never would have come up—he would have shot first. And if Johansson got the same question he would probably have smiled evasively, said that the question was far too sentimental for his taste, but that he might possibly imagine loaning Jarnebring the money for a new car.

Johansson lived on Wollmar Yxkullsgatan on Söder. It was close to his regular place, an excellent Italian restaurant that served simple, well-prepared food. When he and Jarnebring met, he was almost always the one who paid the bill, without even thinking about it. In contrast to his best friend he had very good finances, and, true, he did look out for himself where money was concerned, but when it came to those near and dear to him he was generous in a highly spontaneous way. Besides being enthusiastic about both food and drink, especially in the company of Jarnebring.

"Have whatever you want, Bo," said Johansson, handing over the menu. "This evening's on me."

"Thanks, Boss," said Jarnebring. "In that case you can order a beer and a whiskey for me while I'm thinking."

.   .   .

When Johansson and Jarnebring met at the restaurant, their time together would follow an almost ritual pattern. First a summation of the essentials of police life since they last met: colleagues, crooks, and crime. After appetizers they would naturally move on to the topic of fools not present and surprisingly often also active within the police, the prosecutor's office, or the judicial system in general. Only later—over dessert, coffee, and cognac—would they concentrate on those more personal, intimate questions such as old buddies, their own children, and above all, women. Both those they had already met or were just meeting now and those they still only intended or hoped to meet.

Because Jarnebring had a purpose this evening, he had also decided on a certain approach so as not to disturb their time together unnecessarily. Even before he stepped into the restaurant he had concluded that the news about his impending marriage could suitably be deferred until the coffee and cognac. Possibly even until the highball and the often obligatory midnight snack at Johansson's place on Wollmar Yxkullsgatan. That's how it'll be, Jarnebring decided. No need to excite Lars Martin before he has food in his stomach.

But this time that wasn't how it turned out.

In recent years Lars Martin Johansson had led a transient existence within the police department. First he had taken a leave of absence for some university courses, and when he returned to the National Police Board, after having completed his academic work with customary efficiency, he had been immediately promoted to police superintendent and become a fill-in resource for the Board. After the murder of the prime minister a few years earlier, personnel turnover at the top of the police pyramid had increased dramatically, and Johansson was now a fixed point in a changeable and uncertain world.

For that reason he also had to wander between brief temporary positions as police chief filling in for whichever colleague had most recently bit the dust, as well as serve on more and more study commissions and accept recurring assignments as an expert in the Ministry of Justice and the prime minister's office. He had certainly not lacked for work, and for the past few months he had been sitting in the Ministry of Justice with a new investigation that Jarnebring had only heard rumors about, despite the extensive police station gossip.

"Tell me, how are things in the corridors of power? Or is it secret?" said Jarnebring with curiosity as soon as they had finished the first schnapps with the baked anchovies au gratin their Italian restaurateur served as an appetizer. Presumably for lack of herring, but damned good anyway, thought Jarnebring.

"It's not really a secret," said Johansson in his contemplative Norrland dialect. "You only have to watch TV or read the papers. Although this one came up a bit quickly of course."

One month earlier the Iron Curtain had suddenly been raised with a bang, just like when you fiddle with an old-fashioned window shade that has stuck. On any TV channel whatsoever in the Western world you could follow, day after day, the stream of refugees from the former Soviet satellite states who were pouring westward and the story about how the inhabitants of the former East Berlin had torn down the wall with their own hands.

"The socialist paradise," said Jarnebring, smiling contentedly. "Can you imagine how wrong it turned out."

"Oh well," said Johansson. "The idea was good in and of itself, and you hardly needed the gift of prophecy to realize that sooner or later something like this would happen. But maybe it went a little fast. A little too fast for my taste," said Johansson. He smiled and shook his head, seeming despite everything rather contented.

"Yes, up till now we seem to have managed," said Jarnebring, who preferred not to wind up in any political quarrel with his best friend despite the fact that he certainly was the closet social democrat the majority of his colleagues suspected. "Those Eastern Bloc hooligans we've taken in seem mostly to have shoplifted at NK and Åhléns."

"Yes," said Johansson. "Although a few of us have an idea that this might be different."

Continuing along that track they talked politics far into the marinated pork with garlic and pesto that was their entrée, and it was only when Johansson asked what Jarnebring himself was up to now that the conversation returned to normal.

"Now let's forget about politics," Johansson decided. "Tell me! What are you doing these days?"

"I'm in the middle of a murder investigation," said Jarnebring, and just as he said that he saw the momentary regret in his best friend's eyes.

"I would happily trade with you," said Johansson. "If it's not Palme, of course," he added quickly and smiled. "I have had enough of that mess as it is. I could keep investigating colleagues until I was put in my grave."

"No, God help me," said Jarnebring. "No, this is a completely regular Joe Six-Pack, apart from the fact that he seems to have been a nasty character. But it's hardly the first time."

"Sounds good," said Johansson. "Joe Six-Pack and a real character. If I haven't forgotten everything I learned it sounds a lot like something we usually clear up." Why don't I do something smart with my career too? he thought suddenly.

"There are certain problems, however," said Jarnebring, leaning forward.

"Tell me," said Johansson. "Start with the biggest one and don't make things unnecessarily complicated," he added, suddenly looking rather pleased.

"Bäckström," said Jarnebring with a sneer.

"Bäckström," said Johansson. "Do you mean Bäckström at homicide?"

"One and the same," said Jarnebring. "Bäckström is the leader of the investigation."

"Sweet Jesus," said Johansson with feeling. "I ran into that nitwit the other evening, by the way. He came flying out of that club, you know, that's farther down on the street where I live, and if it hadn't been him I would have thought he was involved in indecent activities."

"He has the idea that this is a so-called gay murder," said Jarnebring.

"I seem to recall he mentioned that too," Johansson recalled. "Why does he think that? Because it's Bäckström, or is there any factual reason?"

"There is a noticeable lack of women in the vicinity of the victim," said Jarnebring. "So the thought even occurred to me—"

"But," said Johansson, leaning closer too.

"I have the wrong feeling in my fingertips," said Jarnebring, holding up his big right hand and rubbing his thumb against his fingers. "In gloomy moments I get the idea that this is more complicated than that."

"Aye, aye, aye," said Johansson, shaking his head in warning. "Watch yourself carefully now, Jarnie. Don't complicate things. Never, never complicate things."

"I get the idea this isn't about sex at all," said Jarnebring.

"What is it about then?" asked Johansson.

"Money," said Jarnebring. "What do you think about money?"

"Money is good," Johansson agreed. "Intoxication and ordinary insanity are best, then comes sex, and then comes money. Money is not bad at all," said Johansson, who for some reason raised his wineglass as he smiled and nodded.

"Although my new colleague thinks that it could be more about power. Well, not political power but power over people that you know and mostly for power's own sake. It's a woman of course."

"Imagine that," said Johansson delightedly, for this had just been his own thought.

"Yes indeed," said Jarnebring. "Although when I was on my way here I got the idea that maybe she's right. This victim of ours is actually a really strange little creep. Not anyone I'd want to share an office with."

"Is she good-looking?" asked Johansson. "Your new colleague, is she good-looking?"

"Yes," said Jarnebring. "You might say so, a little too thin for my taste maybe . . . but sure."

Of course she is, he thought. Anna Holt was a very enticing woman, and the fact that she wasn't his type wasn't exactly her fault.

"Thin women are an abomination," Johansson decided, although he had never met Jarnebring's new colleague. "What do you think about a little dessert, by the way?"

For dessert they had almond torte. Johansson had some kind of sweet Italian dessert wine, but because Jarnebring did not drink wine on principle and could not really have yet another beer, not with almond torte, he jumped the gun with an ample cognac. As the waiter set it down in front of him he decided that now it was high time to let the marital bomb explode. Johansson seemed to be in a splendid mood—he always was when he got to sit and talk about some old murder that he was now too fine to investigate—and personally Jarnebring felt both calm and collected despite the fact that this was a very serious story. A life-changing step, Jarnebring thought solemnly.

It turned out completely wrong. It was his own fault, and it lay in the fact that he got the idea he should warm Johansson up further, despite the fact that things were fine as they were.

"You seem damned chipper, by the way," said Jarnebring. "It's almost as if you've lost a few pounds. Have you started working out?" Oh well, thought Jarnebring, the things you won't do for your best friend.

"Working out," said Johansson with surprise.

"Your fist," Jarnebring clarified, nodding toward Johansson's left hand, which was adorned with an ample adhesive bandage around his ring finger. "I thought you'd caught your little fist in a barbell."

"Oh that," said Johansson self-assuredly, holding up a hand that in size could almost compare with his best friend's. "Depends on what you mean by little . . . no . . . not an exercise injury exactly . . . It's more like it concerns my heart, I guess."

"You haven't been sick, have you?" said Jarnebring, exerting himself not to show how worried he had suddenly become. "I've told you, you have to think about getting some exercise." Advice which of course you've completely ignored, he thought.

"Never felt better," said Johansson, pulling away the adhesive bandage and showing the broad gold ring on his left ring finger. "I just didn't want to spoil your appetite, so I decided to wait until we were through eating."

"Huh," Jarnebring exclaimed. "Are you engaged?" What the hell is happening? he thought in confusion. Is this *Candid Camera* or what?

"No," said Johansson, shaking his head contentedly. "I got married." Engagements are for the cowardly and irresolute, he thought, but naturally he would never dream of saying that to his best friend, who more or less made a habit of getting engaged to avoid taking the great, life-changing step.

"You got married?" Jarnebring repeated with equal emphasis on every word and syllable in that short question.

"Yes," said Johansson, with manly firmness.

"Is it anyone I know, a colleague?" This is not true. Say that it's not true, thought Jarnebring.

"No," said Johansson. "No one you know, not a colleague."

"When did you meet her then?" asked Jarnebring incredulously.

"Fourteen days ago," said Johansson with delight.

"Fourteen days ago? Are you pulling my leg?" In his haste Jarnebring was about to treat his best friend to the same look that he normally reserved for the worst sort of hooligans.

"I talked to her briefly a few years ago; it was in the line of duty," Johansson said evasively. "But then I hadn't seen hide nor hair of her until I ran into her down at the grocery store fourteen days ago and then we got married a week ago. I actually called to tell you but you weren't home."

This is not true, thought Jarnebring. What the hell do I do now?

Jarnebring did not get home until the wee hours and he wasn't sober, not drunk either for that matter, but rather considerably sloshed.

"You seem to have had a good time," his impending wife giggled.

"Yeah," said Jarnebring, sounding even more absent than he felt.

"Did you tell him about us?" asked his impending wife curiously.

What the hell do I say now? thought Jarnebring, and suddenly, when he needed it the most, his poor head was completely empty.

"No," said Jarnebring. It's as though there never was the right time for it, he thought.

14

Monday, December 11, 1989

This time Bäckström took no chances. He personally called Tischler's secretary and set up a time for a meeting on Monday morning, and as he was sitting in the taxi on his way there with his tape recorder as his only companion, he congratulated himself on getting rid of that grinning idiot Alm.

The interview was held at Tischler's lavish office, and their conversation flowed easily and was unforced as happens so often when two men of the world meet to converse with one another, allowing for the fact that in this case they had gathered their experiences from somewhat varying spheres of human activity, Bäckström philosophized.

Tischler proved to be a pleasant fellow. He was sitting in shirtsleeves with his collar unbuttoned, tie loosened, and dressed in wide red suspenders where he evidently placed his flat thumbs while he pondered. A rugged, slightly balding man in his prime, certainly accustomed to being in the thick of things and not completely unlike himself, thought Bäckström. Not reminiscent in the slightest of that pansy he had met at the TV station the week before.

In contrast to Welander, Tischler was also both frank and open, confirming in all essentials what Bäckström had already understood from the very start, and he was not one to toss out a lot of rubbish in Latin either. When Bäckström brought up the subject of Eriksson's sexual orientation, Tischler winked at Bäckström, leaned back in his leathered desk chair, and almost compassionately shook his head.

"I can imagine what Sten said. It can't be easy to work at a place where the hags wear both trousers and skirts."

Then he quoted an Icelandic saga.

"I'm sure you know what the Icelandic Vikings said: One thing I know that never dies . . . the reputation of a dead man. That's the unvarnished truth," Tischler declared.

Personally he could very well imagine that Eriksson lived a secret life in his own little closet, but because he did not understand the sort of people who had such inclinations he didn't waste his time wondering about their motives or how they arranged their business.

"I've been to his home a few times and seen how he lives." Tischler smiled wryly and wiggled the palm of his hand a little. "Not really my taste, if you know what I mean."

"You don't have the name of anyone he may have spent time with?" Bäckström asked carefully.

Tischler shook his head.

"No," he said. "Kjell was a secretive type, so if he was doing any butt-surfing at home in the bedroom then I'm sure he was careful to pull down the shades first."

An amusing fellow, and rich as a troll, Bäckström thought with delight.

Then Bäckström naturally brought up Eriksson's finances, and there was nothing strange there at all according to Tischler. It was clear that he was the one who had helped Eriksson. No big deal about that either, and he had done it despite the fact that Eriksson had really been Welander's friend to begin with. If he could help someone with such simple means then he made no distinction between friends and those who were only friends of a friend.

"You shouldn't exaggerate the level of difficulty," said Tischler. "Up to this point in the eighties the companies on the Swedish stock exchange have increased in value by almost a thousand percent. That's what you would have earned if you had closed your eyes and thrown a dart at the stock exchange list. Personally I usually squint a little with one eye," said Tischler, "so those companies that we've worked with here at the firm have doubtless improved on that."

Why am I not a buddy of this man? thought Bäckström with genuine regret.

"Kjell was a rather frugal type, if I may say so," Tischler continued, grinning. "When he came to me about ten years ago he had scraped together ten, twenty thousand that he had in a savings account—watch out for savings accounts, by the way, because they're pure robbery. I loaned him some money and bought a few shares for him. Of course he had to leave those as security—and then I guess it has just rolled on from there. We have bank confidentiality at this place, but if you just pick up the papers from the prosecutor, I'll tell my coworkers to give you a proper analysis of his finances."

It would be better if you loaned me some money and gave me some good tips, thought Bäckström, and for a brief moment he even thought about asking Tischler flat out.

"That probably won't be necessary," he said instead. "It's not that he's suspected of anything."

"It's never a mistake to have a little money," Tischler grunted, looking as though he knew what he was talking about. "You and I both know what women cost . . . and without knowing about it in detail—I haven't seen this with my own eyes—then I imagine that if one were to prefer little boys in sailor suits that's not free either."

Fucking nice guy, thought Bäckström, who almost forgot to ask the customary routine question about Tischler's alibi until Tischler himself reminded him.

"Well then," said Tischler, looking at his watch. "It was nice to meet you, even if the reason is sad to say the least. . . . So if you don't have anything else, I have a few things to take care of. There's a lot of money out there that I have to place in the right hands," said Tischler, winking.

A purely formal matter, and Bäckström truly hoped that Tischler would not take offense. What kind of alibi did he have for Thursday evening the thirtieth of November?

"That was when those damned hooligans tried to tear down the city," Tischler declared. "I read about it in the newspapers the following day. I was in London the whole day. I flew home the morning after. If you speak with my secretary she can give you the details."

At the meeting of the investigation group that afternoon Holt reported what she, Jarnebring, and the meritorious Gunsan had produced about the victim Kjell Eriksson's background. For the sake of simplicity Holt had compiled half a page with the most important information, which she handed out to all those present.

Eriksson, Kjell Göran, born 1944, single, no children, father unknown, grew up in Hjorthagen in Stockholm with a single mother who died in the mid-1980s, no siblings. The mother worked as a cleaning lady, building manager, etc.

E. completed secondary school in 1961 and then began university-track high school studies, which however were interrupted in 1962. Completed military service '62–'63, so-called fatigue duty with the air force with placement in the Barkaby wing. Started working as a substitute mail carrier in 1964 and was hired permanently a few years later as a mail carrier.

Began adult studies at night school in 1965, finished his degree in 1967. Politically involved in the Swedish Communist Party (SCP) and the so-called NLF movement at the end of the 1960s. Took part in the occupation of the student union building in 1968.

Studied sociology, pedagogy, and criminology at the university. Received his degree in 1974. While studying at the university he met Sten Welander, who was his instructor in sociology. Through Sten Welander he also got to know Welander's schoolmate Theo Tischler in the early 1970s.

In the fall of 1975 he applied to and was given work as an assistant statistician at the Central Bureau of Statistics where he worked with labor market statistics. In 1984 he was given the position of assistant director at the Bureau.

At the end of the 1970s, exact time not known, Eriksson left the SCP to join the Social Democratic Party, and had been a member since the spring of 1979. Eriksson had been active in the union at his place of employment since he started there and held several union positions, including safety representative on TCO's behalf.

Apart from the above-mentioned Welander and Tischler, Eriksson seems to have had few friends and for the most part lacked private social interaction. According to what several of his coworkers have reported, he was not especially popular at his place of employment. He is described as antisocial, conceited, unreliable, gossipy, etc.

Eriksson had very good private finances considering his income. A preliminary calculation indicates that during the last ten years he built up a fortune of about four million kronor. The apartment on Rådmansgatan where he lived is a condominium that he purchased about ten years ago and that currently is estimated to have a market value of over a million kronor. Other assets consist primarily of stocks plus bank balances of about 300,000 kronor.

All of these assets seem to originate from extensive stock market investment activity, in which according to reports he received advice and help from his acquaintance Theo Tischler. These transactions he has also conducted at the latter's brokerage firm.

"Well then," said Holt, looking around. "This is in brief what Gun, Bo, and I have been able to produce about Eriksson's background. If anyone has any questions I will gladly answer them."

No one had any particular questions, so Bäckström took over and started developing his homo lead, which had been confirmed for him by "two sources independent of each other," namely Welander and Tischler, who were also the only acquaintances worth the name that Holt and her coworkers had managed to produce.

"To me this is fucking simple," said Bäckström. "The guy was a closet fairy—there's not the least doubt on that point. What we have to do is to find the little boyfriend he was drinking with that evening, before they started fighting with each other and his bum boy stuck the knife in him. Am I right or am I right?"

At first no one said anything. Not even Jarnebring, who only sighed and looked at the ceiling.

Finally Holt spoke up. Clearly no one else intended to do so, she thought.

"I don't think it's that simple," she said.

"It doesn't seem to have been that fucking simple," snorted Bäckström. "I'm still waiting for you all to give me a name."

"Do both of his buddies confirm that he had that disposition?" asked Jarnebring, who naturally enough had not read the as yet unwritten interview reports.

"Of course they do," said Bäckström with a certain vehemence. "In the way those sort of people talk. Welander spoke in tongues, but between the lines at least I understood what he was muttering about." For some reason Bäckström glowered sourly at Alm at the far end of the table.

"And what does Tischler say?" asked Jarnebring.

"He talks almost like a normal person," said Bäckström. "Sure enough he thought Eriksson was a queer, one of those secretive types that mostly stay in the closet."

"And they themselves have alibis?" asked Jarnebring for some reason.

"Of course, and they're chiseled in stone, so to me this whole thing is fucking simple and has been all along." Bäckström glowered at Holt and Jarnebring in succession, and thus they were no further along on this particular Monday in the middle of December.

Soon it would be eleven whole days since the death and still no perpetrator. This is going down the toilet, Jarnebring thought gloomily. As far as he was concerned Bäckström could stick his so-called homo lead up his own fat ass. But you didn't say that sort of thing. Not even to someone like Bäckström, not when there were other colleagues present. It was the sort of thing you said face-to-face to the person it concerned. At least Jarnebring would do it that way.

15

Tuesday, December 12, 1989

On Tuesday Jarnebring and Holt concluded their careful search of Eriksson's residence. The results were thin, bordering on nil. In the desk in the office a telephone book had been found, including even the number for his old mother, although she had been dead for several years. Also Welander's and Tischler's numbers obviously, but otherwise basically nothing.

In the desk and bookcase there were also twenty or so pages and scraps of paper with notes written in Eriksson's finicky handwriting. Mostly he seemed to have devoted time to calculating how many kronor and öre he had earned on one stock trade or another. Why he did this was unclear. The same information would arrive with the sales note from his broker the next day.

Seems to have been extremely anxious, thought Holt. A very lonely person struggling all the time to have absolute control of those sorts of things over which control was possible, she thought.

In the desk they also found a photo album bound in a pair of simple green covers of stiff cardboard. It contained a total of twenty-one photos. Eriksson's mother when she was young, middle-aged, and old. A picture of the house in Hjorthagen where they had lived when he was growing up. Mostly pictures of Eriksson himself. As a little baby who didn't smile, from first grade in school, in the back row and at the far end, without a smile and with a shy look toward the camera, surrounded by happy classmates. Group photos and a portrait when he got his high school diploma, the same from his college graduation, in which he actually smiled for the first time. A pasted-in official letter from the Central Bureau of Statistics, which stated that Eriksson, Kjell Göran, had been given a position as temporary assistant director at the agency. And basically that was all.

Poor thing, Holt thought gloomily. He doesn't seem to have had it easy.

But there was one photo that stood out from the others. It was not even pasted into the album, just loosely inserted between two pages in the middle. It was a summer picture of three young men about twenty-five years of age and a little girl who seemed to be ten years old at the most. Green grass and glistening water in the background. The three men were in short-sleeved shirts, shorts, and sandals. Two of them smiled openly at the camera, one seemed more reserved. The pluckiest was the little girl. She had her hair put up in Pippi Longstocking braids and stuck her tongue out happily at the photographer.

Swedish archipelago, late sixties or early seventies, thought Holt. Welander, Tischler, and Eriksson, she thought, and was reasonably confident. The little girl held Tischler by the hand, and despite the differences in size and age there was a striking resemblance between them. Something in the posture itself, the self-assured expression in body and face.

That could hardly be his child, thought Holt. Probably a sibling, or half sibling perhaps, and in the back of her head she had a vague memory that Gunsan had said something about Theo Tischler having inherited not only the brokerage firm but also his view of marriage from his long-dead father.

On the back side someone had written in a childish handwriting, "The gang of four. Sten, Theo, Kjell, and me."

"You know what we're going to do now?" said Jarnebring as he sealed the door to Eriksson's apartment.

"I'm listening," said Holt, looking almost as plucky as the little girl in the photo.

"We're going to go back to the office, unplug the phone, lock the door, and sit down in peace and quiet and try to work out what the hell this is really about."

"Sounds good," said Holt. "Only I get to make coffee first."

First they discussed Bäckström's so-called homo lead in detail. On that they had somewhat different ideas. Holt simply didn't believe in it. She was convinced that the murder was not about sex at all, regardless of what orientation anyone wanted to ascribe to their victim. Jarnebring was in agreement with her "in principle," while at the same time he had a hard time letting go of the idea that Eriksson could have been completely uninterested in sexual matters.

"Personally I have a very hard time understanding that," said Jarnebring. Despite what that Polish woman said, he thought.

"I can very well imagine that," said Holt cheerfully. "But if you disregard yourself—"

"Wait now," said Jarnebring. "Don't interrupt me. I'll buy what you're saying about Eriksson being a disagreeable bastard who was snooping around all the time to try to get power over people—you only have to listen to his coworkers—but the one thing doesn't rule out the other, does it?"

"I don't really know," said Holt. "I guess I'm not particularly good at guys."

"You'll just have to work on that," said Jarnebring unperturbed. "Where was I . . . yes . . . there's something about the act itself that I have a hard time letting go of. It's completely obvious that the person who stabbed Eriksson was someone he both knew and trusted. Or in any case was not the least bit afraid of. But that can hardly have been Welander, Tischler, or his cleaning woman. Who was it then? We haven't found anyone."

"Some neighbor that we've missed," Holt suggested. "Some casual acquaintance that we've also missed."

"It doesn't appear to be so," said Jarnebring, shaking himself uncomfortably. "Eriksson seems to have been one highly suspicious bastard, not to mention anxious as hell. Here he sits on the couch drinking a highball in peace and quiet while our perpetrator calmly and quietly stabs him from behind, and then he crawls around on the floor and raises holy hell—if we're to believe his neighbor—before he folds up and dies. Who the hell would he let get that close to him?"

"Correct me if I'm wrong," said Holt, "but aren't so-called gay murders usually dreadful stories? With a lot of aggravated assault, lots of emotions and hatred?"

"Yes," said Jarnebring. "As a rule it's like that but far from always. They're just like all other stoned, jealous, crazy people. But it wasn't like that here."

"What do you mean?" asked Holt.

"The whole thing seems both cowardly and random. Just a stab from behind . . . normally he wouldn't even have died from it. And then the perpetrator darts into the bathroom and vomits, making a nice little mess. Doesn't seem to be one of our motorcycle-riding friends exactly."

"No," said Holt, who had been thinking along the same lines.

"So what have we got?" Jarnebring continued.

A lonely person, a scared and suspicious person, a dissatisfied person, a person who felt unjustly treated by life, a person who should have had considerably more if there had been any justice in this world and if he himself had been the one to decide.

"A snoop," said Jarnebring.

"Someone who wanted to acquire power through snooping, to get emotional power over people around him by ferreting out their weaknesses," Holt continued.

"Who exploited the friendship and feelings of others, who even profited from them if he got the chance," Jarnebring added.

"It's certainly not out of the question that he extorted money from them if he felt sufficiently confident," Holt concluded.

"Snoop, profiteer, extortionist," Jarnebring summarized. Not the type I'd want to share an office with, he thought.

"I have a buddy," said Jarnebring, sounding pretty much as if he was thinking out loud. "He's also my best friend. We shared a front seat here on the squad a helluva lot of years ago . . . and a lot of other things for that matter, but we can leave that aside."

"I can almost guess who it is," said Holt. "What is it our colleagues at the riot squad call him? The Butcher from Ådalen? Police superintendent at the National Police Board, Lars Martin Johansson."

"People here in the building talk too much shit," said Jarnebring. "Do you know what's remarkable about Lars Martin?"

"No," said Holt. "Tell me. I'm listening."

"He's downright fiendish at figuring out how things stand," said Jarnebring. "Sometimes it's uncanny."

"What are we waiting for?" said Holt, nodding toward the telephone. "Call him and get him over here." It's never too late to meet God, she thought, and if only half of what she had heard about Johansson were true then it was high time.

"I don't think so," said Jarnebring. Even if it would be fun to see Bäckström's face, he thought. "One thing that Lars Martin always used to nag about where murder investigations are concerned is that you should forget about the motive."

"You shouldn't worry about the motive?" Holt was surprised.

"Nope," said Jarnebring. "According to Lars Martin, the motive is either something obvious or else some out-and-out craziness that you would never figure out in a million years no matter how much you thought about it, and uninteresting in any event. Johansson used to say that it's like the cherry on the cake, and the court can put it there if it's really necessary once the cake is baked and ready. It doesn't help us police officers. Other than in thrillers and TV series and that kind of shit."

"Sounds maybe a little too simple," Holt objected, being seriously fond of at least two police series that were showing on TV.

"Lars Martin is a very simple man," said Jarnebring, smiling contentedly. "That is what's so strange about the whole thing. I mean with the head that he has. Lars Martin is almost always right," said Jarnebring. "We've talked through dozens of these kinds of cases over the years and I cannot think of a single time when he was wrong."

"But," said Holt noncommittally.

"But this time it seems to me that he actually is wrong," said Jarnebring.

"What do you mean?" said Holt.

"What I mean is that just this once it suddenly seems to me that if we can only figure out why Eriksson was murdered then we're also going to find who did it," said Jarnebring. "Simple and obvious and in the twinkling of an eye we just go pick him up."

"You think so," said Holt.

"Yes," Jarnebring repeated. "And do you know what's even more annoying?"

"No," said Holt. "Tell me."

"I'm convinced we've already stumbled across our perpetrator, but we've simply missed him," said Jarnebring.

"But there isn't anyone," said Holt with surprise. "Not Welander, Tischler, or Eriksson's cleaning woman or—"

"Of course's there's someone," Jarnebring interrupted. "It's just that we haven't seen him. It's no more difficult than that."

16

Wednesday, December 13, 1989

Up at the homicide squad they celebrated Lucia Day according to ancient custom, and during the rest of the day, also according to custom, not much was accomplished. With the exception of Gunsan, who was diligently active at her computer, most of the staff seemed to have sought isolation in their offices.

The flame of diligence was not shining with any marked intensity among the detective squad either. True, Jarnebring had seemed chipper enough when he arrived in the morning, but then he excused himself with a "I have to help the guys with something" and that's the way it was.

Which left a somewhat listless Holt, who even before lunch was starting to feel the effects of the Lucia celebration at Nicke's day care, and mostly for lack of anything better was going through the box with Eriksson's telephone book, photo album, and other private notes.

If the perpetrator is here he's hidden himself well, Holt thought gloomily, for she had a hard time letting go of what Jarnebring had said when they had been talking the day before. It would be simplest to go through the victim's notes with someone who knew him, thought Holt, and because it was Bäckström who was the boss and careful about police etiquette, he was the one she would have to ask for permission.

Bäckström sounded surly and distant. But sure, if she wanted to waste her life on that kind of shit then he wasn't going to stop her. True, he had personally investigated the whole matter, but if that had escaped her . . . then sure.

"Don't forget to look extra carefully from *A* to *Y*," said Bäckström. "On the other hand, you can forget about *Z*."

"*A* to *Y*," said Holt.

"Yes, in his telephone book. From anal acrobat on up. Look extra carefully under *B, F, G, H, P, Q, R, S* and—"

"I hear what you're saying," Holt interrupted guardedly.

"As in butt-surfer, fairy, gay boy, homophile, pederast, queen, rump gnome, sausage prince . . . and under *V* . . . *V* as in Vaseline. Call me right away if you find anything," said Bäckström, who suddenly sounded a good deal more energetic.

"Thanks for the tip," said Holt, hanging up the receiver. That man is not all there, she thought.

She could forget Welander. She spoke with the secretary at his office, and according to her he was away in connection with a feature story he was working on. He would be home right before Christmas. Thanks for that, thought Holt.

She had better luck with Tischler. When she called the number she found in Eriksson's telephone book, he was the one who answered. Holt explained her business and asked him to suggest a time because he was certainly a very busy man.

"Now," said Tischler. "Just give me five minutes so I have time to powder my nose. Do you have the address?"

Five minutes later she had arranged a lift with one of the detective squad's cars, and in another ten minutes she was walking into his office.

"Please have a seat," said Tischler, pointing to the antique armchair on the other side of his large desk. "Are you Inspector Anna Holt?"

"Yes," said Holt. Strange man, she thought. Small, balding, at the same time rugged, his body almost square, with completely attentive eyes that looked at her with undisguised appreciation and without seeming to be the least bit embarrassed on that account.

"I'm Theo," he said. "May I call you Anna?"

"That's fine," said Holt, smiling faintly. Watch yourself, Anna, she thought.

"What can I do for you, Anna?" said Tischler. "You can ask whatever you want, and keep in mind that I am immeasurably wealthy, extraordinarily talented, extremely entertaining, and when need be even quite charming."

"I want you to help me go through these papers," said Holt, taking out the file box with Eriksson's telephone book, photo album, and private notes and setting them on his desk.

"That sounds so dreary," said Tischler, sighing. "But we certainly have to start somewhere, and if it's Kjell's private notes that shouldn't take all of our life together.

"I forgot to ask if you'd like anything to drink," said Tischler as he glanced quickly through Eriksson's handwritten notations. "Champagne, wine . . . perhaps a glass of fresh springwater."

"Later," said Holt. He's rather dashing in his particular way, she thought.

"Ah," said Tischler. "A ray of hope scatters the darkness around my unhappy, solitary soul, and as far as these notes are concerned," he continued soberly, "it looks like Kjell's own compulsive calculations of the most recent deals he's made with us here at the firm. He has shown me hundreds of similar calculations over the years, and if you go through all those binders in his little office I'm sure you will find corresponding statements from us. And if you just give me a note from the prosecutor I'll let our computers do it for you at once."

"This is good enough," said Holt. "You confirm what I already thought."

"The harmony of souls," said Tischler, sighing romantically. "The harmony of souls."

The telephone book didn't take much longer than that.

"This number in Hjorthagen was his old mother's," Theo explained. "Although she's been dead for many years."

"Did you ever meet her?" asked Holt.

"One time I actually ran into her and Kjell in town," said Tischler. "He was on his way with her to the clinic at Odenplan. The old lady must have been over eighty. She was certainly no spring chicken when she had little Kjell."

"Did you get any impression of her?" Holt asked.

"Frightful hag," said Tischler, smiling happily. "I talked with her for only five minutes but that was enough for me."

"What do you mean by that?" said Holt.

"Let me put it like this," said Tischler. "She held her little Kjell in a veritable iron grip. If there's anyone who puts a face on the dominating mother it would have been Kjell's dear mama. You didn't need to be a psychologist to understand that. Strong enough that he would still have had her telephone number even though it's been many years since she died."

"Do you have any idea who Eriksson's father was?" Holt asked.

"No," said Tischler. "If I were to venture a guess, I'd think after the coupling the old lady immediately murdered him and then devoured him."

"Well then," said Holt.

When Tischler saw the photo of the gang of four, he looked like a happy little schoolboy. Extremely charming, thought Holt.

"This is me, Sten, and Kjell. The little lady in braids is my delightful cousin—this must have been during her Pippi Longstocking period—and the photo was taken at the family's so-called summer paradise out on Värmdö—an establishment completely in August Strindberg's taste as far as family relationships are concerned."

"Do you remember when this was taken?" Holt asked. He actually is rather entertaining, she thought.

"End of the sixties, early seventies. I don't really recall. If you want we can drive out and take a look at the guest book. If we find Kjell then the mystery is solved. He was there only one time as far as I remember. We sailed out to the island on Papa's boat. It was in Saltsjöbaden. Sten, Kjell, and I and a frightening quantity of jars and bottles."

"So little Pippi wasn't along," said Holt.

"What a sight that would have been," said Tischler. "No, not really, she was on land with her mom and dad and all the other relatives from nine to ninety who were always hanging around out there."

"The gang of four?" asked Holt.

"Ah," said Tischler. "You intend to convict me of youthful radicalism, Inspector. Chinese opposition politicians, conspiracies against the Great Helmsman Mao, and so on."

"Why would I do that?" said Holt, letting her gaze sweep across the furniture in the room in which they were sitting.

"But here I'm afraid it was much simpler," Tischler interrupted. "My dear cousin was at that time insanely fond of mysteries and adventure novels, she was rather precocious for her age, and the gang of four, I think, alludes to that novel by Conan Doyle . . . *The Sign of the Four,* I believe it's called. The gang of four was a secret society that the master detective Sherlock Holmes was tracking down."

"Who took the picture?" Holt asked, mostly to change the subject.

"It was taken with a self-timer, and my dear cousin got the camera from her kind uncle Theo, as she called me. She ran around for days taking the most unflattering pictures. At times there seems to have been sheer panic out there. I remember that her mother—my aunt, that is— scolded me. Personally I kept away as much as possible. It was hardly suitable for a young radical to spend his summer in the country villas of the bourgeoisie. But certainly sometimes I was weak, much too weak."

"Maybe it's not really so bad," said Holt, smiling, "but I know what you're talking about." Maybe a little tedious, she thought.

"I know what you mean too and I confess unreservedly," said Tischler. "All reasonable young people were radical at that time. We were socialists and communists with all the imaginable acronyms. We were always marching to the American embassy, and then there was quite a lot of balling too. Excellent for the health, both of them, and driving your old father up the wall was a pure bonus."

"I saw in our papers that Kjell Eriksson was politically committed," said Holt. Balling, she thought. When had she last heard someone use that word? A hundred years ago?

"Oh well," said Tischler, smiling. "We actually called him the wet thumb, so maybe it wasn't just commitment."

"What do you mean?" asked Holt.

"There was a certain amount of opportunism, perhaps," said Tischler thoughtlessly, "and perhaps certain problems with timing. I remember when he became a social democrat in the spring of 1979 and went on and on for a whole evening about how as soon as the election was over his union fortune would finally be made and now the bourgeoisie would be gone. Whereupon they won with a tie-breaking vote in parliament and stayed until 1982."

"You were all young socialists at that time," said Holt.

"I'm still a socialist," said Tischler, sounding almost offended. "I've always had my heart to the left . . . and my wallet to the right," he added with a broad smile. "As I said, we were all radicals back then, socialists or communists. For the same reason that today all reasonable people have left that behind them as soon as they realized where it was going."

"But you're not an opportunist," said Holt.

"That is patently absurd," said Tischler solemnly. "Hell, I was born with a whole set of silverware in my mouth. I've never needed to be an opportunist."

"But Kjell Eriksson needed to be," said Holt.

"Yes," said Tischler, suddenly sounding serious. "And the way things were for him when he was growing up I have a very hard time holding that against him. People try to adapt themselves to the time they live in, and when times change their lives change too. There are very few of us for whom things are so ordained that we, like a strong current, can ride our own waves through the sea."

"Nicely put," said Holt.

"I know," said Tischler, grinning. "I have to confess I swiped it from a book."

"What do you say about having dinner in Paris, this evening?" said Tischler, keeping hold of Holt's hand in his when she was about to leave.

"Unfortunately," said Holt, smiling, "I'm afraid that won't work. In another time and another life maybe," she said.

"I live in hope," said Tischler, looking at her with his very attentive eyes.

17

Thursday, December 14, 1989

At the investigation team's last meeting before the weekend the opposing factions came into the open.

Out-and-out fucking mutiny, thought Bäckström as he marched out of the room, his face bright red, after they were through quarreling.

Bäckström started pushing his homo lead again, for the umpteenth time, and now even the three younger colleagues who were on loan from the uniformed police were starting to give audible expression to their doubts.

"You don't think there's a risk we'll get locked in?" the first one of them began cautiously. She was the only woman of the three. "In school we learned that it was crucial to have a broad and open attitude to this sort of thing."

Stick it up yours, you little sow, thought Bäckström, but he wasn't going to say that when there were witnesses present, so it had to be something else instead.

"I'm listening," Bäckström said smoothly. "What did you mean to propose instead?"

"I don't know," she continued hesitantly, "but what is there that actually indicates that Eriksson was homosexual?"

"Apart from what the forensic doctor and his two best friends for twenty years say," sneered Bäckström, "is there anything in particular you're missing? Sailor costume, Vaseline jar, mesh stockings way back in the dresser drawer? Some good porno tapes with well-oiled butt princes?" Or maybe you want Uncle Evert to grease your little mouse for you, he thought.

"Hang on," said Jarnebring, giving Bäckström the same look he always did when he had decided that enough was enough. "Me and my colleague Holt here," said Jarnebring, nodding toward her, "have turned Eriksson's apartment inside out. If anyone thinks we've missed something, then he or she is welcome to try themselves. We haven't found a damn thing that clearly indicates that Eriksson had any sexual orientation whatsoever. We've even checked his sheets—because colleague Wiijnbladh apparently forgot that small detail—and just like his cleaning woman for the past two years—because we've also talked with her—we haven't found the slightest little trace of sperm whatsoever. Much less a strand of hair from anyone other than Eriksson himself, or anything that indicates that any sexual activity whatsoever has occurred in that bed or in that bedroom or in that apartment.

"Personally," Jarnebring continued, raising his right hand slightly when he saw that Bäckström was thinking about saying something, "I would have felt considerably more comfortable if we'd found something of the sort you usually find. Not to mention all those accessories you keep carrying on about all the time."

"Correct me if I'm wrong," said Bäckström, "but wasn't it you who had the idea that someone had cleaned up and removed some stuff from Eriksson's apartment? A whole suitcase if I remember rightly?"

"I don't know," said Jarnebring. "That may be so, doesn't need to be, but I think it was papers in any case. Not his old sheets or his corset, if he had something like that." Jarnebring smiled wryly and exchanged a glance with Holt.

"I hear what you're saying," said Bäckström defensively, for there was something in the eyes of the gorilla-like psychopath that made him feel extremely ill at ease. "If you hear me, all I'm saying is what his two closest acquaintances have said—and what the forensic doctor said."

"When I read the interviews," said Jarnebring, "I wonder what *was* actually said. Welander possibly makes an insinuation, and that applies to Tischler too, even if otherwise he appears to be a motor mouth, but neither of them knows anything. One of them possibly thinks something; the other may possibly imagine something. After twenty years' acquaintance. Talk about buddies."

"The forensic doctor then," said Bäckström. I didn't know you could even read, thought Bäckström sourly, and who the hell gave that half-ape my interviews anyway?

"Don't interrupt me," said Jarnebring. "I'm getting to her. First let's finish with our witnesses, and the way I see it there are three possibilities. Either it's the way at least one of them suggests, in which case we've missed something. Or else it's just that they've imagined things. Or else they've tried to get us to believe that their friend Eriksson was . . . well, homosexual. And if that's the way it is, then it suddenly becomes damned interesting, considering what you've said to them."

Never underestimate a colleague, even if he looks like something that lives in a cave and woke up on the wrong side of the bed, Holt thought, smiling almost sweetly at Jarnebring.

"My colleague Jarnebring and I are in complete agreement," said Holt. "We've both read the interviews, and as you know I've talked with Tischler myself. He was not exactly taciturn, but it was mostly noise and little substance." My colleague Jarnebring, thought Holt, who a moment earlier and in a most unequal manner felt that she had received a major distinction.

"Glad to hear you're in agreement," said Bäckström. "To return to reality for a moment, what do you say about the forensic doctor's report? Has he only been imagining things too?"

"I've actually talked to her," said Jarnebring. "I happened to be in the neighborhood on another errand and I ran into her at the forensic lab. Briefly, she hadn't the faintest idea of what either Esprit or Wiijnbladh are running around fabricating. Esprit hasn't had anything to do with Eriksson whatsoever. And he's on sick leave. Because she is Esprit's boss, she needs to talk to him as soon as he locates his cane and finds his way back to work."

"You've talked with the forensic doctor?" said Bäckström. This is complete mutiny, he thought.

"Yes," said Jarnebring, looking at him. "Do you have a problem with that?"

"No," said Bäckström quickly. The guy is lethal, he thought. How could someone like that run around loose? And what the hell was going on when he became a cop?

"Good," said Jarnebring. "Where was I now . . . yes," he continued. "She had also spoken with Wiijnbladh, and he simply asked her if there was anything to indicate that Eriksson might have been homosexual in the sense that it actually showed up in the forensic inspection and the autopsy. Do you know what she said?"

"No," said Bäckström. Where the hell was Wiijnbladh anyway? Typical of the little rat to sneak away in a situation like this, he thought.

"No," said Jarnebring. "She said no. And if you want I can trot over to Wiijnbladh and take it up directly with him."

"That won't be necessary," said Bäckström. Even if it would be funny because he would probably shit his pants, he thought.

"That's good," said Jarnebring. "Glad to know we're in agreement."

"I'm listening," said Bäckström. "Give me a name."

"He's here," said Jarnebring, tapping his finger on the investigation files binder on the table in front of him. "You can bet your sweet ass he's here, but we've missed him because we've been looking for the wrong things."

The guy is completely insane, thought Bäckström.

18

Friday, December 15, 1989

The reason that Wiijnbladh had been absent from the meeting the day before was that he was saddled with a poisoning. A medical student who lived at home with his elderly father had been having problems with his studies. He had missed a number of exams, fallen seriously behind, and after a period of brooding decided to solve his academic problems by lacing his dad's breakfast yogurt with an ample dose of thallium. His success far exceeded the progress of his studies. Considered as a motive, this was an excellent illustration of Lars Martin Johansson's thesis of the cherry on the cake.

Now the former future doctor was sitting in the jail at Kronoberg. On Wiijnbladh's workbench at the tech squad was the bottle of thallium that the perpetrator had swiped from the chemistry department at the Karolinska Institute, and there was enough poison remaining to depopulate half the police headquarters on Kungsholmen. In Wiijnbladh's pleasure-filled fantasies, this enchanted bottle with its death-bringing genie was a gift from above that probably, within the not too distant future, would solve his problems as well.

Wiijnbladh's difficulties were not related to his studies, for he had never really devoted himself to any such things. Apart from six years of elementary school, less than a year at the old police academy, and a few weeklong courses for crime technicians, Wiijnbladh had studiously avoided all theoretical extravagances, and just like the majority of his colleagues on the squad he was firmly convinced that the only abilities worth the name were those he had acquired by practice.

"We have to distinguish between theory and practice the same way we distinguish between imagination and reality," as his legendary boss Commissioner Blenke had so eloquently summarized the matter when, in connection with a review of the squad's operations, he explained to the inspectors from the National Police Board why the entire library appropriation was spent on fingerprint powder.

Wiijnbladh's problem was different, and relatively simple in the sense that it made up approximately 99 percent of all his problems.

It was bad enough that Wiijnbladh's wife cheated on him quite openly, which was contrary to the basic idea. Worst of all, however, was that she preferred to do it with other police officers, and because this had been going on for a number of years there was not a division nowadays within the Stockholm Police Department that didn't contain one or more coworkers who had put horns on their colleague Wiijnbladh.

Like his spiritual brother, the former medical student, after lengthy speculations Wiijnbladh had come to the conclusion that the only way to solve the problem was to eliminate his wife. Because Wiijnbladh deeply disliked both blunt trauma and knife attacks, was nauseated by their consequences, and obviously did not want to go to jail, he had decided to poison her. Murder by poison was a completely unknown practice at the tech squad where he worked, and the fact that the case of the medical student was solved was not due to dogged fieldwork by the squad's collaborators but rather to the perpetrator himself, who in complete confidence had told an even larger number of classmates about his little caper with his dad.

What could be more certain than using poison, thought Wiijnbladh, for it was common knowledge that lightning never strikes twice in the same place.

Wiijnbladh was now a rich man. He had had both motive and opportunity for a long time, but only one day ago he had secured the means required. So he was also a happy man and decided it would be best to wait for a long weekend or perhaps even until summer when all police officers worth the name were on vacation and only Bäckström and his constantly moonlighting fellow prisoners were left behind.

. . .

Chief Inspector Danielsson at the homicide squad did not sound equally happy when he called Jarnebring and asked if he wanted to have lunch with him out in town. Jarnebring had immediately figured out why he sounded like he did. But sure, lunch was still lunch. They had mashed potatoes and rutabaga with pickled pork and each had a light beer. Apart from the latter this was food for real policemen, and even before Danielsson stuck the fork into the large piece of meat on his plate he got to the point.

"You don't need to say anything, Bo," Danielsson grunted. "I talked with Gunsan this morning and she told me what happened at the meeting. I haven't managed to get hold of that fat little shit because he's hiding out as usual. Which is just as well, because otherwise I might have done something to him I would regret."

"Have you read the material?" asked Jarnebring.

"Some of it," Danielsson nodded. "Then Gunsan filled in the rest. If I understood it right both Welander and Tischler have alibis. It's completely ruled out that either of them were holding the knife?"

"Yes," said Jarnebring, shaking his head. "There isn't a chance. Welander's witnesses are too good for that, regardless of what you might think about their TV programs, and as far as Tischler is concerned Holt has checked with the airline and the personnel out at Arlanda."

"Could they have used an accomplice?" asked Danielsson.

"Don't think so," said Jarnebring. "That seems both unlikely and far-fetched."

"Why are you so in love with those two?" Danielsson wondered.

"Because I think they're both lying," said Jarnebring. "Even if they themselves are innocent of Eriksson's murder, and perhaps didn't even know that it would happen, I still get the idea that they know what went on."

"Why do you think they're lying then?" asked Danielsson. Perjury, conspiracy, protecting a criminal, he thought unhappily.

"Why in the name of common sense would two people like them keep associating year after year with a miserable character like Eriksson if it wasn't because he had some kind of hold over them?" Jarnebring countered. "Take Tischler, for example. As far as I'm concerned he can have all the money in the world. I still don't believe he helped Eriksson earn a few million just because he wanted to be nice to him. Without even having met Tischler, I really don't think he's the type."

"Eriksson blackmailed them?" Danielsson looked questioningly at Jarnebring.

"I think that at the very least he had some kind of hold over them," said Jarnebring.

"How do we open this up?" said Danielsson.

"Bring them in, lock them up, and pound the shit out of them," said Jarnebring, smiling like a wolf. While the prosecutor climbs the walls, he thought.

"That won't work," said Danielsson, "and you know that as well as I do. So what do we do instead?"

"Don't know," said Jarnebring. Because if I had any idea we wouldn't be sitting here, he thought.

"Let's think about it," said Danielsson. "We'll talk after the weekend."

19

Monday, December 18–Friday, December 22, 1989

For a Swedish police officer—which was the standard by which he should be measured—Detective Inspector Bo Jarnebring had been involved in a great many murder investigations. On a few occasions he had also happened to be present when a breakthrough occurred. That blessed moment when all the question marks straightened themselves out, when you went from total darkness to radiant insight, when the entire investigation force could bask in glory. All within the course of a few hours.

Even more often, and especially in recent years, he had been involved with just the opposite. The laborious, hopeless, drawn-out process by which you didn't move forward no matter how long you kept trudging; in which suggestions and tips, initiatives, drive, and ordinary, simple, routine work dried up and ran out, and everyone's combined efforts, all the good suggestions and sure tips as well as ordinary delusions, wild chances, pure shots in the dark, and completely excusable mistakes were transformed at last into mere paper, all of which ended up in the name of justice in the same binders on the shelf for unsolved crimes.

So too this week in December 1989 Jarnebring once again experienced how a murder investigation quietly went dormant and died, and his new colleague, Inspector Anna Holt, was involved in the same thing for the first time.

. . .

As early as Tuesday morning their boss at the detective squad called Danielsson and said he had to have his detectives back. That he completely understood his colleague Danielsson's problems, but he cared even more about the ones that were being heaped on his own desk in a growing mass. Danielsson didn't even try to protest. He just took a quick glance at his bookshelf and ascertained that there would surely be room to squeeze in one more binder.

On Wednesday evening the twentieth of December yet another murder occurred in a porn shop on Söder. The next day the tabloids had already made it the fifth in a series in which Eriksson appeared as victim number four. During the past year an unknown perpetrator had knifed three men, all of whom had in common that they worked in various stores that sold sex merchandise, showed porno films, and sometimes went the whole way and broke the law against procurement. This was bad enough in itself, especially as most of the details argued for it being the same perpetrator on all three occasions, but every thinking police officer also realized that the murder of Kjell Eriksson did not belong in that grouping because—simply put—there "was zero in common with the porn murders."

With one exception no one on the homicide squad even considered linking the lapsing Kjell Eriksson investigation with the porn murder investigation. The exception was Bäckström, who went head-to-head with Danielsson in his office on Thursday morning. Bäckström had discovered that the porn murderer's third victim (a) was working in a shop that catered to homosexual customers, and (b) was homosexual himself, and for the detective inspector the whole thing was suddenly as plain as the nose on his face.

During the first five minutes Danielsson just sat quietly and glared at Bäckström while the vein on his temple wriggled like a worm just set on a hook. Then he suddenly got up and despite his bad knees leaped over the desk to grab his coworker by the throat, finally put an end to the madness, and get a little needed calm in his own existence. Bäckström managed to dodge him, wriggled out through Danielsson's door, was transformed into a gazelle, and fled down the corridor of the squad offices while Danielsson was hanging on to the door handle and howling at him as he disappeared into the stairwell of the police station.

"I'm going to kill you, you fat little bastard!" Danielsson roared, and despite the fact that this actually had nothing to do with it, in reality it also put an end to the investigation of the murder of Kjell Eriksson.

Danielsson put yet another binder on his shelf, but considering "all the old shit that was already there" it was basically more of the same. Besides, it would soon be time to take off for the holidays. Personally he would be going away over Christmas and New Year's, and when he came back he could start counting the days until retirement.

20

Wednesday, December 27, 1989

On Wednesday the twenty-seventh of December, Wiijnbladh received a courier package from the National Laboratory of Forensic Science in Linköping. In it was the hand towel that his colleague Bäckström had found at the bottom of the laundry basket in Eriksson's apartment on Rådmansgatan.

With the package also came a written report that confirmed what Wiijnbladh had already figured out by using his nose, namely that some-one had vomited in the hand towel. Knowing that a relatively short time before vomiting this individual evidently had consumed a meal consist-ing of fish, potatoes, vegetables, and a cup of coffee would scarcely advance the investigation, thought Wiijnbladh. Nor would the findings that the hand towel also bore traces of a lot of chemical rubbish that no normal person would have the faintest idea about, but that he, through practical experience, knew was always found on hand towels and similar places where people dried themselves off.

Stuck-up academics. What use are such people in the police depart-ment? thought Wiijnbladh sourly, setting both the package and the report aside. He himself had more important things to do. For some time he had been gathering considerable information about the element thallium. Unfortunately this research was still only theoretical and thereby unusable in a purely practical sense, but soon . . . soon, thought Wiijnbladh, it would be time to take the next step.

. . .

Criminal Inspector Bo Jarnebring went to work on Wednesday morning and would be filling in as the on-duty chief inspector until the day before New Year's Eve, after which he had requested vacation to make the life-changing move and enter into marriage with his beloved fiancée. He had forgiven his best friend for secretly getting there ahead of him, and police superintendent Lars Martin Johansson and his spouse would be witnesses and honored guests at the wedding.

Jarnebring had not given further thought to the now dormant investigation of the murder of Kjell Göran Eriksson. Naturally he'd heard the story about Bäckström, who had unfortunately saved his skin owing to Danielsson's bad knees; it was already a classic in the Kronoberg block. Jarnebring had even called Danielsson to offer his own legs in the event Danielsson considered it necessary to try again. Even though it had been more than twenty years since he last represented Sweden on the national team in the four-hundred-meter relay, he did not think catching Bäckström would pose any serious problems.

"On one condition," Danielsson had chuckled. "That you just catch the bastard for me. I want to tear him apart myself."

Because there was a lot to do despite the Christmas week lull, Jarnebring had lunch at the restaurant in the courtyard of police headquarters. It was basically empty, so he chose a table in a far corner where he could leaf through the newspaper in peace and quiet with his coffee. As he was sitting there an older colleague who worked with the patrol cars came up and asked if he might sit down and exchange a few words.

Wasn't his name Stridh? thought Jarnebring, searching in his memory files. He never forgot a face but it was starting to take longer to come up with the names.

"Stridh," said Stridh and sat down. "We met when you were the head of the bureau at Östermalm, if you remember that."

"Have a seat," said Jarnebring, nodding at a vacant chair.

Stridh had an errand. Jarnebring had figured that out even before his colleague sat down, but it had taken a good deal of hemming and hawing and beating around the bush before he spit it out.

"Do you remember our colleague Persson who worked in break-ins, who went to SePo later?" Stridh asked.

Do I remember? thought Jarnebring, nodding. A real policeman and one of the surliest colleagues he'd ever met.

"I remember him," said Jarnebring. "Why do you ask?"

"I had a visit from him last week," said Stridh, leaning forward as he said this. "Strange," he added, shaking his head.

"I'm listening," said Jarnebring, setting aside his newspaper.

Stridh twisted uncomfortably and looked around.

"Actually I can't say anything," said Stridh, "but I thought I should talk to you anyway."

Do it then, thought Jarnebring, even if he wouldn't have done it if he had been in Stridh's place and Persson had told him to keep his mouth shut. Persson was not the type you did that sort of thing to, thought Jarnebring.

"Am I suspected of spying?" Jarnebring asked, grinning.

"No, not at all," said Stridh deprecatingly. "It wasn't about you at all."

"What did he want then?" said Jarnebring. I don't have all day, he thought.

"He wanted to talk about the West German embassy," said Stridh. "Yes, you were there too, I guess," he added. "Didn't you almost get shot by the way?"

"People talk a lot of shit," said Jarnebring.

"Yes, that was a dreadful story," said Stridh, almost looking as though he was thinking out loud.

"What does this have to do with me?" asked Jarnebring. There must still be a hundred officers here in the building who were there at the West German embassy, he thought.

"Nothing so far as I understand," said Stridh, shaking his head. "It was about another matter. That homosexual murder on the thirtieth of November," said Stridh. "Isn't that your investigation?"

"Bäckström's," said Jarnebring curtly. It's just senseless how much shit gets talked about here in the building, he thought. "It's Bäckström's investigation. If you want to talk about it, then he's the one you should take it up with. I've been taken off the case."

"Bäckström," said Stridh hesitantly. "Isn't that a real misfortune?"

"Do Turks have brown eyes?" said Jarnebring, smiling.

"I know what you mean," said Stridh, and he smiled too. "Although I actually read somewhere that lots of Turks have blue or gray eyes. Whatever that's supposed to mean."

No, thought Jarnebring.

"What can I help you with?" said Jarnebring briefly, sneaking a glance at the clock to be on the safe side.

"Here I sit taking up your time," said Stridh, shaking his head. "Most of what you hear is just gossip," he continued. "But this is still not cleared up . . . that murder from the thirtieth of November I mean," Stridh clarified.

"No," said Jarnebring. If it had been, I'd have heard about it, he thought.

"Was he homosexual then," asked Stridh, "the victim, that is?"

"People talk too much," said Jarnebring, shrugging his shoulders, "but if you ask our colleague Bäckström, he has no doubt had that thought."

"Him, yes," said Stridh. "But what about you?" he asked.

"What do you mean?" asked Jarnebring.

Stridh sighed again and looked almost unhappy.

"You don't think it was something political then?" Stridh asked carefully.

Political, thought Jarnebring. "What do you mean?" he asked. What is this guy after? he thought.

"Whatever. Let's forget it," Stridh said, shaking his head deprecatingly.

I see, thought Jarnebring, looking at the clock. We'll forget it. What's five minutes when you have an entire life, he thought.

"Well," said Stridh, sighing. "That West German business was a shocking story. They were caught napping out there at the embassy. The ones who worked there I mean."

"Yes," said Jarnebring. "I guess it was all a little too easy for my taste."

"It was in the newspapers that the guys at SePo had received a tip long before that something was up," said Stridh. "But apparently the Germans didn't pay attention."

"No," said Jarnebring, getting up. "That doesn't seem to have worked too well." Or else the guys at SePo forgot to mention it to them, he thought.

"Yes, really," said Stridh, moving his head and sounding mostly as though he was talking to himself. "I was thinking what Churchill used to say during the war . . ."

"Well," said Jarnebring. "If you'll excuse me—"

"Sure," said Stridh, and he got up too. "I'm the one who should say excuse me for disturbing you during your break. What I was thinking of was what Churchill used to say: 'He who is forewarned is also fore-armed.' 'He who is forewarned is also forearmed,' " Stridh declaimed again. "Although that doesn't seem to have applied to the Germans exactly," he declared, shaking his head.

Part 3

Another Time

V

In the late 1980s the democracy movement within the Eastern Bloc quickly advanced in the Soviet Union, Poland, Czechoslovakia, and Hungary. East Germany was an exception. The head of state and leader of the East German Communist Party, Erich Honecker, stubbornly resisted all reform efforts, and when he lost the struggle, the final price that both he and his country had to pay was far higher than the toll paid by the countries that had previously been his allies.

The German Democratic Republic would soon cease to exist, the actual breakdown occurring at roughly the same time that the nation's fortieth anniversary was being celebrated. The formal acknowledgment came less than a year later. October 3, 1990, marked the end of forty-one years as—officially anyway—an independent nation; after that the former GDR was transformed into five new states that were subsumed by the Federal Republic of Germany.

Honecker himself would die in exile in Chile on May 29, 1994, isolated, terminally ill with liver cancer, deprived of all political power, eighty-two years of age, in self-imposed exile on the other side of the globe. Honecker was from the Saar region, the son of a miner from Neunkirchen, where he was trained as a roofer and played shawm in the rock blasters' wind orchestra. When the Nazis marched into the Saar in 1935, the twenty-three-year-old communist had been forced to flee for the first time. That time he ended up in Paris. His last journey was considerably longer than that.

In retrospect, in the pale glow of the night-light of history, Western historians and journalists have portrayed the fall of East Germany as the result of a gigantic information error committed by its leaders, a collection of hidebound old-line communists, desperate, blinkered, unable to comprehend the new world outside. Their spiritual father Karl Marx would certainly have dismissed this writing of history as idealistic, romanticized, and factually absurd—and he would have been completely correct—but considering what happened later this is also uninteresting. According to these Western observers—and it is well known that history is first written by the victors—it was "a little slip of paper that started the landslide rolling" (*Ein kleiner Zettel löst die Lawine aus*), to quote the headline of an article in *Berliner Zeitung* on the fifth anniversary of the fall of the Berlin Wall. The slip of paper in question was presented to the assembled world media at a press conference in Berlin, in connection with the meeting of the Central Committee, right before seven o'clock on Thursday evening the ninth of November 1989. According to the same story it had been delivered by Honecker's successor Egon Krenz to the Politburo's head of information Günter Schabowski just over an hour earlier, and before this much had happened that would have been more to Karl Marx's taste had he been the one writing the historical description.

In May 1989 the Hungarians had started tearing down the barbed-wire fence along the 161-mile-long border with Austria. The fence that had divided Europe for three decades was torn down, and after that everything moved very quickly. It took less than six months to disperse the gloomy inheritance of the Second World War.

During the summer of 1989 the stream of refugees from East Germany increased dramatically. Thousands of East Germans traveled on vacation to Budapest and stayed a few days before the majority of them made their way farther via illegal routes into Austria and from there to West Germany and freedom in the capitalist paradise.

On August 19 Hungary opened one of its border crossings to Austria for a few hours, in order to temporarily ease the pressure, and during that time six hundred East Germans took the opportunity to leave the country and cross via Austria to West Germany. The border was then closed again, and for a few days returned to the old restrictions, with desperate attempts at flight, gunfire, and in the best cases refugees who were only wounded.

By the twenty-fifth of August the Hungarians had had enough, and the country's prime minister announced that Hungary had decided to give all East Germans permission to leave the country. On the tenth of September Hungary then broke its agreement with East Germany, and in the ensuing weeks tens of thousands of East Germans traveled to West Germany via Hungary. The Soviet Union had in any event not raised any active objections. During the prior year, Gorbachev had instead talked about other matters, about the need for openness, renewal, and political reforms, and within the new Eastern Bloc the Hungarians' decision was now seen as a welcome initiative.

At the same time Hungary was not the only way out. In the month of September thousands of East Germans also traveled to Czechoslovakia, where they sought asylum as political refugees at the West German embassy in Prague. At the end of September those who had taken refuge there were unexpectedly given exit permits to the Federal Republic, and within the course of a day four thousand traveled on to West Germany, which had always been their ultimate destination.

Then the landslide began. Before the end of the year more than half a million East Germans, 3 percent of the country's population, had left for a new life in the West, and as so often before it was younger people who took the first step. It was the youth and thereby the hope of the future that had abandoned the fatherland.

The literal-minded may be wondering about that slip of paper. And what was it that actually happened at the meeting of the East German Central Committee on Thursday the ninth of November 1989?

The main issue at the meeting was a given, namely how they could gain control over the flight of the people to the West. What had been specifically discussed over the previous few months was a proposal from Wolfgang Herger, head of the security department within the East German Communist Party's Central Committee, which contained two opposing alternatives. Either close the borders of the country to the outside world or grant every East German citizen the opportunity to apply for an exit visa on their passport, and thereby an opportunity to freely leave the country.

The proposal for the new travel edict was presented for the first time to the members of the Politburo during a break in the proceedings, between twelve o'clock and twelve-thirty on Thursday the ninth of November. During the afternoon it was agreed to let the proposal circulate among the members of the Council of Ministers as well, before being considered by the Central Committee. At four-thirty in the afternoon Egon Krenz read the proposal, there was a brief, rather confused discussion, some changes to the text were made on the spot, whereupon the proposal was accepted in its entirety and without qualifications.

At five-thirty the head of information, Schabowski, came into Krenz's office to hear if there was anything in particular that Krenz wanted him to announce to the media at the press conference that was to begin in half an hour, and that to be on the safe side would also be broadcast live on East German TV.

According to Krenz himself Schabowski was supposed to "emphasize" the decision about a new travel policy. This was world news, a sensation. According to Schabowski he was "not supposed to emphasize anything in particular" but rather simply hand out a bundle of papers with the usual mixture of high and low, mostly just verbiage.

If the latter version is true, this at least explains Schabowski's peculiar behavior during the press conference. Toward the end of it he was asked whether the new travel policy, which had been discussed publicly for the first time a few days earlier, should not actually be seen as a great mistake.

The reply Schabowski gave was verbose, hard to understand, beside the point, and astounding in its significance. In brief he said that the Central Committee had decided that every East German citizen was now free to leave the country. The people's police had been instructed to immediately issue visas for foreign travel to those who so desired, at all border stations between East and West Germany including those in Berlin. And considering what happened later, this was not bad news.

VI

Major Manfred Sens of the East German border police was free that evening. He was sitting in the living room at home in his apartment on Strassburger Strasse in Prenzlauer Berg in the north part of East Berlin, and was following the broadcast of the Central Committee's press conference on his TV. Toward the end of the broadcast, after the customary questions of typically variable quality, something happened that, according to what he himself is reported to have said, caused him to choke on his evening coffee. It was when Günter Schabowski spoke about the new travel policy that had just been adopted.

Major Sens was assistant head of the border post at Bornholmer Strasse in Prenzlauer Berg, not far from his home, which was convenient considering that he immediately put on his uniform and went there. When he arrived, his colleague and chief, Lieutenant-Colonel Harald Jäger, was already on the scene, as growing hordes of Berliners started to stream in. A large number of them Sens recognized too because they were his own neighbors. What was worse was that neither he nor Jäger had any idea what to do, and the situation quickly threatened to get completely out of control.

At nine o'clock in the evening Jäger phoned the minister of security to ask for advice. The minister's spokesman suggested that the most belligerent should be let through, miserable advice that for lack of anything better was followed nonetheless. The agitation in the mass of people had only increased as the pressure on the guards became more intense, and at ten-thirty in the evening Major Sens capitulated and personally opened the border gate to West Berlin. During the first hour twenty thousand people are estimated to have crossed the border at Bornholmer Strasse alone, at the same time as corresponding scenes played out at all the other border crossings in the city.

It was Major Sens's last duty at the border post. As a citizen of the Federal Republic he would receive new employment as a ticket-taker in the subway, which in any case was a freer, better-paid job than the position as a coat checker at the historical museum on Unter den Linden, which is what his old colleague Jäger got, right next to Neue Wache where Jäger, at one time in the bad old days, had commanded the military honor guard.

And for none of them—whether in a status-related or in an economic sense—was their experience of capitalism much like the paradise that many of their countrymen had imagined. On the other hand, both of them got considerably more than the generally allotted fifteen minutes of fame that was also said to characterize free life in the West.

VII

Within the leading intelligence services of the Western world the situation that became a reality in the fall of 1989 had been predicted going back ten years, and the only mistake that had been made was that the majority of the analysts who worked with the issue had set the breaking point even a few years earlier.

The one who had done best at the CIA was Mike "The Bear" Liska, despite the fact that he was neither an analyst nor working at that time with any of the departments responsible for the member states of the Warsaw Pact. In the spring of 1984 there had been a large internal conference at headquarters in Langley during which the invigorating question of the timing of the opponent's collapse was at the top of the agenda. Over two cram-packed days featuring primarily economic analyses the nation's combined intelligence elite were present in full force.

At the usual follow-up gathering on the last evening, bets were made on the timing of the fall of the Berlin Wall, and it would be Liska who both kicked their asses and made himself a decent pile of cash to boot. "Give the motherfuckers five years and their usual bonus for getting it wrong twice," said Liska, and when the list of wagers went around he put a hundred dollars on "late autumn '89, most likely November." The majority of those standing around shook their heads and thanked him for the money and all the beer they would drink at his expense long before then.

.   .   .

Michael Liska was born in 1940 and grew up in a suburb of Pest some twelve miles south of the Hungarian capital. When the Hungarians fomented an uprising against the Soviet Union in 1956, he took part in the armed struggle on the streets of Budapest, and when the whole thing was over he fled by the usual route. Crossing the northern border with Austria and via a refugee camp in West Germany he ended up in Akron, Ohio, having just turned seventeen in his new homeland, the United States, where he was taken care of by fellow countrymen who had emigrated two generations earlier.

After completing university studies he applied to the Marine Corps, trained as an officer, and even before graduation day was directly recruited for the fleet's intelligence service. He remained there for almost ten years until the CIA made contact and made him an offer he could not refuse. In addition to his native Hungarian, he also spoke fluent Russian and German, so his mission was also a given. During the following ten years he would spend more time in West Germany, Scandinavia, and the rest of Europe than in his second homeland, the United States.

Liska was a classic operator, an intelligence officer with responsibility for a large number of field agents who were working behind enemy lines, and his successes finally became so numerous that his supervisors no longer wanted to risk having him out there in the field; instead they brought him home to headquarters in Langley, Virginia, and made him head of the Scandinavian division. And it was in that capacity that he participated in the "collapse seminar" in the spring of 1984.

Four years later, in the spring of 1988, he suggested to his top superior that he should be relocated to one of the working groups that had been trying for the past several years to put some order into the logistics needed before the opponent's impending breakup.

"We're close now," said Liska, and because his boss had an excellent memory and knew that Liska's was now the only name remaining on the renowned betting list, he had asked him to propose his mission himself. "East Germany," said Liska.

"Why East Germany in particular?" his boss asked in surprise.

According to the analyses he had studied, the GDR was more likely the hard core of the collapsing Soviet empire. "What do you have against Hungary, by the way?" With his background, wouldn't that be almost an ideal area to tackle? "Or Poland, or Czechoslovakia too for that matter? Why East Germany, for heaven's sake?" Because it was the GDR that would be the first domino to fall, answered Liska. "They're going to break like a dry twig," said Liska, and that was how it turned out.

Liska was given money to set up his own movement. His first step consisted of putting together the ten or so colleagues he had come to rely on most over the years, and he located the head office for his little firm in Stockholm, just close enough but at the same time far enough away. He felt comfortable in Stockholm. It had a little of both Akron, Ohio, and south Pest, Liska thought, and he would know, having lived in Sweden's capital for a few years in the late seventies when he was posted to the American embassy in Stockholm.

"Okay," said Liska at the first meeting with his colleagues. "I guess you're wondering what we're doing here." From the expectant nods he understood that this was a completely correct assumption. "I've got the idea," he continued with a deliberately drawling Midwestern accent, "that our dear comrades in the German Democratic Republic are going to be turned upside down." He deliberately paused and dug in his left ear with his ballpoint pen. "And then I thought we should take the opportunity well in advance to buy their lists of the various collaborators they've made use of over the years." Liska took the pen out of his ear and inspected it thoughtfully. "So what this is about in concrete terms is that we have to find some person or persons on Normannenstrasse willing to earn a few bucks," he said and smiled. It was no more difficult than that.

VIII

The East German security service, Ministerium für Staatssicherheit, or Stasi as it was called in everyday usage, was without comparison the largest security organization within the Eastern Bloc. In relative terms, and depending a bit on how you counted, it was between ten and thirty times larger than the Russian KGB.

At the time of the collapse of the German Democratic Republic, the Stasi had 102,000 employees and about half a million so-called external colleagues—informants, infiltrators, provocateurs, and not counting plain old gossips—in a country with a population of seventeen million people. When the defeat of communism became a fact and there was a green light to inspect the Stasi's registry of individuals, it turned out that security files had been compiled on more than six million of the Republic's own citizens and almost a million foreigners.

It was information about the latter that interested Liska and his comrades in the security agencies of the Western world. It was enemies of Western democracies they wanted to get at, and what they were searching for above all else was the information being stored at Stasi's own foreign intelligence service HVA—Hauptverwaltung Aufklärung—with 4,286 employees, headquartered at Normannenstrasse 22 in East Berlin, under the leadership of the legendary "Carla," Lieutenant General Markus Wolf.

The Germans had a well-founded reputation for being precise to the point of pedantry, and the filing of various types of information had long been one of their best areas. In the HVA register, according to what the CIA thought it knew, the names of fifty thousand individuals in round numbers were stored who in various ways had helped the East Germans with their "foreign affairs" over the years, from the most qualified spies to the most vacillating sympathizers; it helped that the registry was computerized.

Thus it was not a matter of having to move tens of tons of files, which would have been an impossible task; instead the desired information fit comfortably on large-format computer tapes. At the same time the data was not too big to fit into an ordinary briefcase or even under a uniform jacket in a pinch, obviously assuming the carrier was sufficiently well motivated.

Liska knew from his own experience that almost anything—and anyone—could be bought with money. The disposition of this information was a matter, quite literally, of power over fifty thousand lives, and not just any lives. Assuming that the Western intelligence agencies could find out who these individuals were and what they had been working on, there was also the possibility of affecting the existence of hundreds of millions of other people in both a positive and a negative direction. And for that no price was too high, thought Liska.

Liska was of course not the only one who had this idea. There were a number of others who had been thinking along the same lines for several years, and not least within the organization to which he himself belonged. Therefore the usual bureaucratic catfights had also started to break out within the organization, and when the fog finally cleared, the visible results consisted of a steering group of three individuals who had the power and the money; a reference group of experts and those people who simply had to be humored; a project group that would do the job itself; as well as a number of auxiliary groups, one of which Liska headed; these latter groups would be responsible for the coordination of various field efforts: the one goal, a number of people, a bag of money that for once was ample, and of course the highest imaginable level of secrecy. Everything was, in other words, for the most part as usual, and of course it had been given a project name, Operation Rosewood.

When the Wall fell the Stasi also fell apart like a house of cards. Suddenly everything was for sale, and because it was a matter of getting there first if there was going to be any money worth talking about, it was the seller who made contact with the buyer. At the end of November 1989 an officer of the Stasi, who was not particularly high ranking but was stationed in the right place, brought a copy of the computer tapes with the names of all the GDR's spies and contacts abroad to a Russian colleague at the KGB office in Berlin-Karlshorst. From there the computer tapes were sent by air to the KGB in Moscow so that the sellers from the Stasi and the KGB could finally meet the purchasers from the CIA and calmly and quietly do business in person. On Tuesday the fifth of December 1989 everything was ready. The computer tapes were exchanged for dollars, hands were shaken over the deal, toasts were made with Russian vodka and Russian champagne.

The tapes had been acquired at a bargain-basement price, which did not surprise Liska, who had experienced the Second World War as a small child and the Hungarian Revolution as a teenager and had observed with his own eyes that sometimes a human life was not worth anything at all. Here in any case the sellers reaped a hundred dollars a head, he thought, shaking his own sympathetically.

The evening when Major Manfred Sens was about to choke on his coffee in his apartment in Prenzlauer Berg in Berlin, Liska had been invited to dinner in the fashionable Stockholm suburb of Djursholm more than six hundred miles to the north, but in contrast to Sens, Liska would not have time for any coffee that evening. Something he could live with, by the way, because his waiting would soon be over.

His host was an old acquaintance from the early seventies who was now working as an adviser in the Swedish government offices, where he was officially occupied with research and future issues, but in reality functioned as the prime minister's extended arm whenever a matter concerned Swedish national security.

Their acquaintance had been far from unproblematic. During the early years it had even been so complicated that the slightest official scrutiny would have meant serious problems, not only for those most closely involved but also for their superiors and the national interests they represented. Now, however, the situation was different, and the fact that the Russian bear was on the ropes had also in a very tangible and positive manner eased the association between Liska and the Swedish government's top security adviser. "To put it simply, the Swedes don't need to be so damned moody anymore," as Liska himself summarized the geopolitical background when he was discussing it with one of his bosses at home at Langley.

Liska and his host had reserved the entire evening for good drink, good food, and agreeable conversation about old memories, the brightening future, and the current geopolitical situation, but they hardly had time to sit down at the table before they were interrupted. Just as the host's red telephone was ringing, Liska's driver and bodyguard knocked on the door, and then it was back to work—for both of them, each in his own sphere, but for the same reason.

Before they went their separate ways, Liska's host quoted Churchill with an easy smile and the reservation that the value of being forewarned obviously depends on the possibility of being able to defend oneself. Liska then went to his borrowed office at the American embassy out on Djurgården. There he spent the night mostly talking on the phone and wandering back and forth between his desk and the TV over by the window. "Poor bastards," he thought as he looked out into the black November night, and it was the fifty thousand people whose lives had just been put on the market that he had in mind.

Part 4

Another Life

21

Autumn 1999

It was Bureau Chief Berg, head of operations for the Swedish secret police, who asked the question.

"Could you see yourself doing it, Lars?" Berg asked.

Could I? thought Johansson. Could I see myself doing it?

"Yes," said Johansson.

And that was how the whole thing started.

A good many things had happened in the secret police since the prime minister was murdered in February 1986. The fact that the murder had unleashed a number of re-evaluations of the secret operation was the least important. Where wriggling out of such things was concerned, the people at the agency had decades of practice. In secret police–related work, it was also the case that every investigator with a minimum of instinct for self-preservation realized the importance and value of proceeding carefully.

As this concerned things that were secret by nature, it was extremely important in the process not to damage an operation of decisive public significance, for that could only profit the enemy and in the final analysis even risk the well-being of the entire nation. Therefore the object of the re-evaluation, just like always, escaped with the usual mixture of cosmetic measures and minor personnel changes. All in accordance with the old, proven rule of giving the idealists peace of mind and the cannibals the pound of flesh they were always coveting.

In order to "underscore a more civilian and democratic direction," the operation changed its name from the security department of the National Police Board—Sec—to the Security Police, or SePo, as nowadays even police officers called it. For the same reason the operation was also given greater independence in relation to its immediate parent body, the National Police Board. In order to finally make the head of the Swedish secret police the formal equivalent of his foreign colleagues he had been elevated to the position of general director. Finally, a number of individuals had been kicked diagonally upward or moved around within the upper police bureaucracy, while just one had to step right out into the cold, though he retained his salary.

At the same time other things had happened that had considerably more far-reaching consequences, the most important being the collapse of the Soviet Union and the breakup of the Eastern Bloc. The old "Russian squad," which historically had claimed more than half of all combined resources if properly calculated, was now not even a shadow of its former self, and if it hadn't been for Bureau Chief Berg's bureaucratic creativity the entire organization would have been in serious danger even as the enemy lowered the flag.

Berg was without comparison the shrewdest operational head in the history of the secret police, and instead of coming to a stop when the old main road was closed off, he quickly found new paths in the terrain of security politics: the situation in the Balkans, European and international terrorism, the new threat from the extreme right, the nation's own growing need for Swedish constitutional protection, and best of all the assassination of Olof Palme, which created a veritable boom in the personal security industry.

The same year that the Berlin Wall fell, SePo's bodyguard squad passed the agency's old Russian squad in personnel strength, and after that the demand for bodyguards only increased. Upper-class people felt threatened as never before, and right or wrong this was useful to SePo. So far all was well and good, but other things were considerably more worrisome.

The threat against Swedish democracy nowadays came from the right and not from the left. It would have been simple enough just to turn your head, but the problem was the historical inheritance from the days of the cold war collected in the archives of the secret police. A

workforce of hundreds who had worked doggedly for decades register-
ing hundreds of thousands of Swedish citizens because their political
sympathies were to the left of the Social Democratic regime. A sad
story, but unfortunately only one side of the problem.

Another side of the problem was that the political powers that be from
the days of the cold war who had authorized SePo to collect all this
information were now on their way out. The majority of the older ones
had already died a natural death or had long since retired. The prime
minister had been shot and his contemporaries who still remained in the
corridors of power were a shrinking few who were counting the days to
the end. Thus the basis for the exchange of services between the secret
police and its political client had been demolished.

The burden of guilt still remained, and in a moral sense it was
greater than ever, but there were no old clients to go to for help paying
the claims that would be raised against the secret police. Much less anyone with whom you could exchange services when you ended up with
your beard in the mail slot through your own fault. Nowadays the whole
system was rotten through and through, in Berg's opinion. Humanly
and morally rotten to the core, and deeply unjust to him and his colleagues, who had only been doing their jobs.

And as if this wasn't enough, there was a third side to the matter. The
new powers that be—historically unburdened by this sorry story—were
obviously also strongly overrepresented in SePo's old archives from the
radical sixties and seventies. This Berg knew from his own experience,
because he'd had to play fireman on a number of occasions when new
individuals, who were now living other lives and operating in a different
time, had been appointed to high-ranking official positions. And thanks
for the help was the last thing he could expect. Instead it was a matter of
keeping his lips sealed and hoping for the best.

This complication also happened to be one of the first issues that Berg
brought up during his conversation with Johansson, and the reaction
had of course been as expected.

"If you want me to clean up after you then I think you've come to the wrong person," said Johansson, who suddenly appeared both expectant and guarded.

"No, God help us," Berg answered, making a deprecating gesture. "I intend to take care of that myself. I thought you should start with a clean desk." Thanks to me cleaning up after others. It was that unjust, he thought.

"A lovely thought," said Johansson. "That we'll all get to go into the new millennium with an empty desk."

"That's pretty much the point," Berg clarified, still sensing Johansson's hesitation.

"So that's why you've turned to a predecessor of the '68 generation," said Johansson, smiling.

"Oh well," said Berg soberly. "You understand what I mean."

"What do the ones who decide think?" Johansson appeared genuinely curious about the reply.

"The government offices thought your name was an extraordinary suggestion," said Berg. "I've talked with the responsible undersecretary . . . you must have met him, by the way, around the time Palme was shot. As you know it's the government that controls the appointment, and we were in complete agreement."

"That's a relief," said Johansson, who now seemed rather amused. Times are changing, he thought. "What does the GD say then?" said Johansson. The new general director was nonetheless head of the secret police.

"The general director," said Berg, who had a hard time concealing his surprise. "There's never been any problem with him." It didn't matter what title they gave these high-level bosses (and personally he was now on his fifth), though naturally he couldn't say that, he thought. Johansson would certainly figure that out all on his own as soon as he got his feet wet.

"As head of operations you're the one who will lead the work itself, and in the government offices they have great confidence in you as an individual," Berg clarified, nodding seriously.

And I'm easily flattered too, thought Johansson.

After that they talked about other things that Johansson wanted said before he decided. That he wasn't a politician but a police officer. That for him it was about putting people who were involved in serious crimes in jail before they had a chance to cause even more mischief, and that the only reason for him to change jobs was that he wanted finally to get involved in a few serious operational assignments.

That was no problem at all, according to Berg. On the contrary, the political client, top-ranking police leadership, and, obviously, Berg himself were of the exact same opinion.

"I think you're going to appreciate this job and I'm quite certain that you're going to be pleasantly surprised. I know that a horrifying lot of nonsense gets talked about us among our colleagues in the open operation, but that should be taken with a large grain of salt," said Berg, nodding decisively. "This is a job for a real policeman." Someone like you and me, he thought.

A real policeman, thought Johansson. That sounds good.

Then they proceeded to practical details. Higher rank? Yes. Salary? Obviously higher, which by the way was a natural consequence both of the higher rank as well as the fact that those who worked in the closed operation had always earned more than those who were part of the regular police.

The possibility of choosing his own coworkers? Of course. Assuming that Johansson only spit out a little three-letter word he was the one who was the boss and it was no more difficult than that.

Despite everything, one somewhat sensitive detail remained.

"How long do you intend to stay?" said Johansson. You look tired, he thought. You've lost a lot of weight too.

"I can go tomorrow if you want," said Berg, smiling. Today if it were up to me, he thought, but naturally he didn't say that.

"And here I was hoping for a guided tour," said Johansson, smiling.

"I'll be glad to give you one," said Berg. "I was hoping you'd ask, actually." What's a few weeks more or less after all these years? he thought.

Johansson nodded. He really seems worn out, he thought.

"Oh well," said Berg, looking almost a little solemn. "What do you say? Could you see yourself doing it?"

"Yes," said Johansson.

And that was how the whole thing started.

Johansson's existence as a transient resource within the police department was over. He was no longer a police jack-of-all-trades whom the
government offices and National Police Board could call in whenever it
was time to clean up after some highly placed colleague who had been
discreetly dismissed or had simply thrown in the towel because he'd had
enough. Now he was an established man with operational management
responsibility for what was called the closed operation in police talk, and
for anyone who coveted police authority there was no better place to be.

He himself did not give much thought in particular to that part of it.
He had plenty to do recruiting coworkers to the free investigation and
detective team he intended to have in his immediate vicinity. He would
need the help of his best friend Bo Jarnebring because it had been years
since Johansson had worked in the field himself and there must be many
capable new people whose existence he didn't even know about. In that
way he acquired ten or so new coworkers, and the only fly in the oint-
ment was that Jarnebring himself steadfastly resisted all his friend's
attempts at recruitment.

"I don't look good in a fake beard," said Jarnebring, shaking his head.
"Besides, I'm starting to get too old."

"Say the word if you change your mind," said Johansson. I guess we
all get old, he thought.

"Not this time," said Jarnebring. "On the other hand I wonder what's
happened to you?"

"What do you mean?" asked Johansson.

"How long have we known each other? How long is it since you and
I met for the first time out at the old police academy?"

"Thirty years," said Johansson, shrugging his shoulders.

"If I don't remember wrong you were the class socialist. You were
more or less alone in that besides, and I seem to recall that you wanted
to shut down the secret police."

"You don't say," said Johansson. How time flies. It actually is more
than thirty years now, he thought.

"If I don't remember wrong, you couldn't have something like the
secret police in a democratic, lawful police organization. It was abso-

lutely unthinkable, and if anyone had asked you at that time if you could imagine working as a spook, I know exactly what would have happened."

"What?" asked Johansson, despite the fact that he already knew the answer.

"The person in question would have been socked on the jaw," said Jarnebring, not mincing words.

"Oh well," said Johansson, shrugging his shoulders.

"And because you've never been particularly good at such things, I would have had to jump in and help you, too," Jarnebring declared.

"Sure," Johansson agreed. "I'm sure I would have been counting on that."

"But now you'll be head of the whole thing," said Jarnebring. "What's happened?"

"These are new times now," said Johansson. New and I hope better times, he thought.

"I don't believe that for a moment," said Jarnebring. "Possibly these are different times."

22

Autumn 1999

Of course Johansson spoke with his wife before he decided to change course in his police life. Ten years earlier, after almost fifteen years as a divorced man—or a single man or a bachelor or whatever you want to call it—he had proposed to her after an emotionally charged week of basically uninterrupted togetherness. In that way he had settled accounts with the solitude he had come to consider a natural part of both his individuality and his existence. Disregarding the fact that he might still miss that solitude when their togetherness became too much or when he simply felt like being by himself for a while.

She had said yes despite the fact that he couldn't offer her a new job but only his heart, and because Lars Martin Johansson was a person who knew how to distinguish between great and small he had subsequently devoted himself to his "marital community"—that was how he looked at it—with great seriousness and considerable energy. It hadn't been easy, not all the time, but who ever said we humans should have it easy? We make a choice, and important choices have major consequences, thought Johansson. Like now.

"What do you think, dear?" asked Johansson.

"What do *you* think?" Johansson's wife countered in that way he sometimes had a hard time with. "I'm not the one who's going to be a secret agent," she added, smiling in that other way he had never had any problem with whatsoever.

"If he had asked me twenty years ago I would have thrown him out," said Johansson, whatever that had to do with it, given that the question had been asked a few days ago.

"Do you think we need a secret police force?" his wife asked, looking at him with curiosity.

"It's clear we need a secret police force," said Johansson with a conviction that didn't feel quite genuine. For we do need it, don't we? he thought. Of course we need SePo, don't we?

"Okay then," said his wife, shrugging her shoulders. "Because we need a secret police force and you're an excellent police officer—and a respectable person who lives a respectable life, at least since you met me—then I guess the only answer is yes."

Why does she look so amused? thought Johansson. I don't understand women. They're not like us, he thought.

"You're not pulling my leg?"

"Would I ever pull your leg?" his wife teased. "What does Bo say, by the way?"

"Jarnebring," said Johansson with surprise. "Why do you wonder that? I don't care what he thinks about it."

"Aye, aye, aye," said his wife, shaking her head at the same time that she seemed highly amused. "Little Bosse doesn't want to play with his best buddy anymore."

"He says I'm too old," said Johansson curtly. There she goes again, he thought.

"Do you know something?" His wife looked at him.

Johansson just shook his head. Best to bide your time a little, he thought.

"Do you remember that old comic strip about those two rascals, Knoll and Tott?"

"Yes," said Johansson hesitantly.

"That's you and Bo," she said. "You're just like Knoll and Tott. Or were their names Pigge and Gnidde?"

"I don't remember," said Johansson. Women are definitely not like us, he thought. "On a different note," Johansson continued, suddenly feeling the need to change the subject. "Forget about that for now. What do you want to do this evening? Dinner? A movie? Or . . ." Johansson moved his shoulders in a manner that was clear enough.

"First I think we should go out to eat—we have to celebrate your new job. Then maybe we can go to a movie—there's actually one I want to see. And then . . . a little . . . or what? Was that what you said? You're shy too. Do you know that? Yes, maybe . . . we'll see."

"Good," said Johansson, getting up quickly. "That's what we'll do then. I just have to shower first." How beautiful she is, he thought, and then he leaned over and placed his hand on her slender neck. She had a hollow there, right at the hairline, that seemed made for his right thumb.

"Go shower now," said his wife, releasing herself from his grip. "I have to start powdering my nose if we're going to make it to the movie too."

Wonder what kind of film it is? thought Johansson as he stood in the shower. Say what you want about her taste in films, it wasn't much like his own and at the most recent one he had been on the verge of falling asleep in the middle. Shouldn't I get to decide which film? he thought suddenly. This celebration is for me, isn't it?

23

March 2000

The cleaning out of the Swedish secret police archives, before the truth seekers from the nation's academic institutions were let onto the premises, became one of the most extensive operations in the history of the organization, and a good illustration of the fact that the fruits of persistent police work could be an end in themselves. Disregarding the fact that the reason for the original efforts and the motivation behind the later measures were diametrically opposed

Obviously not all of what was filed could be cleaned out—or even a significant portion of it—because to do so would scarcely have contributed to the improvement of the secret police's reputation. At the same time, certain individuals must by necessity be rescued from the eyes of the review commission. Primarily this concerned the most important informants used over the years. All in all there were thousands of individuals who appeared under various aliases, cover names, and code designations, and who were almost always found in more than one file, and who in practice were almost impossible to clean out.

It was Chief Inspector Wiklander who found the first big dust bunny. Wiklander was head of the detective group that was part of Johansson's new "free resource," the combined investigation and detective squad that was intended to become his primary weapon in the struggle against those who most urgently and unexpectedly threatened the security of the realm. Johansson had become acquainted with Wiklander during his time as acting head of the National Crime Bureau, and as soon as

Johansson settled down in his new chair as boss he had contacted him. Wiklander was one of the best policemen Johansson had encountered during his long career. Almost as competent as he himself had been at the same age, and just as taciturn. After less than a month on Johansson's team, Wiklander had requested a special meeting with his top boss.

"Do you remember the West German embassy, Boss?" asked Wiklander.

"Sit down," said Johansson, nodding toward his visitor's chair. Do I remember the West German embassy? he thought, and the feelings that suddenly arose were mixed to say the least.

The reason that Wiklander had started looking into the occupation of the West German embassy on the twenty-fourth of April 1975 was mostly a coincidence. In one of the secret police's many incident files the embassy occupation was entered as two murders; both the military attaché and the trade attaché had been murdered. Because the statute of limitations on murder was twenty-five years and it was already the end of March in the year 2000, the crimes associated with the embassy occupation had turned up on the special computerized review list of serious crimes that would soon be free of judicial consequences and relegated to the national archives. "The final twitch" was the expression used in the building to refer to those cases on the list of impending nullification.

"I wasn't there personally, I was still in school, but I remember that my buddies and I were glued to the TV," said Wiklander, smiling and shaking his head.

Me too, thought Johansson with sorrow in his heart, but he didn't intend to talk about why he felt that way, not with Wiklander in any event.

"I'm listening," he said instead, leaning back in his chair.

The reason the embassy drama was still on the list of crimes not yet past the statute of limitations was that there were certain questions remaining. It was thus still an open case. True, no one seemed to have given a thought to it during the past more than twenty years, but the filing of an incident did not always bear any logical connection with the work that was put into it.

"The reason it's still there is that we're pretty sure the Germans inside the embassy must have had help from people on the outside," Wiklander clarified.

"Sure," said Johansson dryly. "You didn't need to be Einstein to figure that out."

"No," said Wiklander. "I realized it when I was watching it on TV. Even though I was still in school."

Right man in the right place, thought Johansson contentedly, nodding at him to continue.

Thus it was mostly out of personal curiosity that Wiklander had ordered the old binders from the archive. Among the first things he noticed were the traces of Bureau Chief Berg's sanitary efforts a few years earlier.

"First," said Wiklander, counting on his long, bony fingers, "there have been suspects noted in the files. Second, they were removed during a review that was done by Chief Inspector Persson a little more than two years ago. Persson—wasn't he the one who was Berg's confidant?" And a man who was uniquely perverse, thought Wiklander, who had met Persson and was far from as ignorant about what was going on as he tried to pretend to be.

Bureau Chief Berg and his right hand, Chief Inspector Persson, they were real policemen, thought Johansson with warmth, and now both were out of the building. Persson had retired a year before Berg turned things over to Johansson.

"What's the problem?" asked Johansson. "Were they Swedes? The accomplices, that is," he clarified. He at least had thought as much twenty-five years ago as he sat on the couch in front of the TV in the company of his two runny-nosed children. Despite the fact that he had only been a single observer high up in the grandstand.

"I think so, but I don't know for sure," said Wiklander, shaking his head. "As I said, they're cleaned out of the file and I intended to come back to this. On the other hand I'm fairly certain there must have been four of them."

"You don't say," said Johansson. "How can you be so sure of that?"

Wiklander's suspicions were based on a combination of three factors. For one thing, the same entry appeared in several different registers, which gave a sufficiently clever person with access to all the registers a chance to trace at least some of the erasures that had been made in the register. Obviously—and this was the second factor—assuming that the one who did the cleaning was not as shrewd or careful as the one who checked the cleaning. The third thing was the use of a certain standard format for personnel notations in one of the registers of operatives for the secret police.

"It's this standard format in one of our registers of operatives that makes me pretty certain it must concern four different individuals," Wiklander explained. "I don't know how much you know about computers, Boss," he added hesitantly.

"Enough," said Johansson curtly. "I'm listening." Who do you take me for? he thought.

The connections hadn't exactly been easy to explain. Wiklander was compelled to run through them twice before Johansson was quite certain he understood how the whole thing stood.

"I'm a hundred percent sure that these four people must have wound up in the current register of operatives," said Wiklander. "Everyone who's entered in there has the same format. Simply put it's a matter of a standardized page for each individual, and it's the same for everyone regardless of how much information there is about the various individuals in other registers or in their personnel files, if there are any. The link is made the same way for everyone with a reference code of ten characters."

"But they can't be so fucking dense that every individual who's registered or removed is loaded as a separate entry," said Johansson with a hint of indignation.

"No . . . not really," Wiklander replied, shaking his head. That would have been almost criminal, he thought.

"But you've figured out anyway that just four individuals have been cleaned out," said Johansson. "Four forms in a standard format, each of which contains one individual?"

"Yes," said Wiklander, seeming not entirely displeased with himself.

Around this time two years earlier there had been some rather energetic cleaning in the relevant register of operatives. The various cleaning persons even had to be put on a waiting list while the computer operators executed their orders and the quantity of characters stored in the computer was reduced at the same tempo as the orders were taken care of.

Because each order was signed both by the person who requested it and the person who carried it out, it had been no great challenge for Wiklander to find Chief Inspector Persson and his business on the day in question. Not to mention the colleagues ahead of and behind him on the list of secret police officers in need of cleaning.

"This is where they messed up," said Wiklander. "The character count in the computer is recorded consecutively. So to put it briefly, it's possible to see how many characters colleague Persson alone had ordered removed. And because I know the number of characters on each form—down to a few dozen—he must have cleaned out exactly four individuals who had been entered in the register because they were included in the event file for the West German embassy."

"Sloppy damn computer nerds," said Johansson gloomily. "I hope you stuck the pointer into them."

"Yes," said Wiklander. "They were very grateful for the help."

I can believe it, thought Johansson sourly. What the hell choice did they have?

"Four individuals have been cleaned out—that much is clear—but we have no idea who they were?"

"No," said Wiklander. "That we don't know."

"It can't have been one of those little elves who were going to take revenge for the West German embassy by kidnapping Anna-Greta Leijon," Johansson speculated. "If I remember correctly there were at least thirty individuals in jail at various times. Both Swedes and foreigners as I recall. Do any of them seem to have ended up in parliament a few years later?"

"Kröcher and his comrades," said Wiklander, shaking his head. "No, it can't have been any of them. As far as the member of parliament is concerned, his name is Juan Fonseca. He was completely innocent, by the way. Got damages as a consolation."

"You're quite certain," said Johansson, looking questioningly at his visitor. Damages my ass, he thought. In certain regards Johansson was an extremely old-fashioned policeman.

"Quite sure," said Wiklander. "For one thing they've been checked out this way and that, and for another they're still in our registers. There are thousands of pages about them, so there's enough for a whole raft of dissertations. They come into the story later, after the West German embassy—to take revenge on Anna-Greta Leijon, who was the minister of labor, in charge of immigration issues and the cabinet minister responsible for terrorist legislation. She was the one who in a formal sense made the deportation decision about the German terrorists."

Forget the law, thought Johansson, who was well aware that to carry out real police work in a crisis situation, you couldn't run around with a statute book under your arm.

"So we have four individuals who've been cleaned out," he summarized. "We don't have a clue who they are, despite the fact that this seems to concern one of the most serious crimes that has been handled in this department. Pretty strange," Johansson concluded.

"Yes," said Wiklander. "Although that's not even the strangest thing."

"Then what is?" asked Johansson, looking guardedly at his visitor.

What was most strange according to Wiklander was that only a few months ago, right before Johansson took over from Berg, two names had suddenly appeared in the file on the West German embassy. What's more, they were Swedish citizens who were supposed to have helped the terrorists in the embassy in their planning and preparations before the occupation, and who in a formal judicial sense were guilty, among other things, of being accomplices to two murders, some ten cases of kidnapping, destruction constituting a public danger or sabotage, as well as a few other goodies.

"I'll be damned," said Johansson. More than enough for life imprisonment, he thought judiciously.

"Yes," said Wiklander. "Not exactly a recommendation."

"So what are their names?" said Johansson. I'm still a policeman, he thought.

"They're both dead, actually," answered Wiklander. "One was a TV journalist who was rather well known in his day—we're talking the late seventies and eighties. His name was Sten Welander, born in 1947. He died of cancer five years ago."

"I have a faint memory," said Johansson. A skinny fanatical type with designer stubble and all the opinions that were correct at the time. They were all like that anyway, regardless of when, he thought.

"The other one worked at the Central Bureau of Statistics over on Karlavägen as some kind of official . . . assistant director . . . nothing remarkable . . . Eriksson, Kjell Göran, born 1944."

"Died from a stroke of course," Johansson grunted contentedly.

"No," said Wiklander. "He was murdered in November 1989."

"You don't say," said Johansson. "You don't say." This is getting better and better, he thought with delight.

"Yes," said Wiklander. "I've requested the investigation files from Stockholm. It's still unsolved, but no one has worked on the case since the spring of 1990. After that it went down into the archives . . . no investigation results, according to the decision."

"I have some faint recollection," said Johansson hesitantly. "Eriksson?" What was that about? he thought.

How had Welander and Eriksson, suitably enough both dead, turned up in the file on the West German embassy, and how was it that it had happened when it did? Hardly six months remained before the case would lapse when the statute of limitations ran out, and without anyone seeming to have lifted a finger to investigate the case for more than twenty years. Of all this, and this was what was so strange, there was not the slightest hint in the files that Wiklander had gone through.

"It must have been Berg who put them in," said Johansson. "Have you talked with him?"

"No," said Wiklander. "I thought I would wait until I knew a little more."

"Smart," said Johansson. "Find out how they wound up in the file." If for no other reason than to satisfy our curiosity, he thought.

"Yes . . . it's doubtful there will be any indictment against them," observed Wiklander, who was not particularly interested in jurisprudence either as long as real police work was involved.

24

March 2000

Whether Wiklander was only almost as good a police officer as his boss, the legendary Lars Martin Johansson, was actually of no interest, because he was good enough. When the binders on the unsolved murder of Kjell Eriksson on the thirtieth of November 1989 came up from the colleagues in Stockholm, Wiklander closed the door to his office, unplugged the telephone, and, to be on the safe side, turned on the red lightbulb outside his door. Then he set to work.

Before he left for the day he was becoming certain he had figured out how the whole thing fit together, even if he was far from clear about why he felt that. Police intuition, Wiklander thought philosophically, leaning back in his chair to summarize his thoughts before he went home after a long day.

If I try not to make things unnecessarily difficult, thought Wiklander, then the most likely explanation is that both Eriksson and the now deceased TV reporter Welander were two of the four names that had been cleaned out of the registry just over two years ago. But who were the other two?

Personally he was more or less convinced that the broker Tischler must have been one of them, and according to the searches he had already made Tischler was still alive, allowing for the fact that he had left the country ten years ago and was currently registered in Luxembourg. The simple, obvious explanation for Tischler's generosity toward Eriksson must have been that they had a history together that would not bear scrutiny and that Tischler would fall considerably farther than Eriksson if their common secret was revealed.

That left the fourth one who had disappeared from the registry, thought Wiklander. Who was he, or perhaps even she? Despite everything, women were considerably more common in political terrorism than in traditional serious crime, and that must be the motive in this case, he thought.

One of Eriksson's neighbors? It didn't seem particularly likely based on the material he'd found in the investigation. One of his coworkers whom the detectives investigating the murder had missed because they didn't know what they were looking for? Not at all impossible, thought Wiklander, who as a real policeman had a very strong opinion about university graduates in Eriksson's generation. Eriksson's Polish cleaning woman? She was in a good category, thought Wiklander, but the problem with her—he had already checked on his computer—was that she hadn't come to Sweden until 1978, three years after the events at the West German embassy.

It'll work out, thought Wiklander. In any event, he had already turned over lists of all the neighbors, coworkers, and everyone else who appeared in the investigation to his colleagues at the group for internal surveillance. By the time he arrived at work the next day the names would have been checked against the secret police's registry of politically motivated hooligans and of everyone else who just happened to be there. Despite all the truth commissions that the outside world persisted in foisting off on him and his hardworking comrades.

But that wasn't the question that was really interesting. If someone had gone to the trouble of cleaning out those four names just over two years ago, why had two of them been re-inserted in the same registry only a few months ago, and at a time when the top priority was flushing as many names as possible? And why had Tischler avoided making the same round-trip if he had been in the registry from the start, which most of the investigation suggested that he had? Because Tischler, in contrast to the other two, was still alive? Because he had his own channels to power? Because . . .

This'll work itself out too, thought Wiklander, getting up and flexing his computer-stiffened shoulders. As soon as he figured out who the fourth one was, there would be only one completely uninteresting detail remaining, which his colleagues in Stockholm could take care of: who had murdered Kjell Göran Eriksson?

When Wiklander returned to his office the next morning, the lists with the search results were already on his desk. They contained nothing that he had not already figured out or suspected. Only one of the neighbors had produced a hit in SePo's registry. An old Nazi-tainted major who, granted, lived on the same floor as the murder victim. But the mere thought that he could have had anything politically in common with Eriksson, Tischler, and Welander was preposterous. He couldn't have murdered Eriksson either, because the Stockholm Police Department's detectives had given him a better alibi than he really deserved: He had taken part in the celebration of the anniversary of Charles XII's death on the same evening Eriksson was murdered.

You lucky devil, thought Wiklander, whose political views were different from the major's.

A check on Eriksson's former coworkers had produced considerably more hits in the registry. The number was even higher than expected for the office in question, but none of the five individuals whose names came up made Wiklander particularly excited. They had been ordinary members of the far left back then; two were now social democrats, one a liberal, one a conservative, and one a Green; all of them were living in a new era and evidently unworthy even of being rescued from the eyes of the review commission.

Only Eriksson's Polish cleaning woman remained. Even she had her own file up at SePo. Not because she cleaned but because she was Polish and had apparently been involved with at least seven of Wiklander's colleagues within the open operation, who also seemed to have in common the fact that their discretion left a good deal to be desired. Nice-looking woman, thought Wiklander, looking appreciatively at the picture of Jolanta that was in her personal file, but just now you leave me cold, he thought, as he closed it.

· · ·

So instead he tried a different route. Who had reinstated the information about Eriksson and Welander in the file on the embassy drama, despite the manifest lack of interest in the case itself and the fact that both Eriksson and Welander were long dead?

Not Persson, because he'd already retired. Not Berg either, thought Wiklander, though without really knowing why. It doesn't seem like Berg, taking them out and then putting two back in.

Could it have been someone else in the building? After getting the necessary permissions from Johansson he had simply gone around and asked.

Behind the third door he knocked on was a chief inspector with the terrorist squad, who happened to be sitting on the answer.

"It was me," he said, nodding happily at Wiklander. "I was the one who put them in the file."

"May I sit down?" Wiklander asked, looking inquisitively at the vacant chair in front of the desk.

"Of course," said his colleague with the terrorist squad cordially. "Would you like some coffee?"

Half an hour later Wiklander had consumed two cups. In addition he now knew how the names of two corpses had been reinstated in the as yet inconclusive investigation of one of the most serious crimes in Swedish history. On the other hand, he had not become any wiser. Definitely not wiser, thought Wiklander.

Analysts at the military intelligence service had sent in the tip. The chief inspector with the terrorist squad who received it had obviously noticed that the two individuals in question had been dead for some time, but because his informant had also said that there would probably be more tips concerning the same matter, involving individuals who were both alive and not at all uninteresting to SePo, the guy from the terrorist squad had chosen to put them back in.

"You know how finicky our analysts can be," he added by way of explanation.

Was there anyone else, Berg, for example, who had reacted against this measure? Wiklander asked. No one, his colleague summarized, and obviously not Berg, since considering the order of command in their mutual workplace the information wouldn't have been filed over his objections.

"Berg must have approved it," said the chief inspector with the terrorist squad. "A mere chief inspector like myself . . ."

"Yes," said Wiklander. Berg must have approved it, he thought.

"From the fact that you're here I'm guessing that our friends up in the gray building have gotten in touch again, so this doesn't seem to have been completely wrong," said Wiklander's host, winking slyly.

Wiklander nodded in such a way that a sympathetic observer might perhaps have understood as agreement. What rock did they dig you out from under? he thought.

"I have a slight difficulty right now . . . as you'll surely appreciate," said Wiklander evasively. "What we're trying to do is to assess our previous information . . . in light of the new material we've come up with, if you know what I mean."

"I understand perfectly," said the colleague with a smile of mutual understanding, in spite of the fact that he hadn't understood a thing.

"It's true I haven't been here very long," said Wiklander, "but it seems like it's pretty unusual for us to get any tips from those quarters. From the military, I mean."

"Tell me about it. What do you think I was thinking?" The colleague at the terrorist squad nodded with emphasis. "So I asked them straight out where they'd gotten it from—the information they were submitting, that is."

"And?" Wiklander tried to appear eager and appropriately curious.

"They said they got it from the Germans," the chief inspector said, leaning forward and lowering his voice. "From the lads at the BND. And because it wasn't any of their business, they handed it off to me . . . well, to us that is."

"The BND," said Wiklander, who was new to secret ops and had not yet gone through any courses.

"Bundesnachrichtendienst," answered the chief inspector. "Which as you surely know is the Germans' counterpart to the CIA."

"You don't say," said Wiklander, making an effort to appear at least somewhat shrewd. "Any idea how they got hold of it? The BND, that is," he clarified.

The chief inspector wiggled his right palm.

"Nobody's talking about it, as you can appreciate. But some things you figure out for yourself and some things don't need to be said. That part was more implicit," Wiklander's host replied.

"Wait a second," said Wiklander. "Did anyone say . . . or did anyone not say—that they got the information from the BND?"

"That's not the kind of thing you say," said the chief inspector deprecatingly. "It would be a real dereliction of duty if you said that sort of thing."

"You figured it out anyway?" asked Wiklander.

"Of course I did," said the chief inspector contentedly. "I don't know if you know, but around that time the Germans found some previously unknown material in the old Stasi archives. It was the so-called SIRA archive, which, among other things, contained a lot of names of their old spies and political sympathizers abroad. There was also quite a lot of information from the seventies and eighties, so that even a child could figure out what had happened—when the Germans found out about it, I mean. Well, and then we got it. Of course it was here in Stockholm that the shit hit the fan. And I can't rule out that this was just their way of tweaking our noses. Even if it'll soon be twenty-five years since those leftist maniacs blew up the West German embassy."

"You'll have to excuse me," said Wiklander, "but why in the name of God didn't Stasi get rid of the papers in that SIRA archive?"

"The official explanation is that they didn't have time. They had a shortage of shredders," the terrorist chief inspector said comfortably. "Fate bestows her favors unevenly. They should have called me. They could have borrowed as many as they wanted."

This is getting stranger and stranger, thought Wiklander as he returned to his office. High time to talk with the boss.

Johansson immediately made room in his schedule, and a few hours later Wiklander reported his findings.

"This is getting stranger and stranger," said Johansson. "Here's what we'll do," he continued, nodding encouragingly at Wiklander.

"I'm listening," said Wiklander.

"I think you're completely right about Eriksson, Welander, and

Tischler," said Johansson. "Try to find out who the fourth one is, and then I'll see if Berg has any ideas. At least he'll be able to tell me why he removed them from the file two years ago."

"If you're going to talk with him anyway you might as well ask him how common it was back in his day for us to get help from the military," Wiklander suggested.

"Well, I know what it's like these days," said Johansson with a wide grin. "They seem to finally understand that these are new times. Nowadays we're greeted with standing ovations. I had dinner with the supreme commander last week."

"And it was nice," said Wiklander neutrally. Whatever that has to do with anything, he thought.

"Yeah," said Johansson. "I got the impression that attitudes have changed somewhat." Although the food was only so-so, he thought.

"Let's hope so," said Wiklander. "We still owe our salaries to the same taxpayers." Although they seem to have considerably better per diems than we do, he thought. At least that's what he'd heard at one of the courses he'd taken since getting his new job.

"Joking aside," said Johansson, suddenly looking serious. "If they're just fucking with us, they won't get away with it. I didn't have that good a time. Find the fourth man for us, and I'll take care of the foreign policy. And see if Jarnebring has any ideas. I just remembered he was involved in the investigation of Eriksson's murder," said Johansson, who had finally put the pieces together after Wiklander had recounted the case from 1989.

"The fourth man," said Wiklander. "I'm on it."

As soon as Wiklander left, Johansson called Berg at home. It was high time, even just for social reasons. It had been more than a month since they'd last talked.

Berg's wife answered. She sounded tired and depressed. Her husband was not at home and might be gone for a few more days. Could she ask him to call Johansson when he came back? She would ask, but she couldn't promise anything. And as soon as she had said A she also said B.

Her husband had been admitted to a radiation clinic for treatment. He had been several times during the past six months and she did not want Johansson to tell anyone about it. She herself had promised her husband that.

"Erik has cancer," she said. "We have to hope for the best."

"If there's anything I can do . . ." said Johansson. What do I say now? he thought.

"I promise to tell him that you called," Berg's wife interrupted, "and if it's something to do with work then maybe you should try talking with Persson," she suggested.

Johansson sighed as he hung up, and suddenly he felt gloomy, even though Berg wasn't exactly a close friend. I'll have to try Persson, he thought, looking up the number on his computer. At least he isn't dying of cancer, thought Johansson. Not with all that fat and that blood pressure.

"Yes," said Persson, succeeding in a single word at sounding as cheerful as Berg's wife had when she had answered the phone.

"Do you have time to meet?" said Johansson, who was more like Persson than he realized and wasn't going to risk any small talk.

"If you want, you can have roast pork and brown beans in an hour," said Persson morosely. "If you want a drink you'll have to bring it with you. I'm all out here at home."

"I'll stop at the liquor store, then I'll see you in an hour," said Johansson heartily. That's a real old-time policeman there, he thought. He himself had all the time in the world. His wife was away at a conference, and the alternative would have been to eat alone or in the company of the TV. Without having any idea of Persson's domestic talents he was willing to take the risk.

25

March 2000

Persson lived in Råsunda, in one of the old fin de siècle buildings north of the soccer stadium. On the way there Johansson had his taxi stop at Solna Centrum while he trotted into the state liquor store and bought some strong beer, a bottle of pure aquavit, and half a bottle of Grönstedts cognac. No reason to be stingy, thought Johansson. If his meeting with Persson didn't produce any results he could always enter it as a work expense, to be forwarded to that myth-enshrouded blue book, the royal realm of Sweden's most secure storage place for such information.

I never cease to be amazed, thought Johansson half an hour later as he sat in the kitchen of Persson's small two-room apartment while his host was just pouring a refill in their shot glasses. If Johansson remembered correctly, Persson had lived as a bachelor since separating from his wife in the early seventies, and at work he had been known for going around, regardless of the season, in the same gray suit, same yellowing nylon shirt, and same mottled tie.

At his place there was the smell of cleanser and polished floors. It was as tidy as a dollhouse, and not much bigger. Given that Persson weighed close to four hundred pounds, he was like an elephant in a china shop. An elephant, however, who had the gracefulness of a ballerina and who was as skilled in the art of cooking as Johansson's beloved aunt Jenny. In the good old days she'd been in charge of the bar at the

Grand Hotel in Kramfors and had supplied both lumber barons and ordinary gamekeepers with the finer things in life.

"This is damned good," said Johansson emphatically, and because his wife was at a safe distance at a conference in southern Sweden he was finally free to let loose both his genetically inherited Norrland taste buds and his always tight-fitting belt.

"Real men should have good food," Persson muttered, rocking his shot glass meaningfully. "By the way, I heard you got married."

"Yeah," said Johansson. "Although it's been a while now." A little over ten years to be more exact. You're your usual self, thought Johansson, feeling almost moved by Persson's concern.

"Personally I've had the same thought since I got divorced," said Persson, as if thinking out loud. "But it never worked out. Though I do have a lady friend I see now and then."

"Oh yeah?" said Johansson. What the hell should I say? he thought. I can't really ask if she's nice.

"She's a good woman," said Persson, reading Johansson's mind. "She's Finnish. Works in home services, but she's going to retire soon too. We've talked about buying something in Spain."

"It's supposed to be a little warmer there." Persson in Spain, thought Johansson. Where the hell do people get such ideas?

"Yes, I guess I'm afraid of that," Persson sighed. "Skoal then."

Then they toasted, turned their attention to the food, made coffee, and went to sit in Persson's living room to talk police work.

"You're a good fellow, Johansson," said Persson. "Aquavit and Grön-stedts," he continued, nodding at his large cognac glass. "It's risk-free sending you to the liquor store. I knew that all along. What can I help you with?"

"The West German embassy," said Johansson. Just as well to get this cleared up now so we can talk old memories, thought Johansson.

"If you mean the West German embassy in April '75, well, that was before I came to SePo," said Persson. "I was working at the old burglary squad at the time. With a lot of tattooed idiots who were high as kites and rummaged around in people's apartments all day long."

"After that," said Johansson. "Since you came to SePo?" I wonder why he doesn't ask why I'm asking? he thought.

"I was in on that case in '89," said Persson. "It was Berg who asked me. It was at the very end of '89, in December."

Johansson just nodded. More's coming, he thought. You couldn't rush Persson.

"It was in connection with a murder," said Persson. "Berg wanted me to check up on a Kjell Göran Eriksson who had been killed on the evening of the thirtieth of November. It was roughly the same time as those bastards were about to burn down the whole city to celebrate that Charles XII was dead." Persson shook his head and took a substantial sip from his glass.

"Why was he interested in him?" asked Johansson.

"It had something to do with the West German embassy," said Persson. "I don't know how much you know, but—"

"A little," said Johansson, nodding at him to continue.

"You didn't have to be much of a policeman to figure out that the Germans inside the embassy must have had help from some of our domestic talents . . . on the outside. I did that myself when I was working at burglary and trying to knock a little sense into the thieves," said Persson.

"How did Eriksson come into the picture?" Johansson asked.

"He was one of the ones who helped the Germans," said Persson, looking almost surprised at the question. "Berg figured that out almost immediately. He was a capable cop, Erik. At that time," said Persson, and for some reason he grinned at Johansson. "Before he became a fine fellow . . . if you know what I mean, Lars?"

"I know what you mean," said Johansson, and he smiled too. "I know exactly what you mean," he added with more emphasis than he perhaps had intended.

"Are you wondering why Eriksson didn't get sent to prison?" asked Persson, who could definitely read minds. "Him and his other buddies."

"Yes," said Johansson. "Why didn't he?"

"Yup," said Persson, sighing. "That was before my time. You should really ask Berg about it, but . . ."

"I'm asking you instead," said Johansson.

"I know," said Persson, suddenly looking rather mournful. "Erik's wife called before you showed up."

"How are things with him?" said Johansson.

"He's dying," said Persson. "So . . . that's how it is with him. And since you're asking, as far as I'm concerned he should have been able to live to the end of his life. Sixty-five is no great age, is it?"

No, thought Johansson. Sixty-five is no great age. Not when you've passed fifty, like he had, or would soon turn sixty-seven, like his colleague Persson in the armchair across from him.

"There were certainly several reasons that Eriksson and his friends were not brought in," said Persson. "I'm a policeman, so politics has never been my strong suit, but if you ask me . . ." Persson shook his head and poured another cognac.

"You went in and looked at the murder investigation," Johansson reminded him. "Why did you do that?"

"If you ask me," said Persson contemplatively, "it was for the same reason we didn't put little Eriksson away for his collaboration at the West German embassy."

"And that was?" asked Johansson.

"I guess it had become a little awkward for others besides Eriksson," said Persson. "Because he was working for us—among other things, trying to keep track of all the other student bastards who weren't content with just throwing tomatoes at people like you and me," said Persson.

I thought as much, thought Johansson. It was what had struck him as he sat in the taxi en route to Persson's place.

Then they talked about Eriksson's past as an informant for the secret police, an assignment he had devoted himself to during his entire active period within various parts of the acronym-ridden and lunatic left, counting the time from the late sixties to the mid-seventies.

"Then they hung him out to dry," said Persson. "It was after the West German embassy that Berg decided he should be hung out to dry."

"But you made no attempt to confront him?" Johansson asked.

Allowing for the fact that Persson himself had not been involved at that time, he was nonetheless certain that no such attempt had been made. Eriksson had been far too mixed up with the secret police for any-one to dare risk something like that. He had even been on the salary list for so-called external coworkers at Sec for a rather long time.

"The bastard swindled us out of several thousand in the midst of all this," Persson sighed.

"You think he was playing double?" asked Johansson.

"Yes," said Persson. "True, I never met him, but I understood from what people said that this guy was a real little dung fly. If there was any shit anywhere, he'd be sure to land on it."

"It can't have been the case that he was the one who infiltrated you all," Johansson asked. And let you pick up the tab to add a little spice to the arrangement, he thought.

"No," said Persson. "He was just the kind of guy who likes to keep his options open. We had other informants too, thank God, and you should have heard what they thought of Eriksson. At the time of the West German embassy takeover it was probably as simple as Eriksson abandoning us because he got the idea that it was probably the Red Guards who would win the day. He doesn't seem to have been a great political thinker, and he wasn't exactly faithful either."

"I understand he wasn't particularly pleasant," said Johansson.

"A jerk," said Persson with conviction. "Pity he was already protected when I started."

But it was good luck for Eriksson, thought Johansson, sneaking a glance at Persson's right hand wrapped around the cognac glass.

Eriksson had accomplices. They got off too. Johansson wanted to know why.

"There was no way to get around Eriksson, it seems," Persson sighed. "How would that have looked? They didn't want to bring him in, so the others he'd been in league with get off the hook too. Besides, they weren't really much to hang on the Christmas tree . . . well, with one exception of course."

"You mean Welander," said Johansson, who had figured out a few things himself after his conversation with Wiklander.

"Fucking Red Guard," said Persson, riled up. "For a long time I was hoping that malignant asshole would take a false step, but he was a clever bastard. He got out while there was still time."

"What about the other two," said Johansson with an innocent expression.

"Who do you mean?" said Persson, suddenly sounding normal again.

"Tischler and the fourth guy," said Johansson as if he had simply forgotten the name.

"Tischler," Persson snorted. "He only got involved using his father's money, mostly because it was an easy way to meet willing ladies. True, I wasn't the one who did that investigation, but if there's anything I've learned it's to separate good police work from bad, and there were no major faults with the investigation Berg ordered done. I thought you'd read it?"

"No," said Johansson. "I'm guessing it disappeared two years ago when you pulled it out of the file."

"Orders from Berg," said Persson curtly, "and this isn't me gossiping. He and I have already talked about it. And what do you mean by 'pulled it out' anyway? I put together what I was told to put together, placed it in a couple of binders, and gave it to Erik. It's not my business to have opinions about what he did with it later."

"And you have no idea what he did with it?" asked Johansson with an innocent expression.

"No," said Persson. "You don't ask about that sort of thing."

Although you seem to have managed to do quite a bit anyway, thought Johansson.

How had they found out about Eriksson, Welander, Tischler, and that mysterious "fourth man" almost twenty-five years ago?

"I wasn't there, like I said," said Persson. "Not when it started anyway."

"But you've read the investigation," said Johansson.

"Sure," said Persson. "I've spent a few hours looking at it, and like I said it was not a bad investigation. Berg ran it, and at that time he was no slouch. That I can assure you."

"Tell me," said Johansson.

It had not even been particularly demanding, according to Persson. Welander had evidently driven the car when the terrorists' messages were turned over to TT and the other news agencies in the Hötorg skyscraper. Eriksson was the one who got to take the elevator up and put the message in the mailbox while Welander stayed behind in the car out on the street and waited.

"Welander was moonlighting at the TV station at that time, so it was actually a journalist at TT who was working in the Hötorg skyscraper where the TV station had an officer who recognized Welander outside the building and thought it was a strange coincidence. He tipped us off, and then Berg and the other colleagues were on a roll. Erik set up the whole apparatus," said Persson, seeming not exactly displeased.

"The whole apparatus," Johansson nodded, sounding just as delighted as he suddenly felt.

"The whole apparatus," Persson nodded, "plus a lot of things that not even you and Jarnebring would have dreamed of trying."

"So what did they do besides delivering mail?" asked Johansson. That particular detail must have suited Eriksson to a T, he thought.

"They were the ones who arranged all the practical details for the Germans," said Persson. "Room and board, local knowledge, transport, even some of the explosives they used most likely came from their Swedish contacts. It was ordinary Swedish-made Dynamex from Nobel—our technicians figured that out—mixed with that Czech grease they always used. Welander was the boss and Eriksson was the helper, running around like a rat on fire. He also got paid, the bastard. The Germans gave him thousands of deutschmarks to buy food and drink, but for some reason it was mostly hash he put on the table for them."

"How does Tischler come into the picture?" asked Johansson.

"The Germans were staying with him before the embassy occupation. Tischler's dad owned some big-ass summer place out on Värmdö where they were all having sex while they organized the final details. It was pretty ideally located, isolated and discreet and just half an hour into town by car. Although Tischler's own role in this whole thing is actually a little unclear."

"What do you mean by that?" asked Johansson.

"A few weeks after the West German embassy he looked up

Welander—by then we already had surveillance on Welander. Tischler was more or less crazed, screaming and yelling that Welander had exploited him. . . . He was extremely agitated. Our colleagues reported that they didn't even have to plant any microphones to listen to the conversation. Tischler seems to have been living under the delusion that this plot was about helping some German comrades—the usual student radicals—by keeping them away from the West German police. He had no idea they were going to blow up the West German embassy and try to kill the personnel."

"In any event he seems to have figured out how things stood afterward," said Johansson.

"Sure," said Persson. "In that regard he was a hell of a lot smarter than the member of parliament who helped Kröcher escape, because he had no idea what he was mixed up in, and after having read the interrogations with him I think I believe him. Even though it goes against my usual inclinations," said Persson. "He seems to have been your typical aspiring socialist member of parliament," he summarized, chuckling so that his massive belly was jumping.

"The fourth man then," said Johansson.

"Even more unclear than Tischler," said Persson. "I would go so far as to say I would have left him out if it had come down to it."

"Better safe than sorry," said Johansson.

"More or less," said Persson. "There were slightly unusual circumstances. Besides, in that case you should probably talk with Berg," Persson concluded.

"It's pointless to ask you about it," said Johansson.

"Yes . . . even you couldn't manage to bring that much aquavit here," said Persson.

Don't say that, thought Johansson, but naturally he didn't say it. Better to come back, he thought.

Why had Berg decided to remove the two names from the file two years ago? For a couple of reasons, according to Persson. They were linked to an investigation that had been stone dead for more than twenty years and that no one wanted to touch anymore, for one.

"Times are a little different now," said Persson.

Although the Germans could probably still keep from laughing if they found out about Eriksson's background and his involvement in the occupation of the West German embassy, thought Johansson. But he hadn't come to Persson's place to quarrel, so he decided instead to wrap things up and get what he came for.

"Welander and Eriksson were put back in the file again a few months ago," said Johansson. "Were you aware of that?"

"No," said Persson, sounding genuinely surprised. "I had no idea. I don't know why Erik would go along with that."

"Why do you think he did?" asked Johansson.

"Maybe because they were the ones it was really all about," said Persson. "The other two were just along for the ride. Welander was the driving force and Eriksson was his assistant. That Welander was one unpleasant bastard. There was a good deal of material on him that wasn't about the West German embassy, and there was no question that he had some very peculiar contacts."

"With West German terrorists?" asked Johansson.

"With the circles around them in any case. Their sympathizers, and there were quite a few at that time. Besides, our counterparts at counterespionage were pretty sure he had contacts with the East Germans . . . well, with the Stasi then. So he was lucky he got a job in TV, because that way he was safe from us," said Persson, sighing. "If you only knew, Johansson . . ." Persson shook his head. "For a while we could have put handcuffs on half the workforce at that fucking place. If we were to believe what was in our own papers, that is."

"Exactly what I'm avoiding," said Johansson.

"What else would you expect?" said Persson with conviction. "If Berg promised he would clean up for you, he will. If he has put Welander and Eriksson back in the file, he must have had good reason for doing so."

"Let's hope so," said Johansson piously. I'll believe it when I see it, he thought.

"Well . . ." said Persson with a sigh, taking the opportunity to fill his glass again.

"They were dead anyway, which is a good thing if you want peace and quiet in the midst of a disclosure. The truth commission . . ." Persson snorted. "A lot of crazy academics who don't know a rat's ass about police work."

"One more question," said Johansson, saving the last drop in his glass. "You'll have to excuse me for harping on about this, but who was the fourth one? The fourth man?"

"So that's what you're wondering about," said Persson, grinning. "It was pure chance that we stumbled on the fourth one in the group, and it actually happened in my time. If we were going to put the first three in jail, naturally we would have done so right from the start. But we didn't do that of course."

"So who was it?" said Johansson.

"You know what," said Persson. "From what I've heard over the years, you are said to be the absolute shrewdest person ever to set foot in our beloved police station on Kungsholmen, so I think it will be more than enough if you get the same tip that I got. Just to keep an old retiree from getting dragged into your investigation. And besides, you can get it straight from the horse's own mouth."

"You're the one who figured out who it was?" asked Johansson.

"Of course," said Persson self-assuredly. "Although it wasn't some inner inspiration. That has never happened to me so far," Persson chuckled.

"You got a tip," said Johansson. That hasn't ever happened to me either, he thought.

"I found a memo from a colleague that wound up in the wrong binder. It was as simple as that," said Persson, grinning contentedly. "Talk to our colleague Stridh. You know that lazy ass who worked in the patrol cars. He's still there, isn't he?"

"Stridh," said Johansson. "Do you mean Peace at Any Price?" He's pulling my leg, thought Johansson.

"The very same," said Persson. "Although he himself probably hasn't understood how things really stood, if you ask me. No sir," Persson continued. "Now let's have a good time and have a little whiskey. I have a fine old bottle in the pantry out in the kitchen. I got it from my lady friend the last time I had a birthday, so there's no need to panic. Tell me about your new wife, by the way. I've heard that she is one outstandingly fine-looking lady."

"Sure, she's good-looking," said Johansson, "she is that." And she's nice too, he thought. Stridh, he thought. Could that fuckup Stridh have figured out what both he and Wiklander, and his best friend Bo Jarnebring too for that matter, had missed?

26

March 2000

It was Wiklander who, on orders from Johansson, went to question Stridh at home about the fourth man. It had been a late one for Johansson the night before—many old memories to be aired—yet there must be limits to what liberties a top-level boss like Johansson could take. Working out in the field was all well and good, and eating roast pork and brown beans at home with a former colleague was probably fine, but conducting an interview with yet another colleague the very next morning was a little too much. Besides, in Johansson's case he had hundreds of coworkers available, and Wiklander was certainly better suited for the task than anyone else.

Stridh was home, of course. Within the corps he was known for being something of a comp time equivalent to soccer's Diego Maradona, so it was obvious that he would be home on a Friday when even a child could figure out that there was likely to be a lot of police work over the weekend.

"You're probably wondering why I want to talk with you," said Wiklander collegially when the introductory preludes were over and the mandatory coffee was on the kitchen table.

"I have my suspicions," said Stridh.

"You do," said Wiklander.

"Yes," said Stridh. "I've worked more than thirty years as a cop, and all that time I've had a visit from SePo only once before—that was

Persson—that big fat guy, you know—and that was more than ten years ago, so I'm guessing you're here for the same reason. West German embassy?"

"Yes," said Wiklander. "I want to talk with you about your observations in connection with the events at the West German embassy in April of 1975. Unfortunately I can't go into why and you can't tell anyone that we've even seen each other either—much less had this conversation—but I'm sure you already know all that," Wiklander concluded, softening the whole thing by nodding and smiling.

"Yes," said Stridh. "I've been around awhile so I do know that. As I'm sure you're also aware, I wrote a few pages about the matter, it was the day after—let's see, that would be the twenty-fifth of April 1975. I assume you've read them?"

"Unfortunately not," said Wiklander, who had decided to save time and put his cards on the table as far as possible. "Your papers seem to have disappeared in one of our archives." You could put it that way, he thought.

"Yes, that's really strange," said Stridh. "The very idea of an archive is that it should be a way to ensure that that sort of thing doesn't happen, but sometimes you almost wonder if it isn't the other way around. I have a certain interest in history," said Stridh. "To be completely honest, it's probably my major interest in life."

"You wrote a memo," Wiklander reminded him. Pull yourself together, old man, he thought.

"I even made a copy of it," said Stridh smugly, "so in this case I can actually help you repair the damage . . . as regards the failure in the archiving," Stridh clarified. "This is perhaps not completely in accordance with the rules, of course," he continued, "but considering it's for a good cause . . . Besides, I had the idea that maybe I had been involved in a historic event and because history is my big interest—"

"That's just great," Wiklander interrupted, smiling amiably. "But perhaps you should start by telling me a little about the background, and then . . . we can look at the papers later."

"Sure," said Stridh. "I'm happy to do that."

Then Stridh talked about the mysterious car that he had stopped. About his conversation with the doorman at the Norwegian embassy and the purely general speculations he'd had before, during, and after what had happened on Thursday the twenty-fourth of April 1975. Not unexpectedly, he took his sweet time doing so.

"That was a dreadful story," Stridh declared. "I remember I was thinking about what Churchill said to his countrymen during the war. The Germans probably should have taken that to heart a little more than they did."

"What do you mean?" asked Wiklander, who happened to think of his old history teacher from secondary school at home in Karlstad. Stridh could be a brother to old Nightcap, thought Wiklander.

"Well, if you believed the newspapers, the colleagues at Sec—or SePo, as it seems to be called these days—warned them that something was up," Stridh clarified.

"I was thinking about what you said about Churchill," Wiklander reminded him. Just as confused as old Nightcap, thought Wiklander. They must be twins or at least spiritual brothers.

"Yes, him, yes," said Stridh, nodding. "What I was thinking about was how he said that 'he who is forewarned is also forearmed.' 'He who is forewarned is also forearmed,' " Stridh quoted solemnly. "I think that what happened to the Germans shows—if nothing else—what can happen if we don't learn from history. Or what do you think?"

"Well . . . yes," agreed Wiklander. "Maybe we should look at those notes you wrote." And preferably before summer gets here, he thought.

In its essentials, the memo Stridh had prepared was exemplary. One might have opinions about the organization, use of language, and his typing skills, but if you disregarded that and directed yourself to the police-related meat and potatoes, it was basically unobjectionable.

He had noted the license number of the car he had stopped as well as the time and place. He had looked up the car himself in the vehicle registry. A large 1973 Mercedes that was registered to a pediatrician in private practice by the name of Rolf Stein whose address at that time was on Riddargatan in the Östermalm neighborhood.

The driver's name he had evidently committed to memory well enough that the following day he managed to find him in the driver's license registry. His name was Sten Welander, and he was born in 1947 and got his driver's license in 1965.

All this was good enough, but Stridh had done more than that; he had made a serious attempt to identify the younger female passenger Welander had with him. According to Stridh "the young woman in question was probably one Helena Lovisa Stein, known as Helena, whose registered address was the same as the above-named Stein, Rolf. Helena Stein, born on September 10, 1958, was the daughter of the above-mentioned Stein, Rolf."

"Perhaps you're wondering why I think that?" Stridh asked.

"Wonder what?" said Wiklander, who was starting to experience a certain lack of concentration.

"That the girl in the car was the same as a certain Helena Stein," Stridh clarified. "Perhaps you're wondering why I think that?"

"Yes," said Wiklander, nodding energetically. "How did you come to that conclusion?" I've got to pull myself together, he thought. I'm the one who's doing the questioning.

"Well," said Stridh, clearing his throat, "as I told you, she mentioned something—when I stopped their car—about it being her parents' car, or else she said that it was her father's car—but it was one of the two— so that was my starting point, and then—"

"So you looked her up in the census," Wiklander quickly interrupted.

"Exactly," said Stridh, actually looking a bit disappointed.

"But that's just great," Wiklander said sincerely. "I'm very grateful for your assistance."

"As you see in my memo I tried to make a description of her features," Stridh added, "so my suggestion is that you try to retrieve a school photo or something of her from that time and compare it. But I'm actually rather sure—Stein had only one daughter and it was Helena. Extremely cute girl actually. I have a very good memory for faces, so if you produce a photo of her you're welcome to come back."

"I thank you for that offer," said Wiklander evasively, and he had already stood up. Come back here? God help me, he thought.

. . .

When Wiklander finally returned to the relative safety and peace of his desk he pondered the conceivable "fourth man." Wiklander had no great problem with the fact that "he" would probably prove to be a young woman. Many of the most active members of the European terrorist movements at that time had been women.

On the other hand she was far too young even for that, Wiklander thought. Sixteen years old when the embassy drama took place, or sixteen and a half if you were to be exact the way little children always were when stating their age. Regardless of which, she was too young in a strictly criminological sense, and the only reasonable explanation must be that she had been dragged into something she didn't completely understand, for in that case it was more of an advantage the younger you were, he thought. A radical, politically involved sixteen-year-old? Sounded both probable and correct. A sixteen-year-old who could have taken an active part in the most spectacular political attack in Swedish postwar history and the cold-blooded murder of two people? Forget it, thought Wiklander, who had a daughter the same age himself. She must have been taken in.

In the simplest version of events, she was involved with and had been exploited by a boyfriend almost twice her age. A twenty-eight-year-old academic and TV reporter who was involved with a sixteen-year-old doctor's daughter from a good family during the liberated seventies? It could happen—but there were still limits, Wiklander thought as he filled in his list of questions for internal surveillance. It'll work out, thought Wiklander, who felt secure in his conviction that regardless of what the explanation was, his coworkers would dig it out for him.

Wiklander devoted the rest of the afternoon to routine tasks mostly related to things other than the West German embassy. After an hour his assistant head detective called on the phone to report that she and her colleague had just retrieved a photo of Helena Stein from the photo studio that in the seventies had taken pictures for the French School on Döbelnsgatan in central Stockholm.

"Excellent," Wiklander grunted, returning to his quickly receding pile of papers. This is going like a dance, he thought.

After another half hour the same detective phoned and reported that Helena Stein was now identified as the "fourth man." A photo identification had been conducted at Stridh's kitchen table at home, and he had immediately and without hesitation pointed her out from among a dozen different photos depicting her classmates, which had been obtained from the same photographer.

"Brilliant," said Wiklander. We're going like gangbusters now, he thought.

Only fifteen minutes later there was a knock on his door, despite the fact that the red light was on.

"Come in," Wiklander called.

In the door stood yet another of his many female coworkers, this one from their own group for internal surveillance. Despite the fact that she looked like a little girl in an old Swedish folk ballad, she was a detective inspector whose name was Lisa Mattei. Her mother was a detective chief inspector with the personal protection squad of the secret police, thirty years older and far from the female ideal of the folk ballad.

"This is about this Stein," said Mattei.

"Yes," said Wiklander energetically. "Are you through with her?"

"Depends on what you mean by through," said Mattei, raising her slender shoulders in a gesture of indifference. "In any event, she seems interesting enough," she said, handing a computer printout to Wiklander. "Read the top lines and you'll see what I mean."

This can't be true, Wiklander thought as he read. Then he set the paper down on his desk and looked at his coworker.

"Do you know whether the boss is here?" he asked.

"Which one do you mean?" Mattei said, looking rather impertinent.

"Johansson," said Wiklander. No messing around now, he thought.

"He just came in," said Mattei. "I'm guessing he's sitting in his office having Danish pastries. On several previous occasions I've noted remnants on the lapel of his jacket that indicate such activities."

It's always something, Wiklander thought, but naturally he didn't say that.

"Not a word," he said. "Not a word to anyone."

. . .

It was true that Johansson also had a red lamp beside the door to his office, but it was almost never lit. This was because if you wanted to go into his office, you first had to pass the office where his secretary sat, and there was no red lamp in the world that could compare with her.

"Is the boss in?" said Wiklander to Johansson's secretary, nodding to be on the safe side at the closed door behind her back.

"Yes," the secretary said coolly. "But he's occupied and doesn't want to be disturbed."

"It's like this, you see," said Wiklander, looking as if he meant it besides, "I have to see him immediately."

"Has the enemy landed on our coasts?" the secretary asked, giving Wiklander a very cool glance as she tapped on the keyboard in front of her.

"Something along those lines," said Wiklander, nodding.

"Then it's okay to go in," the secretary said, gesturing toward the closed door behind her back at the same time as a discreet click of the lock could be heard.

Johansson was sitting in the chair behind his large desk, drinking coffee and munching on a sizeable Danish pastry.

"Sit yourself down," said Johansson jovially, pointing toward one of his three visitors chairs. "What can I help you with? Unfortunately you can't have any Danish because I just took the last one, but I'm sure I can arrange coffee."

"It's fine," said Wiklander, hoping he didn't sound the way he felt.

"You seem harried," Johansson asserted. "Do we have a problem?"

"Depends on what you mean by problem," said Wiklander, sounding rather evasive. Is it a problem if all hell's broken loose? he thought.

"We've identified the fourth man," said Wiklander. Best to take this in an orderly sequence, he thought.

"But that's just great," said Johansson. What's the problem? he wondered.

"The fourth man is a woman born in 1958," Wiklander continued.

"And we're quite sure about that," said Johansson. Forty-two years old, an excellent age for a woman, he thought; he himself had a wife who was only a few years older.

"As certain as we can be," said Wiklander.

"What's the problem then?" asked Johansson. Sixteen, seventeen years old at the time of the West German embassy, a bit on the young side, thought Johansson.

"This," said Wiklander, handing over the same computer printout he had received five minutes earlier.

"So what's this?" said Johansson, not making the slightest motion to reach out for the paper.

"I asked one of the gals in our internal surveillance squad to do a complete search on her, but when she started on it our internal warning system came on, because the colleagues who do background checks are already in the middle of a complete workup on her."

"So why are they doing that?" Johansson asked.

"The woman in question is named Helena Stein and she's an undersecretary in the defense department," said Wiklander. "She's an attorney, and before she became an undersecretary in the defense department she worked for a number of years in the prime minister's office and at the ministry of foreign trade on issues dealing with our manufacture and export of war matériel. She took her current job in the defense department two years ago. A background check was made on her then as well, and she seems to have passed without any problems. All undersecretaries have a high security clearance as you no doubt know, Boss—and in her particular case it's even higher than the majority of other undersecretaries. Maybe that isn't so strange considering her job," Wiklander concluded.

"I should damn well think I know who Stein is," said Johansson, look-ing almost amused. In his case it would have been dereliction of duty not to know the name of the undersecretary in the defense department, and that she had apparently disappeared from their files at roughly the same time she was appointed undersecretary did not of course make the matter any less interesting, he thought.

"But that's not the problem," said Wiklander.

"So what is it?" asked Johansson. This is getting better and better, he thought.

"The reason they're doing a new background check on her now is that the prime minister's office requested one yesterday. This concerns the absolute highest existing level of secrecy, and they want it to be done with the greatest possible speed and well in advance of the government meeting in fourteen days."

"So why do they want one?" asked Johansson, despite the fact that he already sensed the answer. There aren't that many jobs to choose from, he thought, and his own was already taken.

"Because the prime minister apparently intends to appoint her as a member of the government," said Wiklander, "and considering her new security level she wouldn't be handling consumer issues or social insurance," Wiklander added. What in the name of God should I do? he thought.

Christ, thought Johansson. It was already pretty late anyway, he thought, but naturally he didn't say that. Acting prime minister . . . coordination minister . . . or perhaps even foreign minister or defense minister? And it didn't matter which, considering the problem that had just surfaced.

"Not a word to anyone, Wiklander," said Johansson, pointing at his coworker with his whole hand. "Not a word to anyone. Is that understood?"

Now it was a matter of thinking, and thinking sharp, thought Johansson.

27

March 2000

Seems like old shit has landed in a new fan, thought Johansson half an hour later when he was through thinking. Then he quickly made three decisions, which he made sure to carry out immediately.

First he informed his boss, the general director, of the unfortunate coincidence between his and Wiklander's investigation and the prime minister's impending appointment. Johansson was not stupid, and because he intended to go further, he wanted to make sure he had all the clearance he could need.

The GD might not have been as cunning as Johansson, for he had seemed almost energized by the news, and when he stated his one, concrete wish, which was to be informed of developments as the case proceeded, it was with curiosity shining from his eyes.

"Of course, Boss," said Johansson, who could not have asked for more.

Next Johansson had a directive issued to his coworkers who were conducting the background checks on Stein. Not a comma—regardless of content or intent—that concerned Helena Lovisa Stein could now leave the building without his approval. And if anyone in Rosenbad was wondering about anything—even if they just wanted to know what time it was—they should be referred to Johansson.

I need people too, thought Johansson. Not that many, but enough, and only the best. People who can work uninterruptedly until this is cleared up and who can fulfill their assignments despite the fact that the person who leads the assignment may be compelled to withhold information that the team members, for various reasons, may not or should not know about.

"Do you think you can arrange it?" said Johansson, nodding at Wiklander.

"Yes," said Wiklander. "It's already done. I've already assigned everyone we need."

The third decision was the most difficult, and so it had to wait until last. Johansson steeled himself and called Berg at home, and surprisingly enough Berg himself answered.

"I'm sorry to disturb you," said Johansson, "but I need to see you immediately."

"Then I suggest you come over to my place," said Berg. His voice sounded tired and muted, but he did not seem particularly surprised.

"Sit down," said Berg half an hour later, pointing toward the empty armchair in his office. "Would you like coffee?"

"Not unless you're having some," said Johansson. You're dying, he thought, and it was more a statement than an expression of sorrow or even emotion. Pull yourself together, Johansson thought, and it was himself and not Berg he was thinking about.

"Then we won't have coffee," said Berg, smiling wanly as he carefully sat down in a straight-backed chair across from the armchair he had shown his guest.

"What can I help you with?" Berg asked.

"Putting some order into old recollections from another time," said Johansson.

"It's about the West German embassy, isn't it," said Berg, and this was more a statement than a question.

"Yes," said Johansson.

"Then I'll tell you the whole story," said Berg.

Part 5

Another Time

IX

Erich Honecker had fooled them all. They never believed he would have dared, but he'd done it, and considering the life he'd lived and the dangers he had undergone, maybe it wasn't really so strange that he had taken the risk. After that, everything he had done followed a simple logic, and in principle it was all based on keeping his opponents in the dark. He had succeeded far beyond expectations, most likely because of something as simple as the fact that those he fooled had lived different, more secure lives than he had.

At the Party conference in Dresden in September 1977, in his speech to the members, Honecker had distanced himself firmly from West German terrorism, and the old shawm player had not minced words when he did so: "These despicable hordes of anarchists and terrorists who are wreaking havoc in the Federal Republic make it possible for the West German regime to silence the political left in the country under the pretext of battling so-called terrorist sympathizers."

Predictable rhetoric, to be sure, but also an official confirmation of what the Western security agencies, all the way from those most closely affected—the West German Federal Crime Agency and Federal Intelligence Service—to the Americans at the CIA and NSA, already thought they had figured out. It was the Arabs who were helping the European terrorists. The Russians, certain of their satellites in the Warsaw Pact, might possibly be suspected of having supplied them with money, weapons, and explosives on some occasion—in a pinch, and by complicated paths—but not the East Germans. They would never have dared. And now Honecker had put his honor at stake that his country was not involved with such things.

Actually, the West German terrorists had been helped in ways both great and small for several years—with money and weapons, of course, but also with hiding places and training camps and military trainers from the People's Army who drilled their West German comrades in advanced weapons techniques. Obviously Honecker himself had not been involved in such primitive activities in the slightest. Not Erich Honecker. That wasn't how it worked. He had on the other hand given his approval for his old comrade in arms Erich Mielke, the head of the Stasi, a member of the government, and minister of state security, to take charge of the practical details.

For Mielke this was an obvious stage in the struggle against the capitalist opponent, and a man with his background had no problems whatsoever with the way the West Germans used the skills and resources he put in their hands. Not the young Communist Erich Mielke, who at the age of fourteen had already taken part in an armed revolt on the streets of Berlin against the conservatives in general and the Nazis in particular. Not the Communist Mielke who was only twenty-one years old when he committed his first political assassination and together with a comrade fatally shot two police chief inspectors and wounded an inspector in broad daylight in Berlin. Not Erich Mielke.

For Mielke it was a matter of helping comrades in the common struggle, and of the help they in turn could give him. Toward the end of his life, when everything had collapsed around him and he would be held accountable for what he saw as his cause and his life's work, he had been content to say that perhaps he did not share their outlook on certain strategic and tactical questions, but that in any event they had been close to him in their view of capitalist society. Mielke and his closest collaborators considered the West German terrorists a kind of reserve force, which could be mobilized as resistance men and saboteurs in any war against West Germany and its allies. It was no more complicated than that.

Men like him and Honecker could keep their opponents in the dark because in all essentials they had a different background from their enemies. Horst Herold, for example, was the legendary head of the West German Federal Crime Agency (the BKA), a highly talented intellectual, a scholar of Marx, political philosopher, socially engaged crime researcher, and also the hawk that flew highest and farthest and most often caught its prey, and who at last in a purely literal sense would be the death of the West German terrorists. There was a different distinction. Mielke and his comrades had themselves spilled the blood on their own hands. Herold sat behind his desk and let others take care of practical matters.

"The East Germans fooled the pants off us," Berg summarized, smiling and nodding to his guest. "Maybe it's not so strange that they fooled a simple country boy like me," he continued, smiling again. "But they actually fooled us all. The Americans, the English, the Israelis, the West Germans . . . they even fooled Herold, who knew them best, who had them closest to him, and who was probably the most talented person I've met in this business."

Just imagine, thought Lars Martin Johansson, who himself was not to be played with and almost never fell for pretty words.

"Stasi registries," he said. "Can you tell me about them?"

X

"Do you know about Operation Rosewood?" asked Berg, choosing to start with a question.

More or less, thought Johansson.

"It's been described to me on two occasions," Johansson replied. "So in broad terms I guess I do." The problem was more that the descriptions he'd been given also diverged at various and not completely uninteresting points, he thought.

"Then you'll get it a third time," said Berg, nodding.

And this time of course it'll be completely true, thought Johansson, but of course he didn't say that.

"I'm listening."

The relevant registry in this context comprised only a small portion of all the information that the Stasi had collected over more than forty years of operation; it concerned their foreign activities and was managed by the HVA, Hauptverwaltung Aufklärung. In concrete terms, in a purely archival sense, it was divided into forty different registries containing information about individuals, events, financial transactions, purchase of materials, and everything else that had to be organized to run, as HVA did, a large movement with espionage as its core activity and political terrorism as a secondary pursuit.

"What the Americans bought when they conducted Rosewood was simply a list of names," said Berg. "It was the list of all of HVA's foreign contacts. Everything from qualified spies to ordinary idiots one might have use for in certain situations. Plus names of a number of individuals who were used by their comrades in the Soviet Union and the Warsaw Pact and whom the Stasi had not used themselves but of whom they had nonetheless become aware, and therefore whose names they had chosen to record," Berg clarified.

In total the deal had included more than forty thousand different names and almost thirty-five thousand different individuals; the discrepancy was explained by the fact that in this context some of the individuals were entered under several different names, code names and aliases. What the CIA had purchased was the names and nothing else, because if you wanted to figure out to what extent and in what manner a certain individual had contributed to HVA's operation, you had to search further in other registries by means of the reference codes that were included with the list.

Yet the registries and archives being referenced were not part of the deal. As a consequence, among other things, certain epistemological problems cropped up, since the name of one of HVA's most qualified spies might be listed right above or below someone who had only attended a party at an East German embassy and after having a little too much to drink said that he thought "Honecker was a damned amusing guy." Provided that the spy's surname was sufficiently similar to the partygoer's, of course.

"Nonetheless," said Berg judiciously, "the Rosewood registry became an indescribably powerful weapon, a fantastic basis for continued intelligence work. . . . I'm willing to bet my professional reputation that Rosewood was the only straight deal that has ever been made with the information that was in Stasi's registries."

Over the years since the collapse in autumn 1989 a number of such deals had been made, most of them very small and very obscure. But Rosewood was by far the biggest, the first, the only straight deal that was made, and the best.

"What was procured at that time was gold," said Berg. "Pure gold for people like us," he added collegially, nodding at his successor.

Oh well, thought Johansson with the mixed feelings that easily followed from his not having had the time to get accustomed to who his new friends were. To whom did "us" refer?

Things were more complicated with the SIRA archive.

"System Information Recherche der Aufklärung," said Berg in his impeccable German. "System for Information Search within the Espionage Service," he translated prudently, because he was far from certain of how simple and rural his successor really was. It's probably just that he looks that way, so I'll have to hope he doesn't take offense, thought Berg.

The SIRA archive held not only names of spies, collaborators, and ordinary fellow travelers, but also information about their various contributions. The problem was the reliability of the information. There were even highly placed evaluators in the Western security services who maintained that the entire SIRA archive was a gigantic swindle, an enormous disinformation campaign in which what was true in the material—and that was of course most of the information—was only included to grant credibility to what was not.

Berg did not share the latter opinion. That was "seeing ghosts in the light of day," according to Berg. Who would the initiator behind the disinformation have been? he asked. Since the Eastern Bloc had fallen apart, there was simply no such entity left. At the same time there was a lot in the original SIRA archive that had been eliminated or changed. Quite certainly there was also fabricated information that had been added to the material, and the reasons were not particularly hard to understand.

When East Germany fell apart in late autumn of 1989, the more than a hundred thousand employees at the Stasi had no problem whatsoever keeping a straight face. The most common topic of conversation in the break room was how many years' imprisonment one's coworkers would get, and alone at home there was plenty of time to ask the same question on one's own account. What could be found in the archive was of course not uninteresting in that context, and for once it was so fortuitous that their political employer had given them the responsibility to see to the destruction of the Stasi archives themselves.

Undoubtedly there were a good many opportunities both to improve their own individual legal situation and—for those employees who were more entrepreneurial—to earn a few bucks at others' expense or even to garner a small profit by rescuing a fellow human being or two from impending misery. But there was a shortage of time. You didn't need to be a political theorist to calculate that soon the enemy would have taken over the operation, and then it would be too late for either one thing or the other, and definitely too late for deal-making.

"According to information in the media," Berg scrunched his long nose, "an employee at the Stasi archive—he has a different superior nowadays—right before Christmas 1998 is supposed to have succeeded in procuring extensive computer files that should have been destroyed after the Wall came down in 1989. And just a month before the new millennium this news became public knowledge.

"Of course this is pure nonsense, as you know," said Berg. "It's enough to visit an ordinary Swedish public library to understand how twisted such a story is. It doesn't work that way. I don't understand how these journalists think. Is he supposed to have stumbled across some box that was hidden away, perhaps way down in the cellar?"

What was called the SIRA archive in the media was material that was originally found in various Stasi registries that for various reasons had escaped being destroyed. The history of the archive was shrouded in darkness, and the only thing that could be said with certainty was that the data, in the form in which it was recovered, could not have existed as a separate archive or even as working data. It must have been compiled late in the game, perhaps even after the Wall came down. Hence, there were suspicions about its reliability. After it had been obtained, the deciphering and analysis of the data went on for several years before it was decided that it was time to "let the media get wind of the matter."

"Personally I've known about Rosewood since the early nineties," said Berg, "and the first time I got information from the Americans that they had gathered out of the Rosewood data was in 1993."

"That was nice of them," said Johansson, who at one of the courses he had attended had heard that not even the German security service was allowed access to the Rosewood material until the Germans agreed to trade information they had gathered from SIRA, which, according to the same source, would have been only a few years ago.

"Oh well," said Berg dryly. "The first time for me was 1993, and I had a little something to trade for, so it was not purely altruistic impulses that drove them to share the information."

Trade in the information from the SIRA archive had, according to Berg, first begun a few years later, but the commerce had accelerated toward the end of the nineties, and this applied to both Rosewood and SIRA.

"And this is when it gets interesting in relation to the occupation of the West German embassy in April 1975," said Berg, looking shrewd. "Really interesting," he said.

"I'm listening," said Johansson.

In 1993, Berg, mostly out of curiosity, he maintained, had traded for information from Rosewood about Swedish involvement in the West German embassy drama. After analysis that information appeared simple and unambiguous. The Swedish connection consisted of four names. In alphabetical order by surname, Eriksson, Stein, Tischler, and Welander. But naturally there was not a peep about what their involvement consisted of.

"According to the Stasi, it was these four who had helped the terrorists at the embassy," stated Berg. "But how they knew is mere speculation, and as I'm sure you already know I have a somewhat more nuanced view of the issue."

"Welander and Eriksson, to some degree Tischler, but in any case not Stein," said Johansson.

"Just about," Berg agreed. "Two who were active, one who was unwitting, and one who was exploited."

It only began to get really interesting when Berg compared corresponding information from the SIRA archive he came across a few years later. If the information in Rosewood was assumed to be reliable—and according to Berg there wasn't the slightest room for doubt on that point—these four should also be found in the SIRA archive, in the best case with an accompanying description of what their efforts had actually consisted of. It was highly interesting, not least to Berg because it gave him a convenient opportunity to assess his own analytical acumen in retrospect.

"You've surely figured out the answer already," said Berg, looking at Johansson.

"None of them were there," said Johansson. Easy as pie, he thought.

"Exactly," said Berg, nodding. "None of them was there. Not a comma about any of them, and that was pretty strange, because there were a number of reasons, beyond what had happened at the West German embassy, that at least Welander's name should have been there. Eriksson's too for that matter. When my predecessors recruited him, they made a serious mistake."

Oh well, thought Johansson. It's probably not Eriksson and his recruitment that's eating you up inside.

To put it briefly, SIRA was not to be relied on, and someone who had contributed to that circumstance was the now deceased doctor of philosophy and associate professor of sociology at the University of Stockholm, later an employee at Swedish Television, Sten Welander. And in all probability his best friend from childhood, the banker Theo Tischler, had given him the money he needed to carry out the necessary erasures in the original database of the SIRA archive.

"Perhaps you'll have some coffee after all?" said Berg, looking inquiringly at Johansson. "This is not a bad story, but it does take awhile to tell it."

"Yes," said Johansson. "Maybe it's time for a cup." Although a Danish is probably out of the question, he thought.

XI

On Friday the eighth of December 1989, Sten Welander traveled to East Berlin, together with a photographer and a colleague from Swedish Television, to do a feature story on the immediate consequences of the East German collapse and the fall of the Wall. This was an idea that had been in the works throughout that autumn and pursuing the story would have been extremely timely on the evening of the ninth of November. There had been a number of meetings, considerable bickering had broken out on the editorial staff, and several younger colleagues—of which Welander was only one—had felt called to immediately go to East Berlin.

The fact that Welander was finally the one sent off on the first round was owing to his being able to present a proposal for a very specific, and, in terms of content, sensational and disturbing program on the East German security service, the Stasi, which until then had held the population of East Germany in an iron grip. According to Welander, the Stasi had files on millions of East German citizens, had persecuted hundreds of thousands of them, had locked up tens of thousands in prisons and mental hospitals, and, with the utmost secrecy, had had hundreds executed. In addition, Welander had evidently developed contacts with dissidents and persecuted East Germans who could testify to their misery and—as icing on the cake—people from the Stasi who had already promised to come forward and let themselves be interviewed. In brief, the proposed coverage was almost too good to be true.

In the wake of management's consent and the curses of some of his colleagues, Welander and his little team got on the plane and flew to Berlin. What they didn't know was that on the same plane were people from both SePo and the Swedish military intelligence service, or that for the past twenty-four hours SePo had been listening in on his and Tischler's home phones, and that people had even been assigned to shadow Tischler on his ever more restless walks between his apartment on Strandvägen, the office down on Nybroplan, and the central city's finer restaurants.

When Welander arrived in Berlin, he immediately snuck out of the hotel and met his Stasi contact at a nearby beer hall in West Berlin, a captain by the name of Dietmar Rühl who had never been involved with operational activities, since his area was administrative issues and personnel matters. The surveillance of Welander and the contacts he made had been taken over by the local division of the West German secret police as soon as they landed, and as a friendly gesture their Swedish colleagues had been allowed to follow along.

Welander and his East German Stasi contact appeared noticeably stressed, almost harried, and from time to time they acted as though they were playing in some old spy film from the days of the cold war. They sat with their heads close together at the back of the place and palavered for more than an hour before they got up, shook hands, and left a few minutes apart. Rühl was seen to be carrying a thick brown envelope, contents unknown, and walked quickly back to East Berlin. A relieved Welander snuck back to his hotel. The whole meeting was well documented with photos taken by BKA's counterespionage department.

During the next few days Welander met with Rühl a few more times in East Berlin. Welander seemed to have more or less foisted the TV reporting onto his two colleagues. On the third evening a shouting match erupted between him and the other two in the photographer's hotel room, whereupon Welander excused himself by saying that his contact at the Stasi had demanded to meet him alone, a necessary condition for his cooperation. The editorial discord that broke out at the hotel was of course recorded on BKA's surveillance tape.

During the next two days the hatchet got buried. The photographer and Welander's colleague interviewed happy East Germans who willingly let themselves be filmed while they cursed at more or less everyone who had previously cast a pall over their lives—from Erich Honecker and his Stasi to the concierge in the building where they lived, who was *"ein Arschloch und Polizeispion,"* to the next-door neighbor who was an ordinary *"Polizistenschwein und Petze."* In brief, things went well for Welander's colleagues.

For Welander himself, on the other hand, life appeared more problematic. After five days an inebriated Theo Tischler called Welander's hotel room in Berlin in the middle of the night from his apartment on Strandvägen in Stockholm. There was a brief conversation, taped, of course, by both SePo and BKA. SePo's transcript read as follows.

TT: How the hell are things going for you guys? Do you need
    more ammo or what? Hello . . .
SW: You must have the wrong number.
TT: Hello? Hellooo . . . What the hell . . . Don't hang up now. . . .
(The conversation ends.)

After a little more than a week, the feature story was pretty much done. Or at least the photographer and Welander's colleague felt they had done their part and could do no more. What remained was the promised interview with Welander's secret contact at the Stasi. A noticeably stressed Welander managed to negotiate an additional twenty-four hours from his team members, and on Sunday the sixteenth of December the interview finally took place. An almost exhilarated Dietmar Rühl showed up at the agreed-upon meeting place in West Berlin.

First he spoke alone with Welander, who appeared considerably happier after their meeting, and then the interview was conducted. With his back toward the camera, and his voice rendered mechanically distorted, "the secret Stasi agent and major Wolfgang S."—which is how the secret contact was introduced in the program—in a monotone tried to avoid answering Welander's questions and assertions about various atrocities that his employer was supposed to be guilty of. The interview took an hour, Wolfgang S. received the agreed-upon compensation of fifteen hundred deutschmarks in advance, and that very same evening Welander and his team packed up and went home to Sweden.

That night a highly intoxicated Welander phoned Tischler from his apartment in Täby and said that he was feeling fine, that it was lovely to be home again, that his reporting trip had been a complete success, that he hoped he and Tischler would be able to meet soon and have a bite to eat, since it was almost Christmas . . . and . . . Whereupon Tischler had slammed down the receiver.

Welander's feature story ran without much notice. Most of their competitors had already purchased, and broadcast, considerably more substantive stories than the material Sten Welander could offer the viewers of public television in the middle of January. Welander's bosses were annoyed. What he had delivered had little in common with the promises he had laid out in his proposal. For some reason those colleagues whose suggestions had been rejected in favor of Welander's were the happiest.

Another person who seemed to have reason to feel content was Welander's contact in the Stasi, who quickly made the transition to capitalist society. Dietmar Rühl, the former Stasi captain, did not have to check tickets in the subway or stand in the coat check at the German Historical Museum. In a relatively short time he acquired three different stores in the former East Berlin selling pornography and sex accessories. According to reports business was booming.

Despite the lackluster reviews, Welander and even Tischler appeared both satisfied and much calmer. After a month SePo withdrew its surveillance of them and ended the audio surveillance on their phones. Because they already had a definite idea of what had happened, and because there was no intention of taking measures against any of them, the whole thing was put to rest. In hindsight Welander might just as well have stayed home. What he did not know was that the Americans had already confirmed the interesting information and none of them even gave Welander and his comrades a thought.

"Do you have any idea what Tischler had to pay to get their names removed from SIRA?" asked Johansson, who knew how to look out for himself where money was concerned.

"No idea," said Berg, shaking his head. "A few hundred thousand kronor if you ask me. Certainly no more than that. The rates for such things had already started to tumble. Whatever it was, it seems to have been enough for Rühl to be able to establish himself in a new business," Berg stated with a hint of a smile.

"How did you get wind of Welander's little excursion to Berlin?" asked Johansson.

"Ahh," said Berg contentedly, looking almost as if he were tasting a fine wine. "If you only knew how many informants we've had at Swedish Radio and Television all these years . . . not to mention the newspapers," he said. "It will be interesting to see if our dear intelligence service commission dares let the veil drop when they account for this aspect of their noble mission in the service of truth."

"So types like Welander are still in our files," Johansson asserted.

"What else did you expect?" said Berg, sounding almost a little resentful. "That would be the last thing I would attempt . . . withholding such information and thus hindering the remaining part of the fourth estate in their important journalistic mission." Although I don't expect I'll live to see the day, he thought, and suddenly he felt rather lousy.

XII

Only one question remained for Johansson.

"There's one more thing I was wondering about," he said.

Berg just nodded. He suddenly looked rather tired, and for the first time during their conversation Johansson felt sympathy for him. I need to stop, he thought. The man must have more important things to deal with than sitting here and answering my nagging questions.

"I'll buy your reasons for having cleaned them out of the files two years ago. Besides, the only two who were interesting were dead. But what I don't really understand . . ." Johansson hesitated. Should I just forget about it? he wondered.

"Go ahead and ask," said Berg. "I promise I'll answer if I can."

"What I don't really understand is why you restored the information on Welander and Eriksson to the files on the West German embassy only a few months ago," Johansson concluded. At the same time you retired and promised me a clean desk, he thought.

"I honestly admit that I was hesitant," said Berg, nodding. "But it was our colleagues in military intelligence who called and tipped me off. Besides, they let it be known that more might be coming on the same subject . . . so I thought it over again and put them back in."

"What was your line of reasoning?" asked Johansson.

There were pros and cons, and Berg had spent a long time deciding. For one thing, it was actually true: Both Eriksson and Welander had been up to their necks in the embassy occupation. Second, if some sufficiently qualified and careful inspector from the security service commission sat down with the material about the West German embassy, he or she might discover rather quickly that names had been removed from the material. Third, and most important, it was conceivable that new material might be added that he would no longer have any control over for the simple reason that he had retired. Fourth, and finally, he saw the openness in communication as an expression of a changed, more positive attitude on the part of their military intelligence colleagues.

"I don't know how many times we've quarreled about this over the years," said Berg. "I didn't think I should just show them the door when at last they'd come knocking, regardless of what they had on offer. Besides, the people this concerned were dead anyway, and because Welander himself had been a journalist, the wolf pack ought to leave his remains in peace. As far as Eriksson is concerned, if I remember correctly he had no surviving family when he died. And then the military intelligence colleagues suggested that more might be coming, and that sort of thing is always hard to say no to."

"You don't think that's what this was really about then?" asked Johansson.

"What do you mean?" asked Berg.

"About information that might possibly come later," said Johansson.

"You mean they wanted to open a doorway through which they might deliver someone other than Welander and Eriksson," said Berg.

"Yes," said Johansson. Like Stein, for example, he thought.

"The idea has certainly occurred to me, and I know who you're thinking of," said Berg, smiling weakly. "No," he added, shaking his head to underscore what he said. "The information actually came from our own military intelligence service, and in the prevailing security climate I have a hard time believing they would conspire against their own undersecretary. I have a hard time seeing the motive, quite simply."

So you have a hard time believing it, thought Johansson, but of course he didn't say that. Instead he asked about something else, interesting in itself, related but at the same time far enough away if, like him, you preferred not to waken the bear that had gone into retirement, and would be dead soon anyway.

. . .

"According to one of my coworkers, the guy at the terrorist squad who received the tip got the impression that it came from the Germans and the SIRA archive," said Johansson. "But that can't be what happened, if I'm to believe you, since Welander had already made sure that he and his comrades were cleaned out of that archive in December 1989."

"Yes, he must have had that all turned around. Personally I'm convinced that the military must have gotten the information from the Americans, and that it derives from Rosewood. There's just no other possibility."

"What I still don't understand is why anyone took the trouble," said Johansson. "Why in the name of heaven does someone tip us off about a matter almost twenty-five years old? About two individuals who are already dead and a preliminary investigation that will be null and void in six months?" What interest could the American intelligence service have in that? he thought, but of course he didn't say it.

"As I just said, I've wondered about that, too," said Berg. "I have no idea, actually, but it's definitely a bit strange."

"The only explanation, as I see it, is that they're trying to build a doorway," Johansson persisted. And that it's about Stein, he thought.

"And that's where we don't agree," said Berg, smiling weakly.

Not if I'm to believe what you're saying, thought Johansson.

"Just one more thing," said Johansson, looking at his watch. "Eriksson's murder . . . do you have any idea who might have been behind that?"

"Not the faintest," said Berg, "and to be honest I've really been trying not to get involved in what our colleagues in the open operation are up to. I've tried to take care of my business and let them take care of theirs, regardless of how good they've been at it. But since you're asking, if only a fraction of what I've heard about Eriksson in connection with our operation is true, then the only mystery is why no one killed him sooner. The man seems to have been an exceptional little jerk. There must have been lots of people with different reasons for wanting to get him out of the way. But that it had anything to do with the West German embassy"—Berg shook his head—"that thought has actually never occurred to me."

"So you don't think his old comrades, Welander or Tischler, may have had anything to do with it?" asked Johansson, who did not seem to have heard what Berg had just said.

"I remember I discussed it with Persson when he was looking at the murder investigation on our behalf, and he was convinced that neither of them could have done it," said Berg.

"Did anything about Eriksson emerge in connection with the surveillance of Welander and Tischler in December 1989?" asked Johansson.

"No," said Berg. "He wasn't even mentioned, which is interesting considering the timing—the man had just been murdered and Welander and Tischler would still have been his closest friends. We thought that was a little strange. Especially as Tischler seemed to spend half his time talking on the phone with more or less everybody about everything in the world and in the most astonishingly indiscreet way. It was as if the fellow . . . Eriksson, that is . . . had simply ceased to exist."

"Then I won't disturb you any longer," said Johansson. What else do I say? he wondered. I have to say something, don't I, because he's dying.

"You take care of yourself, Erik," said Johansson, looking seriously at his host. "And you shouldn't worry about this, because I'm going to take care of it."

"That's nice to hear," said Berg, and he looked as though he meant it.

Part 6

Another Time, Another Life

28

Friday, March 31, 2000

When Johansson arrived back at the office a package was awaiting him.

"You've got a package, Boss," the guard in the reception area said, lifting up an ordinary brown grocery bag on the counter.

"Anything that's ticking?" Johansson asked routinely.

"Just papers, but they were to be given to you personally, Boss," said the guard.

"Are they from anyone I know?" said Johansson.

"Came by courier," said the guard. "Seemed to be a nice guy. Looked like people mostly do."

"But no one you recognized," Johansson confirmed, smiling.

"No," said the guard. "But he said they were worth reading. Then he wished you a nice weekend."

"That was nice of him," said Johansson, taking the bag.

In the brown paper grocery bag were two letter-size binders with investigation files from the seventies and eighties, and a large envelope that contained an old-fashioned audiotape of the kind SePo had already stopped using in the early eighties, as well as a one-page summary of the essentials of the Swedish involvement in the occupation of the West German embassy almost twenty-five years ago.

Persson, thought Johansson as he sat leaning back comfortably behind his large desk, no matter that the brief, typewritten summary was unsigned. It was both explanatory and edifying, and although it was accompanied by several hundred pages of investigation materials and a number of tape-recorded conversations, the essentials were clear to Johansson within an hour. Besides, on the audiotapes he had heard the voice of innocence, with its distinctive tone, in two conversations captured on different occasions, and this was not overly common at his place of employment, and especially not when it came to conversations monitored by the secret police.

The first conversation was from early May 1975. A confused, furious, and very young Helena Stein calls Sten Welander at his office at the university, screaming that he had duped and betrayed her, calling him a murderer and a traitor, and threatening to go to the police and report herself, him, and all the others. The latter, by the way, seems to disturb him considerably more than do her moral condemnations of him. He seems most discomposed that she could be "so fucking dense" as to call him on his phone. When he can't get her to be quiet he finally hangs up, and when she immediately calls back again, no one answers.

The second conversation took place more than three years later, in the autumn of 1978, at a better restaurant in Stockholm. The law school graduate Helena Stein, who has just turned twenty, reads the riot act to Theo Tischler, eleven years her senior. She gives vent to her well-controlled and well-articulated wrath, and a very remorseful Theo Tischler simply cowers and takes it. Considering the secret police's persistent denials that they had ever been involved in concealed electronic eavesdropping, the high technical quality of the recording is both astonishing and admirable.

I have to talk with someone, thought Johansson, and considering what he needed to discuss there was basically only one person he could turn to, his own general director and highest superior. It'll have to be Monday, he thought after a quick look at his watch. It was late Friday afternoon, and usually high time to call it a day, but he had people waiting for him, both in the conference room a few doors down the corridor and at home on Söder.

My wife still comes first, thought Johansson, and called her to say that he would be a few hours late and that he hoped she wouldn't be upset.

"Not if you do the grocery shopping," said Pia.

It was a reasonable price to pay, thought Johansson as he hung up. In the worst case he could have his driver wait out on the street while he rushed into the Söder food hall and picked up the weekend necessities.

They were running short on time, he thought. In a few hours it would be exactly three weeks and three days until the statute of limitations ran out and the case lost its status as a practical legal matter—and, at least in theory, as the basis for indictments for complicity to murder and various other atrocities. Finally the case files would become something else, source material for research in history and political science. Forget the West German embassy, thought Johansson. Regardless of what had happened there he didn't intend to put a manure fork in that heap of shit, and in Helena Stein's case he hoped her entanglement was mainly a matter of youthful indiscretion.

The government offices wanted to have a background check done at the highest security clearance for the designated cabinet minister candidate in ten days latest, and evidently there was such assurance that she would get a green light that the undersecretary in charge of security in the prime minister's cabinet did not even seem to react when Johansson called him and said that unfortunately—for various practical reasons, heavy workload, events over which one had no control, and so on and so forth—he could not promise to deliver until the very last day.

"I see," the undersecretary said. "We'll have to try to live with that." Then he wished Johansson a pleasant weekend and put down the receiver, despite the fact that normally he could be both inquisitive and demanding.

What are you really up to? Johansson asked himself as he sat down at the narrow end of the conference table. Chasing figments of your imagination? You're doing your job, he thought, for now it was a matter of liking the situation. You're doing your job without sneaking a glance upward or downward or to the right or the left, with a clean desk, unsullied by history, with the greatest conceivable competence, in the national interest and in the good spirit of the new era, so you're sitting here because you intend to do your job.

"Welcome," said Johansson. "There's something I wanted to ask you to help me with. I hope I've got the whole thing turned around, but in any event I wasn't going to miss a chance to ruin your weekend." That sounded pretty good, he thought. Pleasant and democratic, and everyone already sitting around the table waiting suddenly appeared both happy and expectant. What a great guy that Johansson is, thought Johansson.

Not too many, not too few, and only the best, he had told Wiklander before he had left to meet Berg, and he hoped it was that directive and that alone that explained why there were only four people waiting for him and why three of them were women. Besides Wiklander, there were Detective Chief Inspector Anna Holt and Police Inspectors Lisa Mattei and Linda Martinez. Or maybe it was a reflection of the new era, thought Johansson, feeling almost hopeful.

First he gave a brief explanation of why they were sitting there.

"We've taken over a security classification from the folks at background checks," Johansson began. "It concerns an undersecretary in the defense department by the name of Helena Stein. Without knowing for sure, we have reason to believe that the intention is to promote her by appointing her as a member of the government, and so far all is well and good," said Johansson as he served himself a cup of coffee, apparently without the slightest thought of passing the coffeepot on to any of the others.

"Where was I," Johansson continued. "Yes . . . the reason that Stein ended up with us is that our esteemed colleague Wiklander here discovered by pure chance that in her youth Stein featured in the occupation of the West German embassy—as one of the four Swedish citizens who at that time were suspected of complicity. In that connection she is now acquitted and has been eliminated. My predecessor Berg conducted an, as far as we can judge, unobjectionable investigation that shows that in all probability she was unaware of what it was all about and she was possibly exploited as well. She was only sixteen years old at the time, and considering that the statute of limitations on the embassy case will run out in less than a month I have no intention of taking up that matter in this context."

Nor in any other context for that matter. God preserve us all, he thought.

"I'm sure you're wondering why we're sitting here," said Johansson, smiling amiably at his coworkers. "I hope the reason," he continued, "is only that I'm starting to get old and tired and occupationally injured and paranoid and have begun seeing ghosts in the light of day, but regardless of all that—and not least considering that I want to be able to sleep at night—before we put a grade A stamp of approval on Ms. Stein, I still want to be sure she's not carrying any old skeletons in her baggage."

"You have nothing specific, Boss?" asked Inspector Martinez.

"Not at all," said Johansson with more conviction than he actually intended to show. There was an unpleasant feeling growing in the back of his head that he intended to keep to himself for the time being. "Wiklander, perhaps you should explain what we've been thinking," said Johansson, nodding at the person who had started the whole thing.

"There were four Swedes identified in connection with the West German embassy occupation," said Wiklander. "It seems two of them were actively involved, Sten Welander and Kjell Eriksson. The other two, Theo Tischler and the just-named Stein, were probably not, and as far as Stein is concerned it appears, as the boss has already said, quite certain that she wasn't." Although God knows where Tischler is concerned, thought Wiklander, who was a real policeman with an old-fashioned view of things. He took the opportunity to pour fresh coffee for himself and of course passed the coffeepot on as soon as he'd done so.

"Two of those involved are dead. One of them, Kjell Eriksson, was murdered in 1989. The case is still unsolved, and I thought we should go over his murder if only for the reason that both Tischler and Welander appear in the investigation. Neither of them is a suspect, however, and anyway Sten Welander died of cancer in 1995. In addition, it so happens," said Wiklander, nodding at Holt, "that Anna here was involved in that investigation from the beginning, so I thought she could outline the case for you."

"How nice," said Johansson with surprise. I had no idea, he thought. Could Holt have been around already at that time? Jarnebring of course . . . whatever that has to do with it, he thought.

"Oh," said Holt, smiling hesitantly. "True, I remember Eriksson, because that was my first murder investigation, but I don't really think it was all that successful."

"But Stein wasn't part of the Eriksson investigation," said Mattei. "Have I got that right or not?"

"No she wasn't," said Holt. "Given that the investigation left a lot to be desired, and based on my own memory—it was more than ten years ago—I'm pretty sure about that. Stein was not mentioned at all in the investigation."

"What business do we have getting into this?" asked Martinez, looking at her top boss with curiosity.

"Yes," said Johansson, smiling weakly and shaking his head. "Good question . . . what the hell business do we have getting into this? I really want to emphasize this: This is not about clearing up an old murder, and least of all about whacking our colleagues down in Stockholm on the fingers. It is simply one last check . . . to be on the safe side, so that we haven't missed anything. Go ahead, Holt. We're listening," Johansson concluded, leaning back in his chair and lacing his fingers over his stomach.

Given all the years that had passed since Eriksson was murdered, Holt gave a clear, composed, edifying summary of the case. First she briefly recounted the factual circumstances: where, when, and how Kjell Eriksson was murdered. Then she described the victim's character: unpopular, solitary, almost strangely isolated. The investigation had revealed only two friends—Tischler and Welander—both of whom had watertight alibis, but because this was not about solving a murder mystery she wasn't going to go any deeper into that aspect.

As far as the motive was concerned, Holt continued, opinions had diverged sharply within the investigation team, and she recounted Bäckström's perception and her own and Jarnebring's opposing view of the matter: namely, that the case had to do with Eriksson's personality, not his possible sexual orientation; that he had been trying to bully someone, extort money, exploit someone.

"You shouldn't judge your own case," said Holt, "but Bäckström's so-called homo lead probably says more about Bäckström than it does about who murdered Eriksson."

"Motive," Johansson snorted, holding up both palms in a deprecating gesture. "I don't understand this constant nagging about motives. It's completely uninteresting. I can't remember a single case in which the motive has given us the perpetrator. You need harder goods than motives if you're going to solve a murder."

"Your friend Bo Jarnebring told me what you thought about motives in connection with the Eriksson investigation," said Holt, smiling rather broadly for some reason.

"And a good thing too," said Johansson. At least one person has listened to me, he thought.

"Just this one time he thought you were wrong," said Holt, who was still smiling.

"You don't say," said Johansson, suddenly sounding guarded. Et tu, Brute, he thought. "Well, what do you think, then?" said Johansson.

"Just this one time I agree with Jarnebring," said Holt, looking steadily at her top boss.

"You do, do you," drawled Johansson. What the hell are the police coming to, he thought. She must be at least ten years younger than I am and her practical experience of murder investigations fits on half the fingernail on my little finger, and still she sits there and contradicts me. "It'll work out, Holt," said Johansson. "It'll work out, and what we do now, to be on the safe side, we go through and check the Eriksson case one more time, just to see that we haven't missed anything. . . . Obviously I also want to have the usual complete rundown on Stein. How you divide that up among yourselves isn't my concern, but I want it done no later than next Friday evening, which gives you seven days." So that even I get a little time to think, thought Johansson.

"At the risk of quibbling," said Holt, "Stein is not part of the Eriksson investigation. On that point I'm certain."

That's just great, couldn't be better, thought Johansson, who saw the chance to conclude the meeting, get out of the office quickly, and leave the rest to his colleagues. If it weren't for Mattei, who, judging by the hesitant expression on her face, clearly had something on her mind. She seemed to be ruminating, thought Johansson. Or was that just because of her horn-rimmed glasses?

"Mattei," Johansson asked, "is there something you're wondering about?"

"Maybe," said Mattei, "in and of itself it's a little far-fetched. Maybe . . ." She was leafing hesitantly in a binder with computer print-outs as she pushed her glasses up on her forehead.

"Yes," said Johansson, exerting himself not to appear impatient. Shoot, man, he thought, but he couldn't very well say that. Well, he could to Jarnebring and Wiklander, but not to his colleague Mattei.

"Before I got here I did a few searches on Stein," said Mattei. Instead of just sitting and twiddling my thumbs waiting for my boss, she thought.

"And?" said Johansson. Get to the point, woman, he thought, in which he was evidently not alone, judging by the facial expressions of the others.

"I see in my notes here that Theodor Tischler and Helena Stein are cousins," said Mattei. "He's the same Tischler who's part of the murder investigation of Eriksson."

"What?" Holt blurted out, and because no one else had said a word, it echoed. "They're cousins?"

"Yes," said Mattei. "According to my research they are. Stein's mother is the sister of Tischler's father. So Tischler and Stein are cousins. It has to be."

"Jesus," Holt moaned, throwing out both arms. "The gang of four . . . How stupid can you be?"

"Excuse me," said Johansson, "I'm afraid I don't really understand."

"Forget everything I just said," Holt moaned. "Jesus, I didn't get it . . . how stupid can you be?"

"I'm still not getting it," said Johansson.

"Excuse me, Boss," said Holt, pulling herself together. "I take back what I said. Stein *is* part of the Eriksson investigation. I looked at a photo of her myself."

"I see," said Johansson. "That's all well and good, but I still don't understand—"

"The reason I never considered her is that in the picture she looks ten years old at most," Holt explained. "But sure, she's there in the evidence."

"The gang of four," said Johansson doubtfully. "Is that something political?" Sweet Jesus, he thought. Please don't let it be something political.

"No," said Holt. "Not the Chinese. It's a reference to characters in a novel by Conan Doyle—you know, Sherlock Holmes."

"Jonathan Small, Mahomet Singh, Abdullah Khan, and Dost Akbar," said Johansson, who had devoted hundreds of hours of his early youth to the adventures of Sherlock Holmes and even now could recite long passages by heart.

"Excuse me," said Holt. "Now I'm the one who's not following."

"Forget about that for now," said Johansson politely. "The gang of four in the novel by Doyle. Those were their names. But I still don't understand."

"Then I'll explain," said Holt, and she did.

Holt told about Eriksson's photo album and the picture she'd found, about the questioning of Tischler and what he'd said about his "delightful little cousin."

"And that was all," said Johansson.

"Yes," said Holt.

"But for crying out loud," said Johansson, who suddenly felt calmer again. "She was ten years old in the picture, you said—"

"About that," said Holt.

"If Eriksson was out at Tischler's summer place, I guess it's not so strange that he had a picture of it," said Johansson. "Someone like Tischler must have hundreds of cousins, and if I've got it right basically the whole extended family used that summer place."

"Over sixty of them according to my searches, if you count both full and half cousins," Mattei interjected after a quick glance at her notes.

"There, you see," said Johansson, nodding toward Holt. Typical shot in the dark, he thought.

"No, no, no," said Holt, shaking her head.

"What do you mean no, no, no?" said Johansson, who was starting to feel a trifle irritated.

"She could very well be the one who did it," said Holt, looking steadily at her top boss. "I hate chance. If she turns up at the West German embassy, then she must have known Eriksson when she was a lot older than ten, and unfortunately we missed that."

"Did what then?" said Johansson, who was no longer trying to conceal his irritation. "What do you mean you hate chance?"

"That it was Stein who killed Eriksson," said Holt. "You're the one who said it, Boss. That we should hate chance."

"Now let's take it easy here," said Johansson. What I might have said is that we should be skeptical of random coincidences, he thought.

"Sure," said Holt, "and because now she suddenly shows up in the Eriksson investigation, I assume we have to check her out as a potential perpetrator."

"Sweet Jesus," said Johansson. "What in the name of heaven is there to indicate that?" And if we're talking about probability, how often does it happen that women knife someone to death? One time in twenty? Tops, thought Johansson heatedly.

"Nothing," said Holt. "It's just that I suddenly have this unpleasant feeling that Stein evidently knew Eriksson and that she may have had something to do with the murder."

"Yes, yes, yes," Johansson interrupted, now sounding very tired. And two minutes ago you were a hundred percent sure that she didn't even feature in the investigation. And this is just too awful to be true, he thought sourly.

"It might very well be her," said Holt. Don't back down now, Anna, she thought.

"Listen, Holt," said Johansson, fixing his eyes on his coworker. "And this concerns the rest of you too, for that matter," he added, locking eyes with them too. "Now let's take it easy. Before we do anything whatsoever that might cause the least trouble for anyone, and not least for me, we need to call and ask for permission first. Is that understood?"

"Understood," said Holt, who did not seem the least bit dejected.

As soon as the meeting was finished Johansson took Wiklander with him to his office and asked him to investigate certain things that were to stay between him and Johansson. Wiklander was a male like himself, not from Norrland to be sure but from Värmland, and in this situation that would have to do. Besides, what choice did he have?

"Women have a unique ability to get worked up about the least little thing," Johansson explained, without naming names.

"Our colleague Holt is one of the best police officers we have," Wiklander said.

"So you say," said Johansson curtly. Not you too, he thought, and then he put an end to the conversation and took the elevator down to the garage to drive home.

If this is a background check, then the direction it has taken is somewhat disturbing, thought Johansson as he sat in the car en route to Söder in the dense inner-city traffic. It has to work out, he thought. Where do I stand now? I still like the situation, even if I liked it better just a short while ago than I do now. We needn't make things unnecessarily complicated. It should be possible to find a fellow who stabbed Eriksson to death. If that really was the problem, he thought. It always worked out, well, it almost always worked out, he corrected himself, so why wouldn't it work out here? Besides, this wasn't about solving an old murder for the homicide squad in Stockholm.

He had to admit that he was troubled by what Holt had said about hating chance. It didn't seem to be simply a matter of chance that among a large number of Tischler's cousins this particular one had probably been involved with his best friend Welander when she herself was only a child, and that she had shown up in the Eriksson investigation too. That was not good. It was bad enough that she appeared in the investigation on the West German embassy. Enough and more than enough. Damn it all, thought Johansson.

"You seem worried, Boss," his driver noted, and when Johansson looked up he saw that he was being observed in the rearview mirror. "Is there anything I can help you with, Boss?"

His driver was named Johan—Johansson had forgotten his surname but he wouldn't forget Johan—and looked like a twenty-years-younger copy of his best friend Bo Jarnebring. When he wasn't carting Johansson around, Johan worked at SePo's bodyguard squad. I'm sure there's a great deal you can do, thought Johansson as he encountered his driver's narrow, watchful eyes.

"You wouldn't be able to shoot Holt for me?" said Johansson.

"Holt," said Johan with surprise. "Do you mean Chief Inspector Holt, Boss?"

"One and the same," said Johansson.

"What has she done?" asked Johan.

"Talked back," said Johansson.

"Well, in that case," said Johan, grinning.

"Let's forget it," said Johansson, smiling wryly. "It's the weekend after all, so I'll let her live."

29

Friday evening, March 31, 2000

After an irritated Lars Martin Johansson had marched out of the meeting to have a private talk with Wiklander and then go home to sulk over the weekend, and the others had escaped to their respective offices to try to get something accomplished, Holt stopped by to see Mattei.

Mattei was sitting in front of her computer, pecking with concentration at what would eventually become the supporting structure of the biography of Helena Stein. "Little biography" as it was called in police Swedish, although in this particular instance there was reason to believe it would be rather lengthy.

"Can I help you with anything, Anna?" Mattei asked without taking her gaze from her computer.

"If you could make a copy of what you've got," said Holt.

"Sure," said Mattei.

"You see, I have an idea," Holt continued, "that it might—"

"Be easier to find Stein in the Eriksson investigation if you know what you're looking for," Mattei interrupted, without taking her gaze from her screen.

"Exactly," said Holt. Lisa is probably the smartest person in this place, thought Holt.

"If you go and check your e-mail, it's already there," said Mattei.

"Thanks," said Holt. She's almost a little too smart, she thought.

. . .

Wiklander had already ordered the binders on the Kjell Eriksson murder to be brought up from the archives in Stockholm, and Holt didn't need to think for very long to realize that it was unlikely anyone would miss them. There was nothing that even hinted that anyone had worked on the investigation since she and Jarnebring left it in December 1989.

There were ten letter-sized binders with several thousand pages of text. Mostly it was interviews, file searches, and other computer lists, plus the forensic investigation, crime scene investigation, and various technical reports, which, based on experience and at such a late date, were usually more interesting than anything else. In a context like this ten binders with several thousand pages were almost conspicuously little.

The papers were neatly organized, and it was quite obvious that Gunsan had done it. The traces of the leader of the investigation, Bäckström, primarily consisted of a long list of searches on individuals who came up in connection with various violent crimes directed at homosexual men, and quite certainly it was Gunsan who had made sure that this list also ended up in the right place in the investigation materials.

What an indescribably dreadful person, thought Holt, and she was thinking about her colleague Bäckström.

Because Holt knew that it could be as tricky to find things in binders as in a house search, she started by printing out the information on Stein that Mattei had e-mailed to her.

If you were going to search for something you might as well do it properly—for some reason she happened to think about what Jarnebring had said about checking the curtain rods in Eriksson's apartment. Because it was Stein she was searching for, it ought to be simpler to find her the more she knew about her, assuming that she was there in the investigation for an important reason and not simply because at the age of ten, through the luck of the draw and ordinary human interaction, she had wound up in Eriksson's photo album.

Maybe she's another Mary Bell, thought Holt, smiling to herself.

Helena Stein was born in the autumn of 1958 and graduated from the French School in the spring of 1976, not yet eighteen years of age. Then she matriculated at the university in Uppsala, became a member of the organization of students from Stockholm, and studied law. She earned her degree in three years compared to the usual four and a half, and she had the highest grades in all subjects except two. After that she did her internship at the district court in Stockholm, practiced at an upscale law firm on Östermalm, was hired as an assistant attorney at the same firm, and just over five years after her degree she was accepted as a member of the Bar Association. At twenty-seven years old Stein was the youngest attorney that Holt had ever heard of. Having come this far in Stein's biography, Holt suddenly realized what she was searching for, and it took her only five minutes to find the papers she hoped would be in the files.

This is almost a little ridiculous, thought Holt. It's so damn easy as soon as you know what you're looking for.

In her hand she held three papers that she herself had entered into the investigation in the middle of December over ten years before. It was a program from a SACO conference held in Östermalm in Stockholm on the thirtieth of November 1989, the same day Eriksson was murdered. Between ten o'clock and ten-thirty in the morning attorney Helena Stein had given a presentation on a case she had conducted on SACO's behalf at the Labor Court in Stockholm. According to the conference program her talk was the third item of the day, right before a fifteen-minute break. A list of participants revealed that one of those sitting in the audience listening to her was bureau director and TCO representative Kjell Eriksson.

Holt had read through the same papers herself when she and Jarnebring had had lunch on the day after Eriksson's murder, and she was the one who had made sure to conduct the fruitless search in the police department's files of all the participants, presenters, and conference organizers. But because she had not known who she was looking for, Helena Stein had been invisible to her.

What a strange feeling, thought Holt, weighing the papers in her hand. I wonder if my fingerprints are still there after ten years, she thought.

"How's it going?" asked Mattei, who had suddenly appeared in the door to her office.

"I've found her," said Holt.

"That conference," said Mattei.

This is not true, thought Holt.

"Yes," she said. "How did you know that?"

"An idea I had. That's why I'm here. I thought I'd give you a tip about what you should be looking for. It struck me suddenly when I was running Eriksson's biography and the log of what he'd been doing on the day of the murder against Helena Stein's biography. Conference on labor law issues, then-attorney Stein—if you want I can make a copy of the computer hits I got—I got two hits, one on 'attorney' and one on 'labor law.' It's pretty interesting software actually. First you enter the documents you want to search in plain text and then you run them against each other."

"I believe you," said Holt, smiling. Lisa is unbelievable, she thought.

"You're the one who found her," said Mattei, shrugging her shoulders. In this building that's the only thing that counts, she thought.

"I'm satisfied," said Holt. So there, she thought, and the person she was thinking about was her top boss, Lars Martin Johansson, who right now was probably settled on the couch in front of his TV dreaming his way back to the good old days when he was a legend who was never contradicted.

"In any event you've connected Stein with Eriksson on the day in question," said Mattei. "I actually had an idea too."

"I'm listening," said Holt.

While Mattei sat and waited for Johansson to show up at the Friday afternoon meeting, she had taken the opportunity to read the two interviews with Eriksson's closest neighbor, Mrs. Westergren. The reason she had chosen them in particular was simply that after quickly thumbing through the otherwise rather thin binder, she judged them to be the most interesting.

"Those interviews with his buddies were really worthless," Mattei said. "That Bäckström doesn't seem quite healthy. He's trying to direct them the whole time, get them to confirm that Eriksson was homosexual. I don't understand why he didn't just question himself?"

Mrs. Westergren, in Mattei's estimation, had made at least one interesting observation, namely that Eriksson had shown signs of increased alcohol intake during the months preceding his death. That was how she had expressed it: "increased alcohol intake."

"Personally I hardly ever drink," said Mattei, "but sometimes when I'm really wound up I have a small one when I come home, mostly to get my head to quiet down. I got the idea that Eriksson increased his alcohol intake because he was nervous about something and that this was happening during the autumn—the same autumn he was murdered."

"Jarnebring and I thought so too," said Holt. "Yes, that was the colleague I was working with at that time. The problem was that we couldn't find anything. One idea we had was that it must have involved his business dealings, but they seemed to be going better than ever."

"That was probably because you weren't aware of Eriksson's involvement in the occupation of the West German embassy," said Mattei.

"No," said Holt. "I only found that out today." Typical for this place, she thought.

"What I was thinking," said Mattei, as if she were working on it out loud, "is that if I had been involved in that incident, I would probably have been going out of my mind in the autumn of 1989."

"What do you mean?" asked Holt. "Fourteen years later? Why then? Shouldn't you have been used to the idea that you would get off?"

"East Germany," said Mattei emphatically. "East Germany collapsed in November 1989. The Stasi, their secret police, collapsed. The Stasi's archives were suddenly everyone's property. Hordes of people like our esteemed boss Johansson poured in from the Western powers and started rooting through their papers. What I mean is simply that if I had been involved with West German terrorists in the mid-seventies, wouldn't there be a high probability that my name was somewhere in the Stasi's files? The Stasi and the Red Army Faction and the Baader-Meinhof gang and all the rest were buddies. They helped each other, it has been shown. It's clear that the Stasi knew who the terrorists were."

"It's as plain as the nose on your face," said Holt. "And if my name was Eriksson, Welander, Tischler, or Stein I would have been really nervous." Not least if my name was Stein and someone like Eriksson knew something about me that he could exploit, thought Holt. And now you can shove it, old man, she thought, rerunning the conversation she'd had with her boss, the legendary Johansson, only a few hours before.

"That is a possible motive," said Mattei thoughtfully. "A little speculative, perhaps, but completely possible. They needn't have been in the Stasi archives—it would have been enough for them to believe that they might be there. For them to be nervous, I mean."

"But they were there," said Holt. "Both Johansson and Wiklander have confirmed that."

"Of course," Mattei objected, "but they didn't need to know that for certain. If they simply believed it they would start getting worried." Anna seems mainly practically oriented, she thought.

"How's it going, gals?" Martinez asked, after suddenly materializing in the door to Holt's office. "Now there are three of us, so it's a girl party. All the boys have gone home to knock back a few beers and stare at the TV."

"It'll be ready soon," said Holt. "Just wait till you hear—"

"Easy, easy," said Martinez, raising her hand in a gesture meant to hold off further discussion. "I'm completely starved. I was thinking about ordering a little junk food, the sort of thing our male colleagues are always stuffing themselves with in all the detective movies. You know, hamburgers and hot dogs and doughnuts. What do you think?"

"Maybe not hot dogs," said Mattei. "That's pure poison. Can't we have sushi instead? I'm trying to eat as little meat as possible. I can run down and get some sushi."

"Sushi," said Martinez. "Real detectives don't eat sushi."

"We do," said Holt. "I want sushi too."

"Okay then," said Martinez, shrugging her shoulders. "I'll get sushi."

When Martinez returned half an hour later bringing sushi and mineral water, the three of them held their first war summit.

"I think you're on the right track," said Martinez after she had listened first to Holt and then to Mattei. "For one thing you've managed to connect Stein with Eriksson. For another you've produced a plausible motive for Stein to stick the kitchen knife in Eriksson. I hardly think Johansson is going to do the wave when he hears what you've come up with," said Martinez, smiling broadly. "Do you want to know what I've been thinking?"

"Yes," said Holt.

"Yes," said Mattei.

"All right then," said Martinez. "I've been looking through the technical reports. But you should know I did it without even glancing at Stein. It was before I knew about that conference where she ran into Eriksson. But while I was waiting for all the rice balls you just stuffed yourselves with I happened to keep thinking about her."

"Yeah," said Holt.

"Yeah," echoed Mattei.

"We have to be able to place her in Eriksson's apartment," said Martinez. "I think there are two good chances. For one thing there are a few prints that were picked up but couldn't be identified. A few of them could be the perpetrator's. They belong to the same person, and both are sort of semi-good if I can put it that way. One is on the kitchen counter and the other on the inside of the cupboard door under the sink where he kept the wastebasket."

"Sounds good enough," said Holt. You can't have everything, she thought, and before her she saw the bloodied Sabatier brand kitchen knife.

"The other thing I was thinking about was that hand towel," said Martinez. "That's good too. If the perpetrator threw up in it, it should still be possible to lift DNA from it, because that hasn't been done. It wasn't done at the time."

Helena Stein's vomit on Eriksson's hand towel, thought Holt, and suddenly it became so tangible as they sat talking that she felt slightly nauseous.

"Assuming that the hand towel has been preserved in a freezer as it should have been, it's worth a try," Martinez said.

"Both the fingerprints and the hand towel are probably down at the tech squad in Stockholm," said Mattei.

"Then we'll have to bring them here so our own technicians can look at them," said Martinez. "Who'll call Johansson and ask for permission?"

"I can do that," said Holt, feeling instantly more energetic.

"I guess it will have to be tomorrow anyway," said Mattei hesitantly. "It's almost ten o'clock."

"Sure," said Holt. "Personally, I was thinking about going home to see the sandman."

"Me too," said Mattei. "I got up at six this morning. Fridays are my jogging day."

"If we were real detectives we would go down to the bar and knock back eight beers, do a little arm wrestling, and bring home a real hunk," said Martinez. "Either of you ladies in the mood for that?"

Holt and Mattei shook their heads.

"Typical girls," Martinez sighed. "Shall I take this to mean that we continue to be useful idiots and meet here first thing tomorrow at eight o'clock? Before you fall asleep you can ponder a practical problem, by the way."

"Which is?" said Holt.

"How we get hold of Helena Stein's fingerprints and DNA without Johansson having a hissy fit," said Martinez.

30

Friday evening, March 31, 2000

"You look tired," said Johansson's wife.

"I am tired," said Johansson. "There's a little too much going on at work right now."

"Anything you want to talk about?" said his wife, who seemed both energetic and suddenly curious.

Peppy Pia, thought Johansson, smiling unwillingly.

"Do you want me in jail?" he asked.

"Let's assume," said his wife as she served herself the last drops from the bottle of red wine, "let's assume that you told me about your job the way I tell you about everything that happens at my job—the sort of ordinary, harmless stuff you tell each other when you live together—about what so and so said and did and what you're up to right now—what would happen then? Could you end up in jail?"

"Without a doubt," said Johansson. Which would have been completely justified considering the rules that applied to him and the papers he'd signed, he thought.

"That doesn't make sense," said his wife, shaking her head with astonishment.

"Actually, it's better that way," said Johansson, who had already started to feel a little happier. I'm going to forget about that damned Holt, he thought. Your own wife is better looking, smarter, and funnier, he told himself, so stop feeling sorry for yourself because one of your coworkers doesn't unreservedly agree with you all the time. "It's a little hard to talk about," Johansson continued, clearing his throat. "But let me put it like this: There are even situations where I could end up in jail just for answering yes to the question you just asked."

"That still doesn't make sense," said Johansson's wife. "That's crazy. Do you get any financial compensation for that? Special bonus for marital silence?"

"I think it's completely okay if I argue with you," said Johansson, smiling contentedly. "Just as long as I don't do it over something that happened at work. Try to imagine the opposite. That we sat here and I babbled about everything to do with my job and it was completely okay for me to do that. That could have terrible consequences. For you personally."

"Tell me," said his wife, putting her head to one side with her right hand as support. "Give me an example," she said, twirling her wineglass.

"You can't get around me that easily," said Johansson, smiling. "But okay then—I'll try to describe what I mean. It's true that I'm tired. I'm worried too—and I think you've already figured out that it has to do with work—so I don't need to answer either yes or no to that. But if I were to be more specific, it would have consequences for a number of individuals, one of whom might also be you."

"Enemy agents would carry me off and torture me to get me to tell what you said and then they would murder me," said his wife, sounding almost expectant as she said it.

"Definitely not," said Johansson, "but regardless of whether what I told you was true or false—I don't know myself, because that's what I'm in the process of finding out and that's what's worrying me. But regardless, if I told you, it would completely change the way you saw certain individuals."

"So it's someone I know about," said Johansson's wife, looking slyly at Johansson. "It's some celebrity then. Some politician of course. It can't very well be Carola or Björn Borg."

"I don't know what you're talking about," said Johansson with a deprecating smile.

"In a way that's too bad," she continued. "Someone like you should really have some kind of use for someone like me."

"I do," said Johansson.

"In your work I mean," his wife clarified. "As you've certainly already noticed, I would be a very astute detective."

"Although perhaps a little too eager for discussions," said Johansson. Be careful not to say "loose-lipped," he cautioned himself.

"But that would suit you perfectly," said his wife, looking at him expectantly.

"What do you mean?" said Johansson.

"You're not exactly talkative," his wife declared. "In the beginning you were—the first years—but then you got more and more silent, and since you started this new job, well, mute is maybe a harsh word, but you're *almost* mute then. . . ."

"I'll try to pull myself together," said Johansson. Almost mute—that doesn't sound good, he thought.

"Good," she said, leaning forward and taking his hand. "Start by telling me who this famous politician is."

"Okay then," said Johansson, throwing out his hands. "If you make coffee, get me a cognac . . . fluff up the pillows on the couch, and massage my neck while I watch the news on Channel 4, then I promise to tell you who this is about and what it's about."

"Are you sure?" said his wife, looking at him. "Do we have a deal here?"

"Definitely," said Johansson. "You arrange coffee, cognac, neck massage, and pillow fluffing, and I'll tell you who it's about."

"Okay," said his wife, "but I want a down payment before I go along with the deal."

"Dost Akbar," said Johansson as he lowered his voice and leaned across the kitchen table, "member of a secret society known as the Gang of Four."

"Nice try," said Johansson's wife, "but no deal. I've read *The Sign of the Four* by Conan Doyle too."

"Maybe you should become a police officer anyway," said Johansson. "I know—apply to the police academy. You're never too old to apply to the police academy." Wasn't that what they said in those recruiting ads he used to see in the newspapers?

"I'm just fine at the bank. I had enough of the public sector when I worked at the post office," she said curtly, shaking her head. "I'll make coffee, you fluff up the pillows, you can get your cognac yourself—have I mentioned you're drinking too much cognac, by the way?"

"Eat too much, drink too much, exercise too little, talk too little—yeah, that sounds familiar." Johansson nodded in confirmation. I'll have to do something about that, by the way, he thought. What if he were to start on Monday, it being the first Monday of a new month? Maybe that would be a good day, because starting over the weekend was inconceivable.

"Good," said his wife. "Then I won't nag you. Now let's celebrate the weekend, and if we have to watch TV then I want the remote control."

"No flipping," said Johansson. Don't eat, don't drink, don't flip between channels.

"Exactly," said his wife, nodding.

"Heavens," said Johansson contentedly, letting his Norrland dialect break through as he said it. Now let's observe the Sabbath. Just like a typical weekend evening in the log cabin without liquor, food, and TV, he thought.

"Try and talk to me instead," said Johansson's wife, looking at him urgently. "You won't die from it—I promise."

Sometimes I miss my solitude, thought Johansson. Not right now, but sometimes. But he couldn't talk about that in any event.

31

Saturday, April 1, 2000

Holt was already at work by quarter to eight, but she still wasn't the first to arrive. When she stepped into the corridor she could hear the diligent pecking from Mattei's keyboard.

"There's fresh coffee in the kitchen," Mattei called without turning around.

"Do you think it's too early to call Johansson?" Holt asked hesitantly.

"Johansson," said Mattei with surprise. "He's from Norrland and a hunter, so I'm guessing he's the type who gets up in the middle of the night."

Johansson was sitting in the kitchen at home on Wollmar Yxkullsgatan reading the second of the two morning papers. In the past he'd been content with *Dagens Nyheter,* even if he would have preferred *Norrländska Socialdemokraten,* where at least they could write comprehensibly and had something important to say, but since taking the new job he suddenly and quite unexpectedly received a free subscription to *Svenska Dagbladet,* so nowadays he read two morning papers instead of one. He turned down the free subscription of course, and instead he paid for the paper himself.

Clever accountants over at *Svenskan*'s marketing department, Johansson thought as he scrutinized their stock listings to see how his investments were doing. Just as he was noting that both Skanska and Sandvik stood like solid rocks in a time of change, his phone rang. Holt, thought Johansson.

"Johansson," he answered. Maybe a little more abrupt than necessary, he thought.

"Anna Holt. I hope I'm not waking you, Boss." He woke up on the wrong side of the bed, she thought.

"No," said Johansson. "I assume you're calling to tell me that you've connected Stein with Eriksson."

"Has Martinez called?" Holt asked with surprise. Must be Linda, she thought, wherever she was hiding herself.

"I'm a cop," said Johansson, sounding extremely abrupt. "You're the only one who has called."

"I see," said Holt, who had a hard time concealing her surprise. "I was just wondering if—"

"Here's a little homework assignment for you," said Johansson, who suddenly sounded considerably more cheerful. "Start by thinking about how often you've called me at home before eight o'clock on a Saturday morning, and then about what I said to you yesterday."

"I think I get it," said Holt. "Yes, I've placed them together on the morning of the day he was murdered."

"So now you want to get her fingerprints to see if you can place her in his apartment," Johansson surmised.

"Yes," said Holt. Now he sounds more like what I'd heard about him, thought Holt. Obviously mornings are the best time to talk with him.

"Where are the prints you want to compare hers to?" asked Johansson.

"At homicide," said Holt. "On the handle of the kitchen knife, and the best of them were left in Eriksson's blood."

"I'll be damned," said Johansson. What do I do if they're Stein's fingerprints?

"April Fool," said Holt, sounding rather upbeat herself. "Sorry, Boss, I couldn't help myself. Kidding aside. On the kitchen counter and on the inside of the door under the sink."

They're like children, thought Johansson, but naturally he wouldn't dream of saying that to a female coworker who was a decade younger than he was. No one's that dense. Not me in any case, thought Johansson.

"So what's the problem?" asked Johansson. The kitchen counter and the door under the sink will have to do, he thought.

"Is it okay?" Holt wondered.

"Do like we always do," said Johansson curtly. "Is Martinez there?"

"She's on her way in," said Holt.

"Ask her to arrange it," said Johansson. "Linda's a whiz at that sort of thing." I can tell you, he thought, because that's why I hired her.

When Holt went into the break room the first person she encountered was Martinez, who was gulping down a large glass of water with audible enjoyment.

"Ahh," said Martinez, wiping her mouth with the back of her sweater sleeve.

What happened to those eight hours of sleep? thought Holt.

"Sleep well?" asked Holt neutrally as she poured a cup of coffee for herself. "By the way, would you like coffee?"

"Sorry, sorry," said Martinez, actually looking a bit guilty. "I'm weak, so it was the bar as usual."

"Was it any good?" asked Holt, handing her a coffee cup.

"It was shiiiit," Martinez moaned. "Eight beers and no hunks."

"I spoke with Johansson," said Holt. "It's okay for us to get Stein's prints. Can you arrange it?"

Martinez nodded and already seemed considerably more alert.

"I could do that in my sleep," she said. "Easy as pie. But you and Mattei have to help me with the practical stuff in the event we've got a moving target."

"No problem," said Holt. It will be nice to get outside, she thought. It's the first real spring day too, sun, blue sky, at least fifty degrees out.

Johansson and his wife did not have the same biological clock. This was a mild understatement because he seldom got out of bed later than six o'clock, yet his wife could spend the day there if she had the choice, and in any case she was scarcely approachable before ten on a Saturday morning such as this one.

So he had managed to shower, have breakfast, and read two morning papers in peace and quiet before he tiptoed into their bedroom at nine-thirty. The only thing he saw was a lump under the blanket, a black tuft of hair sticking up under the pillow, which for some reason was covering the face of the person lying there, and a rather small, naked foot sticking out down below.

"Are you asleep, darling?" said Johansson, who didn't always act like the police officer he was.

"Hmmnuu," moaned his wife.

"I've made breakfast for you," said Johansson. "Fried ham and pan-cakes."

"What?" said his wife, suddenly sounding wide awake.

"April Fool," said Johansson. "If you move over a little then there'll be room for me, too," he said. She's fallen asleep again, he thought in amazement. This can't be true.

"Pia . . . honey," said Johansson. "It's amazing weather. What do you think about a long walk on Djurgården?"

"Not right now," his wife moaned.

They're like children, Johansson thought affectionately, making room by her side.

First Martinez stopped by their tech squad and organized a beer can, specially emptied for the purpose, which she stored in a sealed plastic bag. Then she made a prank call to Stein at home on a prepaid cell phone that couldn't be traced, and as soon as Stein answered she excused herself, saying it was a wrong number, ended the call, and took Holt and Mattei with her down to the garage.

"We'll take my vehicle so we don't stick out unnecessarily," said Martinez, opening the door to the driver's seat of an unbelievably crappy, small, older-model Japanese car of a make unknown to Holt. "Get a move on, ladies, we're in a hurry," said Martinez, waving them impatiently into the car.

"Isn't it best if I drive?" said Holt doubtfully. Eight beers, she remembered.

"Fine with me," said Martinez, shrugging her shoulders. "You'll have to sit in back, Lisa," she decided, giving Mattei a critical glance. "Damn, don't you look tidy," she said disapprovingly, shaking her head.

"Excuse me," said Mattei, guiltily.

"It's okay," said Martinez to smooth things over. "No one's going to believe you're a cop anyway, and if you have to get out and move around I have some things in the trunk you can borrow."

Johansson gradually breathed some life into his wife, saw to it that she got a cup of coffee and a glass of fresh-squeezed orange juice, and then led her out into the beautiful spring weather. They walked down to Slussen and took the ferry over to Djurgården. Johansson stood in the front and let the sea breeze caress his Norrland cheeks while he hummed an old popular song from Jussi Björling's repertoire. Then they strolled all the way down Djurgården, continued back along Strandvägen, Nybrokajen, and Skeppsbron, and when they got back to Slussen a few hours later, Johansson was in a terrific mood and suggested a late lunch at the Gondola.

"Awesome," said his wife, who was influenced by the many young coworkers at the bank where she worked. "I'm dying of hunger."

And I am a fortunate man, Johansson thought, who had already decided to have both an appetizer and an entrée, since he must have burned tons of calories while he and his wife made their way around half the inner city at a brisk pace.

At the same time Martinez was carrying out her mission with all the accuracy that made her famous, and right before the eyes of Holt and Mattei.

Helena Stein lived on Kommendörsgatan in Östermalm, at the end where it met Karlaplan. When Martinez saw that Stein's car was parked outside the building where she lived she quickly decided how to proceed.

"Stop here," she said to Holt. "Then drive down a bit, but stay close enough so you can keep an eye on the outside entrance. I'll try to get it over with so we don't have to waste half the day."

"It's cool," said Holt. I was working as a detective before you started at the police academy. Who do you take me for? she thought.

Martinez walked down the street, and as she passed Stein's car two things happened so fast that neither Holt nor Mattei had time to understand what had taken place.

Suddenly the beer can was on the roof of Stein's car, and the car alarm was going off.

A minute later a woman in her forties came out of the building. It was apparent that the car alarm had brought her out. After looking up and down the street, she caught sight of the beer can on the roof of her car, shook her head, turned off the electronic alarm, and carefully lifted the beer can off the roof with an ungloved right hand.

"Record time," said Martinez contentedly from the backseat into which she had crawled half a minute earlier.

Helena Stein, thought Holt. It was a strange feeling seeing her with her own eyes. She was a trim, good-looking woman, forty-two years old, Holt's own age, and just like Holt she looked younger than she was. Her thick red hair was pinned up in a bun at her neck, and she might have been planning to spend the day outside, because she was dressed in jeans, sturdy walking shoes, a checked shirt, and a jacket that she must have draped over her shoulders when the car alarm lured her out onto the street. She wore good-looking, expensive, discreet clothing, the kind that Holt could only dream of owning. Clearly she was a conscientious citizen too, for instead of simply tossing the beer can away in the gutter she placed it in a trash can at the crosswalk more than twenty yards farther down the street. Then she went back with quick steps and disappeared into the building where she lived. I hope I'm wrong, Holt thought suddenly, and the thought was so unpleasant that she immediately dismissed it. Pull yourself together, Anna, she thought.

"Okay," said Martinez, "drive around and pick me up at the next intersection, and I'll bring home the bait."

She patted Holt on the shoulder before she got out of the car, stopped at the crosswalk, and then, after a quick glance in each direction for cars that weren't there, crossed the street and disappeared around the corner out of their field of vision.

"Linda is just unbelievable." Mattei sighed. "She could get a job as a witch."

. . .

Johansson did not get an appetizer, and it was his wife, Pia, who explained why he couldn't.

"I don't care how many calories you've walked off. It's completely meaningless if you're going to stuff yourself with caviar and potato pancakes."

"No fish, please," said Johansson, putting his head to one side and trying to look like a little boy from the great forests north of Näsåker in the province of Ångermanland.

"You can have grilled beef and boiled potatoes," his wife declared from behind a menu. "Doesn't that sound good?"

"What's wrong with au gratin potatoes?" said Johansson, sounding whinier than he intended. Other than that they taste so much better? he thought.

"They're bad for you," said his wife. "And because I love you so much I want to protect you from dangerous things. We're very much alike in that regard, you and me," she declared without raising her eyes from the menu.

"Okay then," said Johansson manfully. "Grilled beef, boiled potatoes, and a strong beer."

"What's wrong with light beer?" his wife objected. "Or plain water for that matter?"

"Don't contradict me, woman," said Johansson, "or I'll order a shot of aquavit too."

"All right then," she said. "Personally, I think I'll have fish. And a glass of white wine."

"Fine by me," said Johansson. "Have fish, dear." You're a woman, he thought.

When the three investigators returned to the police station, Martinez took her beer can trophy—now bearing Helena Stein's fingerprints—and disappeared to the tech squad to arrange the remaining practical matters.

Mattei went back to her computer, and Holt sat down in the break room to have another cup of coffee while she pondered how she should proceed. At the same time her thoughts started wandering off again in a direction she didn't like.

Assume that she's the one who did it, thought Holt, who had suddenly started having doubts in a situation where she reasonably ought to have been strengthened in her spontaneous conviction. Then we're going to crush her for the sake of someone like Eriksson. What was it he'd said, that doorman at Eriksson's office that she and Jarnebring had talked to more than ten years ago? That Eriksson was both the absolute smallest person and the absolute biggest asshole he had ever met. From the little she'd seen of Helena Stein, she didn't seem to match that description, thought Holt.

Boiled potatoes are actually not that bad, thought Johansson. Not if they are really fresh like the ones he'd just had. True, French new potatoes are not in a league with Swedish ones, but these were completely edible. What did you expect at this time of year, and what did the French know about potatoes anyway?

"There was something I was thinking about," said Johansson's wife, looking at him with her spirited dark eyes.

"I'm listening," said Johansson. So you've finally woken up, he thought.

"Is there someone who works with you named Waltin?" she asked.

"Waltin," said Johansson with surprise. "You mean Claes Waltin? A little dandy who used aftershave and pomade in his hair," said Johansson. And a real little asshole if you ask me, he thought.

"He was some kind of police superintendent," said Johansson's wife.

"A deputy police superintendent," said Johansson as he shook his head. "No, he's not around anymore. He disappeared a long time ago. Why are you asking?"

"Nothing special," said his wife, shaking her head. "I went out with him a few times, but that was long before we met." So you don't really need to look that way, she thought.

"No, he's not around," said Johansson. "He quit many years ago—I think it was in '87 or '88, a year or two after Palme was shot. Now I'm getting curious." There's something she's holding back, he thought.

"Is he still working with the police?" his wife asked.

"No, not really," said Johansson with surprise. "He's dead."

"He's dead?" she said, suddenly looking rather strange. "What did he die of?"

"Yes," said Johansson. "It was an odd little story. It happened several years after he quit the police force. I don't know the details since I heard it only in passing, but it happened sometime in the early nineties—'92, '93 maybe—four or five years after he quit. They say he drowned on a vacation in Spain. Did you know him well?" Good old retroactive jealousy. Still, she couldn't have known him that well if she didn't even know he was dead, thought Johansson.

"Since you're asking," said Johansson's wife. "I saw him four, five times actually. The first time I was out at a restaurant with a girlfriend. Then he called me and asked me to dinner at the same restaurant, and then I remember he got a little kiss in the doorway before we parted. He drove me home in a taxi. He was enormously attentive and polite. Not your typical Swedish man if I may say so. Well . . . we met a few more times—the last time was at his place. Then I stopped seeing him and he called me about ten times before he gave up."

"So why did you stop seeing him?" asked Johansson, thinking, Something here doesn't add up, without really knowing why.

"I found out he wasn't a good person," his wife answered, shrugging her shoulders. "So I told him I didn't want to see him anymore and that was that."

"So what was wrong with him?" asked Johansson. Apart from the fact that he looked and acted as if he had a spruce twig stuck up his ass, he thought.

"Forget about it now," said his wife, shrugging her shoulders. You don't want to know, she thought. "He just wasn't my type," she said. "Is that so strange?"

"No," said Johansson. The same sort of thing has happened to me too, he thought. "That has actually happened to me too," he said, smiling.

"He drowned, you say," said his wife, suddenly looking extremely curious. "Are you absolutely sure?"

"Sweet Jesus," said Johansson. "Either you explain or we change the subject, okay? According to what I heard, our former colleague Waltin is said to have drowned during a vacation in Spain. I heard it in passing. I didn't know the guy. I hardly ever met him. And from the little I saw and heard I didn't like him. Is that enough?"

"You don't think he could have been murdered then?" asked Johansson's wife, looking at him with curiosity.

"Murdered?" said Johansson with surprise. "Why in the name of God should he have been murdered?"

"Well," said his wife, who didn't appear particularly disheartened by Johansson's reaction, "considering his old job and all that."

Sigh, thought Johansson. It must be all those mysteries she reads, but naturally he couldn't say that.

"The only motive I can think of is that he must have been careless about paying his tailoring bills, which really didn't have anything to do with his job," Johansson said, grinning.

"I know what you mean," said Johansson's wife, and she smiled too.

"And what's that mean then?" said Johansson.

"That it's high time we change the subject," said Johansson's wife.

She's not only lovely to look at but also fun to talk with—she's smart too, thought Johansson. As soon as they got home after their little Saturday excursion he called Wiklander and gave him yet another task: to find out what had really happened with former police superintendent Claes Waltin, since he was going to be talking with former colleague Persson about the other things Johansson had asked about.

"Waltin?" said Wiklander, sounding surprised. "That dandy who drowned on Mallorca a while back?"

"That's the one," said Johansson. "He quit us a few years after Palme and then he drowned during some vacation in Spain a few years later."

"Sure, I can do that," said Wiklander with surprise. "Do you think he has anything to do with this, Boss?"

"Not in the slightest," said Johansson emphatically. "Why should he?" Just a little private question I have, thought Johansson, and why I'm asking has nothing to do with you.

"Sure," said Wiklander. "I'll take care of it." I wonder what this is really about, he thought.

32

Sunday, April 2, 2000

At eight o'clock on Sunday morning, Holt called her boss Lars Martin Johansson at home to obtain permission to proceed with Helena Stein via the methods she had learned during her more than ten years as a detective—shadowing, wiretapping, and the whole ballet, so something would finally happen. Others could sit and peck at a computer or bury their heads in a pile of binders, like her colleague Lisa Mattei, for example, who loved that sort of thing and was better at it than almost anyone else.

In contrast to the morning before, Johansson didn't answer until the third ring, and he was if anything even more direct than the first time Holt had called him at home that weekend.

"Good morning, Holt," Johansson muttered. "How can I help you?"

"I'd like to initiate external surveillance of Stein," said Holt. I don't want him to get the idea that I've become fond of him, she thought. Calling two mornings in a row is perhaps a bit too much?

"Forget it," said Johansson politely. "Call me again when you've placed her in Eriksson's apartment. Give me three good reasons, and then I promise to think about it."

So a wiretap is out of the question, thought Holt.

"And you can also forget about tapping her telephone," said Johansson, who despite his nonexistent social skills was apparently a mind reader.

"Then I'll have to say thank you, Boss," Holt said politely, "and I do hope I haven't disturbed you on a Sunday morning." And how would I manage without you and people like you? she thought sourly.

"Forget about that too," said Johansson. "And a piece of advice: Someone like me doesn't bite on something like that," and he hung up.

Oh my, thought Holt. But there isn't much time.

Martinez too had gotten stuck in the bureaucratic mud. All the technicians who were on duty at SePo's tech squad were fully occupied with a matter that had suddenly come up, top priority and so secret that they wouldn't even say when they might be returning to the building on Polhemsgatan.

It wasn't possible to get hold of on-duty technicians at the police department in Stockholm, though in a way it was simpler with them because no one was even there to answer the phone, much less anyone else who could tell her anything at all.

"Don't ask me, they're probably out running around somewhere, as usual," said an irritated chief inspector at the City squad's detective unit when Martinez finally got hold of him.

"Thanks for your help," Martinez said politely, putting down the receiver. Idiot, she thought.

Both Holt and Martinez had to resign themselves to their fate—keeping Mattei company in front of the computers and piles of binders that were neatly arranged in the project room they'd moved into in order to be left alone with their mission. Mattei was happy as a clam and promised to show them some interesting new software after lunch—"Assuming you're interested of course," she added. Holt decided to make the best of her circumstances and, for lack of anything better to do, refresh her knowledge of the Eriksson case. What Martinez was actually up to at her computer was less clear, but she mostly seemed to be surfing on the secret police's own network and taking full advantage of her temporarily expanded access.

Johansson had devoted the day to his wife, Pia, or Peppy Pia as he called her at home when he was in the mood.

The first time he had met her was almost fifteen years ago. He had run into her when he was investigating a mysterious suicide he had been dragged into, an American journalist who supposedly took his own life by jumping out of a sixteenth-floor window. The reason he had started to pay attention to Pia was more private than professional.

He had spoken with her as one of several witnesses, and because she looked the way she did and was the person she was, he immediately became interested in her, considerably more interested than he normally would have been. This was highly unfortunate given the way he had met her. On that point Johansson was very old-fashioned. Women he met in connection with his job, even in a situation like this, which was somewhere in between personal and professional, he did not meet as a man but rather as a police officer.

When he had finally put the case of the dead journalist behind him, not suicide but murder, he looked Pia up again, not as a police officer but as a man. But at the time she'd had something else going on, and what that was he never asked, because he knew anyway. He had hidden Pia far back in his mind among all the other things that certainly could have been significant in his life but for various reasons never were because he had never made up his mind. He had thought about her sometimes when the solitude that he all too gladly resorted to became too tangible. Then he thought about her with a special sense of loss that did not feed on all that had happened but only on the things that hadn't but perhaps might have.

Several years later, when he had basically stopped thinking about her, he accidentally ran into her in his own grocery store, in the neighborhood where he lived. Luck of the draw, thought Johansson happily, and despite his estimable talents as a detective, for once he had no idea how things really stood.

Less than a month earlier Pia, who often thought about Lars Martin Johansson for more or less the same reasons he thought about her, happened to read a lengthy interview with Johansson in a tabloid, and immediately decided that if anything was going to happen in that area of her life, she was probably the one who would have to take the initiative. It was just a sudden impulse that she followed because over the years she had caught herself thinking about a man she had met only twice in her life. She found out just as quickly where he lived and that, at least in a legal sense, he was as single as could be. After that she figured out where he probably did his grocery shopping, and because she too lived on Söder it wasn't difficult for her to change to a different store. On the fifth visit, just when she was thinking the whole project was starting to seem a little ridiculous, she had run into an absent-minded Johansson standing in deep contemplation in front of the meat counter. And that's the way it was.

"What are we doing today?" asked a pleased Johansson as he squeezed grapefruit and oranges for his still half-asleep wife. "What do you think about starting the day with a long walk? The weather is almost as good as yesterday," he added.

"What do you think about coming back to bed?" Pia proposed. "Then we can think about it while we're considering something else."

"Yes," said Johansson. "Do you want juice now or do you want to wait?" Not a bad idea actually, he thought, and they could always go for a walk later.

"Later," said Pia, suddenly looking very attentive.

"Good," said Johansson, reaching out his hand for her slender neck.

After ordering out sushi for the second day in a row, Holt, Martinez, and Mattei devoted the afternoon to their daily war council.

"I'm starting to put together quite a bit on Stein now," said Mattei, pointing to an impressive pile of computer printouts and other papers. "I almost feel she and I are getting to know each other in some way. This is really exciting."

"You've never thought about writing a novel?" asked Martinez innocently.

"Sure," said Mattei, nodding thoughtfully. "This is a problem I have when I do this kind of job. I have to downplay the literary element of my work. I don't know how to explain it, but to me it's often been the case that a really good novel has more to say about what we're really like as human beings than the gloomy accounts of people and their lives that we compile here."

"I'm sure Stein would be delighted to know how much you want to cuddle up with her," said Martinez, smiling wryly. "If she only knew . . . imagine how happy she would be. Perhaps you should—"

"I know exactly what you mean," Holt interrupted, nodding seriously at Mattei. "There are some truths about other people that we can only discover by means of our imagination. The problem is this place where we work, because they don't much like that sort of thing here; in fact they're actually scared to death of it." Prejudices on the other hand, she thought. They're always nice and safe.

"You must be a fortunate person, Linda," said Holt for some reason, and then they returned to their respective piles of papers, and it was not until it was time to go home that a friendly male colleague called from the tech squad and said that he was now back in the building and was of course at their immediate disposal.

Martinez got up at once, took her beer can and her basis for comparison, and vanished in the direction of the tech squad. Half an hour later she was back, and when Holt saw her come through the doorway to the room where they were sitting she did not even need to ask how the work had gone.

"Yeeesss," said Martinez, raising her clenched left fist in a victory gesture from the suburb north of Stockholm where she had grown up. "Those are her fingerprints. Both on the kitchen counter and on the door under the sink."

It was too late to call Johansson and get yet another dose of cynicism and sarcasm, thought Holt as she looked at the clock.

"What do you think about seven-thirty tomorrow morning?" she asked instead.

"No beer, no hunks, fine with me," Martinez summarized.

"That suits me fine too," said Mattei. "I'm actually a morning person."

Instead of going home to sleep, Holt borrowed an unmarked car and took the route past Helena Stein's residence on Östermalm. Parked discreetly a little way down the street, she sat in the car for an hour while she kept an eye on the windows in Stein's apartment. There were lights on in there somewhere in the inner regions, and at one point she saw someone go past behind the curtains in the room that she now knew to be Stein's living room. But she wasn't able to see whether it was Helena Stein or someone else.

What are you up to? thought Holt with irritation. Then she drove straight home and went to bed. What kind of a life are you living anyway? she thought as she fell asleep.

33

Monday, April 3, 2000

When Holt reached work on Monday morning she immediately went to see her boss to report on the latest developments. Johansson was not there. According to his cool and correct secretary, the boss might show up after lunch, assuming of course he didn't have anything else going on. Reaching him on his cell phone was out of the question as well, because he was in important meetings where he could not be disturbed. Johansson's secretary suggested that perhaps Holt should try speaking with Wiklander instead. And if he wouldn't do, then she would just have to be patient and wait until Johansson came back.

Wiklander was also conspicuously absent, and because he didn't have a secretary who refused to say where he was, all that remained were Holt's closest coworkers, Martinez and Mattei.

"Okay," said Holt. "The boys are staying out of sight as usual, so what do we do while we're waiting?"

"I have more than enough of my own work to do," said Mattei, nodding at the piles of papers towering beside her computer. "But if you want I can help you look for connections between Eriksson and Stein at the time of the murder."

"Good, Lisa," said Holt. "If you look for any financial connections—and for God's sake don't forget her cousin Tischler—then Linda and I will try to check the phones."

"Almost eleven years ago," said Martinez doubtfully, shaking her dark-haired head. "The AXE system wasn't completely built at that time, and almost nobody had cell phones. I don't even know how long Telia saves its call lists. Surely not for ten years."

"We have to at least try," said Holt. "The lists of Eriksson's calls are included in the investigation, but if I remember correctly it was like you say, pretty slim. But we have to check again anyway."

"You do that then since you're the one who knows the case," said Martinez, "and I'll talk with Telia and the other cell phone companies." It has to be done anyway, she thought, and she might even get the chance to get out and move around.

Chief Inspector Wiklander met with former chief inspector Persson, and it was Johansson who had arranged the contact. The substance of Wiklander's mission was simple enough. He would interview Persson for informational purposes and make sure that everything Johansson and Persson had talked about that evening when they had brown beans and roast pork—and a drink or two, and as the time passed quite a few—ended up on paper and was read out loud and approved by Persson. Because if Johansson was getting ready for war, he wanted to be well prepared.

The business between them had been taken care of both quickly and painlessly. Considering that Persson looked like an old, red-eyed male elephant who might at any moment drive his tusks through the person he was talking with, he had been both obliging and talkative. Wiklander's extra assignment remained.

"There was one more thing," said Wiklander, trying to sound as if he had just happened to think of it. "It was Johansson who asked me," he added to be on the safe side.

Persson just nodded.

"It's about your former colleague Claes Waltin. The one who quit a few years after the Palme assassination, when you shut down the so-called external operation."

Persson nodded again, but without saying anything.

"Johansson was wondering if you had anything interesting to say about why he quit and what happened to him later—they say he drowned," said Wiklander, and for some reason he felt slightly uneasy when he finally squeezed out the question.

Persson on the other hand reacted in the most unexpected manner. He looked almost delighted, and considering how he usually looked this was a frightening sight for Wiklander.

"I never talk about colleagues," Persson growled. "I don't even talk shit about them if I don't like them, but where that little asshole Waltin is concerned I'll be glad to. Do you want to know why?"

"Yes, please," said Wiklander, for he did want to know, and it was one more reason why he was where he was. Besides, Persson wasn't the type you said no to, regardless of what you wanted personally.

"I never considered him a colleague," Persson snorted. "Waltin was no policeman; he was an ordinary little gangster dandy with police chief training and good manners. So I hope you have enough tape with you so it doesn't run out," said Persson, nodding toward Wiklander's little tape recorder, which he had set on the table between them.

And then Persson told him about former deputy police superintendent Claes Waltin.

"We actually received the tip from our American friends," said the colonel. "We get together occasionally and exchange a few common experiences," he added evasively, "and when we had a session at the beginning of December this case came up. They were the ones who offered it to us actually."

"There wasn't anything that caused you to wonder then?" asked Johansson.

"What do you mean?" the colonel counter-questioned.

"A twenty-five-year-old case on which the statute of limitations was due to run out and that no one seems to have given a thought to for decades. Besides, if I've understood this correctly, you got tips about a couple of people who have already been dead for many years. Eriksson and Welander, I seem to recall," said Johansson, despite the fact that he knew quite well who he was talking about.

"So that's why you think we shared this with you," said the colonel, smiling. "You can have two old corpses to be forwarded to our dear truth commission. Was that what you were thinking, Johansson?"

"The thought may have occurred to me," said Johansson, and he smiled too.

"But it wasn't that way at all," said the colonel, looking at him with his honest blue eyes. "The fact is, I asked the exact same question you did, and the answer I got was convincing enough."

"What was that?" said Johansson.

"That there would be more," said the colonel. "And that we might need Eriksson and Welander for our background analysis, if nothing else. The Americans have devoted a good deal of time to analyzing the data they got when the Germans took possession of the SIRA archive, and among other things they've been running it against their own Rosewood material and a few other goodies they've collected in boxes over the years. However it was, they seemed pretty convinced that names would be produced of individuals who are still highly interesting. To both you and me," the colonel concluded.

And if you think they've produced these with the help of the SIRA archive then they've been holding out on you, thought Johansson, who had no problem whatsoever believing his predecessor Berg's story of what had gone on when Welander removed himself and his comrades from the Stasi files.

"Did they say anything about who would be included in future deliveries?"

"Young radicals from the seventies who have become established citizens and come up in the world," said the colonel. "But who perhaps haven't really made a clean break with their past and who might therefore be interesting both to you and to us. Far more interesting today, by the way, than at the time when they were just marching in a lot of demonstrations and giving you hell," he added.

Not someone like Tischler, but quite probably Helena Stein, thought Johansson.

"And you don't think this may be part of a disinformation campaign from their side?" he asked.

"No," said the colonel. "For the simple reason that there is no reason to carry on with that sort of thing anymore. We're living in a new era," said the colonel credulously.

So that's what we're doing? The hell we are, thought Johansson.

"Give me a name. Who was it who gave you this information?"

"I'd rather not," said the colonel, squirming. "And you know why as well as I do."

"Then I'm afraid I'll have to ask you again," said Johansson, who was suddenly reminded of Berg's old hand, Chief Inspector Persson. If you don't want to keep company with your former colleague Wennerström of course, thought Johansson.

"Normally it doesn't work like that," said the colonel evasively, "but I'll make an exception because they gave us the go-ahead to share this with you."

How did the CIA get the idea that they could decide that sort of thing for us? thought Johansson, who could already feel his blood pressure rising.

"As I said, we get together occasionally, and this time it was more of a social event, I guess, it being almost Christmas and all, so we had a nice dinner at the old mess out at Karlberg and listened to a darned interesting lecture that one of their guys gave us. A real old legend in the industry actually, and what he had to tell was both highly informative and highly entertaining. He was the one who came up and asked me after dinner if we were interested, and when I said we were he promised to get back to me. Then one of our regular contacts at their embassy contacted us within just a few days and did a presentation for us. Our analysts were obviously included, so we're entirely in agreement here, they and I," said the colonel, nodding. "It was the genuine article we were offered."

"Has anything else arrived?" asked Johansson. How naive can he be? Or is he pulling my leg? he thought.

"Not yet," said the colonel, shaking his head, "but there's nothing strange about that, because even then they said it might take a good while."

"The legend," Johansson reminded him, "what was his name?"

"Since you're the one who's asking," sighed the colonel, "Liska. Michael Liska, born in Hungary during the war, fled as a teenager to the U.S.A. after the revolution in 1956. Big burly guy in his sixties. Called the Bear actually, Michael 'The Bear' Liska," said the colonel, nodding with the sincere expression of one who did not need to unburden his heart.

"What a fucking story," said Wiklander, despite the fact that he almost never swore. Persson had just finished talking about the former police superintendent Claes Waltin.

"I told you he was a fucking jerk," said Persson. "And if you want a piece of good advice to take with you, by the way," he added. This Wiklander seems to be a real policeman in any case, thought Persson.

"Yes, please," said Wiklander. He's actually quite pleasant once you get to know him, thought Wiklander.

"This job," said Persson, "be sure to keep your distance, otherwise you'll go crazy, start seeing ghosts in the light of day."

"Sure," said Wiklander. "I've already sensed that." Because I really have, he thought.

"Never forget you're a policeman," said Persson, nodding seriously. "Keep your distance from the crooks, don't make things complicated, and never start compromising with them."

Johansson's first task when he returned to work was to call in his head of counterespionage and ask him to find out as soon as possible, preferably immediately, what information the group had about an old CIA agent by the name of Michael "The Bear" Liska.

Then his secretary stepped in to report that Chief Inspector Anna Holt was looking forward to seeing him as soon as possible.

"She can come in now," said Johansson. War it would be.

"They're Stein's fingerprints. Both the one on the kitchen counter and the one on the inside of the door under the sink," she said laconically. What can you say to that? she thought.

"What do we do now?" asked Holt, looking at her boss inquisitively. "You're the one who decides after all," she said, smiling weakly.

"How do you interpret her prints?" asked Johansson. "Even an old man like me can see that she's been in Eriksson's apartment, but do you have any idea when her fingerprints ended up there?"

Now you're sounding like the Johansson I've heard about, thought Holt, and then she spoke about the pedantic, demanding Eriksson, about his Polish cleaning woman who certainly had to earn her meager pay, and about the window of opportunity this left for her and Johansson.

"She cleaned every Friday. Eriksson was murdered on a Thursday evening. I have a hard time believing that the kitchen counter was sparkling clean every time the cleaning woman had been there, so we have at the earliest Friday after lunch the week before—when the cleaning woman left the apartment the last time before the murder—and at the latest the same evening Eriksson was murdered, which gives us a little less than a week."

"Was there anything interesting in the wastebasket?" asked Johansson.

"Not according to the report from the crime scene investigation," said Holt, shaking her head, "but personally, I'm pretty sure the impression on the inside of the cupboard door ended up there at the same time as the one on the counter."

"I'm inclined to agree with you," said Johansson, nodding. "Too bad there isn't a date stamp on the impression." The clouds are gathering over little Ms. Stein's head, but the lightning bolt has not yet struck her, he thought. "Do we have anything else that might lead us closer?"

"Martinez is checking the phones," said Holt.

Johansson shook his head doubtfully.

"I think you can forget that," he said. "We had a similar case a while ago and I'm pretty sure that this is too old for either Telia or Comviq. They were the only cell phone operators in the market at that time, weren't they? Unless there's something saved in the investigation about Eriksson?"

"Nada," said Holt. "I've checked that myself. He hardly ever called anyone, and there was almost no one who called him. Stein hasn't in any event. He didn't have a cell phone."

"Money then," said Johansson.

"Mattei is in the process of checking that part," said Holt, "but I don't think we should pin our hopes on that either."

"I agree with you," said Johansson, "because even if there had been something like that between Eriksson and Stein, her cousin Tischler would surely have taken care of it."

"We have a hand towel too," said Holt, and then she told him about the vomit-stained hand towel that Bäckström of all people had found at the bottom of the laundry basket in Eriksson's bathroom. "The time-related problem with that is the same as with the fingerprints, I guess, but I'm pretty sure it was Eriksson's murderer who threw up in it after the act," Holt continued.

"I agree with you completely," said Johansson. "We'll have to try to secure DNA on it." Vomit is better than fingerprints when it concerns murder, he thought.

"We've requested it to be sent up to us from the tech squad in Stockholm," said Holt, "so I'm guessing it's already on its way. Vomit is of course even better than fingerprints," Holt clarified.

"I wonder if I can ask you a favor?" said Johansson. "I'd like to look at the pictures from the crime scene, so if you could give me the materials on the crime scene investigation and the forensic investigation, plus everything else you consider to be of interest, I'll try to form an impression of how the whole thing played out."

"Of course," said Holt. He apparently cares in any event, she thought.

"Well," said Johansson, smiling and leaning back in the chair, "do you still think Stein did it?"

"Yes," said Holt, nodding. "Unfortunately we're moving in that direction." And it doesn't feel especially good, she thought.

"And that bothers you," Johansson said.

"Yes," said Holt.

"Because she's a woman?" asked Johansson.

"Maybe," said Holt, "I don't know." Pull yourself together now, Anna, she thought.

"Sometimes it's hard to like the situation," said Johansson. "Especially when Eriksson seems to have been such an outstanding little asshole."

"Where would we be if it was open season on getting rid of assholes?" said Holt. He's actually rather pleasant, she thought.

"There would be a lot less people," said Johansson, who seemed amused by the thought. "Now let's do this," Johansson continued, sitting up straight in the chair and beginning to count on his fingers. "We like the situation, we don't make things complicated, we mistrust chance, and to start with we pull out that hand towel. When we're done with that and everything else," Johansson continued, holding up the fifth finger on his left hand, "then we turn all our worries over to the prosecutor with a clean conscience."

"All right by me," said Holt, smiling involuntarily.

"After all, this isn't actually a murder investigation we're working on," Johansson concluded.

This is going like clockwork, thought Johansson as Wiklander sat down on the chair Holt had just left.

"I'm listening," said Johansson.

Everything that had been discussed between Johansson and Persson over their roast pork and brown beans was now noted in an interview, a copy of which Johansson would receive the next day. In addition Persson extended his greetings to the boss and looked forward to seeing him again in more pleasant circumstances.

"You've got a real old-time policeman there," said Johansson with an extra dollop of Norrland dialect. "So what did he have to say about little Waltin?"

Quite a bit, according to Wiklander, but nothing that was particularly flattering to former deputy police superintendent Claes Waltin.

"Spare me no details," said Johansson, leaning comfortably back in his chair.

Claes Waltin had as noted already quit the secret police in the spring of 1988 because the so-called external operation, of which he had been the head, had finally been shut down. He was the one who had resigned, but if he hadn't done so it was most likely that he would have been removed anyway.

"Financial irregularities," Wiklander summarized. "The auditors were furious with him, but because he was who he was Berg was content that he turned in his resignation and quit."

"He seems to have been pretty well off," said Johansson. "If I've understood things correctly he had a lot of inherited money?"

A great deal of inherited money, according to what could be determined. As well as an even greater amount whose origin was less clear but could probably be attributed to various shady transactions made during his time with the secret police. Another portion of his wealth he had buried abroad, and no one ever really got a handle on that, but it probably originated from the same sources as the majority of the money that had been found.

"Waltin seems to have been a real gem," Wiklander summarized.

"And think how well dressed he was," said Johansson, grinning contentedly.

Not when he died, according to Wiklander. Not even a bathing suit was left on what the Mediterranean birds and fish left behind of the former deputy police superintendent.

"He was on vacation in Mallorca," said Wiklander. "It was October of 1992. He had checked into a really extravagant luxury hotel that he visited every fall—it's out on the furthest northern point above Port de Pollenca—and every morning he was there he would take a dip in the Mediterranean before breakfast. But one morning he didn't come back, and when he was finally found almost fourteen days later, it was only his remains, bumping against the seawall a couple miles away from the hotel."

"I see," said Johansson. "Was there anything strange about that?"

"Not according to the Spanish authorities," Wiklander replied. "It was written off as an ordinary accident. In any case no bullet holes were found in the little that was left of him. Not according to Persson anyway."

"So what did Berg say," Johansson wondered.

"Berg was apparently his usual self," said Wiklander. "He immediately took over the domestic investigation as soon as he found out that Waltin was dead. Among other things he had a really thorough search done at Waltin's residence. He had a large apartment on Norr Mälarstrand, as well as an old family estate down in Sörmland."

"And it's quite certain that those remains were Waltin's?" asked Johansson, who was meticulous about such things.

"According to Persson they were one hundred percent sure. They had access to his DNA, and when the remains came home to Sweden they compared that DNA with what they already had, so it had been established beyond a doubt that it really was Waltin."

We'll all have to try to live with the sorrow, thought Johansson piously.

"So was anything interesting found at his home?" he asked.

"That's what was so strange," said Wiklander. "With the exception of some mysterious will that was in his safe-deposit box and which I'll come back to, more or less nothing was found of a more private nature. There were a lot of expensive paintings and furniture, but nothing more personal."

"That must have been a downer for Berg," Johansson chuckled.

"Yes," said Wiklander. "Among other things Waltin was known as a ladies' man, so I guess everyone was a little surprised that no traces of that part of his life were found. For a while they had the idea that he'd cleaned up after himself and gone to Mallorca to commit suicide. He had started drinking rather heavily after he quit working with us," Wiklander added. "According to the colleagues who ran into him in town he was starting to look rather moth-eaten toward the end."

"Is that what he did?" asked Johansson. "Took his own life I mean?" Nice to hear he was a ladies' man, he thought, and for some reason it was his own wife he was thinking about.

"I don't know," said Wiklander, shrugging his shoulders. "There was never any real clarity on that point, but according to the Spaniards it was a pure accident. They naturally talked with the personnel at the hotel, and according to them he was exactly the same as usual the morning that he drowned."

"There were no witnesses?" asked Johansson.

"No witnesses," said Wiklander, shaking his head. "It was mostly Spaniards who stayed at the hotel, and they lounged in bed until late in the morning in contrast to Waltin, who apparently was a morning person. The hotel had its own beach too, discreet and separate from the hoi polloi."

"I see," said Johansson. "We'll have to live with the uncertainty. So what was there with that will?" he wondered.

"A real shocker," said Wiklander. "It was in his safe deposit box, it was handwritten, and it had been established beyond a doubt that he wrote it himself. You'll hardly believe it's true." Wiklander shook his head.

"What was in it then?" asked Johansson impatiently.

"All the money he had—and there was quite a bit—was to go to a foundation to support research on hypochondria among women, in memory of his old mother, and the foundation would bear her name. The Foundation for Research into Hypochondria in Memory of my Mother, Aino Waltin, and All Other Hypochondriacal Old Hags Who Have Ruined the Lives of Their Children—that was what he wanted it to be called."

"Sounds nice," said Johansson, whose mother would soon turn ninety. She had given birth to seven children and got up with the rooster the day after every birth. Dear Mama Elna. It's high time I called to ask how she's doing, thought her youngest son Johansson affectionately.

"That was far from the worst." said Wiklander. "He wrote down a detailed explanation too. He said his mother had apparently promised she would die for as long as he could remember, from basically every conceivable illness to be found in a medical book, and finally he got so tired of the old hag and her unfulfilled promises of an imminent departure that he pushed her off the platform at the Östermalm subway station."

"That sounds completely insane," said Johansson. Not even Waltin could have been that crazy, he thought.

"In and of itself, yes," said Wiklander. "The problem is that the old lady appears to have died in exactly that way, sometime in the late sixties when Waltin himself was about twenty-five years old and studying law at the University of Stockholm."

"So did he do it?" asked Johansson.

"It was written off as a pure accident," said Wiklander, "but our colleague Persson was completely convinced that he was the one who killed her. According to Persson she wasn't the only one either, but he didn't want to go into who the others were, so I think that was mostly bullshit."

Amazing story, thought Johansson.

"So what happened with the foundation?" he asked.

"It didn't happen," said Wiklander. "The will was declared invalid and the money went to his old father. They hadn't met since Waltin was a little boy, because the old man had taken his secretary, fled his home, and moved down to Skåne, but he got the money in any event. Whatever he could do with it, because he was pretty well heeled himself, and besides he was already ancient when his son died. The old man is said to have died a year or two ago, just before he turned a hundred."

"I see," said Johansson. "This was a rather amazing story."

"Yes," said Wiklander. "It's got just about everything, but what I don't really get is what this has to do with our case. With Stein, I mean?"

"Nothing at all," said Johansson. "I promise and assure you that it has nothing whatsoever to do with our case. I was simply curious about what happened to Waltin," said Johansson.

Should I believe that? thought Wiklander, who was a real policeman and had already forgotten the good advice his predecessor Persson had given him.

When Johansson arrived home that evening, after mature deliberation, and against his oath of secrecy—after all this matter did not bear directly on the security of the realm—he told the whole, sorrowful story of Waltin and his demise to his wife, Pia.

"I knew that something would happen," said Pia agitatedly. "He was just the type to be murdered."

Sigh and moan, thought Johansson. Wonder if it can be all the vegetables she eats. For according to his clear understanding, based on common sense and far too much experience, Waltin was exactly the type who would never be murdered.

"I've just told you that he drowned," said Johansson with emphasis on every syllable. "So why do you persist in saying that he must have been murdered?"

"He was the type," said Johansson's wife. "I'm quite sure. I can feel it. That's just how it is."

"What do you think about sleeping on it?" Johansson suggested, pointedly turning off the light on his nightstand. Another one that's like a child, he thought, and it was his good fortune that his wife was not a coworker of Anna Holt.

34

Tuesday, April 4, 2000

Holt devoted half of Tuesday to searching for a vanished hand towel, but the only thing the tech squad in Stockholm came up with was yet another copy of the forensic report already in the investigation file confirming the existence of the hand towel in question, and they gave a number of strangely evasive responses when she talked with them on the phone. Meanwhile her colleague Martinez, who had promised to help her, had disappeared.

"Okay," said Holt when she finally got hold of Martinez, in their own break room of all places. "We'll have to hop down to Stockholm and question that fuckup Wiijnbladh, who was responsible for the hand towel debacle."

"I don't think it's going to be easy," said Martinez, who had already investigated the matter.

Wiijnbladh had scarcely been a giant at the time Holt had worked with him on the investigation of the murder of Kjell Göran Eriksson. He was currently a fragment of his former self, and had been working for several years at the Stockholm Police Department's so-called lost-and-found. The alleged purpose of the job was to hunt for stolen and missing goods, though everyone who knew anything worth knowing also knew that this was one of the agency's many assignments for warehousing colleagues for whom things had gone badly but who for various reasons could not simply be kicked out.

Mere months after the murder of Kjell Eriksson, Wiijnbladh had suffered an accident at work under peculiar circumstances. One day he had simply fallen apart at work—cramps, vomiting, crazed outbursts—and his terrified colleagues had carted him off to the ER at Karolinska, where he was immediately sent on to intensive care.

At first no one understood a thing. The assembled medical experts stood by scratching their heads, until a senior physician in the department with a good memory recalled a recent, very sad story at the Karolinska Institute about a young medical student who had stolen a bottle of thallium, which he had used to poison his father. From the notes in Wiijnbladh's medical record it appeared that he worked as a crime technician with the Stockholm police, and the doctor quickly added one and one together and got to two. Because there was no way to talk with Wiijnbladh himself—in plain Swedish he was completely gone, and was wandering back and forth in the borderland between life and death—his doctor called the head of the Stockholm Police Department's disciplinary unit, whom he knew due to a previous, similar story, and reported his observations directly to him.

The bottle of thallium was found locked up where it should have been at the tech squad, but the quantity it contained was less than what it should have been according to the confiscation report, and the remainder, more than ten grams, was found on the shelf in Wiijnbladh's locker at work. Someone, most likely Wiijnbladh himself, had poured it into a can that originally held instant coffee.

Considering that a few hundredths of a gram was sufficient to kill, and that even a few microscopic grains on the skin were more than sufficient to make you feel like Wiijnbladh, the potential for harm was frightening and the agitation at the tech squad had been great. They were worried not so much about Wiijnbladh as about what might have happened to other, completely normal colleagues in Chief Inspector Blenke's valiant battalion.

"But what would he do with ten grams of thallium?" Holt asked with surprise.

"According to a colleague at internal investigations, Wiijnbladh was going to use it to kill his wife," Martinez explained.

"What?" said Holt. That little twit, she thought. Who knew he had that much backbone?

"Although that problem solved itself—they say she'd already left him before he was discharged from the hospital. I hardly think he's in any condition to kill her with anything he can swipe from all the old shit he has access to down at the lost-and-found department," said Martinez. "It's mostly stolen bicycles and TVs," she clarified.

"So what happened to the hand towel?" asked Holt.

According to Martinez the hand towel had been lost to forensic science in the general disorder that had broken out in the wake of Wiijnbladh's sudden bout of ill health. In normal circumstances Wiijnbladh would have placed it in one of the tech squad's freezers for storage to await any future needs—such as now, for example—or until the case was closed and it could be discarded. But things did not go as usual.

Instead it had remained lying on Wiijnbladh's work bench, and because it was well packaged it had managed to rot considerably before the odor finally forced its way through the plastic, alarming Wiijnbladh's colleagues—who by that time were rather sensitive where he was concerned—and one of them took immediate measures.

"Someone simply threw it in the garbage," said Martinez, shrugging her shoulders. "It's unclear who, but it was someone who worked there."

"I see," said Holt. "Have you spoken with Wiijnbladh?"

"Yes," said Martinez, "and the reason I didn't take you along was that you were sitting talking to our beloved boss."

"So what did Wiijnbladh say?" Holt wondered. Typical, she also thought.

"Not much," said Martinez, shaking her head. "The guy's only a remnant. No hair, hardly any teeth left, his whole body shaking like he's playing maracas. I could hardly hear what he was saying and he didn't remember any hand towel or any murder of any Eriksson. On the other hand he remembered that he had personally solved hundreds of murders when he was working at the tech squad. He just didn't remember Eriksson. Then he asked me to say hello to someone named Bäckström. So I promised to do that. Is he someone you know?"

"Depends on what you mean by know," said Holt, shrugging her shoulders. "He was the one in charge of the Eriksson investigation."

"Omigod," said Martinez. "I wondered. So what's he like?"

"Well," said Holt, delaying her response. "Like Wiijnbladh—only the other way around—and just as bad."

"I get it," said Martinez.

According to Martinez it was still too early for them to throw in the proverbial towel. One of their own technicians had promised to do his best with the report and get back to them as soon as possible, and dear Mattei had had an idea when Martinez told the sorrowful story of the hand towel to her.

"What was that?" said Holt.

"She didn't say," said Martinez, "but it must have been something pretty special, because she left the building before lunch. What's with you anyway? You look strange."

"I had an idea myself," said Holt. "It was just something that struck me." Wonder if he's alive, she thought.

"Spooky," said Martinez. "Real, real spooky."

Mattei returned from her mysterious expedition that same afternoon, with flushed cheeks and a story she simply had to tell.

"Where have you been?" asked Holt.

"I've been out surveilling. I didn't get hold of you because you were sitting in Johansson's office, but I got the go-ahead from Wiklander."

"So where have you been?" Holt wondered impatiently. "With the Hell's Angels in their cozy little clubhouse out in Solna?"

"No, yuck," said Mattei. "I've been with SACO at their main office in Östermalm, and it was just in the nick of time actually."

As she was reading the report on the hand towel Mattei had gotten an idea.

"The person who vomited in the towel had evidently consumed fish, vegetables, and coffee," said Mattei.

"Yes, I saw that too," said Holt.

"And considering that the traces were visible, I realized the meal must have been consumed relatively late in the day," Mattei explained. "But it would be before the person vomited into the hand towel," she clarified.

"Yes," said Holt. Even I realized that, she thought.

"And then I happened to think about that conference," said Mattei.

Considering that it was an all-day conference, it did not seem entirely unreasonable that at the end of the day those who had worked at the conference—organizers and presenters, for example—might have been offered a meal as thanks for their efforts, even if this was not listed on the printed program that Holt had collected for the investigation more than ten years earlier.

"They did have such a meal, of course, because they always did," said Mattei. "It was in their own executive dining room, and there were only ten or so participants. Stein was there at the dinner as an invited presenter. And they still have the menu and a list of the participants, since you need those for accounting purposes and you have to save the records for at least ten years according to the regulations. By next week they would have started to clean out the accounts from fiscal year 1989, so I was in the nick of time," Mattei concluded, catching her breath.

"And fish was served at the dinner they were treated to," said Holt.

"Of course," said Mattei. "There was fish as an appetizer—salted West Coast cod on a bed of rucola—and fish and vegetables as an entrée. It was flounder, by the way, with oven-baked root vegetables and lime dressing. Here's the menu," said Mattei, handing over a thin plastic folder.

"Fish as an appetizer and fish and vegetables as an entrée," Holt repeated.

"Yes, it was almost only women at the dinner, so that was probably why," said Mattei. "It actually sounds really good. And Stein was there, as I said, and she ate."

"Yes, I heard you say that," said Holt, "and it—"

"Although on the other hand she declined the snack later," Mattei interrupted.

"How do you know that?" asked Holt with surprise.

"She's crossed off the list," said Mattei. "They had an early dinner at six o'clock," said Mattei, "and there were eleven different participants listed of which one is attorney Helena Stein. But then cheese and fruit and red wine were served as a kind of evening snack at ten o'clock, and seven of them signed up for that. The others had to go home, I guess to take care of the kids, and one of the seven who signed up was Helena Stein."

"But then her name is crossed out?" Holt clarified. For her own sake, she wasn't going to get anything turned around.

"Yes," said Mattei, "and I think she must have declined at the last minute."

"I do too," said Holt slowly.

"She must have been in a hurry if she was going to kill Eriksson at eight o'clock," Mattei observed in a most unsentimental manner.

Fifteen minutes later Martinez called Holt and reported that her contact at the tech squad had called and wanted to share his findings regarding the hand towel, provided they could come to see him at the tech squad of course.

Nice to get to move a little, thought Holt, who was not accustomed to running investigations from a desk. If anyone had asked her before this strange story got going in earnest, she would certainly have said that solving a case sitting behind a desk was an impossibility. You conquered out in the field—every police officer worth the name knew that. She had never been part of an investigation that had moved with such speed and vigor while she sat in front of her PC or at her desk. We have a break-through, and soon we'll be basking in police department glory. Assuming that Johansson doesn't decide to take the credit, of course.

"Sit down, girls, and make yourselves at home," said the colleague at tech, who had both a beer belly and an old-fashioned, courteous manner.

"Thanks," said Holt, although she actually wanted to say something else.

"Well . . . let's see now," said their technician, pushing up his glasses on his forehead and taking out his copy of the report from the forensic lab, which was now covered with his own notes. "It's rather amusing to be sitting here with three female colleagues in my office—"

"It's nice that you think so," said Holt neutrally, because she was still a chief inspector. She wanted to say something before Martinez could blurt out something less appropriate.

"Yes, considering the conclusions that I've drawn regarding the finds that our colleagues in Linköping SCL secured on the hand towel in question," the colleague continued, looking shrewd.

"I don't really understand," said Holt.

"I'll get to that," said the colleague with a sober expression. "So we have vegetable and animal oils, esters, vegetable fat in solid form, traces of wax plus three different coloring agents, and in addition . . ."

"What he means is that the chemical stuff they found on the hand towel comes from an ordinary lipstick," said Mattei innocently.

The meeting with the colleague from the tech squad had been brief, and in the corridor outside his office Martinez had embraced an embarrassed Mattei and kissed her right on the mouth. Then all three, giggling happily, returned to their project room.

"I had no idea you knew that kind of chemical hocus-pocus too," said Holt, looking at Mattei. Johansson can eat his heart out, she thought. Little Mattei will soon be doing turns around him.

"I don't," Mattei objected. "But I did run it on the computer. There are standard programs for searching chemical finds. This one in particular is a crib sheet I swiped from the FBI."

"This is completely insane," said Martinez happily. "Did you see the bastard's expression? It's an ordinary lipstick," Martinez imitated. "I thought our old colleague was going to freak out."

"Oh well," Mattei objected. "We shouldn't be unfair. He actually has pulled out both the color of the lipstick and the most likely brand. Dark cherry red, cerise, high quality, expensive, probably French manufacture, and in any event not American, because their health laws prohibit the use of one of the coloring components. Probably Lancôme bought in France and not intended for export," Mattei stated with the help of the technician's handwritten notes.

And regardless of the price, it was hardly something that the blonde

Jolanta would use, thought Holt, who to be on the safe side also intended to ask the cleaning lady about it.

"I think it's high time we have a chat with our esteemed boss," said Holt. "What do you think about that?"

Holt had to have her conversation with Johansson without the company of her closest coworkers, because both Mattei and Martinez decided they had other, better things to do.

"Shoot," said Johansson. He leaned back in his chair and nodded encouragingly at his female chief inspector and assistant chief detective, who recounted the status of the investigation in less than five minutes.

"So, that's the situation," Holt concluded. And what do we do now? she wondered.

"It's starting to lean toward our needing to have a talk with Ms. Stein, I'm afraid," said Johansson.

"Isn't it a little too early?" Holt objected.

"Will we get much further then?" asked Johansson. "Wouldn't it be perfect if we could get her to deny that she ever set foot in Eriksson's apartment?" Regardless of the fact that this is not a murder investigation we're involved in, he thought, and besides, his best friend Bo Jarnebring and a few hand-picked colleagues of his from homicide in Stockholm could take care of that work. Nothing could be better than to solve this in such a fashion, he thought.

"I understand how you're thinking," said Holt. "The risk is that then she'll suddenly remember that sometime before—but she's not sure which day it was—she happened to stop by Eriksson's by pure coincidence. Perhaps because she saw her cousin Tischler and he was the one who suggested it. And I can imagine that he'd be willing to swear to that."

"Yes," said Johansson, "but she's going to think of that explanation sooner or later no matter what, if this gets serious." And at least then she will have talked with her attorney, he thought.

"You're looking for an opportunity to be rid of the whole case and send it down to Stockholm," said Holt. Say that you aren't, she thought.

"Yes," said Johansson seriously, "I actually am, because this is starting to look suspiciously like something that shouldn't be on our table anymore. But I've also realized that you really, really want to have a talk with Stein, so I'm willing to discuss the matter."

"Then I have an idea," said Holt.

As soon as Holt had left, Johansson told his secretary that under no circumstances did he want to be disturbed. Then he ordered coffee and a much too large bag of Danish pastries from a nearby bakery, and because his wife was traveling for work he had the whole afternoon and evening to himself to go through the crime scene investigation from Eriksson's apartment and the autopsy report in peace and quiet.

When he got up from his desk a few hours later to stretch his legs, he was completely convinced that he knew what had gone on down to the slightest detail when Kjell Göran Eriksson was murdered almost ten and a half years ago.

Oh shit, thought Lars Martin Johansson, who had never really been able to come to terms with the experience of holding another person's entire existence in his hands. Maybe I could call Jarnie. After all, he was the one who found Eriksson, he thought, and the mere idea made his mood feel lighter.

"The murder of Kjell Eriksson," said Johansson. "Do you remember it?"

"I was the one who found him, so I guess I remember a few things," Jarnebring answered. "Bäckström got to play investigation leader and Wiijnbladh was of course the way he was—so the fact that it went the way it did probably isn't so strange."

"A poorly run investigation," said Johansson, and this was more a statement than a question.

"Does Dolly Parton sleep on her back? Does Pinocchio have a wooden dick?" Jarnebring asked. "True, I hoped you might treat me to dinner, but it's clear . . . if you've cleared up a ten-year-old murder for us I might as well treat myself to a hot dog on the way home."

"It doesn't have to be that bad," said Johansson. "I've already reserved a table for us."

"Sounds good," said Jarnebring. "My wife is forewarned and I've got permission. So there's only one thing I'm wondering about."

"I'm listening," said Johansson.

"Why is SePo suddenly interested in Eriksson? I mean, if you've found out that he was spying for the Russians then perhaps you're a bit late, considering the state of both Eriksson and the Russians."

"I've thought about that as a matter of fact," said Johansson. "And I can tell you about it, but then I'll have to ask you to sign a bunch of papers first."

"Then I think we'll forget about that," said Jarnebring, grinning. "Just so we get out of here at some point."

"Good," said Johansson. "Then I thought I'd ask you to look at this picture," he continued, bringing up an image on the overhead projector in his conference room, which showed Kjell Eriksson lying dead on the floor in his own living room.

"Damn, the things you've got in this place," said Jarnebring with involuntary admiration in his voice. "And here I sit, an ordinary, lousy country cop, in my worn-out shoes and my ragged old detective jacket."

"Which you paid for yourself," Johansson observed.

"Life isn't fair," said Jarnebring, slowly shaking his head. "I recognize the picture. It must be one of Wiijnbladh's old pictures."

"Does this agree with your own recollection?" asked Johansson.

It was a picture of Eriksson's living room that had been taken from the door between the hall and the living room. The couch was located a few yards out from the short wall running toward the kitchen, and the door into the kitchen was diagonally behind. The overturned coffee table was flanked on either side by an antique armchair and an amply proportioned wingback chair. Squeezed between the couch and the coffee table was Eriksson, lying on his stomach in his own blood.

"Yes," said Jarnebring. "It looks the way I remember it. Are you going to tell me what happened before he ended up there?"

"I thought we could discuss that," said Johansson.

"I'm listening," said Jarnebring.

"Eriksson is sitting on the couch having a drink with his back toward the door to the kitchen. He has no idea what's going to happen before it happens. The perpetrator comes out from the kitchen and stabs him in the back while he's sitting down. When the perpetrator pulls the knife out of Eriksson's back, blood gushes out of the wound onto the upper edge of the back of the couch. Those are the stains you see here," said Johansson, clicking to an enlargement of the couch, showing the top side of the back of the couch and half a dozen closely spattered blood-stains the size of rice grains.

"I don't recognize this enlargement," said Jarnebring. "I haven't seen it before."

"That's 'cause our technicians developed it, but the original is Wiijn-bladh's," said Johansson.

"What are you saying?" Jarnebring sighed. "Why didn't Wiijnbladh ever do that?"

"If you look at the victim's left shirt sleeve," Johansson continued, clicking to the next enlargement, which showed Eriksson lying on his stomach on the floor with his arms along the sides of his body, "then you see that he has blood on the shirt sleeve right above the cuff, approximately where he dragged his shirt sleeve across the wound in his back to feel it."

"On the other hand I do recall that we talked about this, and for once colleague Bäckström and I were in agreement," said Jarnebring. "Eriksson didn't realize at first what had happened, so he dragged his free arm over the place on his back that had just been stabbed—he was holding his toddy glass in his right hand—and when he realized what had happened, he went crazy and started to raise Cain. Did you read the interview with the neighbor lady?"

"Yes," said Johansson. "But what does he do next?"

"Then he seems to have moved around a bit," said Jarnebring vaguely.

"Seen from the kitchen, with the eyes of the perpetrator, Eriksson is sitting to the right on the couch when the perpetrator comes into the living room," Johansson said. "Closest to the kitchen door where the perpetrator comes from."

"Even I get that," said Jarnebring. "It's apparent from the location of the bloodstains on the back of the couch that Eriksson was sitting there when he was stabbed."

"But nonetheless he first moved to the left between the couch and the coffee table," said Johansson.

"Are you sure of that?" Jarnebring objected. "That's not the way he's lying. He's lying with his head to the right, facing toward the hall. Personally I get the idea he got up, started to raise Cain, and then just folded over—headlong right where he was sitting—he'd been bleeding like a stuck pig so it must have gone fast."

"No," said Johansson, "it probably didn't go quite that fast, because first he took a few steps to the left between the couch and the coffee table, then he turned and went back the way he came, still moving along between the couch and the coffee table. When he was back to the starting point he fell down, pulling the coffee table over as he dropped, and the toddy glass he had put down on the table fell to the floor."

"This sounds serious, Lars," said Jarnebring, grinning. "I'm almost getting the idea you were there when it happened."

"No, but it's enough to look at this to realize how he moved," said Johansson, clicking to an enlargement of the blood traces on the floor. "While he was moving to the left, blood from his wound was splashing on the floor, and he stepped in the blood when he turned in place and moved back to the right."

"When I look at that, yes," said Jarnebring, nodding at Johansson's enlargement. "But when we sat and stared at Wiijnbladh's original, it just looked like the end of the night shift at Enskede slaughterhouse. A fucking lot of blood everywhere."

"So why did he move in that way?" asked Johansson.

"The simple explanation is that he was trying to get out of reach of the perpetrator, I guess," said Jarnebring. "The perpetrator was still standing at the right end of the couch where Eriksson had been sitting when he was stabbed. When Eriksson moved away from the perpetrator, that is, to the left, the perpetrator rounded the coffee table on the other side and Eriksson fled back to the right—and then he fell."

"I think it was just the opposite," said Johansson. "True, I'll buy the location and movements of the perpetrator in the room—on the other side of the coffee table and the armchairs—and first to the left and then back to the right again—but otherwise you're wrong."

"Since I'm the one who's playing the fool here, naturally I wonder what you mean," said Jarnebring.

"What I mean is that it was Eriksson who was trying to get hold of the perpetrator," said Johansson. "It was Eriksson who was following the perpetrator, and the perpetrator who was backing up. Not the other way around."

"The hell it was," Jarnebring objected. "Not that I met Eriksson while he was alive, but I still got the distinct impression that he was a real little coward."

"But not this time," said Johansson, "because he was not physically afraid of this particular perpetrator."

"I see," said Jarnebring, smiling broadly. "You're onto colleague Bäckström's line, that after all it was a little fairy we're searching for."

"No," said Johansson. "It's someone else we're looking for."

"Someone that Eriksson knew, someone he wasn't afraid of, but instead someone with whom even Eriksson could feel big and strong," said Jarnebring.

"Yes," said Johansson. Unfortunately that's the way it is, he thought.

"Damn, Lars, say what you want about old unsolved murders, but they're good for the appetite," Jarnebring said an hour later as they sat at their usual table at Johansson's regular place and had just been served a baked sandwich of Parma ham, mozzarella, basil, and tomato as a little prelude to the lamb filet that would come when it was time to get serious.

"Too bad it has to be an ordinary Tuesday," said Johansson vaguely.

"You're thinking of a small one," said Jarnebring.

"What makes you think that?" Johansson asked evasively.

"I'm a cop," said Jarnebring. "I've been a cop my whole adult life—and I've known you just as long—and because Pia is out of town anyway and I am free myself, I get the idea that you, in your dark Norrland way, are talking about a little shot, despite the fact that it's only Tuesday."

"What the hell should we do?" said Johansson hesitantly. It is only Tuesday after all, he thought.

"Order two good-sized shots and pretend it's Friday," Jarnebring decided.

35

Wednesday, April 5, 2000

It was Holt's suggestion, a sudden idea, a pure hunch that would probably prove to be completely wrong.

"It's worth trying anyway," Johansson said, which was why he was sitting with Wiklander in his office early Wednesday morning, refining tactics. Unusually alert and sober besides, despite the previous evening.

"I see you've already spoken with our colleague Holt," said Johansson, nodding toward the little gold pin in the form of a trident that now adorned the lapel of Wiklander's jacket.

"Old coast commando," Wiklander nodded, not without pride as it appeared.

"Yes, be happy you don't have to wear a fake mustache," said Johansson, who was in the absolute best of moods because he was being let out into the field again. Despite his high rank, and despite all the old rust he was no doubt dragging along with him.

The day before, Holt had suddenly happened to think of Eriksson's neighbor, the major, about whom she had had her suspicions after she and Jarnebring had interviewed him ten years ago.

"I had the distinct impression he was hiding something from us," Holt had explained to her boss. "He was a guarded type, very guarded, and he had peepholes in the door and a good view of both the hallway and the stairwell. Because there had been a lot of racket at Eriksson's the night of the murder, I thought it was more than probable that he had tried to peep out and see what was happening. Possibly he saw the perpetrator when he or she left. At that time I was completely convinced that the person we were searching for was a man," she clarified. "All of us were, not least Bäckström."

"Why didn't the major say so then?" asked Johansson. "About whether he'd seen anything."

"For several reasons, I think," said Holt. "First, he clearly seemed to dislike Eriksson. Second, he didn't like the police. That was probably enough for him to decide to keep his mouth shut. And it may have been much simpler too," she added.

"What do you mean?" asked Johansson.

"He was extremely anxious to show what an old warrior he was. For a while I almost thought he was going to show us an old bullet wound from the Finnish war he was boasting about. But maybe when he saw something he was just afraid, like anyone else would be, or out of cowardice or laziness he didn't want to be drawn into something. I'm sure he would rather bite his tongue off than admit to something like that."

"Yes," said Johansson, nodding. "But isn't it still most likely that he didn't see anything?"

"Yes," said Holt. "That's the most likely—that I'm completely wrong."

"It's worth trying anyway," said Johansson. "But why do you want me in particular to do it?" he added. "You should know it's been a while." Even if I am flattered that she asked, of course, he thought.

"I think you're just the right type to pry open that old cuss," Holt explained.

"Do I look like I might conceivably share his political opinions?" Johansson asked. Think carefully about what you say, Holt, he thought.

"No," said Holt, looking at Johansson, "but you definitely look like a man with strong opinions."

"Nice," said Johansson. And how nice is it on a scale from one to ten, he thought, for he had heard his wife say that.

"He scarcely noticed my presence," Holt explained. "On the other hand he took note of Jarnebring—who doesn't," said Holt, smiling faintly. "But at the same time I think he felt that Jarnebring was maybe a little too simple for him to condescend to take seriously."

"I think I'm starting to get an idea of the type," said Johansson.

So now they were sitting there, at home with the major in his apartment on Rådmansgatan.

"The secret police and the second highest in command if I've understood this correctly," said the major, nodding toward Johansson as he set Johansson's business card down on the desk, behind which he had settled himself. "To what do I owe this honor?"

"It concerns a neighbor of yours, Major Carlgren, a man who was murdered in 1989," Johansson explained.

"That little shit," the major said amiably. "Why in the name of heaven should the secret police be concerned about him? You weren't interested in him when he was still alive."

"As you'll understand, Major, I am prevented from going into any details," said Johansson, looking sternly at the person he was speaking with. "But my colleague Wiklander here and I are following up a tip that we got from our colleagues in the military intelligence service," Johansson concluded, nodding in the direction of Wiklander and the fish spear on his jacket. In a way that is what we're doing, thought Johansson, even if this was the last thing the mysterious informant had had in mind when he brought new life to the Eriksson case.

"Coast commandos," said the major, nodding with approval toward the lapel of Wiklander's jacket.

"I am of course well acquainted with your military experience, Major," said Johansson, who had decided in advance to pour it on thick. "By the way, I had a close relative myself who fought on the Finnish side—"

"So what was his name?" the major interrupted, looking guardedly at Johansson.

"His name was Johansson, Petrus Johansson. He was a commando with the rank of corporal when he fell at Tolvajärvi."

"Was that your father?" asked the major.

"My uncle," Johansson lied. It was bad enough that it had been his father's crazy cousin about whom the older generations in the Johansson family still talked an unbelievable lot of shit whenever they got the chance.

"I know who he was," said the major, nodding. "I never met him but

I know who he was. Corporal Petrus Johansson died a hero's death and you have my sincere sympathy."

"Thank you," said Johansson, who was shaken to his core because an eighty-year-old major had just got the idea that Johansson had been born no later than 1940. I'll have to start dieting, he thought.

"He did not fall in vain," said the major, "as the developments of recent years have no doubt illustrated clearly."

"I would understand completely, Major, if you had seen anything, yet you might nonetheless have chosen to let the whole thing be, considering the victim's past, and considering that the police officers who spoke with you came from the uniformed police with its unfortunately limited insights into security issues. I can reveal this much," said Johansson, who had decided to fire up the boilers as he was picking up speed anyway, "that the individuals we are searching for are cut from the same cloth as Eriksson himself."

"What is it you want to know?" asked the major, who looked as if he had just made a decision.

"I am wondering if you saw the man when he left Eriksson's apartment," said Johansson.

"What makes you think it was a man?" asked the major, and in that moment Johansson knew he had succeeded, because every word he had said had been chosen with care.

"What do you mean, Major Carlgren?" said Johansson, acting surprised.

"It wasn't a man," said the major, shaking his head. "It was a young woman—twenty-five years old perhaps, thirty at most, well-dressed. She was holding a briefcase or something like that pressed against her chest. She seemed rather upset, slammed the door behind her, ran down the stairs, which wasn't so strange in the circumstances."

"Do you recall anything more about her appearance?" asked Johansson.

"She was nice looking," said the major. "Well dressed, neat, I remember I noticed she had a lot of hair—red or maybe more brownish red—not at all that miserable character Eriksson's type. He was much older. When I heard what had happened I got the idea that he had tried to rape her and that she was only defending herself. If that was the case

I hadn't the slightest intention of helping the police lock her up," the major concluded, nodding firmly at Johansson. "Not the slightest," he repeated.

Then they showed pictures to the major. Pictures of twelve different women, of which one was Helena Stein at the age of thirty and another three depicted women of the same age with approximately the same appearance and hair color.

"I recognize that one," the major snorted, setting a skinny, clawlike index finger on Eriksson's cleaning woman, Jolanta. "That's the Polish whore who cleaned under the table for Eriksson."

"Is there anyone else who seems familiar?" Johansson asked. The old man isn't completely gone, he thought hopefully.

The major took his sweet time, spreading out all eleven pictures that remained on his desk. He picked up each and every one of them and inspected it carefully. Then he shook his head.

"No," he said. "I'm sorry. I remember that she had red or in any case reddish-brown hair, so if she's here it must be one of them, but unfortunately I can't say more than that."

You can't have everything, thought Johansson philosophically, and for him personally it was all the same, because he had already figured out how the whole thing fit together.

"Then I must truly thank you for your help," said Johansson.

"Who is it then?" asked the major, nodding toward the pictures on the desk. "Which of them is it?"

"We don't really know yet."

"I hope she gets off," said the major suddenly. "Eriksson was not a good person."

When Johansson returned to work he immediately called in Holt and told her about his conversation with the major.

"I think it's high time you met Helena Stein," said Johansson.

"You've abandoned the idea of turning it over to Stockholm?" asked Holt.

"Yes," said Johansson, sounding more convinced than he actually felt. "There'll just be a lot of unnecessary talk. We'll question her for informational purposes about her contacts with Eriksson without explaining why we're interested in him. If she makes a fool of herself and denies having been in his apartment then we'll call in the prosecutor so he can decide about taking her away." It'll be amusing to see his expression, Johansson thought.

"And otherwise we'll have to see," said Holt.

"Unless you have a better suggestion," said Johansson.

"No," said Holt.

"Okay then," said Johansson as he got up, looking at the clock, and smiled to soften the whole thing. "Then you'll have to excuse me. I have another meeting."

"Helena Stein," said Johansson's boss, the general director, nodding contemplatively. "She's a very interesting woman."

"I understand you've met her," said Johansson.

"Oh yes," the GD confirmed. "She came to the ministry during my time there. True, she has never worked under me, but I've met her several times. For a while I saw her on a daily basis when she was working in the prime minister's office."

"I've never had the pleasure," said Johansson. "What's she like?"

"Intelligent, highly intelligent, and an extraordinarily knowledgeable, sharp attorney. And she looks good too, in that slightly icy way. And she neatly balances her radical opinions with a blouse, pleated skirt, and high heels in well-chosen color combinations," the GD summarized, clearing his throat slightly for some reason as he said the last thing.

"But she's not someone you'd marry—if you were concerned about domestic tranquility," said Johansson, who in the company of his boss had no problem whatsoever playing the role of simple man of the people.

"You said it," said the GD. "Personally I would describe her as very intelligent and at the same time very intellectual. And always ready to stand up for her opinions. Razor-sharp and merciless when she does so. A woman whom the majority of men, especially in our generation, seem to have an extremely difficult time managing."

"Not an easy match for a simple lad from the country," Johansson said with enjoyment.

"Definitely not," said the GD, suddenly sounding rather reserved. "And now I've understood that she has problems."

"Yes," said Johansson. "Now she has problems. The whole thing is rather complicated and hard to understand, and for once we're not the ones who've made it complicated."

"It's just complicated?" asked the GD.

"Yes," Johansson confirmed. "It's complicated."

"Then I suggest you take it very slowly," said the GD. "I have nothing against appearing ignorant in a one-on-one like this, as long as I can be spared more public shortcomings."

"It concerns three connected problems. The first regards her involvement in the occupation of the West German embassy almost twenty-five years ago. The second concerns a number of strange turns in connection with our handling of that case, and those start when she was appointed undersecretary two years ago. The third concerns the murder of one of her acquaintances from the time before the West German embassy. And I suggest we wait with that part."

"Why?" said the GD.

"We need to know a bit more," said Johansson. "On the other hand we probably will fairly soon, so it won't be a long wait."

"The West German embassy," said the GD drawlingly. "She can't have been very old then?"

"Sixteen," said Johansson. "She was young, radical, and involved, but exploited and kept in the dark by her boyfriend, who was almost twice her age."

"In concrete terms," said the GD, "what did she do and why did she do it?"

"She helped the Germans with somewhat simple practical matters. Nothing remarkable. Loaned out her father's car, which her boyfriend, the now deceased Sten Welander, used for transport and reconnaissance missions. She didn't have a driver's license herself, and her father had moved abroad at that time and left the car behind so it was easily accessible. . . . Yes . . . Then she bought food for the terrorists at some point. In addition the Germans stayed for a few days at a summer place that her mother's family owned."

"The Tischler family chateau out on Värmdö," said the GD, who apparently was not completely ignorant.

"Yes," said Johansson. "But the one who actually took care of that was probably her older cousin Theo."

"And that was all," asked the GD.

"Yes," said Johansson. "That was the whole thing."

"So why did she do it?" the GD asked curiously. "Did she know what kind of plans the Germans had?"

"No," said Johansson. "She had no idea about that. She thought it was about helping some radical German students who were wanted at home in Germany to hide from the police. She hadn't heard a word about any terrorists or any violent actions. It was her boyfriend Welander who got her to believe that."

"Helped by a combination of youthful ignorance and radical involvement," the GD added dryly.

"More or less," said Johansson.

"And we are quite sure about this?" asked the GD. "Both what she did in purely practical terms and why she did it?"

"Yes," said Johansson. "There's not the slightest doubt on any of those points."

"If that's so," said the GD while he nodded in the direction of his own ceiling light, "then in Stein's case this concerns the protection of a criminal. Making a rough estimate, without having checked on this, it must be at least fifteen years since the statute of limitations ran out. Probably twenty years."

"Something like that," said Johansson. "Law is not my strong suit."

"But it is mine," said the GD, smiling. "Why did we pull the case out of our files two years ago?"

"For several reasons, according to my predecessor, Berg," said Johansson. "The two who were actively involved, Welander and Eriksson, were both long dead. The statute of limitations had run its course in terms of Stein's involvement and Tischler's probably too. Then the truth commission was going to come in, and considering that the West German embassy was a very conspicuous event that is still interesting in terms of politics and the media—I can imagine for example that the German media would have a few ideas about the Swedish part of the drama—among other things there are relatives of the German victims who are still alive—I guess there was simply a desire for peace and quiet."

"You don't think there were any reasons other than the ones Berg mentioned?" asked the GD.

"Well," said Johansson, "I can think of one."

"Which is what?" asked the GD curiously.

"Eriksson worked for several years as a so-called external collaborator at what was then the security department at the National Police Board. Among other things he was collaborating at the time of the embassy occupation."

"Oh dear," said the GD. "That isn't good."

"Concern for one's own ass is seldom particularly rational," said Johansson, who knew what he was talking about from his own experience.

"Stein then," asked the GD. "The background check on her when she was going to be made undersecretary dates from around the time when the case was cleaned out of the files. What is the connection there?"

"According to my predecessor, the fact that Stein was approved was primarily the result of a strictly legal assessment."

"Of course," said the GD, pursing his narrow lips slightly. "That sounds reasonable, but I have a very hard time believing that Berg would be unaware of the political risk in the event of a leak."

"I think he judged the risk of a leak from his own department to be basically nonexistent, and besides he solved the problem by informing our common acquaintance the undersecretary—the prime minister's own security adviser—about Stein's involvement in the West German embassy."

"So how did Berg describe it?" asked the GD.

"In factually correct and very conciliatory terms," said Johansson.

"And considering that she was appointed, the government seems to have taken the same position," the GD observed.

"Because the information about Stein's involvement in the West German embassy was given orally by Berg to the undersecretary, I get the impression it also may have stayed with him," Johansson clarified.

"Is this something you believe or something you know?" asked the GD.

"It's something that occurred to me," said Johansson.

"Interesting," said the GD. "I was struck by the same thought myself."

"As I've gathered from your description and that of others, Stein's appointment as undersecretary can scarcely have been uncontroversial," said Johansson.

"No," said the GD. "Definitely not, and the general perception among those who consider themselves well informed about such issues was that the government wanted to give the military and defense establishment a tweak on the nose. Considering Helena Stein's personal qualities it was not a bad tweak. She is a creditable opponent, to say the least, and her basic view of defense policy is simple enough to summarize."

"How so?" asked Johansson.

"The four Ns," said the GD. "Nonproliferation, neutrality, and no NATO."

"She can't be entirely alone in that," Johansson objected, having entertained a similar viewpoint himself, despite the fact that he was a hunter and had his appearance against him.

"Among her predecessors in the position this has not exactly been the dominant view, however," the GD said primly. "With Stein it is also the case that as a defense analyst she is far superior to both her sympathizers and her opponents. And it gets really sensitive when we come to the subject of her view of the defense industry and trade in war matériel."

"How so?" asked Johansson.

"For one thing," said the GD, "the basic view she and others have expressed is hardly compatible with the fact that we also export or import defense matériel to or from either the U.S., NATO, or other democracies in the West, not just those economically less interesting non-democracies we've already blacklisted."

"Goodness gracious," said Johansson.

"Yes," the GD agreed. "At Saab and other similar places they can certainly keep a straight face. In monetary terms it comes to more than thirty billion kronor per year if you count both exports and imports and include the civilian element. You see, it's not just about JAS planes, submarines, cannons, mines, explosives, and bomb sights. There's a great deal besides that has economic importance, primarily for civilian production, such as trucks, ventilation systems, electronics, and the packaging of freeze-dried food, one of the most common articles in the military commercial context."

"But that's no joke," said Johansson. "Appointing her undersecretary of defense must be a real blow." Like being knocked down from behind with an iron bar, he thought.

"Helena Stein is more intelligent than that," said the GD, who now appeared visibly amused. "She has always been careful to discuss these issues in principled, ideological terms—not least in terms of legal philosophy. She has raised ideas, brought up issues at a high level, pointed out moral, political, legal, and economic consequences of one position or another."

"I'm sure that didn't make them any less nervous," Johansson objected.

"No," said the GD. "They were completely terrified by the prospect of her appointment. But let's return to the handling of the West German embassy. I understand that a few months ago certain information was returned to our files about the Swedish involvement in the West German embassy."

"Yes," said Johansson. "Reportedly it was because of tips from our American friends, and strangely enough the information specifically concerns Eriksson and Welander, both of whom are dead. On the other hand there was not a word about Tischler and Stein, who are both alive of course."

"What was it that caused Berg to change his mind?" asked the GD.

"There were several reasons, according to him," said Johansson. "That on closer consideration he started to doubt his own cleaning of the files—anyone who is dead can't be affected personally. But mostly it was because he had been promised that more would be coming and he didn't want to take the risk that significant future information would be left hanging in the air. And if you ask me personally, I think his illness was also a contributing factor."

"That he might have lost his edge," said the GD.

"Partly, but also that he had become far too cautious, that he simply didn't dare turn it down," said Johansson.

"But you think this is really about something else," the GD observed.

"Yes," said Johansson. "I don't know if I'm starting to get paranoid, but I get the idea that they actually wanted to open a door so they could send us information about Stein. I have a hard time understanding that this would be about anyone other than her, considering the connection to the West German embassy."

"So what did Berg think about that?" asked the GD.

"That I was wrong," said Johansson. "The fundamental political prerequisites were now lacking, given that the Russians have retreated."

"And what do you think about Berg's view of the matter?" the GD persisted.

"That he's wrong, and after hearing your description of Stein I've only been strengthened in that conviction," said Johansson.

"But has anything else come in?" asked the GD. "About Stein, I mean, because considering her probable appointment, wouldn't it be high time?"

"No," said Johansson. "Nothing yet." It has been as silent as the grave, he thought.

"And how do you interpret that?" asked the GD, who now appeared both interested and amused.

"Either I've got the whole thing turned around," said Johansson, "or else they don't know that she's going to be appointed and they've simply missed the opportunity. Or else they do know about it but are still choosing to wait to turn the screw until she's in her new position."

"So which of those do you think it is?" asked the GD.

"Alternative number three," said Johansson. "That they will let her be appointed—see to it that both she and those who appointed her get raised high enough that it would be a pure catastrophe for both her and the government if any harmful information about her past were to come out—and only then will they start to advance their demands about what she and the rest of us ought to do and not do."

"They don't sound like nice people, if you're right," the GD observed.

"There's yet another complicating factor in that case," said Johansson. "We're talking of course about our American friend, the ultimate bulwark for the democracies of the Western world, a highly esteemed friend raised above all suspicions."

"You've never met her," the GD said suddenly.

"You mean Stein?" said Johansson.

"Yes," said the GD.

"No," said Johansson. "I've never met her." Although I may have to soon, he thought.

"Maybe you ought to do that," said the GD. "Take a discreet look at our object Helena Stein."

"Yes, maybe," said Johansson. A discreet look is never wrong, he thought.

"I'll arrange it then," said the GD, who had a hard time concealing his enjoyment. "A discreet look at Undersecretary Helena Stein when she visits the suspected robber in his own den."

36

Thursday, April 6, 2000

On Thursday the sixth of April, Holt and Wiklander interviewed Under-secretary Helena Stein at the Ministry of Defense. Johansson's secretary decided on the time and place with Stein's secretary, and neither had come as a surprise to Johansson, Holt, or Wiklander.

The undersecretary had an extremely busy schedule, but since the secret police were asking, she nonetheless managed to squeeze them in for half an hour between six and six-thirty in the evening. Because the undersecretary was supposed to be at a reception later that night, she proposed that the police come to her and not the other way around. So the two chief inspectors went to the Ministry of Defense offices on Gustaf Adolf Square in Stockholm.

Helena Stein's secretary conveyed them to the undersecretary's own conference room, asked whether they wanted coffee or water, which they declined, then asked them to sit and wait. After a quarter of an hour Helena Stein strode into the room where they were sitting. She nodded and smiled, apologized for being late. Holt was completely convinced that Stein had no idea what they wanted to talk with her about.

At worst she thinks something has come up in connection with her background check, thought Holt. Something she's prepared for, something she knows she can work her way out of. She's attractive, trim, well dressed, self-confident, and obviously quite intelligent, thought Holt. She could see it in her eyes. Goddamnit, thought Holt.

. . .

After the introductory remarks into the tape recorder, a few words from "Interview leader Chief Inspector Anna Holt" to the effect that "Helena Lovisa Stein is being interviewed for informational purposes in connection with an ongoing security matter," it was finally time to begin.

"We're here because we want to talk with you about an old acquaintance of yours, one Kjell Göran Eriksson," said Holt, trying to concentrate on Stein's reaction.

"Kjell Eriksson," said Stein. "Must be a million years since I saw him. You mean the Kjell Eriksson who was . . . well . . . that awful story from sometime in the late eighties? You want to talk with me about him? I don't even remember what he looked like."

You did it, thought Holt. That tenth of a second when your gaze faltered and then the words came tumbling out. You were trying desperately to keep him away from you, to get control over the situation in which you've suddenly landed. I know you remember Kjell Eriksson. If nothing else, after the West German embassy you must have spent hundreds of hours of your life thinking about Kjell Eriksson, what he was like, who you are. That can't have been easy, she thought.

"We've reopened the case," said Holt. "I'm prevented from going into the reasons why."

"But why in the name of heaven are you asking *me* about him? I hardly knew him," said Stein. "A cousin of mine, Theodor Tischler—I don't know if you know who that is but he was a businessman—worked at a brokerage firm started by his father—he lives abroad now. He was the one who knew him. And . . . it wasn't even really him, either, it was his best friend, Sten Welander. He was an academic to start with . . . worked as a reporter at Swedish Television. He's dead too actually. Died of cancer five or six years ago."

"But you *have* met Eriksson?" Holt asked.

"Yes, of course," said Stein, clearly surprised by the question. "But that must have been more than twenty years ago. During my radical youth," she said, smiling faintly. "I met hundreds of people during those years who were working for the same political goals—Sten and Theo and obviously Eriksson too. I think I even remember him being out with Theo at our country place one summer. I can't have been very old . . . ten maybe . . . but I remember. Theo brought him out to the country."

It's that photograph you're suddenly remembering, thought Holt, and you probably still hope that's the only reason we're here. And you're probably thinking that now you'll have to go on the offensive, she thought.

"You'll really have to excuse me," said Stein, "but I am somewhat surprised. Has someone alleged that Eriksson and I were old acquaintances, or what? In that case I can assure you it's a lie."

"No," said Holt, shaking her head. "No one has alleged that. We're just trying to talk with everyone who knew him."

"Yes, but that's just what I'm trying to say," said Stein, with controlled heat in her voice now. "I didn't really know Eriksson. I only met him a few times when I was young. I can't have been older than fifteen or sixteen. Eriksson must have been twice as old as I was then—Sten and Theo's age—and they were the ones he socialized with."

Considering that all Eriksson is supposed to have done was get murdered, it's pretty strange you're spending so much energy talking about how little you knew him, thought Holt.

"So Eriksson was Sten Welander's and Theodor Tischler's acquaintance," said Holt, who had decided to let Stein think the worst was over.

"Yes," said Stein, nodding in confirmation. "I know they still saw him up until the time he died. I sometimes talk with Theo and I'm certain he mentioned that to me. We talked about that horrible thing that happened to him, of course. It would be strange otherwise," said Stein.

Just as strange as that you're avoiding the word "murdered" despite having worked as an attorney for almost twenty years, thought Holt.

"If you could really make an effort to remember," Holt continued, "when was the last time you saw Eriksson?"

"As I said," said Stein, "it must have been twenty-five, thirty years ago. Sometime in the mid-seventies."

"Well," said Holt, smiling amiably, "considering we've already talked with people who associated with him at the time he was murdered—it was the thirtieth of November 1989, by the way—it seems you're not the right person to ask."

"No, I'm really not," said Stein. "Even at that time it must have been fifteen years since I'd seen him last."

"Yeah," said Holt, smiling again. "In that case, my colleague and I apologize for taking up your time."

"That was all?" asked Stein, suddenly having a hard time concealing her surprise.

"Yes," said Holt. And now you're trying desperately to figure out if you said anything wrong, she thought.

"Let me think," said Stein suddenly. "There is something floating around in the back of my mind."

"Yes?" said Holt expectantly.

"It suddenly occurs to me there was another time later on that my cousin and I ran into him," said Stein hesitantly.

"Uh-huh," said Holt amiably. So this is suddenly occurring to you, she thought, exchanging a glance with Wiklander, who seemed completely oblivious.

"But when was it?" Stein shook her head as though really exerting herself to remember.

"Seventies, eighties?" Holt suggested.

"Definitely the eighties . . . in the late eighties even, because I remember I was working at the law firm. Theo had invited me to dinner. I had helped him with some legal matter . . . I don't remember what. Then he called and invited me to dinner. It was some Italian restaurant—I think it was in Östermalm."

How close to the truth are you willing to go? wondered Holt.

"Sometime in the late eighties your cousin Theo Tischler invites you to dinner, at an Italian restaurant in Östermalm—and you run into your cousin's old friend Kjell Eriksson," Holt summarized. Now's your chance, she thought.

"Did I say that?" Stein said suddenly. "No, it was like this, we were going to walk home from the restaurant or else take a taxi into town and then continue on foot—Theo likes to party—but when we were walking—I think it was on Karlavägen—Theo pointed out one of the buildings we were going past and said that Kjell lived there—yes, Kjell Eriksson. Then he suggested we ring his doorbell and let him offer us a drink. I guess I wasn't very amused, but that's how it was," said Stein. "Strange I didn't think of that," she said, shaking her head.

Undeniably, thought Holt, who just nodded and smiled.

"You said you and your cousin went to Eriksson's place," Holt clarified.

"Yes," said Stein. "We dropped in and I think he offered us wine or something. . . . I think I drank wine, and not that I remember but I'm guessing Theo had whiskey because he always does." Stein smiled, shaking her head as if the difficulty of recalling her cousin's alcohol habits was her biggest problem right now.

"How long were you at Eriksson's?" asked Holt.

"We just dropped in, half an hour, forty-five minutes maybe . . . at the most," said Stein.

"You don't remember more precisely when it was—you said late eighties," Holt clarified.

"No," said Stein, suddenly sounding very sure. "Any more precisely than that I don't remember."

"Autumn, winter, spring, summer?" Holt suggested.

"Not summer," said Stein, shaking her head. "Autumn or winter, but that's just a guess. I think it was winter."

Sufficiently close, sufficiently far away, thought Holt.

"Of course you could always ask Theo," Stein suggested. "I'm pretty sure he makes notes of dinners and things like that in his datebook, and he didn't go out to dinner with me very often. Talk with Theo; maybe he can help you. I'm pretty sure he saves his calendars too. . . . I remember he told me that for him they also functioned as diaries."

Why is that so important now, wondered Holt. Because if what you're saying is true, it's totally uninteresting to us.

"You wouldn't happen to have his phone number," asked Holt. Not on you in any event, she thought.

"Not on me," said Stein. "I have it at home of course. If you want I can arrange for you to get it tomorrow. This evening unfortunately I won't have time," she added, looking at her watch to be on the safe side. "I promised to go to a reception in a little while."

"I don't think that will be necessary," said Holt, shaking her head. "It's Eriksson we're interested in. We thank you for your help and we truly apologize for having bothered you unnecessarily."

"It's no problem," said Stein, smiling. "I was just a little surprised, as I'm sure you understand."

Scared to death is what you are, thought Holt. Not surprised.

·   ·   ·

"She is scared," said Wiklander as they were sitting in the car en route to the office.

"Yep, but she managed," said Holt.

"She seems to have," said Wiklander. "If we don't come up with anything better, of course."

In the evening Lars Martin Johansson met Undersecretary Helena Stein. True, they didn't talk with each other or even exchange a glance, but he had an opportunity to observe her at a distance, and for him that was good enough. Helena Stein was standing under the crystal chandelier in the middle of a large room, surrounded by men her own age or older. Well-dressed, successful men, conspicuously many of whom were glistening like roosters in their tailored suits, and unlike him they never seemed to need to pull down the cuffs on their shirts or be content with buttoning only the bottom button of their jacket.

Helena Stein in black dress, black jacket with velvet trim, and multistranded pearl necklace, smiling and listening, happy but also serious and very alert. Courted the whole time by the men who came and went. He hadn't seen the slightest trace of the deep ideological battles over defense policy that his boss had told him about.

Noblesse oblige, thought Johansson. He'd read that in a book, long after he'd left the worn-down front seat he'd shared with his best friend during his time with the Stockholm Police Department's central detective squad. And if this was what it was like to make your way up in life, he had come a long way, yet he still remained off to one side, watching.

This particular evening he had made his way to the door near the serving area. Basically the only people who had anything to say to him were the waitstaff constantly hurrying past with routine apologies despite the fact that he was the one in the way. One of the ambassador's many bodyguards gave him a discreet, collegial nod and a faint smile of silent mutual understanding, emanating from the fact that he knew who Johansson was and that he himself was obvious enough in his dark suit, broad shoulders, earpiece, and large hands clasped in the ready position on a level with his crotch.

The only person Johansson really talked with during the evening was his boss, the general director, who came up to him and asked if he was having a nice time. He was having a nice time himself and apologized that he hadn't thought about arranging an invitation for Johansson earlier. But because here he was now anyway, his boss realized that everything had worked out for the best.

"It's mostly us Swedes who were invited here tonight. It's probably meant as a networking opportunity for us and them. And the fact that we're in the ambassador's home is another way for them to send a positive signal," the GD explained.

Exactly, thought Johansson, who would never have dreamed of letting the hoi polloi into his home on Wollmar Yxkullsgatan and completely understood why the American ambassador in Stockholm obviously felt the same way he did.

"Exactly," said Johansson. The crowd was almost strictly old men, military, executives, and diplomats. What the hell could he say about that? He couldn't very well say that the whole affair looked just like the political gatherings in the Arab world he saw on CNN. Apart from the differences in clothing, of course, which were strictly a reflection of climate. But he couldn't very well say that either, even if it was obvious to an old detective like himself.

"Do you want to talk with her?" asked the GD, nodding discreetly toward Helena Stein in the middle of the room.

"No," said Johansson, smiling. "I came here mostly just to look at her. But if you speak to the ambassador you can say hello and thank him for the invitation. I hope I haven't caused any practical problems for him and his wife?"

"Not in the slightest," said the GD. "The ambassador and I are actually old friends. It wasn't any problem at all."

A small world, thought Johansson, and after having observed it for another hour he went home to Pia.

"Did you have a nice time?" Pia asked, and as usual her eyes looked like a squirrel's as soon as she had asked the question.

"So-so," said Johansson. "Mostly just a lot of strange people."

37

Friday, April 7, 2000

"I want you to question Bäckström," said Johansson when he ran into Wiklander in the corridor at work early Friday morning. "I have to run down to Rosenbad for the usual weekly presentation to the government."

"Bäckström," said Wiklander, who had a hard time concealing his surprise. "Boss, do you mean—"

"Exactly," said Johansson, smiling. "It'd be nice to hear what ideas he has about the murder of Eriksson—it was his investigation, after all—so I have what he thinks about it on paper."

"But what if he wants to know . . . why we want to know," said Wiklander hesitantly.

"Say we've uncovered a gigantic homosexual conspiracy," said Johansson. "Or whatever else he might swallow whole. Just don't offer him any aquavit."

"I think I get it," said Wiklander.

So Wiklander questioned Bäckström about the Eriksson case, and what Bäckström said exceeded Johansson's wildest expectations. Bäckström was his usual self. The only thing that had really changed was that a few months earlier he had left the homicide squad in Stockholm and was now working as a chief inspector at the National Bureau of Investigation's homicide commission.

"You want to know what I think about the Eriksson case," said Bäckström, nodding heavily.

"Yes. Perhaps you're wondering why," said Wiklander.

"Actually I think I've already figured it out," said Bäckström, nodding even more heavily. "You only have to turn on the TV to realize what's been going on for a long time now. A person doesn't need to be working for you to understand."

So you don't need to do that, thought Wiklander.

"Queers, queers, queers," said Bäckström and sighed. "They've taken over the whole thing."

Well, maybe not the late-night cable broadcasts, thought Wiklander, who never watched TV himself but had heard a few things in the break room.

"Eriksson," he reminded him. "What do you think about it?"

"Typical homosexual murder," said Bäckström, nodding. "Besides, it was part of a whole series of homo murders—you might not remember them. Some crazy fairy was running around with a big fucking knife hacking down other sausage riders who worked at various porno dives. It was a real samurai sword actually. In total there were five butt princes cut down if I'm not mistaken, and Eriksson was the fourth."

"None of them seem to have been solved, if I've understood the matter correctly," said Wiklander carefully.

"I should damn well think not," said Bäckström. "I was trying to convince the bosses to go further, but it was like banging your head against the wall. Although I haven't let it go. There are certain things I have going now," he added cryptically.

"Yes," said Wiklander, nodding in agreement, "I know what you mean." Bullshit, he thought.

"You see, they aren't afraid of using brute force," said Bäckström with emphasis. "They don't just appear on TV acting like queens. It's nice to hear that at least someone in this building finally gets what's going on."

"Yes," said Wiklander in agreement. "If you're ready, then, I thought I'd turn on the tape recorder so we can get a few questions and answers down in print."

"Always ready," said Bäckström, nodding confidently.

What will Johansson do with this? thought Wiklander an hour later after Bäckström had left and he was sitting listening to the tape of the interview. Maybe he'll try to get him admitted to the nuthouse, thought Wiklander hopefully, because he was an optimistic soul. That's probably it, he thought. Johansson must have blown his stack when he saw what Bäckström had come up with in the Eriksson investigation, and now he's decided to do something about it, Wiklander surmised.

Johansson had no inkling of Wiklander's speculations regarding his intentions vis-à-vis colleague Bäckström. He was sitting among fine folk down in Rosenbad at the presentation SePo held every week for representatives of the Ministry of Justice and the government. In Berg's time it had almost always been Berg himself who represented the secret police, but nowadays the top-level bosses at SePo took turns, and Johansson, who was no great friend of meetings, would usually be there at most a couple of times each month.

The minister of justice was usually the chair, and he always had his director general for legal affairs with him to keep the minutes, which were classified. Sometimes the prime minister's own security adviser would show up, as he did on this occasion. Not only Johansson but others as well immediately noticed the security adviser's attendance and were intrigued because none of the issues scheduled at the meeting seemed particularly exciting. Pure routine, no surprises. Mostly status reports on the standard assortment of long-term projects.

Could it be me he wants to talk with? Johansson wondered.

Johansson and the undersecretary had met for the first time fifteen years ago, concerning various papers Johansson had acquired but wanted to relieve himself of as quickly as possible. At that time the undersecretary was the special adviser at the prime minister's disposal, and he was involved with issues affecting national security including among other things the activities of the secret police.

When his boss was assassinated the undersecretary left Rosenbad. Where he ended up was somewhat unclear—although among those who considered themselves well informed and close to power there was wild speculation. In any event he could not have been sent out into the real cold, because he had come back again quickly and nowadays he was on his third prime minister and things had gone better and better for him. Prime minister number two had retired with a pension and in the best of health, and number three, the undersecretary's current boss, positively glowed with vitality. This special adviser had the same duties he had always had, with a somewhat more elegant title than before and with a suitably harmless nametag he could show to anyone who wondered what he was really up to.

"Research and future planning on behalf of the government offices," he would answer on those few occasions when anyone had the chance to ask. "Mostly future planning actually," he would add, if the person who wondered didn't give up.

Apparently it was Johansson he wanted to meet, because he scarcely opened his mouth during the meeting for anything but the usual sarcasm, but as soon as it was over he took Johansson aside and requested a conversation in private.

"How's it going with Stein?" asked the undersecretary. "No problems, I hope?"

"What do you mean?" asked Johansson, looking roughly like his older brother (who dealt in property and cars) did when he preferred not to answer.

"I was thinking about her youthful sin in connection with the West German embassy," the undersecretary explained.

"Oh yes, that," said Johansson. "I thought you and Berg had cleared that up two years ago."

"Yes," said the undersecretary. "That's why I'm asking."

"I completely share Berg's opinion on that point, and as you know an investigation was done of the matter," Johansson said. "Quite apart from the fact that she was only a child when it happened, she was almost a victim, exploited by her old fiancé, or whatever you want to call him, who was twice her age."

"We human beings live different lives," the undersecretary declared philosophically. "We live one life at one time and another life at another."

"Not everyone," said Johansson, thinking of his old parents and all the other relatives from his home district in northern Sweden. They've been living the same life the whole time, he thought with feeling.

"I understand what you mean," said the undersecretary, who was being almost inexplicably sensible. "The kind of person I was thinking of, to be a little more precise, was rather the intellectual, financially independent, urban type . . . Helena Stein, for example."

Or you, thought Johansson.

"Sure," Johansson grunted. "My understanding is that in those circles you can manage a number of different lives." Because such people seem to have nothing better to do, he thought.

"While the rest of us toil and moil," sighed the undersecretary. "Take our dear German foreign minister, for example. I've met him myself on a number of occasions. He seems completely normal, even pleasant, though that environmental bullshit leaves me cold—and then one day an old picture shows up from some political demonstration during his youth. He's kicking a policeman who's lying on the street, and it isn't at all clear who the real villain is."

The way you talk, thought Johansson.

"Yes, I've seen that too," said Johansson, nodding curtly. "As far as Stein is concerned, I've simply told my coworkers to be extra careful. Neither you nor we and least of all she will be well served if there's any carelessness in that respect. And you know as well as I do that it takes a hell of a lot of time to do something properly. I'm estimating you'll get a report in time next week."

"Sounds good," said the undersecretary, appearing to be almost satisfied as he leaned back among all the pillows on the large couch. "One other thing, by the way . . ."

"I'm listening," said Johansson.

"It would be nice if I had the pleasure of seeing you over a bite of food, when the report does come in," said the undersecretary. "In my own humble abode, with the resources the house can offer."

"I've heard a good deal about them," said Johansson, smiling.

"Nothing bad I hope," said the undersecretary.

"The little I've heard sounded good enough," said Johansson.

"Well all right then," said the undersecretary. "I'll ask my secretary to call your secretary and see if they can find a time that suits us both."

I wonder what he really wants? thought Johansson sitting in the car on the way back to work. It's all the same anyway, he thought. Because if it's important enough it will come out sooner or later. And if not, you only risk becoming like your unfortunate predecessor.

"How'd it go with that fuckup Bäckström?" Johansson asked as soon as he stepped into his department's corridor and caught sight of Wiklander.

"Above all expectations," said Wiklander. "By the way, did you know he has a position as chief inspector at the crime bureau?"

"But that's just excellent," said Johansson, who knew the score when it came to things like that, and had already made note of his impending promotion sometime before Bäckström's appointment. "With those amazing testimonials he had this can't have been completely unexpected, and you have to admit there's something reassuring about a consistent development," he said.

"I've told the others to reserve the afternoon," said Wiklander, who was not really clear what Johansson meant and in any case did not intend to go deeper into the subject.

"Good," said Johansson. "Then I'll see you after lunch."

The entire afternoon was spent on the meeting with the investigation team. First, Anna Holt reported on where they were in her usual efficient manner.

The attempts to chart the dealings among Stein, Tischler, and Eriksson by means of telephone and financial transactions had not produced any interesting results beyond what was already in the old murder investigation, which was meager enough. On the other hand, a number of conversations between Stein and her cousin Tischler had been logged, which indicated that they'd kept in constant touch with each other. For a rather long time Stein had also had a deposit account at Tischler's banking firm, but she had closed it when her cousin formally left the family firm several years ago.

"So my proposal is that we discontinue that aspect," said Holt.

"That's okay with me," Johansson agreed. These lines of inquiry were fucking expensive too, he thought. Telia and the other operators start robbing you blind as soon as you want any information from them.

After that Holt touched on Stein's fingerprints and the forensic analysis of the traces on the lost hand towel. Stein had offered an explanation for how the prints were left in Eriksson's apartment, and it could not be immediately dismissed, even if Holt and Wiklander were firmly convinced that she had been lying to their faces. Same with the traces of vomit and the lipstick on the hand towel. In both cases they pointed to Stein, but at the same time they didn't rule out alternative explanations strongly enough to have legal significance.

"And as far as our witness the major is concerned, he can't point out Stein from among a group of pictures," Holt stated.

"Do you think there's any point in questioning Tischler?" asked Johansson, although he already knew the answer.

"Only if we want him to confirm Stein's version and you want to tip them off that she's the one we're interested in," said Holt.

"And that's all we have," Johansson summarized.

"Yup," said Holt, "and unfortunately it's not very likely we've missed anything either. Not this time," she added, smiling faintly.

"Okay then," said Johansson, who sounded unexpectedly cheerful. "Now I want all of you to close your eyes. . . ."

The four in the room exchanged surprised glances but did as he said, even if Martinez looked like she was trying to peek.

"Everyone who is completely convinced that Helena Stein stabbed Kjell Göran Eriksson to death, raise your hand," said Johansson. After a pause of a few seconds he said, "You can open your eyes now."

There were five raised hands including his own, and a unified investigation.

"Please put down your hands," said Johansson, smiling. "The day before yesterday I took the opportunity to go through the tech report and the autopsy report, as well as a few other goodies that Anna alerted me to," said Johansson, nodding at Holt, "so I'm pretty clear now on how the whole thing went down. If any of you are interested, I can tell you about it," said Johansson.

"I am," said Holt before any of the others managed to say the same thing. We're already sitting on pins and needles, she thought. You don't need to show off.

"Okay then," said Johansson. "Then I'll tell you what happened when Helena Stein stabbed Kjell Göran Eriksson to death."

And he did, with the help of his pictures, in the same way as he had when he talked through the case with his best friend, Bo Jarnebring. It took about half an hour, and whether what he said was true or false—for some of it he couldn't have known without having been there, and in any case he couldn't have known what was going on in the heads of Stein or Eriksson—regardless of that he had mesmerized his audience. When he was finally silent they too sat silently.

Now I understand what Jarnebring and everyone else here was talking about, thought Holt, who had finally experienced the true Lars Martin Johansson. Although naturally she didn't say that.

"I'm in complete agreement," said Holt. "That must have been what happened." At least in the essentials, she thought.

"And that woman is going to get off. . . . It's just too much," said Martinez with poorly controlled anger and her police instincts still intact.

"Yes," said Wiklander with a heat he seldom showed and the ambivalence that naturally ensues when reality is no longer black or white. "This is an extraordinarily gloomy story."

"It's probably the sorriest story I've heard," said Mattei, who looked like she might start crying.

And for some reason it was to her that Johansson turned when he began to speak again.

"Yes, of course it is," said Johansson. "Sometimes it's a real shame about us humans. And this time it's a real shame about Helena Stein. Speaking of her," Johansson continued, smiling at Mattei, "I understand that you, Lisa, have produced quite a bit about Stein. It would be interesting if you'd give us a summary." But not a novel, thought Johansson, for he tried to avoid that sort of thing.

"I could write a whole novel about Helena Stein actually, but for now I'll concentrate on two moments in her life: the mid-seventies when the occupation of the West German embassy took place, and the late eighties, when Kjell Göran Eriksson was murdered."

Sounds good, thought Johansson, but be very careful not to put it in book form and publish it or I will personally see to it that you end up in the slammer.

"Looks like you've uncovered a lot of information about her," said Johansson.

"There's plenty if you know where to look," said Mattei, who had a hard time concealing her enthusiasm. "Not least on her political involvement, despite the fact that she seems to have made an effort to keep a low public profile the whole time. For example, I have hundreds of pictures of her published in various books and newspapers, which I've gathered from open sources. The first one is a book cover that came out in 1975, but the book isn't at all about her. She's not even mentioned by name, which in itself isn't so strange considering her age. The book is called *The New Left* and was published in 1975 by Fischer & Co., and there's Helena Stein on the cover. It's a news photo the publisher used from a demonstration outside the American embassy in 1973, and Stein is only fifteen years old at the time. She's standing in front of the barricades waving a placard, dressed in jeans and one of those padded jackets girls wore back then. The last photo I have is the official portrait taken of her when she was appointed undersecretary a few years ago. There she's dressed in a graphite-colored dress with a dark blue blouse and black pumps. She is extremely attractive. So there are twenty-five years between the first and the last picture, and it gets really amazing when you look at all the pictures of her in chronological order—I've put them on a separate CD-ROM in case you want to do that yourselves," said Mattei with enthusiasm blossoming on her pale cheeks.

"Do you have any more like that?" said Johansson, who himself was passionate about this kind of research. During his most active period as a police officer he used to devote hours to going through photo albums, home videos, and diaries he'd acquired from both crime victims and thugs.

"I have a whole CD filled with film clips of her too. There are news reports and interviews that I downloaded from our various TV channels. Then I have a third disk with the written material and my summary of her biography."

The weekend is saved, thought Johansson, who was already mentally rubbing his hands.

"The mid-seventies and late eighties," he reminded her. "What were things like for her then?"

In the fall of 1975 Helena Stein turned seventeen. Just over six months later she would graduate from the French School, which was one year earlier than normal because when she was little she had been an unusually precocious child and had started school a year before her classmates. But as a teenager she seemed completely normal and displayed a sampling of the usual problems of puberty and conflicts with her parents and teachers.

Her father was a pediatrician with his own private practice; her mother was an art historian and worked for the Nordic Museum. Helena had grown up in Östermalm and the French School was the only school she attended. She was an only child, and when she was seven her parents divorced and had other children with their new partners. Gradually she acquired four half siblings. At the time of the divorce Helena chose to remain at home with her father.

In the fall of 1974 her father was appointed as an expert at UNICEF, the United Nations Children's Fund. He temporarily turned his practice over to a colleague, took his new wife and Helena's two younger half-siblings and moved to New York where they remained for over a year. Helena remained at home in the apartment on Riddargatan, and the contact she had with her mother seemed not to have intensified as a result of her father's absence. Helena seems to have taken care of herself.

That same autumn she started a relationship with her cousin Theo Tischler's best friend, Sten Welander. Helena had just turned sixteen; Welander was twenty-seven, the father of two and still married to his first wife. When he finally divorced her in the fall of 1975, he had also broken up with Helena Stein.

Helena Stein seemed to have devoted most of her time during these years to political activism, which led to recurring conflicts with her mother and some of her teachers.

As a young radical Helena initially hopped among various minor left-wing groups until she finally settled on the Swedish Communist Party. Helena Stein was a young Communist and no one in her bourgeois milieu was particularly happy about that, but it was hoped that this phase would soon pass, and that by and by it would be seen as a youthful aberration in the spirit of the time.

In addition she was involved in a number of other radical groups and societies, the Swedish NLF movement of course but also KRUM, which worked for humane treatment of criminals.

"That's the recurring theme in her life," Mattei summarized, "her strong political involvement, always to the left."

"Yeah," said Johansson with a drawl. "Judging by her upbringing, she sounds like a typical young radical from the happy seventies."

"No," said Mattei, shaking her head. "There you're wrong, Boss. That's actually a prejudice."

"I see," said Johansson, not looking as though he was particularly offended. "How so?"

"It wasn't the case that the young left of the time was dominated by a few upper-class kids. Those involved were a rather representative selection of the populace," said Mattei.

"So Stein was an exception," said Johansson.

"Yes. Her background was unusual within the young left," said Mattei.

"Her involvement then," said Johansson, "how genuine was it?" Given her background, thought Johansson.

"I'm completely convinced that her political involvement was genuine," said Mattei. "Otherwise she never would have thrown herself into it the way she did."

"You mean the West German embassy," said Johansson. "Don't you think that was mostly a desire for adventure? Exciting and romantic, or so she believed. Not at all like what it turned out to be."

"It's possible that was part of it," said Mattei, "but there were other things that might not have been so pleasant for her."

"Such as?" asked Johansson.

"If I've gotten this right, she was pretty badly bullied during her whole time at high school, and the first year she studied law at Uppsala a couple of her male classmates gave her a good beating after a party at the Stockholm student organization," Mattei said in a serious tone. "According to the police report it was a political discussion that went downhill. If you're interested in counting her bruises, I've placed a copy of the medical examination from Academic Hospital in her background material," Mattei said.

You're a lot pluckier than you look, thought Johansson.

"What bastards," he said. "But after that, where was she in 1989 at the time that she helped Eriksson take down the flag?"

"She was a member of the Social Democratic Party. She became a member as early as 1977, and she still is, as you know. She's also a member of their women's caucus and their attorneys group. Belongs to the left wing of the party. Despite her low profile, she is viewed as a very big name."

"That's what *you* see," said Johansson contentedly, because even he suffered from the unfortunately common weakness of gladly judging others by comparison with himself.

"Excuse me, Boss," said Mattei amiably. "See what?"

"You see a person who has moved to the right," said Johansson.

"I guess everyone does when they get older. There are lots of academic dissertations in which that political shift has been analyzed."

"Nice to hear," said Johansson. Nice to hear that people are normal, he thought.

"She hasn't been on the gravy train since she became a Social Democrat in any event," said Mattei.

"She hasn't," said Johansson. Has she had any more beatings, he wondered, but he couldn't ask that of course. That would be childish.

"She has worked very actively in politics and has a number of responsibilities besides her job as undersecretary," Mattei continued. "She even served in parliament for a short time in the early nineties, substituting for someone who was sick."

"But in November 1989 she was working as an attorney?" Johansson asked.

"She got her law degree at Uppsala in 1979, did her internship at the district court, and practiced at a law firm up until 1985, when she became an attorney. She quit in 1991, and since then she has worked more or less full-time in politics and in the government offices since the Social Democrats came back to power in 1994. She's actually somewhat unusual for a Social Democrat," said Mattei.

"In what regard?" Johansson asked.

"Well, partly because of her background," said Mattei. "I guess it's just like you say, Boss. Helena Stein is an upper-middle-class girl—and I'm sure she's had to hear plenty about that too. But there are other things."

"Such as?" said Johansson.

"That she's viewed as an extraordinarily capable attorney, that she speaks several languages fluently, that it seems to be extremely difficult to find anyone who has worked with her who has anything but good to say about her—"

"Is she married? Does she have children?" Johansson interrupted.

"She was married to a classmate for a few years when she was studying in Uppsala and served at the district court. They divorced in 1981. She has no children. She's had a few relationships of varying duration over the years, but since she was appointed as undersecretary she seems to have lived alone."

"Are you quite sure of that?" Johansson asked, and for some reason he was smiling broadly.

"Yes," said Mattei. "In recent years she has lived alone."

"Interesting," said Johansson. "I look forward to going through everything you have compiled once I have some peace and quiet. Is there anything else in particular you think I should look at?"

"That she was appointed as undersecretary in the Ministry of Defense is undeniably interesting," said Mattei.

"What do you mean?" asked Johansson.

"She's had a number of opinions over the years about both the military in general and our export of war matériel in particular," said Mattei. "Not least when she was working in foreign trade. I don't think the military and the defense lobbyists were particularly happy about her appointment."

"You don't say," said Johansson, suddenly looking as if he was thinking deeply. "A new Maj Britt Theorin perhaps?"

"In an ideological sense I believe that describes her rather well," said Mattei, "but what her opponents are probably most afraid of is her capacity as an attorney. She seems to be enormously sharp."

"But nonetheless she becomes undersecretary in the Ministry of Defense," said Johansson.

"Exactly," said Mattei, "and the only reasonable interpretation is that the government, or the person or persons in the government who decide this sort of thing, wanted to give the military establishment a tweak on the nose."

"You don't say," said Johansson. I understand what you mean, he thought.

When the meeting was finished, after the usual questions and the usual empty chatter, Johansson wished everyone a pleasant weekend and thanked them for a job well done.

"Go rest up properly, and we'll meet on Monday to try to make some kind of decision about what we should do," said Johansson, looking both friendly and bosslike.

Then he took Holt to one side and asked her to compile the essentials and make sure the prosecutor got it all as quickly as possible, no later than the following day.

"Then you can celebrate the weekend too," said Johansson. "By the way, don't you have a little boy?"

"Not so little," said Holt, shrugging her shoulders. "He's turning seventeen soon."

"And I'm sure he hates me," said Johansson, "because I've taken his mom away from him."

"I don't think so," said Holt. "If he knew why I haven't been at home lately you'd probably be his hero."

"You don't say," said Johansson, who just happened to think that it was high time to call his own boy, despite the fact that nowadays the good-for-nothing had a fiancée and a child on the way. "But you must have some guy you have to see," Johansson continued, having decided to engage in a little personnel care and cultivate his human relations. Since he didn't have anything better to do.

"No," said Holt, smiling weakly. "Just like Helena Stein, I've been living alone for a while."

"Go out and get someone then," said Johansson unsentimentally. "That shouldn't be so damned hard."

That evening Bo Jarnebring and his wife had come over to Johansson's place for dinner. It had been just as pleasant as always, and when their guests had gone his wife had fallen asleep almost immediately with her head on his right arm and his left arm around her body.

Wonder how it's going for Holt, thought Johansson. Did she sneak out to the pub and hook up with a guy? And then he too had fallen asleep.

38

Monday, April 10, 2000

Johansson devoted the weekend to various activities. Part of the time he spent with his wife. He also went through Mattei's comprehensive material on undersecretary Helena Stein, and when he was done he was in complete agreement with Mattei. If she ever failed to write a novel she couldn't blame lack of research material at any rate.

On the subject of the imagination, thought Johansson, it's probably only when that takes over that even a reasonably good story takes off and the people in it really come to life. What was true and what was false was actually a rather overvalued distinction. Wasn't it the case that the really great truths, the eternal truths, could only be given life and substance by means of the human imagination?

Johansson felt so uplifted by these and similar musings that he decided to reward himself with yet another glass of red wine before going to bed. That evening his wife had gone to see her best girlfriend, and as she was leaving she'd let him know it would probably be a late night and he didn't need to sit up waiting for her.

On Monday morning Johansson was still in a good mood, which was excellent because he would be meeting with his department's chief prosecutor first thing, and he would need all the strength he could summon.

"What do you think?" said Johansson, nodding at the chief prosecutor, who was already squirming in his chair on the other side of Johansson's large desk.

"There are undeniably a number of unpleasant coincidences," said the chief prosecutor, who did not appear particularly cheerful.

"There sure are," said Johansson heartily. As so often happens when against your better judgment you try to make the best of chance, he thought.

"There is no way this constitutes reasonable grounds for suspicion," said the chief prosecutor deprecatingly, holding up both palms. "Far from it, far from it. I've tried to do an ordinary, traditional sifting of evidence, and when I consider the various aspects—both separately and combined—the only reasonable conclusion is that they're insufficient . . . clearly insufficient."

"That's more or less the same conclusion we've drawn," Johansson agreed.

"That's probably the only reasonable conclusion you can come to," said the prosecutor, "and we can't disregard the fact that there are credible alternative explanations for what might have happened when Eriksson was eliminated. In which there is not the slightest room for any involvement on Stein's part, I might add."

"So what are you thinking?" asked Johansson innocently, despite the fact that he had already figured out what the response would be.

"Well," said the chief prosecutor, "I'm thinking for example of the interview with Chief Inspector Bäckström. He does have a completely different view of the matter, and he was after all responsible for the original investigation."

"He certainly was," said Johansson.

"Bäckström is a very experienced, skilled police officer," said the prosecutor. "One of the real old owls," he said, nodding with more emphasis than even Johansson would have expected of him.

"A real old owl," said Johansson heartily. A really thirsty old owl, he thought. "That homosexual lead is definitely promising," he continued. Assuming that you're really stupid, and you definitely are, he thought.

"What do you think about a dismissed with prejudice as far as Stein is concerned," the chief prosecutor said carefully.

"A strong dismissal," Johansson emphasized.

"And that the investigation your people have done—very meritorious, I want to emphasize—obviously stays up here with us," the prosecutor decided, already seeming considerably perkier.

"Yes, of course," said Johansson. "Anything else would be purely defamatory. When do you think you can have the papers ready?" he asked. I'll talk with my people, he thought.

"When do you want them?" the chief prosecutor.

"Preferably now," said Johansson. And if you even think about chickening out at the last minute, I'll kill you with my own bare hands, he thought.

"How about this afternoon?" the prosecutor asked carefully. "I need a few hours to refine some of the wording, but you'll get a decision this afternoon."

"This afternoon will be fine," said Johansson. Refine away, he thought.

"Unfortunately," said Johansson an hour later as he was sitting with his investigation team, "we got the cold shoulder from the prosecutor. The poor guy was scared to death."

"Such is life," said Wiklander philosophically. And I don't intend to lie awake at night on Eriksson's account, he thought.

"Yes, it doesn't seem like Stockholm will straighten out this case," said Holt. Despite the fact that Bäckström apparently quit, she thought.

"Damn it all," said Martinez. Fucking cowards, she thought. If this hadn't been about someone like Stein then the colleagues down in Stockholm probably would have pounded the shit out of her, she thought.

"I think it sounds like the right decision," said Mattei. Because regardless of what Johansson said about the case last Friday, it needn't be the case that Stein killed Eriksson. In any event it had not been established beyond a reasonable doubt, she thought.

"Okay then," said Johansson, nodding. "By the way, on a completely different matter, I want you to close your eyes," he said, smiling. "Then I want everyone to raise your hand if you think we've done all that can be asked of us. Now you can look," said Johansson.

Three hands out of four, he thought, but because he himself was holding up both of his it was all the same.

"I'm sure you'll get another chance, Martinez," said Johansson, nodding. "Thanks for a good job by the way, and that applies to all of you," he said. And now only the hard part remains, he thought.

After lunch Johansson met two of his colleagues from counterespionage, who gave him a presentation on Michael Liska, born in Pest, Hungary, in 1940 and an American citizen since 1962.

"Allowing for the fact that we don't have too much on our American friends—for obvious reasons, as you surely understand," said the police superintendent, who was one of several assistant heads in the department, "we have nonetheless tried to gather together what there is about old Liska. It's on the disk here," he said, handing over a computer disk to Johansson. "All we have on him is there, which as I said is not very much."

Then perhaps, given the way the world is starting to look, it's high time you find out a little more about him, thought Johansson, but naturally he didn't say that to them. Someone besides him would have to do that.

"Can you summarize what's here?" asked Johansson.

"Certainly," said the police superintendent, and then he did.

According to the police superintendent, Liska had been working for almost thirty years at the CIA, and before that with the naval intelligence service. He was a legend within the CIA and the intelligence agencies of the Western world, and nowadays not even a particularly secret one. Among other things he was said to have played a prominent role in the execution of Operation Rosewood.

"Although in later years he has become more of the agency's outward face," the police superintendent explained. "He has made several appearances on American TV, where he sometimes speaks on his employer's behalf. He's a very good TV personality, has a good image, and in recent years he has mostly made the circuit giving talks. Much appreciated as a lecturer, he has even done a few appearances here in Sweden. Most recently he was featured at a dinner that the military gave at Karlberg's castle in December."

During his period as an active agent, Liska had primarily worked abroad, almost solely in Europe, and concentrating primarily on the countries behind the Iron Curtain, although he had also been active in Scandinavia, including Sweden.

"The guy even seems to speak completely comprehensible Swedish—well, Scandinavian maybe. Altogether he seems to have spent at least a couple of years in Sweden and Norway. All at once he would show up at their embassy out on Djurgården," said the police superintendent, seeming almost flattered by Liska's interest in his native land.

"What kind of Swedish contacts did he have?" asked Johansson.

"You mean apart from the regular channels with our own military intelligence service and a few of the real bigwigs in the older generation?" the police superintendent asked. "That part's on the disk."

So it's there, thought Johansson. Several old owls. I really ought to take up bird-watching given my job, he thought.

"Does he have a best buddy here in Sweden I ought to know about?" asked Johansson. Don't be so damn naïve, he thought.

"Well," said the police superintendent, smiling, "he does have one friend who is undeniably intriguing."

"And who's that?" said Johansson, though he had already guessed the answer.

"And you know him well, too," said the police superintendent. "The prime minister's own éminence grise in questions that concern national security—the not entirely unknown former special adviser, nowadays the undersecretary in the government offices."

Strange that people never refer to him by name, thought Johansson. Is it so damn hard to remember that his name is Nilsson? With the usual spelling, too.

"So Undersecretary Nilsson and CIA agent Liska are best buddies?" asked Johansson.

"Depends on what you mean by best," the police superintendent said evasively. "I don't really dare say "best," but that they've known each other forever is common knowledge."

"And the contacts Mr. Nilsson had with this Liska, of what nature are they?" asked Johansson.

"We assume they have occurred with the blessing and consent of the highest authorities," said the police superintendent, nodding piously.

"If I may now be a little nitpicky and boring," said Johansson, "I'm wondering if there is anyone here in the building who during all these years of blessed coexistence has had the good taste, if for no other reason than the sake of good form, to inform the undersecretary of who his American friend's employer is?" said Johansson. "I'm assuming it doesn't appear on Liska's business card."

"Not the ones we've seen in any event," said the police superintendent, who still seemed happy and upbeat. "I don't think it's a secret," he added. "It's clear he knows what agency Liska works for."

"I'm sure he does," said Johansson. "But that's not what I'm sitting here pestering you about."

"You mean whether we in the service have informed him about who Liska is?" asked the police superintendent, who no longer seemed as exhilarated.

"Exactly," said Johansson. "Have we?" Finally he gets it, he thought.

"No," said the police superintendent, suddenly seeming rather gloomy.

"Then we should change that ASAP," said Johansson. "Make sure the documentation is clear so the analysts can make their assessment. Then make a proposal for getting a regular security intelligence report to the undersecretary. And a copy to the minister of justice for his information so they can't put the blame on each other."

"When do you want it?" said the police superintendent guardedly.

"It'll be fine if I get it in a few hours," said Johansson. So I can go through the disk in the meantime, so there, you little bastard, he thought.

"No one is going to be particularly happy," said the police superintendent, who didn't look too happy himself.

"That leaves me cold," said Johansson. "If we assume, and this is purely an academic question, that Liska hadn't been working for the CIA, but instead for the former GRU or KGB at a time when these agencies viewed Sweden as part of their own domestic politics, what would have happened to the undersecretary in that case?"

"Yes, but that's an impossible comparison," the police superintendent objected. "I think that—"

"Answer the question," Johansson interrupted. "What would have happened to the undersecretary then?"

"Then naturally he would have ended up in jail," said the police superintendent.

"Nice that we're in agreement," said Johansson.

"I want you to set up three meetings for me," said Johansson to his secretary.

"As you wish, Boss," she replied, smiling her cool smile, pen already in hand.

"First, I want to meet the GD within the next few hours at the latest, but in any event before the end of the day," said Johansson, beginning to count by raising his right index finger. "I need half an hour."

"Second?" asked his secretary.

"Second," said Johansson, letting the middle finger on his right hand keep the index finger company, "I want to have a meeting in Rosenbad with our esteemed contact the undersecretary sometime tomorrow. Preferably in the morning."

"And third . . . ?"

"Third," said Johansson, but without holding up the middle finger— you didn't do that to women—"and assuming that I've managed to meet the person I just mentioned, I would like to have a meeting with Helena Stein, the undersecretary in the Ministry of Defense. In the evening, just the two of us, and preferably at her home."

"My goodness," said his secretary. "I hope it's nothing like that."

No, thought Johansson. Unfortunately it's just the opposite.

39

Tuesday, April 11, 2000

At ten o'clock in the morning Johansson met with the undersecretary in his office at Rosenbad and turned over the security intelligence regarding the American citizen Michael Liska, which the colleagues in counterespionage had produced the day before and which his own general director had approved the same evening.

"I am grateful for the honor that has been bestowed on me," said the undersecretary, nodding ironically toward the binder of papers he had received but had not even condescended to open. "I will obviously inform my highest superior of your findings."

"You don't seem particularly surprised," Johansson chuckled. He had decided in advance to play along as long as it suited him. And don't try to pressure me with your distinguished acquaintances, he thought.

"I doubt that anyone here in the building will be particularly surprised by how Liska puts food on the table," said the undersecretary.

"If you know about more contacts he's had that we've missed, I assume you'll report them to us," said Johansson.

"Of course, of course," sighed the undersecretary. "I had no idea you were so formal, Johansson."

"I guess you didn't," said Johansson, smiling. "Yes, I am very formal," he continued. "I can be downright frightfully formal in a pinch, and to avoid any misunderstanding I would also like to stress that you should not view me, my superior, or our organization as some kind of free resource for you to dispose of as you choose. That goes against the constitution and I can be terribly sensitive where such things are concerned."

"Oh boy, that last part almost sounded a little threatening," said the undersecretary, unperturbed. "Would you like a cup of coffee by the way? I'm in the mood for one anyway." The undersecretary made an inviting gesture toward cups, coffeepot, and plates on his coffee table. "As you can see I've got an ample supply of pastries."

I see that, thought Johansson, who had already made note of the excess of pastries on the table and immediately decided not to let himself be tempted, not even by a little cognac ring. On the other hand, he thought, those napoleons do look heavenly.

"By the way, how's it going with Stein?" the undersecretary continued as he poured coffee into Johansson's cup.

"Not so well," said Johansson, who had decided that it was high time to turn the screw.

"Not so well," the undersecretary repeated, actually sounding sincerely surprised. "Is it that old story from the West German embassy that's still haunting her?"

"No," said Johansson, shaking his head heavily. "If only it were that good." And if you're going to pour coffee for me, I prefer that you do it in my cup, he thought.

"Now I'm getting worried," said the undersecretary, setting down the coffeepot and looking at Johansson without trying any of his usual grimaces. "As you know, my esteemed boss intends to offer her a position in the government, and if you and your people have a different opinion I'm afraid you'll have to count on us devoting a good deal of time and effort to scrutinizing your arguments."

"Has she already been asked?" Johansson said.

"No," said the undersecretary. "But soon."

"Tell your boss he has to find someone else," said Johansson. "If you don't want to tell him, I can take it up with him directly."

"Johansson, Johansson," said the undersecretary deprecatingly. "Now you really have to tell me what this is all about. And I'm assuming that this doesn't have anything to do with a twenty-five-year-old embassy occupation."

"No," said Johansson. "It doesn't."

"Well," said the undersecretary, attempting a smile, "I'm frightfully curious. What in the world has she done? Is she involved in the Palme assassination too?"

"No," said Johansson curtly as he took a blue plastic folder from his briefcase. "I will gladly tell you what this is about, provided you acknowledge on a paper I have with me that you have had access to this information and that you also sign a special confidentiality agreement on another paper that I also have with me. I have discussed the matter both with the GD and our lead attorney, and the GD told me that if you sign you should be informed, and if you don't, he is going to personally request a private presentation for your boss."

"Give me a pen," said the undersecretary. "Before I die of curiosity."

"Well," said the undersecretary as he set aside the pen and pushed the folder with the signed documents back to Johansson.

"Now I'm going to tell you about two partially connected problems we discovered during our background check of Undersecretary Stein," said Johansson. "Namely, that we have reason to suspect that Liska and his organization, in cooperation with domestic interests within our so-called defense lobby, planned to subject Undersecretary Stein to influence were she to be appointed minister of defense or given a similarly security-related position within the Swedish government."

"Goodness," said the undersecretary. "Correct me if I've counted wrong, but I come up with at least three objections in a single sentence."

"A few months ago Liska managed, with the help of a few useful idiots in the military intelligence service, to activate the case that concerns the embassy occupation—which will soon pass the statute of limitations," Johansson said. "We believe they've opened up a portal through which they intend to convey disinformation in order to influence Helena Stein and people like her." Why do you look so strange? thought Johansson. What happened to your usual trademark sardonic smile?

"Sounds rather daring given the relations between our respective countries," said the undersecretary. "But I hear what you're saying," he continued. "You don't think you could be a little more precise?"

"Not at the present time," said Johansson. "We have decided to follow up on what we have and provide the usual updates as we go forward, depending on how the whole thing develops."

"But that's just excellent," said the undersecretary. "Because we are forewarned, we are also forearmed, and if I were Stein I would be the one who was most grateful. In any event she doesn't need to worry that the Americans will try to yank her chain."

And not yours either, thought Johansson.

"No, neither the Americans nor anyone else is going to yank her chain," said Johansson. In any case not in that way, he thought.

"Okay then," said the undersecretary, who for some reason chose not to question any further what Johansson had just said. "Then I don't really understand the problem. What obstacle is there to appointing her?"

"Unfortunately it won't work," said Johansson.

"What do you mean it won't work?" said the undersecretary, no longer making any attempt to conceal how irritated he was. "Has she murdered someone, or what?"

"Yes," said Johansson.

"What?" said the undersecretary.

You definitely did *not* know that, thought Johansson when he saw the undersecretary's suddenly wide-open eyes.

Johansson then related what had gone on when Helena Stein stabbed Kjell Göran Eriksson to death almost eleven years ago, basically the same way he had told it to his best friend and to his own investigation team.

After that he gave an account of the measures he had taken, all the way from the prosecutor's dismissal with prejudice down to all the top-secret classifications he himself had put in place, not least the little scrap of paper he had put into the shredder with his own hands.

"What a completely improbable fucking story," the undersecretary moaned, shaking his head with dismay.

"Regardless of that," continued Johansson, who had one more point to clear up before he was finished, "completely regardless of that she represents a risk that we advise your superior in the strongest possible terms not to take," said Johansson, and he almost felt solemn as he said it. For a simple boy from the country like himself it was almost as though the eagle of history had brushed him with its wing.

"I see exactly what you mean," said the undersecretary, looking as though he would like to moan audibly.

"For both your sake and mine I would still like to go over the risks we envisage. There are four sources of risk here. The first is leaks within our own closed operation," said Johansson. "It's true we're known with good reason for being taciturn, and compared with all the babbling brooks running around in the open police operation, we're about as talkative as a concrete wall with no cracks. Still I can't overlook the risk, even if I judge it to be the least serious in this context."

"How many at SePo know about Stein?" the undersecretary asked.

"Eight including myself, plus another seven who know parts of it and might possibly figure out the rest themselves."

"And that's as secretive as you've managed to be," said the undersecretary crossly.

"As you already know," said Johansson, grinning. "And with you now, that makes nine."

"What are the other three risks, besides ourselves?" he asked.

Johansson's colleagues at the detective squad in Stockholm were another risk. The files on Eriksson would be returned in exactly the condition they were in when they were loaned out and with all conceivable discretion. Regardless, it was still an open murder investigation, and sooner or later—this could definitely not be ruled out—it might end up in competent enough hands that someone would be forced to start being interested in Helena Stein.

"Just imagine if she were the defense minister," said Johansson. "This would not leak like a sieve. They'd be able to drive her around with a manure spreader."

"The media," Johansson continued. "Here in particular, because there is a very unfortunate possibility that a sufficiently thoughtful investigative reporter might piece together the elements of an already famous, very spectacular event—the occupation of the West German embassy—with Eriksson, Tischler, Welander, and Stein. There is also the remarkable circumstance that one of the members of the 'gang of four' was suddenly murdered. Not all journalists are idiots," said Johansson, "far from it, and with the West German embassy in particular it's probably the case that many of the older journalists were around at the time it happened, and that they had contacts in those circles the four were involved in."

"That's enough, that's more than enough," said the undersecretary shaking his head in dismay. "But there was something else you were thinking about too. You said four risks. . . . I've counted three."

There were Stein's own acquaintances and above all Tischler, who knew down to the slightest detail how things stood. Tischler with his big mouth, his uninhibited indiscretion, and his, to say the least, adventurous life. What might happen the day he became angry at "his charming cousin," or simply let his tongue wag without thinking, or put himself in a position—in relation to the tax authorities, the police, or both—where he might find it expedient to use her as a negotiating tactic.

"Someone like Tischler is a walking bomb, as I'm sure you understand," said Johansson. "We really ought to have someone like him eliminated immediately," he added, smiling broadly at the undersecretary.

"No objections," sighed the undersecretary. "I've never liked his type anyway."

"Well," said Johansson, leaning back in his armchair, forming his long fingers into a church vault, and observing the undersecretary. "Are we agreed?"

"Yes," said the undersecretary. "But doesn't someone still have to talk with Stein?"

So you've already talked to her about her becoming a member of the government, thought Johansson.

"You don't need to say anything, Johansson," said the undersecretary deprecatingly. "We have the same problem that you do as far as the undesired distribution of information is concerned."

"I had thought about talking with her anyway," said Johansson.

"You had?" said the undersecretary with surprise.

"Anything else would be dereliction of duty on my part," he explained. "It wasn't that I forgot to mention her, but it's obvious that in the situation we're now in, she constitutes the greatest risk." She might even be cause for your dear boss to have to return to his childhood home in Katrineholm, thought Johansson.

"Thanks," said the undersecretary. "I understand exactly what you mean." Anyone at all, but not Göran Persson, he thought.

That evening, before he was to meet Helena Stein, Johansson had dinner with his wife, but because his thoughts were elsewhere not much was said. As soon as he set aside his coffee cup he looked at his watch and nodded at her.

"I have to go," he said. "I'll see you in a few hours."

"It's secret, of course," said his wife, smiling.

"Yes," said Johansson, sighing.

"Is she good-looking?" she asked.

"I don't really know," said Johansson. "I've only seen her from a distance and never talked with her. In any event she's not like you."

"That's what you say," said his wife.

"Yes," said Johansson. "I say that because no one is."

"Thanks," she said. "Then you should take care of yourself."

"Yes," said Johansson.

But of course Stein *was* beautiful and not only at a distance, thought Johansson when he was finally sitting in her living room looking at her. Beautiful in the same way as her clothes or the room they were sitting in. Beautiful in a different way than what had been beautiful to him during his childhood, youth, and adult life—the sort of thing that was both beautiful and accessible to him. Helena Stein seemed to be beautiful in an inaccessible way, and sometimes, in moments of weakness, he was seized by a longing for that kind of beauty, because he really did want to live a different life than the life that was his.

"Would you like coffee?" asked Helena Stein.

"No," said Johansson. "I'm fine. I won't be long," he added, thinking he should try to calm her.

"Something tells me this is not going to be a pleasant conversation," she said, looking at him seriously.

"No," said Johansson. "I'm afraid not, but I've carefully considered the existing alternatives, and this is what I think is best for everyone involved." And quite certainly for you, he thought.

"I hear what you're saying of course," she said, "but I sense that this is about that time twenty-five years ago when I was a naïve child who thought that I was only helping rescue a few German students from being murdered by the German police."

"Yes," said Johansson. "I guess that's how the whole thing started."

"And if you think I would have done what I did then if I'd understood what they really intended to do, then I don't think we really have very much to say to each other," she continued.

"No," said Johansson, looking at her seriously. "I have never believed for a moment that you would have cooperated with any such thing."

Because of course I haven't, he thought. Not since he had gone over Berg's and Persson's investigation and spent the weekend reading Mattei's description of Helena Stein's life.

"How many people know about this story?" asked Johansson.

"The ones who were inside the embassy, of course. Four of them seem to still be alive—and they've probably been out of prison for many years now. The first one was let out in 1993. Because I met only two of them, on one occasion, a brief occasion, and one of them is dead, I've never been worried about them. I don't even think the ones who are left remember me. How would they even recognize me? I looked like a child at that time—I *was* a child."

"Then there was your cousin, Theo Tischler, Welander, Eriksson," said Johansson.

"Yes," said Helena Stein, smiling bitterly. "Two are dead and one is my cousin. The older brother I never had but always wanted."

"Have you told anyone else?" asked Johansson.

"Yes," said Stein, and suddenly there was a glimmer in her eyes. "I've told two other men. One of them was a man I had a relationship with, and as soon as I told him he left me. I don't think he's told anyone, if you're wondering about that. I actually think he would be the last person to talk about something like that, simply out of concern for himself."

"So who was the other man?" asked Johansson.

"Two years ago, before I got my current job, I found out in a roundabout way that you people at SePo were interested in this story and I asked a friend—not a close friend, but a person I rely on and who knows a good deal about these kinds of things—I asked if it might not be best to simply talk about what had happened. Tell the whole story straight out and let the world decide whether I was fit to serve the country."

"What advice did he give you?" asked Johansson.

"He almost got upset," said Helena Stein. "It was almost like he'd been involved himself. He advised me firmly against it. According to him, the time wasn't ripe for that sort of thing, and I could forget about my new job as undersecretary—that it was inconceivable that I would be permitted to continue working in the government offices. So I followed his advice. Was that stupid of me?"

"Perhaps," said Johansson. "I don't know. I think that's something only you can answer. But because I know who gave you that advice, there's one thing you should probably know," he continued. "In case you were to turn to the undersecretary again for advice."

Then Johansson told her about the suspicions currently harbored by the secret police that there were advanced preparations "by a foreign power and domestic interests close to this same power" to exert pressure on her in the event that she was given any position worth the trouble. And that it was highly probable that one of those who had helped make the intrusion possible was the very person she had asked for advice.

"Are you completely sure about all this?" Stein asked, looking doubtfully at Johansson.

"Yes," said Johansson. "As sure as you can be in this business."

"Good Lord," said Stein, shaking her head indignantly. "How do you put up with yourself? With the job you have?"

"It's my job," said Johansson. "I knew before I took it that it wouldn't be easy." Although I never imagined this, he thought.

"Fine then," said Stein. "What do I have to worry about? I have people like you and your colleagues to protect me from people that in my stupidity I thought I could rely on."

"There's one more problem," said Johansson. For there is something that can't be put off any longer, he thought.

"Imagine that," said Helena Stein. "I suspected as much."

"It concerns Kjell Göran Eriksson, whom you also got to know over thirty years ago," said Johansson.

"I'd already figured that out," said Stein, looking hard at Johansson. "He's the only truly evil person I've met in my entire life, including both of those insane Germans who later made their way into the embassy. Compared to Kjell Eriksson they were almost respectable. At least they were driven by political conviction."

"I hear what you're saying," said Johansson, gently raising his hand in a forestalling gesture. "But before you say anything else there are actually a few things I have to remind you of, and which I presume you as an attorney are familiar with. I'm a police officer," Johansson continued, "so if people say certain things to me I can be forced to do certain things regardless of whether I want to or not. Therefore I thought I should inform you that we have concluded the investigation of your possible involvement in the murder of Kjell Eriksson. The prosecutor is of the firm opinion that you have nothing to do with his death, and the case has been dismissed. That is his firm, legally grounded opinion. And, true, I'm not much of an attorney, but I share his opinion as far as the law is concerned."

"And in your actual role—you *are* a police officer, aren't you?" asked Stein. "What is your opinion as a police officer?"

"Let me put it like this," said Johansson. "The only possibility of getting you indicted and convicted of Kjell Eriksson's murder, or even reporting you on reasonable grounds for suspicion, would be if you decided to confess. I know that as a police officer, because it's as a police officer that I've inspected the existing material on the murder of Eriksson. But what I think about it, and this is my purely private opinion, is completely uninteresting."

"Not to me," said Stein, shaking her head firmly. "I really would like to hear what you believe about my involvement in the murder of Kjell

Eriksson. And considering that this is about me—and only me, really—I would be very grateful if you would tell me. Strictly privately, and I can assure you that I would not dream of using anything against you, if that's what worries you. And note that I clearly trust you, despite the fact that we've never met before."

"Personally, I'm not the least bit worried," said Johansson, shaking his head. "You're not that type." And we have actually met once, at a distance, he thought. I saw you but you didn't see me, and that's the difference between us.

"Okay then," said Stein. "I want to hear what you think."

"On one condition," said Johansson. "That you just listen. I don't want you to say anything."

"I promise to be completely silent," said Helena Stein. "I'm used to listening to men," she added with an ironic grimace.

And I to women, thought Johansson. Or at least to one woman in particular, he thought.

Okay then, thought Johansson, and then he told Helena Stein what had happened when she murdered Kjell Göran Eriksson.

"Because you're asking now, I think it probably *was* you who stuck the knife in him," said Johansson, and his Norrland dialect immediately became more apparent as he spoke. "But it was not a murder, and if you had only pulled yourself together and called the police yourself, I am completely convinced that no one would have convicted you of anything more than assault and manslaughter. If the knife wound hadn't been where it was, I even think you would have had a good chance of getting off completely by maintaining that you administered it in self-defense when he tried to attack you or rape you."

"But that wouldn't have been true," Helena Stein interrupted. "Because he didn't—he was completely incapable of any sexual feelings whatsoever—"

"Sweet Jesus, woman," Johansson said very slowly and very clearly. "I thought we agreed that I would talk and you would listen. This is for your own sake."

"Forgive me," said Helena Stein and she suddenly looked just as des-

perate as she had sounded on the almost twenty-five-year-old audio surveillance tape Johansson had listened to a few days before.

"If I were to begin with the act itself," Johansson continued, "it occurs
about eight o'clock. Eriksson is sitting on the couch in his living room,
spewing out his usual foulness. He has sent you out to the kitchen to cut
up fresh lemon slices for his gin and tonic. He has probably already suggested that you can be his new, unpaid maid, so he can save on the Polish
woman who's been cleaning under the table for him. And as you're
standing with your lemon slices and his tonic on the threshold between
the kitchen and the living room, where he sits with his back to you, waving his glass demandingly without even condescending to turn toward
you when he's talking to you, you suddenly discover that you're still
holding his kitchen knife in your hand, and without even consciously
making a decision you simply take a step forward and stick it in his
back."

Helena Stein kept her promise. She did not say a word. She simply sat
up straight in her chair, without leaning against the back and without
looking at him. No expression on her face or even a shift in her eyes, very
present and yet very far away.

"When you've done that you back a step out of the room still holding
the knife in your hand and you hardly know what's happened, for it took
only a fraction of a second, and Eriksson seems to have barely reacted.
He turns around and looks at you with surprise, then he runs his left
arm up along his back toward the place where it's starting to hurt, and
when he sees all the blood he has on his left shirt sleeve he sets down the
glass he's been holding in his right hand and gets up and suddenly he's
completely furious and starts to yell.

"Then he tries to get hold of you," Johansson continued, "and you
back straight out toward the window in the living room, because maybe
you have the idea that you might be able to get help by calling out to the
street, but Eriksson gets tangled up in his own furniture. After following
you a few steps to the left he turns in place and takes another few steps
back, yelling at you the whole time. Then suddenly—just like that—he
collapses between the couch and the coffee table, which turns over, and

the glasses and bottles land on the floor. And now he's lying there—and he's not screaming anymore. He's only moaning faintly and he's hardly moving, but a lot of blood is running out of the wound on his back and out of his mouth. And then you run back into the kitchen, throw the knife in the wastebasket, rush into the bathroom, lock the door, and vomit into a hand towel you grab . . .

"That's how it went, more or less," said Johansson, nodding.

"May I say something now?" asked Helena Stein, but without looking at Johansson.

"Sure," said Johansson. "Just think about what you're saying."

"So why would I have done that?" she asked.

"You had run into him earlier in the day. You probably hadn't even seen him since the embassy takeover almost fifteen years earlier, but suddenly he was simply sitting there in the audience listening to your lecture. And when you saw him it was like seeing an evil apparition from another time. You were already nervous. East Germany had just fallen apart, and you were constantly worried about what people like me might find in the Stasi files when we finally had the chance to snoop through them. And when Eriksson came up to you after your lecture he didn't exactly do anything to calm your fears on that score. More likely he tried to get you to think that your whole life was now in his hands. And maybe he also said something to the effect that he was the only one who would get off on the strength of his contacts, once the police finally came knocking on your doors."

"That's what he said to Theo—long before," said Stein.

"Careful now," Johansson warned.

"So what did I do afterward?" asked Helena Stein. "Yes, I promise to be careful," she said, and now suddenly she looked at him again.

"You tried to collect yourself as best you could, cleaned up as well as you could, went through his desk and took a binder with you that he probably had been boasting about earlier in the evening—and that mostly contained a lot of nonsense and his own notes, if you want to know what I think personally—because unlike you I've never seen all that shit he had locked up in his safe-deposit box, mostly for his own sake, so that he could convince you what a remarkable person he was. The following months you weren't doing so well yourself. . . . You told

Theo what had happened, naturally—if he hadn't already figured it out on his own—and obviously he promised that regardless of anything else he would see to it that nothing bad happened to you and that in the worst case you would simply disappear to some tropical island as far away as you could get. But apart from that, well, you were desperate, probably thought about committing suicide. On several occasions I'm convinced you stood with phone in hand and were about to call the police so that it would finally be over, but then time passed, and nothing happened, and now we're sitting here," said Johansson, sighing.

"Why are you telling me this?" asked Helena Stein.

"For several reasons," said Johansson. "Because I think that if someone offered you a new job within the government, you should be given the chance right now to avoid the risk by choosing to do something else. I brought these with me, by the way," said Johansson, taking out the bag with two CD-ROMs containing extracts from Mattei's research that he had carefully edited himself.

"What's that?" said Stein.

"Scenes from your life," said Johansson. "When I look at them, I get the distinct impression that you don't lack alternatives. If you were to decide to live a different life now, of course," said Johansson, looking steadily at her.

"What I don't really understand," said Stein, "is why you're telling me this. Why are you doing this?"

"Oh well," said Johansson. "If I don't remember wrong, it was actually you who asked me."

"You came here to tell me," she said. "I'm quite sure of that, and I've listened to you. I haven't said anything about what you've said that can cause you any problems."

"I'm not the one who has problems," said Johansson, "and I didn't come here to play God."

"Why did you come here then?" she asked.

"Two reasons, as I see it," said Johansson. "It *has* happened that I've been wrong, and I guess I wanted to assure myself that this time I wasn't."

"I don't understand," said Stein. "I haven't said a word about what I think about your story."

"No," said Johansson, "and I was actually the one who asked you not to. Let me put it like this: I guess I've figured it out anyway. Maybe I saw it in your eyes?"

"The other reason then," said Stein without looking at him.

"Justice," said Johansson. "I think what has already happened is good enough. What happens now, you decide yourself."

"Do you want me to thank you?" said Helena Stein, and the bitterness in her voice suddenly came through.

"Why should you thank me?" said Johansson. "If the prosecutor had decided to report you on reasonable grounds for suspicion, we would have turned the case back over to the Stockholm police and let them take care of the formalities. And I'm convinced they wouldn't have gotten very far. Just as I'm convinced that you would have had to run the media gauntlet anyway. So it was solely for that reason I did it this way. How could we have done anything else? The prosecutor chose to write off your case, and with that it's closed for me and my colleagues too. We're not the ones you need to be worried about now; there are completely different interests and different individuals. And if anyone asks me, you and I have never met. For the one simple reason that that's the way I'm expected to answer such a question, and, if I may be personal now, I don't have the slightest problem with that."

"I understand what you mean," said Helena Stein.

"I'm convinced of that," said Johansson. "And for me it's only about justice."

And then he left, walked to Östermalm subway station, and took the subway home to Söder. To another, and better, life, thought Johansson as he strode into the hall to his and Pia's apartment. A new time, and a better life.

Part 7

A New Era

XIII

On April 24, Easter Monday, the media made note of the fact that twenty-five years to the day had passed since six young German terrorists occupied the West German embassy in Stockholm, murdered two people in cold blood, and carelessly or intentionally blew up the embassy building.

The occupation was described as one among a well-known series of events from a different time, and the anniversary provided an opportunity to show the classic images of a now legendary TV reporter screaming at his technicians to start filming him live. He crouches with microphone raised while in the background the embassy building shakes and there are shock waves and flames from the explosions. He too was interviewed on this anniversary, of course, and everything he had to say showed clearly that nowadays he was living a different life and that the exuberant interest of his younger colleagues mostly just made him feel tired.

The legal consequences of the twenty-fifth anniversary were for the most part not touched on. Only in passing was the fact mentioned that in a legal sense, right before midnight the statute of limitations would run out on the legal case based on the occupation of the embassy, and from now on the event would live on only in history. Of the intimation of Swedish involvement in the drama, there was not a peep.

At the beginning of May, Undersecretary Helena Stein left her position at the Ministry of Defense, and according to the briefly worded press release—for the most part passed over in silence by the media—the reason she did so was that she had decided to return to private legal practice. She did, however, intend to retain some of her political involvement on the local level, and she also expressed a hope that the change in her work situation would give her more time for such involvement.

The same day as the press release about her departure became public, the former bureau chief of the National Police Board Erik Berg passed away at a private nursing facility in Bromma.

During the spring the cancer had spread like a wildfire in his body, and on this particular day he had decided to release his hold. Now I'll let go, he had thought. Let go so I can fall freely, like in a dream. And so he did.

Both Johansson and Berg's old squire, Persson, attended the funeral.

Berg's widow was there too, of course, but not many others, especially considering who Berg had been. The undersecretary, on the other hand, sat in the front pew in the church and surprised them all by showing visible signs during the funeral that he was deeply moved. On one occasion he even snuffled audibly and rubbed the corner of his eye with a giant handkerchief.

After the funeral service, when both Persson and Johansson were about to go their separate ways, the undersecretary came up to them and asked if he might invite them to lunch at Ulriksdals inn.

"I need a couple of good shots in the company of someone I can talk to, so I can gather my courage to say goodbye to Erik," he explained. Johansson and Persson did not make any objections, but instead immediately accepted his invitation, and when they thought back on this afterward it really had been pleasant.

The following week Johansson met the undersecretary to ask him for a favor.

"I want a new job," said Johansson.

"I'm sorry to hear that," said the undersecretary, sounding as though he meant what he was saying. "What kind of job do you want?" he asked. "You can have whatever you want." Finally, he thought.

Oh, well, thought Johansson.

"I'm a policeman," said Johansson, "but these last twenty years I've mostly been involved with other things. Before I retire I would like to have a job where I get the opportunity to put away the occasional bad guy who has done ordinary, decent people harm. That was why I wanted to become a policeman in the first place," Johansson concluded.

An extremely honorable ambition according to the undersecretary, and as far as the details were concerned he did not intend to interfere.

"If you give me a proposal, I'll arrange it," he said.

"Thanks," said Johansson.

A week before Midsummer the chief inspector at the National Bureau of Investigation's homicide squad, Evert Bäckström, entered the police hall of fame. The reason was that the almost eleven-year-old murder of Kjell Göran Eriksson had been cleared up after an almost heroic investigation by Bäckström. For once, and in the sphere in which the police department's homicide investigators ordinarily live and act, it was also justified to describe the formidable investigative effort as having been solely thanks to Bäckström. It proved that Bäckström had been right the whole time. The murder of Eriksson was an almost classic gay murder, allowing for the fact that the perpetrator was, fortunately, a highly unusual gay.

The murder of Eriksson was yet another deed in an apparently endless series of senseless outrages with homosexual overtones and motives that had been committed by the now nationally known and even internationally renowned serial killer who went under the name the Säter-Man in the media—named after the well-known mental hospital in Dalarna where, by the way, he had spent more or less half his life.

Bäckström's effort had come in the nick of time. During recent years public doubts about the guilt of Säter-Man had been growing at the same pace as the number of murders attributed to him had increased. As usual the media hadn't picked up on the fact that "the critical voices"— that was how they preferred to describe themselves—consisted of an exceedingly mixed company of professional backbiters who made envy a virtue and raising doubts a meal ticket—but then the media and the backbiters were closely allied. True, the Säter-Man had already been convicted of half a dozen murders, but he had confessed to another thirty, and among those who had worked on the investigation there was a strong conviction that everything argued for this being only the "tip of the iceberg" and that there were thus indispensable values of criminal policy at stake.

A recurring theme in the criticism centered on the fact that the Säter-Man had always been convicted solely on his own admissions and without a shred of either witness testimony or technical evidence. Confessions that were alleged to have little in common with the actions he maintained he had committed. But Bäckström had succeeded where his colleagues had failed for more than ten years. He had silenced the critics and finally managed to create the peace and quiet necessary for continued, successful work.

For several years, long before he came to the National Bureau of Investigation, Bäckström had come, through his own persistent inquiries, to believe that the Säter-Man was also guilty of a series of five bestial knife murders of homosexual men that had been committed in Stockholm in 1989, and of which, moreover, the murder of Eriksson was the fourth. After lengthy questioning of the Säter-Man he got him to confess that in the early nineties he had access to an out-of-the-way, long since abandoned sheep pasture in northern Dalarna. "A holy place" that the Säter-Man frequented when he was "visited by elves and visions of the hereafter," as soon as he managed to obtain the necessary permissions from the mental hospital to make "these pilgrimages to his inner borderland" possible in a purely practical sense.

Bäckström ordered a search of the sheep pasture in question and "in a cabin at the sheep pasture in question" had secured technical evidence that unambiguously and beyond any reasonable human doubt connected the Säter-Man to his victim Kjell Göran Eriksson. For one thing, a leather suitcase bearing the victim's initials, for another a pair of terry-cloth hand towels, and finally a plastic bag from the tax-free shop at Kastrup Airport, that contained an unopened bottle of banana liqueur as well as the signed copy of the credit card receipt that showed that the referenced bottle had been purchased by the victim in September 1989, only a few months before he was murdered.

At the trial the Säter-Man had testified that the suitcase, hand towels, and banana liqueur were not the only things he had stolen from his victim. Besides numerous bottles of Eriksson's alcohol he had emptied in his solitude up at the hut, he had also devoted himself to a number of videocassettes and a large number of magazines containing "brutally sadistic violent pornography of a homosexual nature." He had later brought these pornographic works with him to the hospital after his leave was over, and there they had unfortunately been lost in the general handling. "I guess they were simply read to pieces," he tearfully explained to the members of the court and other listeners.

Johansson and his wife had celebrated Midsummer in the city. The weather had been excellent, and after a nice dinner out at Djurgården they had walked home at a leisurely pace through the empty summer streets to their apartment on Wollmar Yxkullsgatan on Söder. As soon as they came into the hallway Johansson reached out his hand for the hollow in his wife's neck and then . . . when at last they had wound up in bed, and at that point Johansson was already gliding from serene lethargy to deep and undisturbed sleep, his wife had something she absolutely had to say.

"Are you sleeping, Lars Martin?" she asked at the same time as she slowly drew the nails of her right hand through the hair on his neck.

Not any more, thought Johansson, because reality had just jerked him back.

"I was thinking about that Waltin," she said.

"Yes," said Johansson. Not now, he thought.

"The one who was murdered on Mallorca," she continued.

"I remember him," said Johansson, who was suddenly wide awake. "You mean the one that the Smurfs killed when he was down there swimming?"

"I'm serious," said his wife. "Are you listening?"

"Yes," said Johansson. What choice do I have? he thought dejectedly.

"You don't think he might have been involved in the Palme assassination?" his wife asked.

This is, God help me, not true, thought Johansson, sitting up in bed and turning on the light on his nightstand.

"No," he said, shaking his head. "Actually I don't think so. Why in the name of heaven should Waltin have been involved in the Palme assassination?"

"I don't know," said his wife, shrugging her shoulders. "It was just a thought that struck me."

Then everything returned to normal and they didn't talk about it anymore. Not about Waltin, not about the assassination of the prime minister, who nowadays of course belonged to another time and another life, which had nothing to do with Pia and Lars Martin Johansson's lives. They talked about other things. About things going on right then, about things in their lives and in their time.

Leif G. W. Persson is the Grand Master of Scandinavian crime fiction. Over three decades, he has taken a scalpel to the political and social mores of Swedish society in his dark and complex crime novels.

Persson is also Scandinavia's most renowned criminologist and leading psychological profiler, and has served as an advisor to the Swedish Ministry of Justice. Since 1991, he has been Professor at the National Swedish Police Board, and is regularly consulted by the media as the country's foremost expert on crime. He is the author of nine novels, all of which have been bestsellers in Scandinavia. His most recent, *The Dying Detective*, won The Glass Key award for Best Scandinavian Crime Novel 2010. His Bäckström novels have been optioned by Twentieth-Century Fox TV for a major US crime series.

X